John O'Keeffe

The Dramatic Works of John O'Keeffe

Volume 1

John O'Keeffe

The Dramatic Works of John O'Keeffe
Volume 1

ISBN/EAN: 9783337303358

Printed in Europe, USA, Canada, Australia, Japan

Cover: Foto ©Andreas Hilbeck / pixelio.de

More available books at **www.hansebooks.com**

THE

DRAMATIC WORKS

OF

JOHN O'KEEFFE, ESQ.

PUBLISHED UNDER THE GRACIOUS PATRONAGE

OF

HIS ROYAL HIGHNESS

THE PRINCE OF WALES.

PREPARED FOR THE PRESS BY THE AUTHOR.

IN FOUR VOLUMES,

VOL. I.

LONDON:

PRINTED FOR THE AUTHOR, BY T. WOODFALL;

AND SOLD BY

Meſſrs. LONGMAN, ROBINSONS, DEBRETT, CADELL and
DAVIES, NICHOLL, PAYNE, EGERTON, WHITE, HOOK-
HAM and CARPENTER, CAWTHORNE, BELL, London;
ARCHER, Dublin; CREECH, Edinburgh; MEYLER, Bath;
FLETCHER, Oxford; DEIGHTON, Cambridge; HUMPHREYS,
Chicheſter; GREGORY, Brighton; MOTLEY, Portſmouth;
GARDNER, Margate; &c.

[*ENTERED AT STATIONERS' HALL.*]

1798.

HIS ROYAL HIGHNESS

THE PRINCE OF WALES,

HAVING, in the complacent benevolence of his gracious difpofition,
condefcended to fignify his Approbation of thefe Works, and his pleafure
that they might come into the world
under his Auguft Protection ; in
the hope that the degree of lenity
with which his Royal Highnefs has
been pleafed to regard them on the
Stage, will not be affected by a look
over of them in the clofet (if fuch
humble productions, unaided by the
advan-

advantages of reprefentation, can ever be admitted to a place even among the lighter engagements of his Royal Highnefs's leifure moments) they are, laid at his Royal Highnefs's feet, with all humility, duty, and grati= tude, by

THE AUTHOR.

June, 1798.

ADDRESS PREFATORY.

THE AUTHOR regrets that an inconsiderate difposal of the Copy Right of his Pieces, called The SON IN LAW, The AGREEABLE SURPRISE, The YOUNG QUAKER, The DEAD ALIVE, and PEEPING TOM; to the late Manager of the Hay-Market Theatre, prevents their appearance in this Collection*. However, fhould thofe of his compofitions, which he is here enabled to give to the Public, afford any gratification in the reading, it is derived from the kindnefs of MR. HARRIS, (Proprietor of the Theatre-Royal, Covent-Garden) in permitting the AUTHOR to Print them; the Copy Right of moft of them, he alfo having purchafed.

* Had they been fold to a Bookfeller, and confequently then Publifhed, the AUTHOR would, by the laws refpecting literary property, have had a right to print them at the expiration of fourteen years, a term now long elapfed.

To

vi

To that Gentleman, for this fignal in-
ftance of generofity, as well as for many
other acts of friendfhip, the AUTHOR,
thus Publickly returns his moft fincere
and grateful thanks.

*Teddington, Middlefex,
June, 1798.*

LIST

OF

SUBSCRIBERS.

HIS Royal Highnefs the Prince of Wales

His Royal Highnefs the Duke of York

His Royal Highnefs the Duke of Clarence

A.

Her Moft Serene Highnefs the Margravine of Anfpach

Nathaniel Atchefon, Efq. F. A. S.

Miles Peter Andrews, Efq. M. P. for Bewdly, Worcefterfhire

Mrs. Abingdon

Mr. Angelo

F. Dugdale Aftley, Efq. Everley, Wilts

Mr. Attwood

Mr. Adams, 10 copies

F.

LIST OF SUBSCRIBERS.

F. Aickin, Efq. Gower-ftreet
Mr. A——
Mrs. Allen, Errol Houfe, Scotland
Lee Allen, Efq. Errol Houfe, Scotland

B.

Sir George Beaumont, Bart. L. L. D. Dunmow,
   Effex
Sir Charles Burdett, Bart. Acomb, Yorkfhire
Francis John Browne, Efq. M. P. for the county
   of Dorfet, Frampton, Dorfetfhire
Mifs Benfon
M. H. Beach, Efq. M. P. for Cirencefter, Wil-
   liamftrip-park, Gloucefterfhire
Mr. Bannifter, Jun. Gower-ftreet
Dr. Charles Burney
Mr. Blandford, Surgeon, Wincanton, Somerfet-
   fhire
Mrs. Boone, Berkeley-Square
—— Boone, Efq. Berkeley-Square
Mr. Broderip, Haymarket
—— Babbs, Efq.
Samuel Birch, Efq. Cornhill
Luke Birch, Efq. Jun.
Mr. Brandon
Robert Byrne, Efq. Cabinteely, Ireland
Captain Henry Bunbury
Mr. Barker, Bookfeller, 6 copies
Thomas Brand, Efq. Soho-fquare

Captain

Captain Burnell
Charles Bifhop, Efq. Ruffell Place
The Reverend Mr. Burnett, Berkhamftead, Herts
Captain Edward Barlow
Mr. Bellamy, Bookfeller, 2 copies, King-ftreet, Covent-Garden
R. H. A. Bennet, Efq.

C.

The Right Honorable the Earl of Chefterfield, 2 copies
His Excellency Earl Camden, Dublin Caftle
Francis Conft, Efq. Barrifter at Law
Richard Cumberland, Efq.
Robert Calvert, Efq.
Charles Calvert, Efq.
Mr. James Clarke
James Cawdell, Efq. Manager of the Sunderland Company
Lieutenant A. Congalton, R. N.
Mrs. Carey
Mr. James Champ, Chichefter
Edward H. Cruttenden, Efq.
James Cobb, Efq. Eaft India Houfe
Mr. Thomas Crefer
G. Colman, Efq.
Mr. John Carpenter, Wincanton, Somerfetfhire
L. Concannon, Efq.
Mr. Crofs
Mr. Jof. Clark, Hull

b His

D.

His Grace the Duke of Devonſhire

The Right Honorable the Earl of Dorcheſter

The Right Honorable Lady Vifcountefs Dudley and Ward

The Right Honorable Lord Vifcount Dudley and Ward

N. Dalton, Efq. Shanks Houfe, Wincanton, Somerfetſhire

John Dalton, Efq. Pitbcome, Bruton, Somerfetſhire

Mrs. Deacon, 2 copies

Mr. Deacon

Mifs De Camp

The Reverend Dr. Dupré, Berkhamſtead, Herts

W. Dawes. Efq.

The Reverend Mr. Dodd, Weſtminſter, 2 copies

Mrs. Dehany

William Davies, Efq.

Mr. Dowton

Mr. Dignum

E.

The Right Honourable the Earl of Egremont

Mrs. Eſten

F.

The Right Honorable Earl Fitzwilliam

Dr. Fiſher, Doctors' Commons

A Friend

Mr. Fawcett

—— Fielding, Efq. Barrifter at Law
Francis Freeling, Efq. General Poft Office
Mr. Fox
A Friend
W. T. Fitzgerald, Efq. Upper Seymour-ftreet,
   Portman-fquare
R. Frewen, Efq.
The Rev. Brownlow Forde, L. L. D, 2 copies

G.

William Guy, Efq. Chichefter
Mrs. Gardiner, Hampton Court
Mr. Gout
—— Ginnis, Efq. Barrifter at Law, Ireland
Mrs. Grove, Zeal's Houfe, Mere, Wiltfhire
The Reverend Mr. Grove, Mere, Wiltfhire
William Garrow, Efq. Barrifter at Law
Captain Francis Gallini
Edward Grubb, Efq. Great Queen-ftreet
Mr. Henry Gapper, Henftridge, Sharton, Dorfetfhire

H.

His Grace the Duke of Hamilton
Lady Hoare, Barn-Elms, Surry
Prince Hoare, Efq.
The Reverend Mr. Heming, Chichefter
Thomas Hickrott, Efq.
William Hayley, Efq. Eartham, Suffex
Thomas Harris, Efq. Uxbridge

Mr.

Mr. Philip Humphreys, Bookfeller, Chichefter, 2 copies

Mr. Merrick Hoare

Mr. Hugh Hoare

The Reverend Mr. Hobfon

Mr Holman

William Hoare, Efq.

John Hale, Efq.

I.

The Right Honorable the Earl of Ilchefter

The Honorable William Irby

B. James, Efq. 2 copies

Mrs. Jordan

William Johnfon, Efq. Inner Temple

Mrs. Jeffries, Ireland

Mr. Johnfon

—— Jones, Efq. Bloomfbury-fquare

Mr. Jewell

Mr. Incledon

K.

Dr. Kennedy, Great Queen-ftreet

Mr. Kemble

Mr. Kirby, Bookfeller

Mr. King

Mr. King, Jun.

Mr Kelly

Mr. Knight

The

L.

The Moſt Noble the Marquis of Lothian
Sir James Lake, Bart. Edmonton, Middleſex
M. Lewis, Eſq. Devonſhire Place
M. G. Lewis, Eſq. M. P. for Hindon, Wilts
Miſs Lowther
Meſſrs. Latouche, Bankers, Dublin
Meſſrs. Lee and Hurſt, Bookſellers, Pater-noſter-row
Mr. Longman, Cheapſide
Miſs Leak
Beckford Long, Eſq.
H. Lefanu, Eſq. Dublin
Mr. Lewis
Mr. Longman, Bookſeller, Paternoſter-row
Mr. William Lane, Bookſeller, Leadenhall-ſtreet

M.

His Grace the Duke of Marlborough
The Right Honorable the Earl of Miltown
The Right Honorable Lady Mulgrave
The Right Honorable Lord Mulgrave, 2 copies
Mrs. Minchin, Bath
Thomas Morton, Eſq.
Mr. Munden
Mr. Motley, Porſmouth
——— Moor, Eſq.
John Maddocks, Eſq.
William Maddocks, Eſq.
Miſs Mellon

Ruffel Manners, Efq. Burlington-ftreet
The Proprietors of the Monthly Mirror, 2 copies
Mrs. Martyr
—— Minier, Efq.
Mrs. Mitchell
Mr. Morgan
Mrs. Mattocks
Linus Macnally, Efq. Barrifter at Law, Ireland

N.

The Right Honorable Lady Vifcountefs Newark

O.

W. O'Brien, Efq. Stinsford, Dorfetfhire
Dennis O'Bryen, Efq. Craven-ftreet
Lieutenant Orton, R. N.

P.

His Grace the Duke of Portland
The Right Honorable the Earl of Pembroke
The Honorable Colonel Phipps, M. P. for Scar-
borough
Mifs Pope
Mrs. Parker, 2 copies
Mr. James Parker, Efher, Surrey
Mr. Pope, Half Moon-ftreet
Mr. Perfect, Surgeon, Wincanton, Somerfetfhire
Mr. R. Palmer
Walfh Porter, Efq.

William

William Morton Pitt, Efq. M. P. for the county
   of Dorfet, Stinsford, Dorfetfhire
Mr. Payne, Bookfeller, Mews-Gate
Mrs. Powell
Mr. Powell
Percival Potts, Efq.
John Palmer, Efq. Bath
William Henry Pejen, Efq. Portland Place
Mr. Peake

Q.

Mr. Quick

R

His Grace the Duke of Roxburgh
The Honorable John Roper
Frederick Reynolds, Efq.
Mr. Reinhold
—— Riley, Efq. R. A.
Mr. Reeve
Johnathan Raine, Efq. Barrifter at Law, Lincoln's
   Inn
Mr. Ruffel
—— Raine, Efq.

S.

The Right Honorable the Countefs of Shaftefbury
The Right Honorable Earl Spencer
William Shield, Efq. Berners-ftreet

Mr.

Mr. Simpſon

Mr. Suett

Thomas Sheldon, Eſq. Tottenham-court-road

Richard Sullivan, Eſq. Thames Ditton, Surrey.

Mr. Stokes

George Shum, Eſq. M. P. for Honiton, Devonſhire, Berry-hill, Dorking, Surrey

George Stephens, Eſq.

Mr. Shaw

Sir Robert Saliſbury, Bart. M. P. for the Town of
Brecon; Llanwern, Monmouthſhire

Peter Stuart, Eſq.

Charles Stuart, Eſq.

Mr. Sedgewicke

John Sylveſter, Eſq. Barriſter at Law

—— Shepherd, Eſq. Serjeant at Law

T.

The Right Honorable Lord Teynham

John Taylor, Eſq. Hatton Garden

Mr. Tremell

Mr. Townſhend

The Reverend George Threnchard, L. L. D. Hen-
den Houſe, Maidenhead, Berks

—— Townſhend, Eſq. Cleveland-court, St. James's

Mr. Thring, Attorney at Law, Warminſton, Wilts

Edward Taylor, Eſq. Old Burlington-ſtreet

V.

—— Udney, Efq. Teddington, Middlefex
Mrs. Vickery, Ireland
The Reverend Doctor Vincent, Weftminfter

W.

Mrs. R. Walpole, Jun.
Mrs. Weddell
Mrs. M. Ward
Mr. Wathen
Nathaniel Webb, Efq. Round-hill, Wincanton, So-
    merfetfhire
Mrs. Wheeler
Mr. Wheeler
Mr. William Woodfall
Mr. Whitfield
Mr. Whyte, Dublin
Mr. Wilkinfon
Mr. Warburton
Mr. White, Bookfeller, Fleet-ftreet
—— Wickham, Efq. Duke-ftreet, Weftminfter
H. S. Woodfall, Efq.
Mr. F. G. Waldron
Mrs. Mary Wood
Mr. T. Woodfall, 2 copies

☞ Subfcribers whofe names, from diftance of place, cou'd
not be afcertained, and are here omitted, are refpectfully in-
formed they fhall appear in the Second Edition.

c

CONTENTS*.

* A wifh that by chequering and contrafting the pieces, more variety might be given to the Reader, is the reafon they are not aranged according to the dates of their firft reprefentation.

CONTENTS.

VOL. IV.

---

* In the firſt ſcene of this piece the following eſſential lines have by miſtake been omitted.

Darby. But Captain, what brought you into this foreign Pruſſian land.

Capt. P. Why Darby, as it was peace, I thought my paſſing my time here in this excellent ſchool of arms, might give me a better claim, even to half pay, than idly ſtaying at home to ſhine the fluttering hero of a Hampſtead Ball, or à Cork Aſſembly.

LIFE'S VAGARIES;

OR,

The NEGLECTED SON.

IN

FIVE ACTS.

PERFORMED AT THE

THEATRE-ROYAL, COVENT-GARDEN.

IN 1795.

VOL. I.   B

PROLOGUE,

WRITTEN BY JOHN TAYLOR, ESQ.

AND SPOKEN BY MR. MIDDLETON.

'TIS ftrange that authors, who fo rarely find
Their pray'rs can move an audience to be kind,
Still fend, with piteous tone and look forlorn,
The Prologue forth to deprecate your fcorn;
Such doleful heralds, which would fain appear
The timid ftruggles of a modeft fear,
The furly Critic views with jealous fpleen,
As the dull prefage of the coming fcene.
In vain, the dread hoftility to calm,
E'en potent Flatt'ry tries her foothing balm;
Pity's a crime his lofty foul difdains
And his pride feafts upon the poet's pains.
Yet now no critic rancour need we fear,
For lib'ral candour holds her empire here,
Candour, who fcorns for little faults to pry,
But looks on merits with a partial eye.

And fure a bard whofe mufe fo oft has found
The happy pow'r to kindle mirth around,
Though, in her fportive moods, averfe to trace,
The rigid forms of *Action*, *Time*, and *Place*,
While gen'rous objects animate her view,
May ftill her gay luxuriant courfe purfue;
For, mid her whims, fhe ftill has fhewn the art,
To prefs the USEFUL MORAL on the heart;
With juft contempt the worthlefs to difcard,
And deal to VIRTUE its deferv'd reward.

So aim'd the bard * (if haply we may dare,
Our humble fcenes with nobleft ftrains compare)
The bard whofe favour'd mufe could joy afford,
That eas'd the cares of Rome's Imperial Lord,
Who in her fatire frolickfome and wild,
Gave vice the deepeft wounds when moft fhe fmil'd.

* HORACE.
B 2

PERSONS OF THE DRAMA.

Lord Torrendel, ... Mr. BERNARD.
Arthur D'Aumerle, ... Mr. LEWIS.
Sir Hans Burgefs, ... Mr. MUNDEN.
Dickins, ... Mr. QUICK.
George Burgefs, ... Mr. FAWCETT.
Timolin, ... Mr. JOHNSTONE.
L'Œillet, ... Mr. FARLEY.
Robin Hoofs, ... Mr. TOWNSHEND.
Robinfon, ... Mr. ABBOT.
Thomas, ... Mr. SIMMONDS.
Coachman, ... Mr. THOMSON.
John, ... Mr. LEDGER.
Conftable, ... Mr. BLURTON.

Lady Torrendel, ... Mrs. POPE.
Augufta, ... Mifs WALLIS.
Fanny, ... Mrs. LEE.
Mifs Clare, ... Mifs STUART.
Landlady, ... Mrs. PLATT.

TRADESMEN, and SERVANTS.

SCENE, Suffex.

LIFE's VAGARIES;

OR,

THE NEGLECTED SON:

ACT I.

SCENE I.

A Parlour in DICKINS'S; *Breakfaſt laid.*

Enter SIR HANS BURGESS, *and* ROBIN HOOFS.

SIR HANS.

I'LL truſt nothing to the errand cart, you muſt bring up my own waggon; cuts ſuch a figure! a Gentleman's fine team ringing thro' a country town.

Robin. Why it does make folks ſtare.

Sir H. There's the Duke's cart, Lord Mar-quiſs's cart, and why not his Worſhip's cart? and on it written in capitals, " Sir Hans Bur-geſs l Samphire Hall." A ride of ſeven miles, after breakfaſting at eight as I have, is a kind of Whet; but to find Major Talbot there over his breakfaſt at eleven! Shameful! Eh, why here's

another

another Breakfaſt at—*(looks at his watch)* twelve !
Scandalous !

Robin. Now you mention that Sir, don't forget,
that Squire Miller invites you to dine with him to
day.

Sir H. Aye, his dinner hour is two ; you call
and tell him, I'll wait on him.   [*Exit* ROBIN.]
I breakfaſt at eight, Major Talbot at eleven, this
little Shopkeeper at twelve, why a man in his
rounds, according to the degrees of faſhion, may
ſwallow four or five breakfaſts in a morning.—
Ah, Dickins is quite ſpoilt by a Lord's taking
notice of him—aping all the abſurd impertinence
of faſhion ; an inſignificant cur mongrel, ſetting
himſelf up for a greyhound.

Enter DICKINS, *in a morning gown, &c. tying his
neckcloth, ſits.*

Dick. When one ſups at the Caſtle, no riſing
next morning (*yawns, not minding Sir Hans.*)

Sir H. The Caſtle ! ſup with Lord Viſcount
Torrendel.

Dick. His Lordſhip would make me bumper it
laſt night, toaſting ſuch bundles of his fine. girls ;
'pon my ſoul I and Torrendel knock'd the bottle about rarely. How his Lordſhip ſtared at
dinner when I hob nob'd him ; ſays he, my dear
Dickins, are you in earneſt ? 'pon my ſoul, ſaid I
my dear Torrendel I am, that's poz. I'm uſed
to good old black port, and his Lordſhip's pink
Burgundy has given me an immenſe head-ach.
No getting from him, he's ſuch good company.
(*yawns.*)

Sir H. Then I'm not even to be aſked to ſit
down ?

Dick. Sir Hans Burgeſs ! Oh, how do ye do ?
                                                Sir H.

Sir H. Well, this is good, a Gentleman comes to talk about bufinefs, and its " Oh, how do ye do."

Dick. Bufinefs! true, I ride out with my Lord this morning.

Sir H Pleafe, Sir, firft to ftep into your fhop, and weigh out the fugar and tobacco for my fervant, Robin Hoofs.

Dick. (*rifing*) Sir, if you don't know how to behave as a parlour vifitor to me, as a cuftomer, walk into my fhop, and wait there till you are ferv'd. Here John, take this perfon's orders. Weigh tobacco! as you are *now* Sir Hans Burgefs, I may yet be Sir Anthony Dickins; I may be knighted for bringing up an addrefs. You made your money by a contract of hats, and an't I making mine by——

Sir H. Your country merchant fhop of all forts.

Dick. My banking-houfe, agencies, receiverfhips, factorfhips——

Sir H. And coal-fhips. Now *I* have laid out my money in buying a fcope of land; and my grand hobby is to turn it into a fafhionable feabathing place. I have fuch a liberal mind to accommodate the publick, I built firft there a beautiful houfe——

Dick. For yourfelf. As my Lord fays, to ferve a man's felf, has been long the way of doing things for the public good.

Sir H. I raifed as pretty an hotel! and the neat row of lodging-houfes!

Dick. But to give it a name, you muft get a few of us people of fafhion down to it. Suppofe I fay to his Lordfhip, 'pon my foul Torrendel, now you fhould take a houfe from my friend, Sir Hans, he's a good, honeft, ftupid fort of a foul
—why

—why then, fays my Lord, nay my dear Dickens, you are too fevere. Yes, perhaps I may prevail on Torrendel to take one of your new houfes.

Sir H. Not fo much good in you, a pity, friend Dickens, my Lord can't admit you for an hour to his table, but it makes you fo faucy.

Dick. Proud! a proof my Lord ca'n't do without me.

Sir H. Why you are fo clever that I will truft you, becaufe I ca'n't do without you.

Dick. Very civil. (*bows*)

Sir H. I came to confult you.——You know I defign to beftow my ward Augufta Woodbine, with her whole fortune, on my fon George; but I fear the report of her riches will bring all your flafhy, high-titled gentry about her, then——

Dick. Ay! then, indeed, fhe may be for defpifing a fon of yours. Wa'n't Mifs Augufta adopted by her uncle on his difcarding his own daughter for a *faux pas* with fome man of fafhion two and twenty years back?

Sir H. Devil's in your twenty years back! how to bring my fon's marriage about now?

Dick. Make your ward think that her uncle has made a fecond will, and that fhe's not worth two-pence, then fhe'll be glad to fnap at your George.

Sir H. Eh! that's well, I expeét her to-day from London. According to that plan, it will fhew too much attention to go myfelf to meet her—I'll let her down—I'll fend any body—will you go, my dear fellow?

Dick. Civil again; (*bows*) its a doubt to me, if you know how to make a bow, Sir Hans; ha, ha, ha! this morning I, making my bow of leave to his Ludfhip, fliding back, ftumbled upon the
poor

poor Chaplain's toe; my Lud laughed! S'death! cries his Reverence, you've killed me! Huzza, fays my Lud, then the parfon's dead, and has loft his living, ha, ha, ha!

Sir H. Then you are a retailer of his Lordfhip's jefts too.

Dick. But to meet this Lady, I'll fend my daughter Fanny. Here fhe is.

Enter FANNY, *ftops fhort, and makes a low curtefy.*

Why, Mifs, isn't this your fchool hour?

Fanny. Yes, papa, but I've ftept home for a book; did you fee my Pleafing Inftructor? (*looks about.*)

Dick. My dear, you muft ftep over to the inn to receive——

Fanny. Lord! papa, what would our Governefs fay if a young Lady of her fchool was feen going into an inn? befides its now my reading time; then I have my embroidery; then I muft practice my mufick; then fay my French leffon; then the dancing-mafter; then, papa——

[*Exit. courtefying. Sir Hans bows.*

Dick. I muft not take her from her accomplifh-ments—I'll go, and in my way drop this parcel at my Lud's, a trivial thing, but was I to fend it, it would be, Eh, now, Dickins, why didn't you come yourfelf, my dear fellow? always happy to fee you. Muft call, my Lord may think I'm getting proud, pride is fo contemptible.

Sir H. So it is, I defpife it at this moment.

Dick. Well, good bye.

Sir H. Devil's in your good bye! Introduce me now to Lord Torrendel.

Dick. Why, I don't know, his Lordfhip fup-

ports vaſt dignity; but never mind, tho' he is very difficult of acceſs, I'll introduce you, for my
Lud ſays, Dickins, I'll be glad to ſee ſome of
your people; from my reſpect to you, you may
command any ſervice—never mind their aukward
want of breeding, if known to you. Sir Hans,
I'll preſent you to my Lud; expect to ſee all the
importance of genuine old nobility; yet I'm of
that conſequence with him, that once preſented by
me, his Lordſhip and you are hand and glove.

[*Exeunt.*

SCENE II.

A Chamber in LORD TORRENDEL'S

Enter LORD TORRENDEL, *and* L'ŒILLET, *adjuſt-
ing his dreſs.*

Lord Tor. Then you think, L'Œillet, Lady
Torrendel is ſtill in Cumberland. She is too
good a wife—I uſe her ill.

L'Œillet. Oui! mais, mi Lor, dat be de faute
of la nature, vich did give your Lorſhip conſtitution galante, amoureuſe

Lord Tor. No interruption from my wife here,
ha, ha, ha! good deception this of mine, to make
her believe I'm at Liſbon for the re-eſtabliſhment
of my health; never was better in my life!

L'Œillet. Your Lordſhip be robuſte comme
Hercule; vid your ſpindle ſhank. (*aſide*)

Lord Tor. Lady Torrendel, among the lakes,
imagines that I am retir'd hither to this ſcene

of

of darling pleafures; a doubt to me if fhe even knows I've ftill a feat in this part of the country. She is truly amiable, her mind ftored with every delicate refinement, and for perfonal charms has few fuperiors; I like people fhould know fo fine a woman chofe me;—yes, fhe feems the only perfon unconfcious of her fhining qualities; but I cannot help my irrefiftible penchant for variety, (*ringing without*) I'm not at home; except it is the little girl, Dickins's daughter Fanny! isn't her name Fanny? an abfolute Cherub!

L'Œillet. Ah! oui milor—Fanny Dickins, Fanny Cherub!

Lord Tor. But living beauty cannot banifh the fweet remembrance of Emily Woodbine. If her father hadn't difinherited her for coming off with me, and adopted his neice, I fhou'dn't now be troubled with this profligate boy of her's, this *Lord* Arthur, as he calls himfelf—prefumes as if my fon in real *wedlock*. My fitting him out for the Indies was doing very handfome for a chance child.

L'Œillet. Milor, I did vid money, you give me, furnifh him fuperbement for voyage de mer; but he did make fuch a fabat affreux in de fhip, dat he vas turn'd out—(*afide*) fo I did tell you; but your money I have fnug dans ma poche.

Lord Tor. He's well enough, I hear, as to his perfon.

L'Œillet. Oui! il eft fait à peindre, l'image of your lordfhip!

Lord Tor. But mad! I'm abfolutely afraid of him.

L'Œillet. Milor, here come de pretty girl.

Lord Tor. L'Œillet! how do I look this morning? candid now! I always like the truth.

c 2 *L'Œillet.*

L'Œillet. Den, en vérité, milor, you look not above fifty, tho' you are a-quarter paſt.

Lord Tor. Fifty! L'Œillet you are exceedingly coarſe.

Enter FANNY.

Ha, my charmer!

Fanny. 'Pon my word, Sir, my Lord I mean, if you talk that way to me, I won't come here any more; I didn't know you were in the room, or I ſhouldn't have come in I aſſure you, Sir, my Lord I mean.

L'Œillet. Ah, petite badine. Mamſelle Fanny come purpoſe tô ſee my Lor.

Fanny. Monſieur, how can you ſay that.

Lord Tor. Do now, my love, declare and make me happy.

Fanny. Then I only came becauſe——

Lord Tor. What, my angel?

L'Œillet. Ah, pourquoi?

Fanny. Becauſe papa ſays its a boyiſh play, and all the rooms in our houſe are ſo ſmall, and you've ſuch a fine long gallery here, and Jenny the houſe-keeper's daughter is ſo ſmart at—he! he! he! (*produces battledores.*)

Enter THOMAS, *with a parcel.*

L'Œillet. (*ſnatching it.*) Va tén! (*puſhes him off.*)

Lord Tor. (*breaks it open.*) Oh, ſome begging petition. How! my Lady Torrendel's hand! L'Œillet do you read, and write ſome conſiſtent anſwers; date the letters from Liſbon as uſual.

L'Œillet.

L'Œillet. Wile you, milor, play de raquette vid Mifs Fanny.

Fanny. What! can you play, Sir, my Lord I mean?

Lord Tor. (*afide.*) To win a girl one muft comply with all her childifh follies. (*To L'Œillet*) Say the fprain's not better—can't lift my arm—and all that, (*takes a battledore.*)

Fanny. Ca'n't lift your arm! you flourifh it finely, Sir; my Lord I mean.

Lord Tor. Come, my love. (*they play*)

L'Œillet. Ah! bien—trés bien!

[*Exit. admiring.*

Enter DICKINS, *and* SIR HANS, *who ftand amazed.*

Fanny. Oh! my Lord, what a rare old beau the King won'd think you now, and if my papa was to fee me—oh! (*feeing Dickens, runs, he ftops her*)

Dick. So, this is your "Pleafing Inftructor."

Sir H. The dignity of "genuine old nobility!"

Lord Tor. Ah,. hem! what, Sir?

Dick. I beg your Lordfhip's pardon, but I brought a parcel, and am come up to fave your Lordfhip's coming down.

Lord Tor. Impudent intrufion this!

Dick. Mifs, you ftep over to the Swan Inn to receive a young lady juft arrived from London —go.

Fanny. Lord, Papa!—give my battledores to Jenny. (*apart to Lord Torrendel; goes to door, turns, makes a low courtefey, and exit gravely.*)

Sir H.

Sir H. How finely ſhe holds up her head.

Dick. All the good ſhe's got at the boarding ſchool.

Lord Tor. Once you make free with theſe kind of people.

Sir H. The devil's in your ſtrutting! why don't you preſent me?

Dick. Oh, true, my Lord give me leave to introduce——

Lord Tor. Ah! hey! L'Œillet! (*calls and exit. Dickins ſtands confuſed*)

Sir H. Dickins, ſince I have been introduced by you, his Lordſhip and I are hand and glove, ha, ha, ha!

Dick. Get drunk with a man over night, and in the morning its——

Sir H. Ah! hey! 'L'Œillet! (*mimicks*)

Dick. Hem!   [*Exit.*

Sir H. Stop, my Lord ca'n't do without you.

Enter L'ŒILLET *haſtily.*

L'Œillet. Mon dieu! vere be my Lord to tell him of dis beauty lady ſtop at de Inn?

Sir Hans. I ſee the valet's the prime favourite after all. (*aſide*) Monſieur, pleaſe to accept— (*gives money.*)

L'Œillet. Qu'eſt que c'eſt? vat's dis?

Sir H. 'Tis—you are ſo civil.

L'Œillet. Ah! je vous entends—to make me civil.

Sir H. Sir?   [*Bows and exit.*

L'Œillet. Two guinea! very polite! he vant ma Intereſt. In his Lordſhip's ſervice I have been but four year, yet have ſav'd two thouſand

guinea;

guinea ; the guinea flow to my coffer in many channel. My Lor fancy watch-trinket, to prefent as decoy to Lady, I buy at ten guinea, charge him twenty. I wink at de tradefman's bill, ven paid he flip me de guinea:—if tenant want leafe renewed, I fpeak to my Lor, tenant me donne the guinea. De maitre tink we be dere fervants, but when we have got into de love-fecret, pardi! den de maitre become fervant to de valet de chambre.   [*Exit.*

SCENE III.

A Room in an Inn.

Enter LANDLADY, *introducing* AUGUSTA.

Landlady. This way madam.   [*Exit.*

Enter FANNY.

Fanny. How d'ye do, Ma'am, after your journey ?

Augufta. Tolerably well, Mifs—but, pray, who am I to thank for this obliging enquiry ?

Fanny. Why, Mifs, a'n't you the great heirefs, Mifs Augufta Woodbine, Sir Hans Burgefs expected down here from London ?

Augufta. Where is the good old gentleman ?

Fanny. He good ! brought papa upon me juft now ! he, he, he ! I was caught—but pray don't you young Ladies in London fometimes play at fhuttlecock ?

Augufta

Augusta. Ha, ha, ha! why, Miss, you are very agreeable—what a simple thing! (*aside*) but, how came you to know, or expect me?

Fanny. Papa sent me to receive you.

Augusta. I didn't know Sir Hans had a daughter —Miss Burgess I presume.

Fanny. He, he, he! no! no! I am not Miss, but I may be Mrs. Burgess, for young George is quite partial to me; there he's now gone on his travels round Brighton, and Battle, and Hastings, Sandwich, and Margate, and Ramsgate. My dear soul, George Burgess is a very fine creature, I assure you.

Augusta. I ca'n't doubt his taste, Miss, when I understand he's an admirer of your's.

Fanny. Ah! now I see the difference between you and us down here. You are a true Lady, and we are only conceited figures, and so I'll tell all the Ladies in our school, and I don't care if my French teacher hears me too. 'Pon my honour, with all my finery, I'm but a shabby genteel.

Enter DICKINS.

Dick. If my scheme of letting down our young heiress, can bring about a match with Sir Hans's Son George, by agreement I touch the handsome present.

Fanny. La, papa! why don't you speak to the young Lady?

Dick. Welcome, Miss! (*nods familiarly.*)

Augusta. Sir, (*courtesies*) I wish somebody would call my servant. (*going*)

Fanny. Miss, I'll run.

                                             Dick.

Dick. Stop. Now to let her down. (*afide*) Mifs, I've difcharged your fervant.

Augufta. How, Sir !

Dick. And, my dear, inftead of attendance on yourfelf, you muft learn to attend on others, my dear.

Augufta. Sir! very odd and myfterious; this brutal treatment—(*afide*)—my guardian lives but a few miles—the carriage ready ! (*going*)

Dick. Never mind, my dear, you'll be able to walk as far as you've to go; you can walk ! (*abruptly*)

Augufta. What can be the meaning !———

Dick. A word, Mifs; you have been brought up with the idea of a great fortune. Smoke ! your uncle has made a fecond will, and bequeath'd all his property to a—fome Mr. Jackfon, or Mr. Johnfon, no matter who.

Augufta. I don't know who you are, Sir, but if acquainted in my affairs, furely by my uncle's will I am———

Dick. A man's *laft* will is the clincher, tho' he had made fifty before; you are left a trifling legacy, and a handfome education, fo muft now battle it out for yourfelf.

Fanny. I could cry for her misfortune, if I wasn't glad at its making us more equal. Before, I admir'd; but now I fhall love her, dearly.

Dick. My generofity is fuch, that at Sir Hans's requeft, I'll take you into my houfe to be governefs to my daughter Fanny, here.

Augufta. Can this be poffible ?

Fanny, Then I'm to leave fchool ! (*joyfully*)

Dick. You fhall have my protection, you may dine at my table when we have no parti-

cular company. No occafion to acquaint you,
my dear, of my property and fortune—firft
fafhion. (*looks at bis watch*) My Lord may
now have called at my houfe! but let him call
again!

Enter JOHN, *with a large Bag.*

John. Here, Sir Hans's man fays you fold him
better moift fugar for 6d. a pound.

Dick. Get you gone, you rafcal! (*pufhes bim
out*)

Fanny. La, papa, why don't you mind the
bufinefs of the fhop?

Dickens. Hem! yes, I want a governefs for my
daughter. What fay you Mifs?

Augufta. Sir, I am a friendlefs orphan; no
alternative—but fuch an afylum! (*afide, and
weeps*)

Dick. Come, young Lady, don't be caft
down.

Augufta. I am furprifed—perhaps concern'd;
but the profpect of riches gave me little pleafure in the reflection that I was to poffefs what
belonged to an unfortunate relative; the unfor-
giving fpirit of her obdurate parent took the
birth-right from his own lamented daughter,
caft down! I could be happy was I fure my
uncle's wealth would devolve on the offspring
of his child's offence; the poor youth, who
may at this moment be a wretched outcaft,
difown'd by an unprincipled father, and no inheritance, but his mother's fhame.

Dick. Why, a babe was, I heard, the confequence of your Coufin's flip; a boy—this
yourg

young mad Arthur D'Aumerle, (*aſide*) but, dear, nobody knows any thing of the bantling ; it may be dead or drowned, or—well, but, Miſs, 'what think ye ?

Auguſta. Sir, I accept your offer.

Dick. Now, I ſhall have you under my own eye, no more playing ſhuttlecocks with Lords— but, how are you qualified for this office ? what is your idea of the duties, in bringing up a young woman ?

Auguſta. Sir, by the mouth of a parent ſhe receives admonition from Heaven itſelf ; and when he commits that charge to another, it is indeed ſacred. The care of youth is an ardu- ous, and delicate truſt of confidence, and honor ; I look upon truth, cleanlineſs, and frugality, to be the firſt principles in a lady's · education. They preſerve to her mind, perſon, and means, purity; health, and independence of obligation, which latter thro' the devious paths of her future life, to the unſuſpecting female, is often the concealed adder, for the deſtruction of her inno- cence.

Dick. She ſet out pretty well about my hea- venly authority, and my delicate mouth ; but for her concealed adders—(*aſide*) well, in truth, my dear, your quondam guardian, bid me break this affair in a rough way, to lower your ſpirit to your ſituation; but it's my intention to treat you with kindneſs and reſpect. (*aſide*) This will do me no harm, when ſhe finds ſhe has *ſtill* the fortune.

Enter

Enter L'ŒILLET.

L'Œillet. Vraiment oui! here is de charmante inconnue for milor; (*aside*) and Mifs Fanny! ah! ha! (*with freedom*)

Dick. And Mifs Fanny's pa! pa! (*interpofing*) Monfieur—you want now, I fuppofe, to engage my daughter in a match of cricket; but you fhall get all the notches on your pate.

L'Œillet. Non! Monfieur, I did come vid milor's compliments—you ride cavalcade vid him dis morning.

Dick. What! after his affronting me!

L'Œillet. Affront pah! votre interêt.

Dickens. True! intereft is the gold-beater's leaf, for my wounded pride. Come, Mifs, be chearful; you'll dine with us—dinner on table at fix.

Fanny. Why, papa, we always dine at one.

Dick. Fanny, to amufe you, will fhew you our town here.

L'Œillet. I vill fhow de Lady de town. (*bowing*)

Dick. (*Bowing*) Don't you believe it. After you, s'il vous plait, Monfieur.

[*Exit, with* L'Œillet.

Fanny. Yes, papa, I'll take Mifs Augufta to the cathedral, the play-houfe, and fhambles, the beaft-market, and affembly-room, and fhe fhall fee the fine gallery of pictures, in my Lord's caftle too.

Timo'in. (*Without*) Give me my own big bottle of old claret, in my own fift.

Fanny.

Fanny. A man! oh! Lord! I muſt take care of my governeſs. [*Exeunt.*

Enter TIMOLIN, *with wine and glaſs, and Land-lady.*

Timolin. Puppies ! but they couldn't read in my face, that I was gentleman to a Lord.

Landlady. Here, porters, fetch up his Lord-ſhip's, and the Gentleman's trunks, let Dick and Tom Oſtler give a help ; take care how you turn the ſtairs.

Enter WAITER, *with two ſmall bundles.*

Waiter. Here ,Ma'am, is the luggage.

Landlady. And call for claret ! (*aſide*) Your maſter, Sir, is ———— ?

Timolin. The Honorable Lord Arthur D'Au-merle.

Landlady. The Honorable Lord————
[*Exit with Waiter.*

Timolin. (*taking papers out of his pocket*). I hope my Lord w'on't find out, that I colleƈted all theſe tradeſmen's bills, which he ran up in Lon-don ; he'd never have thought of them himſelf. This claret is neat—ſince he did call for it, I may as well drink it ; for he has run out of the houſe. If his father, this Lord Torrendel wo'n't do ſome-thing, no going back to London, for us !

Enter WAITER.

Waiter. Sir, the other gentleman is calling for you, and making a great noiſe.

Timolin.

Timolin. Noife! aye, that's quite himfelf. Then, Sir, this gentleman will wait on that gentleman, and that may happen to fave all the bottles and glaffes in your houfe.

Waiter. He has juft taken lodgings, at the jewellers over the way.

Timolin. What may the price be ?

Waiter. I think, they let them at three guineas a week:

Timolin. (*Whiftles, Waiter ftares*) Don't be frighten'd, it's only a little new tune I was humming.

Waiter. Sir, he defires his luggage to be brought to him. (*Timolin afhamed, looking at the bundles, whiftles*) Sir !

Timolin. What's the matter with you now ? luggage ! have you good ftrong porters here, and a big cart ?

Waiter. For what, Sir ?

Timolin. For—hem! only Sir—I'm afraid our luggage will break down the landlady's ftair-cafe. " And there was three travellers—travellers three."   [*Exeunt. Timolin, finging.*

END OF THE FIRST ACT.

ACT II.

SCENE I.

Before Lord Torrendel's

Enter Lord Torrendel.

Lord Torrendel.

No, the phæton: (*calling off*) I may fee this little girl in the evening, and after an hour on horfe-
back; my limbs, not quite fo fupple, appear rather older than fuch a young creature fhould think
one; but, true—I afked this Dickins to ride out
with me to-day. One fhould hold thefe fort of
people at arm's length, till we want to turn them
into fome ufe.

Enter Timolin, *who takes papers from his pocket,
and thrufts them into* Lord Torrendel's *hand.*

Timolin. There! now you have the whole kit of
them.
Lord Tor. Who are you, Sir? what's all this?
bills!
Timolin. Yes, and by my foul they're not bank
bills, and that's the worft of them; and, they're
not

not play bills, and that's the beſt of them; for there's not a gaming debt in the whole cluſter.

Lord Tor. But, friend, you ſhould have delivered them to my banker, Mr. Dickins.

Timolin. A banker! he'll give me the money! (*joyfully*) by finding you ſo good, oh! how you've diſappointed me. (*going*)

Lord Tor. Stop! (*looks at bills*) " Lord Torrendel, debtor, for goods delivered to Lord Arthur;" ——who is Lord Arthur D'Aumerle?

Timolin. Now don't he in a paſſion, why, I am his ſervant.

Lord Tor. But who is he himſelf?

Timolin. Come, be aify my Lord, don't go to pretend to know nothing of your own child.

Lord Tor. How dare any fellow aſſume—— Lord Arthur!

Timolin. He has the honor of being your ſon.

Lord Tor. 'Tis falſe,

Timolin. Well, he has no honor in being your ſon,—Will that content you.

Lord Tor. A raſcal! run about, contract debts, ſend in his bills to me! I won't pay a ſhilling to ſave him from perdition.

Timolin. Perdition! ſome new-faſhion'd name for the King's Bench.

Enter GROOM.

Groom. My Lord, am I to ſaddle the cheſnut mare for Mr. Dickins? he inſiſts upon having it.

Lord Tor. Yes, yes, ſcoundrel! (*walks*).

Groom. She coſt your Lordſhip two hundred guineas; he's a bad rider, and if ſhe ſhould get any hurt——

Lord Tor.

Lord Tor. Don't trouble me with your quarrels.
[*Exit Groom.*

Timolin. Refufe his child a few pounds, a bit of beef, a feather bed, and a hat and a pair of fhoes, or fo; yet mounts a Mr. Dickins on a horfe coft 200 guineas!

Lord Tor. Can't keep within the allowance that I ——

Timolin. What allowance, My Lord?

Lord Tor. An extravagant ——

Timolin. He *is* extravagant; wicked; he's a devil! but, it's all your fault, my Lord, as a father; not noticing and bringing him up with a fenfe of duty to himfelf and his neighbours. Call to mind how you loved his mother, and inveigled her from her friends, tho' you wasn't married to the poor unhappy lady, that doesn't make the child's little finger a bit lefs your fon.   -

Lord Tor. Emily! *(takes out his purfe)* for her dear fake——

Timolin. Then bleffings on you! befides, Lord Arthur is fuch a gay——

Lord Tor. Lord Arthur again! not a guinea!

Timolin. And as like your lordfhip as a fprightly young buck is like——an auld fhambling baboon. *(afide)*

Lord Tor. I know nothing about him.

Timolin. Thefe they call gallantries, to bring a living creature into the world and then leave him like a wild beaft to prey upon fociety. *(Lord Torrendel walks about enraged; Timolin following.)* Now, my Lord, only fee him.

Lord Tor. Begone.

Timolin. I'll tell you what—you'll drive him defperate; he'll do fome hellifh thing or other; he'll commit a fuicide upon either himfelf or me, for, when once he thinks any thing, he immediately does it, without thinking at all about it.

Lord Tor. Harkye, you fcoundrel! if I hear of your lord Arthur, or yourfelf, being feen about my door, I'll have you taken up.

Timolin. Well, a fmall man taken up, does'nt cut fuch a pitiful figure, as a great man taken down.   [*Exit.*

Lord Tor. This eternal moment!

[*Exit difturbed.*

Enter DICKINS, *dreffed in an uniform of Hunt, and* JOHN.

Dickins. Yes, John, I think I'm very well equipp'd to ride out with my lord.

John. Well, fir, you had a hundred guineas fee with me, and the day may yet come, for my crof-fing a hunter.

Dickins. It may, John; when I was 'prentice in Barbican, and like the houfe dog, flept in the fhop; promifed the watchman a pint, to roufe me, to go to the Eafter Epping Hunt; five a clock and a fine morning! thump comes the pole againft the fhop door; tingle, tingle, goes the little bell behind it; up ftarts me, from my bed under the counter; on with my buckfkin and jemmy jacket; jumps into my two boots; mounts my three and fixpenny nag; but, firft I put my fpurs in my pocket; hey off we go, thro' Hack-ney, Hammerton——I faw the ftag once, but then heard the hounds all the way; find I've a fhort and a long ftirrup: difmount to put them even; forgetting to buckle the girt, down comes me, and the faddle at-top of me; by this I was flung out; but to prove I was in at the death, prefents my kind

miftrefs

miſtreſs with a piece of the ſtag's horn, which
horn ſhe gives her huſband for a tobacco ſtopper,
with ah my dear hubby, I wiſh you were as good
a ſportſman as your 'prentice Tony Dickins, ah
he's the ſmart fellow, ha! ha! ha! and ſo I was,
and dem it ſo I am ſtill.—John you needn't
wait dinner, I ſhall dine with Torrendel.

[*Exit John.*

Sir Hans! curſe it, I can't be plagued with ſuch
a ſilly old fool now.

Enter Sir Hans.

Sir H. Hollo, Dickins! ſo you have ſeen my
ward, Miſs Auguſta.

Dickins. Yes, yes, I have humbled her rarely,
but pray don't delay me now, I'm engaged to ride
out with my lord. I, and Torrendel, may firſt
take a turn or two down the Street, arm in arm,
right ſide, ſo don't hide the ſtar! my dear Hans
don't ſtop to talk to me; if you've people with
you, and you ſhould bow, I'll return it.

Re-enter Lord Torrendel.

Lord Tor. Call himſelf my ſon; keep ſervants
too.

Dickins. Well, my lord, here I am: whip and
ſpur.

Lord Tor. Deſire the porter not to admit either
of them. (*calls off*)

Sir H. Not admit either of us!

Dickins. Poh! hold your tongue. (*puſhing
him*) My lud, I had a little head ache from our
bout laſt night; you look vaſtly well, but a
little chevy will do us both good.

E 2

Lord Tor.

Lord Tor. Pray, Sir, what are you talking about?

Dickins. Why, my lord, you fent for me to——

Lord Tor. Poh! poh! man, I fha'n't ride out to-day.   *[Exit.*

Dickins. Go to the expence of dreffing! view'd by every body in the town, walking out in my leathers, and———

Sir H. Why, Sir, you are equipp'd in your leathers.

Dickins. Poh! poh! man, I fha'n't ride out to-day.   *[Exit.*

Sir H. And, pray, man, who cares whether you ride or walk? big little nobody! I'll introduce myfelf—Gad's curfe! a'n't I a Knight, and if I can effect this marriage with Augufta and my George———

Arthur. (*Without*) Timolin! (*Enters in flippers*) Where's Timolin? Sir, I afk pardon. My rafcal dare loiter and had only to come and bring me a couple of hundred guineas from my father; I'll fee my lord myfelf. (*rings violently at the gate*)

Sir H. Some young fellow of fafhion!

Arthur. I'm run out in flippers; all afleep here.

Sir H. Yes, Sir, they were at a jovial party laft night; Mr. Dickins told me.

Arthur. Who? aye, my father keeps it up here, and I without the price of a bottle.

Sir H. (*afide*) A little civility might make this Gentleman take lodgings at Samphire-hall.

Arthur. So, I'm not to be let in! then I'll have fome of you out. (*rings*)

Sir H. Are you in this way, Sir! (*offering fnuff-box, which Arthur dafhes through a window.*) the devil's devil's in you, Sir! what fort of mad trick's that, to knock a Gentleman's fnuff-box.　　　　　[*Exit.*

Enter a MAN, *with Boots.*

Arthur. Whofe boots are thefe? what do you afk for thefe boots?

Man. They are bought already, Sir, I'm bringing them home to my Lord Torrendel.

Arthur, My father; *(afide)* you could make me a pair?

Man. Certainly, Sir.

Arthur. Thefe are about my fize. *(kicks flippers off, and puts on the boots.)*

Man. Don't put them on, Sir, I can take your meafure.

Arthur. My dear fellow, why fhould I give you that trouble, when here is a pair ready made? that fits, now this, the whole world is made up of this, that, and t'other, I have this, and that, and t'other I don't want, for two boots will do for me as well as fifty.

Man. Lord, Sir, don't walk about in them, his lordfhip wo'n't have them.

Arthur. A paradox! his lordfhip cannot have them, and his Lordfhip has them already.

Re-enter SIR HANS.

Sir H. Only the pebble knocked out of the lid! never faw fuch a ftrange——

Man. The boots are now unfaleable, his lordfhip wo'n't take them off my hands.

Arthur. Nor off my lordfhip's feet.

Sir H. Lord! then I'll pocket my broken box.

Man. They are two guineas, Sir.

Arthur.

Arthur. (*to Sir Hans*) Sir, I beg you a thoufand pardons for my inadvertency.

Sir H. Inadvertency! a man of rank, by not knowing what he does.

Man. We never book fuch trifles, Sir.

Arthur. Well then fet them down to me, to Lord Arthur D'Aumerle; or, carry the Bill to my father; or, Timolin will pay you; or, any body will pay you; or, John Bull will pay you; honeft John pays for all.

Man. I'll fee if the law wo'n't make you pay me.   [*Exit Man.*

Sir H. Sir, I prefume you are Lord Arthur D'Aumerle.

Arthur. Right—who are you? (*afide*) oh! Sir Hans Burgefs! that old fool they were laughing at in the fhop yonder—I hear an immenfe character of you, Sir Hans.

Sir H. Pray, my Lord, what do they fay of me?

Arthur. Ha! ha! ha! what I ca'n't fay to your face : that's my father's houfe.

Sir H. Indeed! why we didn't know Lord Torrendel had a fon.

Arthur. He doefn't like my coming about him—he affects to be thought fo very young, to recommend him to the Ladies: you underftand me, Sir Hans?

Sir H. Not fee you! he's a very unnatural father.

Arthur. And yet I'm quite a natural fon.

Enter THOMAS.

Thomas. Sir, my Lord is very much alarm'd,
                                                        and

and begs you will not commit any more outrage, or attempt to fee him.

Arthur. Did he give the money to my fervant?

Thomas. Why, Sir, I did fee his Lordfhips purfe——

Arthur. Then he has, my profound duty—I afk his pardon. (*exit Thomas*) He's a tolerable father after all—I'll now pay my debts and be a man again.

Sir Hans. I wifh my fon had your fire.

Arthur. You've a fon? I'll fhew him how to knock your cafh about!

Sir Hans. Good morning to you, Sir. (*going*)

Arthur. Not fo, Sir Hans! come and breakfaft with me.

Sir Hans. Two o'clock! Why my dear Sir, I broke my faft fix hours ago.

Enter ROBIN HOOFS.

Robin H. Sir, here bes Squire Miller's man to tell you dinner bes on table. 　　[*Exit.*

Arthur. Pfha—come and breakfaft with me.

Sir Hans. But I'm going to dinner.

Arthur. Well, you fhall have Hams, Tongues, Tea, Coffee, Chocolate, Anchovies, Eggs, and Rafhers. Come along——

Sir Hans. Ha, ha, ha! You hit my humour—I'm very wife and cunning—I'd do any thing to get money: but all only to fee my fon make a blaze.

Arthur. Blaze! a conflagration! I have a bachelor's houfe—that is, I lodge at the jeweller's yonder; I like to have things about me; I've ordered in wine's and relifhes—I want your opinion of a horfe I've bought juft now. How I'll curve

it

it before noble dad's door ! he fhall fee I can fpend
his money like a gentleman.

Sir Hans. What a noble lad, I could never get
my fon to buy a jack-afs.

Arthur. Come, old hock's the word.

[*Exeunt.*

SCENE II.

ARTHUR'S *lodgings. 'New cloaths, linen, faddle,
hat, &c. lying on chairs.*

Enter TIMOLIN.

Timolin. Oh, melancholy is our new home here.
I'd wifh to keep up my poor mafter's fpirits, but
he'll fee an empty pocket in my difmal countenance. If his papa had only given him as much
as would have taken us back to London—well,
we have no debts to lay hold on us in this
town, however—(*fees the things*) oh thunder and
zounds ! whats here ;—been fhopping on the
ftrength of the expected money ! Ordered in wine
too ! Oh, ho, then not a cork fhall be drawn
'till it is paid for. (*Locks the cupboard and takes
the Key.*)

Arthur. (*without*) This way, Sir Hans. Oh,
very well ma'am ; but where's my fervant?

Timolin. Bringing company too !

Enter a Maid-fervant, with Tea-things, &c.

Maid. Sir, your mafter is returned, and is
bringing a gentleman to breakfaft.

Tim-

Timolin. Inftead of a little civil bafon of tea, he has brought the whole Bedford Coffee-houfe about us!

Enter ARTHUR, *and* SIR HANS.

Arthur. Pray Sir, walk in—be feated—fo we've touched? *(joyful)*

Timolin. Yes! we fhall be touched. *(difmal)*

Arthur. Timolin, my friend here has breakfafted, fo get Sandwiches, and Old Hock.

Timolin. Old Hock! I believe you're jumping out of your leather.

Arthur. Ha! ha! ha! very well, Timolin. Sir Hans, that fellow's a treafure: but, when he does any thing clever, fuch as bringing a man a couple of hundred, it makes him fo pert—

Sir H. Yes! my Lord, when once a fervant knows he's an honeft man, he begins to be an impudent rafcal.

Timolin. Poh! what talk's that! Was the devil bufy with you, Sir, to fend in all thefe new things from the tradefmen?

Arthur. Ha! ha! ha! very well—Timolin, the wine! Sir Hans, I never drink in a morning, dem'd vulgar and unfafhionable; but I know you old codgers of Port-foken Ward. You're a Citizen, Sir Hans, I've heard of your gillings round the Royal Exchange.

Sir H. Why if I drink in a morning, it makes me ftupid all day.

Arthur. Oh, Sir Hans, impoffible to make you ftupid.

Sir H. Sir. *(bows)*

Arthur. Come Timolin, unlock.

VOL. I.   E   *Tim.*

Timolin. Indeed I wont.

Arthur. No! Sir Hans, this is the secret history of Old Hock, (*pointing to the cupboard*) and this (*touching his leg*) is the key to it. (*Bursts the door, and brings out wine.*)

Timolin. Broke open the cupboard—Oh, he'll get us both hanged.

Arthur. Sir Hans, without expedient a man's nothing.

Sir H. You and your servant, my Lord, put one in mind of a couple of ghosts. You are all spirit, and he is no body—ha! ha! ha!

Arthur. Bravo!

Timolin. My Lord, let me send these things back to the honest people.

Arthur. Send yourself out of the room.

Timolin. Only hear me.

Arthur: I'll give you such a beating.

Timolin. Well, so you do but hear me, beat me as long as you like.

Arthur. Lay the money upon my bureau and go to the devil. (*Puts him out*) The fellow is so puffed with doing a petty service—Give me leave to stand Lady, and make tea for you.

Sir H. My Lord, I hope for the honour of seeing you down at Samphire Hall, an infant scheme, merely, for the health and convenience of the gentry in this part of the country. I've converted a naked beech into as commodious a sea-bathing place—

Arthur. Then your principle object is—

Sir H. The main ocean!

Arthur. Psha! you want to establish it into a fashion? Its done, I'll be seen there upon your stein or esplanade; my physician shall recommend all his patients from Brompton, and Paddington;

dingdon; a variety of gambling tabbies, honourable black legs, and rickety children.

Sir H. I'll defcribe to your Lordfhip, exactly this fituation of mine.—Here, fuppofe the edge of this Tea-board is the beach, the top of the Coffee-pot, here rifes the look out—

Arthur. Yes Sir, this is the pour-out. (*Overflows Sir Hans's cup.*)

Sir H. Then Sir, here's the Sea—eh!—I'm fcalded!

Arthur. Aye Sir, the fcalding tea.

Sir H. Thefe cups are one of the Rows of Lodging-houfes, this Sugar-bafon, the Chapel and my Houfe—

Arthur. Yes, yes, the fweeteft place for yourfelf.

Sir H. The Saucers are too large, to fhew you the arrangement of the Machines; but, however, fuppofe each of thefe Guineas a Houfe. (*Takes out his Purfe, and arranges Guineas.*)

Arthur. A Guinea a Houfe! very cheap, I'll bring all my Friends.

Sir H. Ha! ha! ha! a pleafant joke!

Arthur. And here's the cream of the jeft.— (*Dafhes Cream over Sir Hans.*)   Ha! ha! ha! This is a moft fociable Breakfaft.

Re-enter TIMOLIN, *with* THOMAS.

Timolin. You told him! then untell him; for he won't hear me at all at all.

Arthur. There again! then, dam'me! now you fhall bring me fome brawn and anchovies.

Ti-

Timolin. Now don't make quite a kiſkawn of yourſelf.

Thomas. Sir, I thought when I told you that my Lord's purſe——

Arthur. Yes! I'm grateful for good news, here. (*puts his hand on his pocket*) Not at home—all abroad. (*ſnatches a few guineas from the table, and gives them to Thomas.*)

Sir H. But my Lord, my guineas.

Arthur. Yes, Sir, a guinea a houſe, neat cottage, ſtable for ſix horſes, coach-houſe, gardens before and behind, pantheon ſtoves, Adelphi windows, geometrical cork-ſcrew ſtair-caſe, kitchen on ground-floor, and fine proſpect from attic ſtory.

Sir H. Bravo! capital for my advertiſement.

Arthur. Here's—I'll reward you. (*taking the guineas*)

Sir H. Stop, you've given him lodging-houſes enough, here my honeſt fellow is the look-out for you. (*gives the Coffee-pot*)

Arthur. Ha, ha, ha! true citizen, ſharp look-out on the guineas.—Tom you ſhall have a bottle. (*gives him one and places him at table. Timolin ſtares, then runs to take it from him.*) What! don't be quite ſo buſy;—ſit ſtill. (*to Thomas*) You march. (*puſhes Timolin out*). Sir Hans, Timolin will pay you your guineas.

Sir H. What a fine model for my ſon! Come, my Lord, I'll give you a patriotic toaſt—Here's ſucceſs to all my undertakings.

Arthur. Patriotic and diſintereſted indeed, Sir Hans! here's——

Thomas. Succeſs to my undertakings!

Arthur. Right, little pigeon—finiſh your bottle by yourſelf, and, if you quarrel with your com-

company, I'll kick you both out of the room. Have you advertifed this place at Samphire-hall?

Sir H. I fancy advertifing might make it better known ; for newfpapers are a fort of thing that's read.

Arthur. Why, yes, Sir Hans, people do read newfpapers; how the deuce did you find out that? Come, I'll draw you up a flourifhing advertifement.

Sir H. I employed a famous auctioneer to draw up one for me. (*takes a paper and perufes*) Mind how he defcribes the beauties—" To the right, the bold cliffs and high bluff heads—at the foot, Sir Hans has built an elegant ftrait row of houfes, called the Crefcent"—Eh! that's very foolifh.

Arthur. Why, yes! your crefcent is a little in the full moon order, ha, ha, ha! no no, I'll try at it. (*gets pen and ink.*)

Enter TIMOLIN, *walks about with his arms folded.*

What do you mean by walking in here with your executioner's face?

Timolin. Well, I didn't run in debt for my face. Step in here, all of you.

Enter feveral Trades-people.

1ft *Man.* Sir, the horfe you bought—I'll be fatisfied with a draught on Mr. Dickins, our banker, for the 50 guineas.

2d *Man.* Neighboours, your goods are undamaged; but, I infift on being paid for my boots.

Arthur. Timolin!

Timolin. Oh! I know nothing at all about it.

Arthur.

Arthur. Pay the people this moment.

Timolin. With what ?

Arthur. What! the two hundred my father gave you.

Timolin. He didn't give me a Manx rap half-penny.

Arthur. No! why, I thought—by Heavens! I'll get into the houfe myfelf.

Sir H. (*rifing*) Oh! my Lord, a thought ftrikes me of great confequence, in the prefent cafe.

Arthur. Well—Sir—quick?

Sir H. That here, inftead of curlews, he fhould have faid fea-gulls. (*looking at paper.*)

Arthur. Damn your fea-gulls, Sir! fee a nobleman baited, by a parcel of mechanical——

Timolin. There's all your goods for you again —what more do you want? (*they take up all their feveral goods.*)

Arthur. Every one of you, lay down my property this moment, in the very fpot from whence you took it. I'll pay you the firft money I receive ; but now, begone, or I'll murder you.

Timolin. Go good people, whatever he fays he'll do.

Thomas. Here's gaiety and innocence! (*drinks*)

Arthur. True, it was you who told me firft, that the money—I'll make you gay, you innocent dog. (*whips him off*)

Sir H. Oh! what a model for my fon. (*Arthur gives him a ftroke.*)   [*Exeunt.*

SCENE

SCENE III.

A Gallery in LORD TORRENDEL'*s hung with whole length Pictures of Women.*

Enter LORD TORRENDEL, *and* L'ŒILLET.

Lord Tor. So very lovely?

L'Œillet. Une beauté celeste! et pauvre—poor, derfore no danger from relations. So, my Lord, think no more of the rich mechanic Dickins's daughter.

Lord Tor. Why, their sturdy Citizens may be troublesome; but you say this young Lady is coming with Fanny to see my pictures.

L'Œillet. Oui, my Lor.

Enter FANNY.

Fanny. This way, Miss Augusta.

Lord Tor. L'Œillet! (*winks, exit* L'Œillet.) well, you have brought your new friend, to see my paintings?

Fanny. Oh yes, Sir, my Lord I mean, but I didn't think you'd be in the way.

Lord Tor. Don't let her be alarmed at my presence.

Fanny. Oh true, I'm not to let out you are a Lord?

Lord Tor. Fanny! I should like to have your picture here.

Fanny. No, my Lord, sure you wouldn't?

Lord Tor. And you shall have mine for a locket.

Fanny. You think me a silly girl, but I know enough, never to give tokens, or accept presents,

but

but from my papa, and one befides, a certain—
not an old Lord! but a young man. As my
new fong fays,

AIR—*Fanny.*

Laffes all are fimple,
  So the wife one's fay:
Caught by blufh or dimple,
  Who is filly pray?
    The ribband, and the ftar,
    One fmile brings on a par,
With ruftic maid, in her ftockings blue:
Squeezing the hand, is the laffes cure.
      For ting, ting, ting, ting,
      I can dance, and fing.
        (*Step Minuet.*)

II.

When the boy we fancy
  Jolly comes to woo:
Lady gay or Nancy.
  All know what to do.
    Tho' mantling cheek denies,
    And language of the eyes,
When the tongue gives you words unkind,
Take in her filence the laffes mind.
      With our ting, ting, ting,
      I can dance and fing.
        (*Quick Step.*)

Re-enter L'ŒILLET.

L'Œillet. Here, my Lord, be de beauté Lady.
Fanny. What a monkey you are, I don't know
what you mean, by making fo much of my governefs.

Enter AUGUSTA.

Augufta. Oh, are you here Fanny, the pictures
in that room are fo fafcinating.

Lord Tor.

Lord Tor. L'Œillet has good taſte, ſhe's a love-ly creature; (*bows*) ſervant ma'am.

Auguſta. Sir! (*curteſies*)

Fanny. Miſs! never mind this old gentleman, he's only the houſe ſteward.

Lord Tor. Old!

Auguſta. (*looking round*) Something in the man-ner of the beauties at Hampton Court—true, I've been told what he is.

Fanny. What do they ſay of my Lord? he, he, he! ſhe's going to abuſe you. (*apart*)

Auguſta. Fancy habits, or drawn in their real characters?

Lord Tor. Both, madam, they are Ladies that his Lordſhip's heart has at times been devoted to.

Auguſt. And his Lordſhip, I preſume, has flattered himſelf into the idea, that he was at times in poſſeſſion of their hearts. (*Lord Torrendel bows.*)

Fanny. Now, what do you bow for? Miſs wasn't ſpeaking of you, Mr. Old Steward.

Auguſta. I was told he's very vain.

Fanny. Yes! he's quite a conceited figure, and as grey as a badger—isn't he, Mr. Old Steward? (*apart*) I ſaid ſhe'd abuſe you.

Auguſta. What a ſweet expreſſion in that coun-tenance! (*pointing to a picture*)

Lord Tor. Her loſs, madam, makes a chaſm in his Lordſhip's heart, never to be filled but by a face, the lovely emblem of this collected group of charms. (*bows to her*) That is Miſs Emily Wood-bine.

Auguſta. My couſin! then am I in the houſe of her baſe deſtroyer!

Lord Tor. What's the matter Madam?

Auguſta. Not much, Sir, I'm not very well.

Come,

Come, Fanny! a ftar! heavens! have I been talking to——

Lord Tor. Stay, my divine girl!

Augufta. My Lord, it ill becomes my youth, and humble life, to offer admonition, where age fhould be the monitor of inexperience; and exalted rank *only* illuftrious in virtuous example. The veil of delicacy drops between my mind and tongue —I cannot fay what I think you: but the bitter reproach will yet reach your heart, when your only hope lies in pardon for a bad life, from, perhaps, a too late repentance.   [*Exit.*

Fanny. What, has my governefs run away! why Mifs! Mifs!   [*Exit.*

Lord Tor. Her words have peirc'd me—but I muft have her—the only being worthy to fupply the place of my loft Emily, and banifh all other purfuits from my mind; from her good fenfe I fhall enjoy rational fociety—and from her beauty—yes, L'Œillet muft finifh, what he has fo well begun.
                                              [*Exit.*

Enter THOMAS *and* ROBINSON.

Robinfon. But how can I help this crazy Lord's getting in.

Thomas. You never ftrove to help it, you're a rare porter for a Nobleman!—Walk away from the Lodge leave the door open, and let people in that my lord has ordered to be kept out.

Robinfon. Well, for my part, I couldn't fee that any body had a greater right than a child, ¿to come into his father's houfe.

Thomas. A bleffed babe this! he treated me with a bottle of wine juft now, but by the Harry he made my back day the reckoning.

                                           Arthur.

Arthur. (*without*) Pack of ſcoundrels!

Thomas. Aye there he is running from room to room.—What a row we ſhall have, I'll keep out of the ſcrape however.   [*Exit.*

Enter ARTHUR.

Arthur. Prevent a dutiful ſon from ſeeing his honor'd parent! where's my father?

Robinſon. Why Sir, my Lord is within that's certain; I'm the porter, and I'm afraid I ſhall get at the wrong ſide of the door, for letting you in.

Arthur. Indeed! you're not fit for a great man's porter—you're too honeſt—when a poor man comes to his gate, your hand upon the churliſh key obeys the voice of pity—begone! you ſhall live with me—you ſhall be my Almoner, and diſtribute my whole roaſted oxen, and buts of ale— you ſhall give away a couple of thouſand a year— when I get them—but its dangerous for you to know me now. Go.   [*Exit Robinſon.* Yes, oh by heaven my father ſhall ſee me, I'll convince him I'm a good boy—and I will be his comfort, and, though he commands me to be gone, I'll ſtay with him to prove my obedience. What a pity that the omiſſion of ſaying a few words, before I was born, ſhould prevent me from being lawful heir to this caſtle! perhaps the pride of my father! the darling of the tenants! favourite of the neighbours, and friend to the poor! now, a wretched outcaſt, ſhunned like a ſavage, foe to mankind, and man at enmity with me! no eſtabliſhment! profeſſion! friend, or character, no gentle word, no complacent ſmile, every tongue is the vehicle of coarſe reproach, and

G 2   every

every face meets me with a chilling frown. Oh!
my father, where are you? (*looks round with
grief*) do not fhun me, I'll kneel, till you fpurn
me from you—that face! (*looks at a picture*) it is
my mother. I heard of his lordfhip's gallery of
beauties—quite an exhibition for every ftarer :
but my dear mother fhall no more be difhonour-
ed, by making one in this unhappy collection—
no, by heavens! her misfortunes fhall be no
longer the topic, for the fneering comments of
vulgarity and ill nature. (*lifts the picture down*)
Timolin! why don't you come up? Timolin!

Enter LORD TORRENDEL, *and* L'ŒILLET.

Lord Tor. What uproar is this in my houfe?

L'Œillet. Sacriftie ! by dis meeting milor will
find out, I did keep all de money, he did give
me for his fon's fupport.

Lord Tor. Have you any bufinefs with me, Sir?
who are you?

Arthur. (*falls on his knee, and points to picture*)
Sir, this was my mother. (*Lord Torrendel looks
at both, puts his handkerchief to his eyes.*)

L'Œillet. Diantre! he is foftened, and I am
ruined—milor, here be Mifs Augufta in de hall
ftill. (*apart*)

Lord Tor. Begone! (*pufhes him off angrily, walks
flowly and then turns*) My fon, the child of Emily!   [*Exit in great emotion.*

Arthur. This our firft interview fince my in-
fancy! my father not to fpeak to me! now where
to turn—I think I have—fome honour but I have
wrong'd the induftrious tradefmen—what muft
they think of me?—fo fanguine in my hopes !—
all blafted by this father's cruelty—he is cruel,
                                          thus

thus to abandon me to the horrors of contempt, fhame, and poverty.——Many have been banifhed their country for what I have done——I deferve it—— it may come to that.——Diftraction! Oh! my father, hear, fave me!——no, no, no! he's deaf to the voice of nature.——Now the ftorm's up, and let it blow me as it will.

Enter TIMOLIN.

Timolin. Well, and you faw your papa? *(joy-fully)*

Arthur. Take that picture to my lodgings—— farewell father. *(Calling off at the fide, turns tender-ly to the picture,)* Oh! my mother. *(burfts into tears)* [*Exeunt. Timolin with the picture.*

END OF THE SECOND ACT.

ACT III.

SCENE I.

A Street.

Enter Sir Hans Burgess.

Sir Hans.

CRAM a fine dashing fellow into their prisons for hats and shoe-buckles! Sha'n't. What a bright model this Arthur for my son George! yet if he had but life and soul to shew it, George is a compleat and finish'd pattern for most of our young men. I don't know any one thing that my boy is not perfect master of, music, dancing, fencing, languages, a magazine of accomplishments: set him to country sports, he excels every body; he's as keen as an attorney, has the courage of a mastiff, generous as the Man of Rofs! but hang it, all his shining qualities clouded by want of spirit to dash! Oh, if I could but see him a bold free dasher!

Enter

Enter Robin Hoofs.

Robin H. Sir, who fhould pafs me juft now but the young fquire.

Sir H. What, my fon George whifk'd by you in a phæton? a chaife and four? a tandem?

Enter George Burgess.

George, why, what the devil's this fort of figure?

George. Sir, how are you? *(calmly)*

Sir H. Spare no expence for you to appear like a prince; give you money to flafh in a fhining tour, to be here and there, before any body can tell where you are, and when I expected you to come, tearing up the pavement, in a phaeton as high as the clouds, over chickens, old women, and pigs, all the people jumping out of the way, with huzza for the young Squire, here you fneak into town, limping like a lame Highlander on a march, covered with duft as if you had been danc-ing in a cannifter of Scotch fnuff. 'Sblood, Sir! what do you mean by this behaviour?

George. Sir, on my leaving home you gave me a five hundred pound note, and fix guineas; there's your note—I've ftill one pound five and feven-pence in bank. *(touching his pocket.)*

Sir H. Devil's in you and your feven-pence! I wifh you were both in the ftocks you pitiful cur. Damn me if I havn't a mind to difinherit you, and adopt Robin Hoofs. Robin, go to the Rofe inn, and befpeak the beft dinner they can pro-vide for I and George and the gallant Arthur, if we can find him. [*Exit Robin H.*

George.

George. Why, Sir, I am a little hungry. *(takes something from his pocket.)*

Sir H. By the Lord! a fon of mine knawing a cruft in the open ftreet!

George. Sir, as I paid for it at the laft alehoufe where I fupp'd——

Sir H. Supp'd at an alehoufe!

George. Yes, Sir, a neat little place, fign of the Goat in Boots.

Sir H. And perhaps fome of my friends, in their coaches. faw you?

George. Yes, Sir, Lady Beechgrove, and the two Mifs Sandfords, drove by in a coach and four; they didn't fee me at firft, but I faluted them.

Sir H. Salute ladies from the Goat in Boots! Where did your noble honour dine? *(ironical)*

George. Sat upon the mile-ftone this fide Salifbury. *(Sir Hans ftares.)* Sir, I had no occafion to fhut myfelf from the open air, as I had a couple of hard eggs in my pocket.

Sir H. And I fuppofe you brought falt in your pocket?

George. Yes, Sir, and a penny roll.

Sir H. His penny roll has choak'd me! and where did your honour take your bottle? *(bows ironical.)*

George. True, Sir, I flipp'd off the bank into the river, as I was getting a little water in the brim of my hat.

Sir H. The devil take them that took you out again!

George. Father, the walking got me an appetite; after my repaft, I was neither dry nor hungry; I drank no wine; but then I was free from an headache,

ache, and, without mixing in company, my heart was chearful.

Sir· H. (aſide) This gay Arthur will make him another thing. But Dickins will have the con-ſtables after him. George, you'll give me what information you've picked up in your tour; how they manage their machines and lodging houſes; what they do, and what they don't do, that I may know what I ought to do.

George. Ca'n't make up that other ſix-pence —oh! the halfpenny to the boy for opening the gate!

Sir H. Dem the boy; come poliſh yourſelf up a little, my ward Miſs Auguſta Woodbine's come from London, and I've a certain reaſon for her thinking well of you. If ſhe ſhould ſee you ſo— *(takes an handkerchief, and whiſks the duſt off)*— ſuch an appearance, by the Lord ſeems as eaſy and ſatisfied, as if dreſt for a ball. Can nothing make you aſhamed?

George. I'll take care to do nothing that can make me aſhamed.

Sir H. Here's the Lady—I'll try what effect an accidental meeting may have. Now to know what they have done with the gay Arthur! *[Exit.*

George. I fear I've loſt my clothes bruſh.

Enter FANNY.

Fanny. Bleſs me! where can ſhe be? if ſhe has run home, and told papa, I ſhall have it in ſtile.

George. Fanny! how do you do, my love?

Fanny. My dear George! when did you come? Lord! I'm ſo glad!

George. You look as charming as ever.

Fanny.

Fanny. Thank'ye; but, upon my word, you don't look fo charming.

George. I fhould make myfelf a little decent.

Fanny. Then run home, and change your drefs.

George. Oh, no·occafion, I've my clothes-brufh in my pocket. *(retires, brufhing his coat.)*

Enter AUGUSTA.

Fanny. Oh! governefs, I've been running about after you.

Augufta. What could induce you to bring me into Lord Torrendel's houfe? fure you know that he is a very dangerous charaćter.

Fanny. Lord, its no fuch thing, who could have told you that? his Lordfhip has no more pride! he's not afham'd at making one in a game of romps, even with his own fervant maids.

Augufta. Ah, Fanny, when our fuperiors of the other fex condefcend to affability, inftead of exalting, it is for the purpofe of degrading us to a ftate of the moft pitiable humiliation.

Fanny. Now don't be angry with me, I'll introduce you to———

GEORGE—*advances.*

Augufta. Oh, no more of your introdućtions, pray.

Fanny. I will, tho'; Mifs Augufta, this is—

Augufta. A Mr. *young* Steward, I fuppofe.

Fanny. Ha, ha, ha! George you don't know what we're laughing at—*(apart)* Mifs, don't go tell him that I play at fhuttlecock with my Lord in the great gallery.

Augufta. A piece of his lordfhip's condefcenfion
                                                    I didn't

I didn't know before. My guardian's fon, I prefume.

George. The defcription of Mifs Augufta Woodbine falls fhort of what I have the happinefs to
behold. *(bows)* .

Fanny. There I told you he was a fmart fellow
fometimes. Come, George, you fhall be our
chaperon about the town, but you are an odd-
looking beau.

George. I'll attend you on your rambles—Madam—Fanny will you honour my arm.

[*Fanny takes his arm.*

Enter ARTHUR.

Arthur. Ha! odds. Madam, my arm is at
your fervice. *(to Augufta.)*

Augufta. Do you know this Gentleman? *(to
Fanny.)*

Enter a Man with fruit.

Fanny. Lord, true, this is Affembly night.

Man. Gentlemen, treat the Ladies.

George. The Ladies don't want—fhall we
walk?

Arthur. Quite a hound! ha! nectarines fo early! Madam. *(offering fruit.)*

Man. Six are a guinea.

Arthur. There! *(gives money.)*

Augufta. Oh! Sir, by no means.

George. Mifs, an apple—Fanny! *(offering)*

Arthur. Thefe are Angels, not Eves, to be
tempted by yonr paltry pippins. *(knocks them
about.)*

George. Sir, what d'ye mean? *(angry)*

H 2   *Enter*

Enter a Woman and Child.

Woman. Good Gentlemen and Ladies, I've a fick hufband lying in prifon.

George. For debt? what is it? *(apart)*

Woman. Above eighteen fhillings.

George. *(loud)* Pray go—don't teize people; their diftrefs is only the confequence of idlenefs. I'd never encourage beggars—there, go—*(gives money apart.)* plaguing one.

Woman. Sir, it's a guinea!

George. Well, don't trouble one now. *(loud)* Get your hufband out of prifon, and comfort your child. *(apart; fings carelefsly, and puts them off.)*

Augufta. What's this?

Fanny. Blefs you, governefs, he is always doing thefe kind of things. He'd grudge himfelf a penny cheefecake, yet maintains and clothes half the poor round; he's king of a fmall ifland near his father's feat, who is fuch a ftingy old curmudgeon.

Arthur. What a pitiful fcoundrel am I. My guinea nectarines, and little penny-worth of pippins, with the benevolent heart of a god! Sir, if I dare beg the honour of your acquaintance— I haven't a card, but I'm over at——

George. Sir, I'll put down your addrefs; *(takes out his pencil)* points broke *(takes out pen-knife)* cutting it away—waftes—*(puts up both)* Oh, Sir, I'll remember.

Fanny. What fignifies your bowing there? come and pay fome attention to me.

Arthur. *(looking at Augufta.)* How charming! what a block am I, talking half an hour to a lady, and never look at her!

Augufta.

Augusta. Fanny, we must be walking towards your papa's.

Fanny. But you hav'n't seen our ball-room here.

Arthur. Ball-room! Ladies, do you know I'm a most capital dancing-master? harkye, my worthy friend, a word.

George. Oh! Sir, as many as you 'please.

[*Exeunt.*

Fanny. Lord! that rattle there has dragged George up into the Assembly-room; I hope its not to fight—if he goes to fight, George will kill him. (*a fiddle heard above.*) That's he! I know his sweet little finger.

Augusta. What an astonishing resemblance! Fanny, did you ever see any likeness of this strange gentleman?

Fanny. Ah! the image of Miss Woodbine's picture! its Lord Torrendel's great boy.

Augusta. The neglected son of my unhappy cousin!

Enter TIMOLIN.

Timolin. To drive him in sorrow from his doors! my poor master now is sunk in grief and woe.

Arthur. (*without*) Bravo! (*enters singing*) Ladies, 'pon my word, my friend is an excellent stick; his respects to you, Miss, and my most humble adoration to you, Madam, we'll have a little dance above.

Augusta. Oh, Sir! no, no! come Fanny.

Fanny. Lud! it would be fine fun, governess don't you see how cloudy it gets; I'm sure there will be a shower, and if I walk thro' the rain, you, as my governess, ought to be very angry with me.

Arthur.

Arthur. Fye, Ma'am, wou'd you fpoil your drefs? we fhall have a dafhing fhower.

[*Fanny holds out her hand.*

Augufta. No, indeed! come Fanny.

Arthur. You, Sir, where's my mother?

Timolin. With your father. I left the picture in the porter's lodge; for the Frenchman has turn'd away the porter for letting you in.

Arthur. Go back, and bring it to my lodgings, or I'll maffacre you. (*a fiddle heard without*) we'll be with you, boy.

Fanny. But, Sir, as that young man plays, where's my partner?

Arthur. I'll whiftle, fing, and dance, all in a breath. (*puts an arm round each, and runs in.*)

Timolin. (*whiftles*) A pity that Chriftians hav'n't a laughing and crying fide to their faces; for in a comfortable fit of forrow, up ftarts fomething to give us an he, he, he! and when the mouth's opened for a grin, up goes the finger in the eye with an ho, ho, ho!—but my face muft take the humour and fortunes of my mafter; in the road of life the fmall muft follow the great, and that's the reafon the big coach-wheel runs after the little one. [*Exit.*

SCENE II.

The Inn.

Enter LANDLADY, *introducing* LADY TORRENDEL, *and* MISS CLARE.

Landlady. Won't you pleafe to reft, Ma'am?

Lady Tor. I thank you, but fo long fhut up in

a

a carriage, one fhould reft walking.   Mifs Clare,
will you be fo kind as to afk the footman if I've
left my memorandum-book in the coach? (*exit
Mifs Clare*) Some handfome equipages about
here! have you many gentry in the town?

Landlady. Oh, yes Ma'am, we've a Lord, and
Knight, and a power of Squires.

Re-enter MISS CLARE.

Mifs Clare. Here, Ma'am, is the book.

Lady Tor. Oh! I thank you.

Landlady. I'll haften the horfes.   [*Exit.*

Lady Tor. My Lord had a feat in this part of
the country, and I think a banking agent of his
lives in this town, (*looks in the book*) Mr. Dickins,
yes, very true.

Mifs Clare. This feems a charming place, my
Lady!

Lady Tor. It is! I wifh my Lord hadn't parted with it! the caftle and its delightful environs
were the tranquil fcenes of my moft happy
hours! after marriage our firft years were pafs'd
here, and tho' there was title on his fide, and
great wealth on mine, yet ours was not a match
of fafhion! neither ambition on my part, or (I
think) avarice on his; very young to be fure,
but then I was a little philofopher, tho' bred in
the full brilliant certainty of every dazzling joy
that riches cou'd beftow, yet my fight was
proof againft the glare of fplendor.   My Lord
was gay, accomplifh'd, and the generofity of a
youthful mind repell'd all idea of advantage in
our union.

Mifs Clare. Ah, Madam! any Gentleman muft
think himfelf poffefs'd of every advantage in a
union with your Ladyfhip.

                                                    Lady

Lady Tor. I wifh I had myfelf gone to Lifbon with my Lord; this journey feems fo tedious, and then the uncertainty of the feas; thro' his indifpofition he may want that tender cordiality, his claim from me; I'm all anxiety to proceed.

Enter COACHMAN.

Coachman. Madam the horfes are too, but does your Ladyfhip know my Lord's here?

Lady Tor. Here! how! what do you mean?

Coachman. In this very town my Lady, I met our old Martha.

Lady Tor. Impoffible! return'd to England! fomething very myfterious——

Dick. (*without*) Well, what is it?

' *L'Œillet.* (*witheut*) I cannot talk my Lor's bufinefs in public entré.

Lady Tor. Eh, why—fure that is my Lord's valet.

Mifs Clare. It certainly is, Madam.

Lady Tor. Hufh, ftep this way, Heavens! oh, my heart—well—Martha you fay—tell me—(*agitated*). [*Exeunt.*

Enter DICKINS *and* L'ŒILLET.

Dick. Really, fince my Lord's lofty conduct to me, I fhall give up his affairs. I've my agencies, and my bank to mind.

L'Œillet. Bank! vat! de little till in your boutique? you had better fend challenge to mi Lor—fwell and puff! ma foi! c'eft comique ça! let mi Lor take his money out of your bank, den vat is your bladder of confequence.

Dick. 'Sblood I don't want any body to take their money out of my bank.

L'Œil-

L'Œillet. Here be a frefh pacquet of letters.

Dick. Which I am to forward, as ufual, to Lady Torrendel in Cumberland.

L'Œillet. I have date 'em, fo as to make mi Lady believe my Lor ftill at Lifbon.

Dick. To keep the unfufpecting wife cool amongft the lakes there, whilft the gallant hufband enjoys his rofe-buds in his pleafure grounds here.

L'Œillet. Mi Lor, to fpare himfelf from writing, ftill fineffe de fprain hand, and trouble me vid de vife—fo dere I ave writ dat whole bundle for her at vonce. I ave upon my mind des affaires d'importance to get de pretty girl for mi Lor.

Dick. And I, as a magiftrate, have to fend this young dog to prifon, who has been taking up the tradefmen's goods.

L'Œillet. Magiftrate! fi donc! petit bourgeois —you huff abaut pah! [*Exit.*

Dick. Who cares for your paw, or your four claws, you outlandifh cockatoo! I muft fend thefe one by one, which firft?

Re-enter LADY TORRENDEL (*unperceived*).

Lady Tor. My Lord in England all this time!

Dick. Dated this day—to Lady Torrendel. (*reading.*)

Lady Tor. How's this! (*afide*)

Dick. Then to give time for her to fuppofe it came from her Lord at Lifbon, where he has not been at all, her Ladyfhip fhall have this in about a month.

Lady Tor. A little fooner, if you pleafe, Sir. (*advancing.*)

Dick. My Lady herfelf! (*drops the letters and*

exit confufed. Enter Mifs Clare; picks them up and prefents.)

Lady Tor. (*opening one*) Separate himfelf from me by fuch a complicated feries of invention, and by fallacious accounts of his ill-health, keep me in perpetual uneafinefs! cruel man! make me believe he had fold his eftate here, yet retain it only for the bafe purpofe of converting a fpot (that brings to my mind the fweet recollection of delight, and innocence) into a contaminated retreat for licentious, guilty, fordid pleafures! you charg'd the coachman not to mention who I am? but I fear that now is too late.

Mifs Clare. No, Ma'am, for his own difcretion fuggefted the neceffity of that, before I mentioned it to him.

Lady Tor. Do you think too, if the people of this houfe know it, I can engage them to keep my arrival a fecret.

Mifs Clare. The woman promifes that, for tho' my Lord fpends fo much money, he's no favourite in the town, from the knowledge of his ill ufage to your Ladyfhip.

Lady Tor. I wou'dn't have him defpifed; but how to gain full and certain proofs? to put beyond all doubt his motive for fecreting himfelf here?

Mifs Clare. So far I have taken the liberty of anticipating your Ladyfhip's wifh. I have afk'd Martha——

Lady Tor. My good friend! a thoufand thanks! I'm charm'd with your zeal. Yes, it is my wifh; what! Martha will convey me privately into the Caftle? delightful! I think none of his fervants know me here, but his French Secretary. Write to me by a fervant! not open my Letters! unkind!

kind! ungrateful! but then, to fteal upon him,
it's a fevere trial—I'm faint! but I muft fummon
fortitude! they'll fee I've been weeping; come—

[*Exeunt.*

SCENE III.

A Parlour in DICKINS's: *large Books lying on the
table.*

Enter JOHN *and* TRADESMEN.

John. Step in, only ftop a moment, my mafter will be in directly, and take all your infor-
mations.   You know I can do nothing in it.

[*Exit.*

1ft *Man.* The young Gentleman is thoughtlefs and wild, but I believe's there not much
harm in him.

2d *Man.* I don't think I can find in my heart
to profecute, if the affair is likely to affect his
life.

3d *Man.* He's but a bad one I fear, yet I'd
not hang a man for all the boots I'm worth.

Enter DICKINS.

Dick. So, the Lady has got into the Caftle.
fhe'll trim his gay lordfhip—yes, fhe has ftole a
march upon him—he fha'n't hear of it from me.
Oh what curtain lectures, perhaps a divorce,
then maybe he'll marry my Fanny. (*afide*) A
pretty bufinefs this young buck—

2d *Man.* If he can raife the money to pay me
I don't wifh to hurt him.

Dick.

Dick. Pay you, oh! I fhall lofe my fees! *(afide)*
You felfifh man, would you compound a felony:
Some revenge upon the father, to have the great
family-name of D'Aumerle down in a Mittimus.

Enter CONSTABLE.

Fellow, where's your pris'ner?

Conft. Pleafe your worfhip, he be dauncing—
he defired me to gi' you this bit of paper.

Dick. I fend you for a thief, and you bring
me a bit of paper!—he be dauncing! *(reads)*
" Lord Arthur D'Aumerle's compliments to Juftice Dickins, is now engaged with fome Ladies,
but after another dance will wait upon"—dance!

Conft. Yez, there bes young Squire Burgefs
got fiddling, and Mifs Fanny, they be jigging it
up rarely.

Dick. My daughter! is this the firft leffon
from her new Governefs! but you ftupid fcoundrel, I fuppofe you took a bribe.

Conft. Noa, Sir, I only took Half-a-crown.

Dick. How dare you, only a Conftable, meddle with the Juftice's bufinefs. A notorious of-
fender; charged with crimes of life and death!
he come! no! he'll abfcond—we fha'n't fee him
in a hurry.

Arthur. *(without)* I want the Juftice!

Dick. Why, that's he, but you find no Juftice
here *(afide)* I muft examine the culprit in form;
you, firrah! John, what are you about in the
fhop, when I want you in my office? weighing
raifins and pepper; down with the fcales and
balance, and bring my great books, and my
ink-ftand, aye! and I'll take my chocolate here.

(Cho-

(Chocolate, &c. brought in; Dickins places books, puts on wig, and sits. ' *[Exit Constable.*

Enter ARTHUR.

Arthur. I've finish'd our Coranto in a quick step, and, with a kiss hand to the Ladies, have flown to receive your commands.

Dick. (*aside*) Now, is this folly, impudence, courage, or generosity?

Arthur. Upon the information of the butter'd muffins, Justice Dickins, I presume——*(sits on the table, and eats.)*

Dick. Sir, upon the information of the Constable, a great rogue I presume—but 'pon honor I didn't expect you.

Arthur. Oh! then Sir, your most obedient! (*going*)

Dick. Stop! stop! is this the man that took your goods?

Tradesman. Yes!

Dick. Enough! write his mittimus.—you all prosecute; what's your name Mr. ——

Arthur. Lord Arthur D'Aumerle.

Dick. Alias Duke of Dunstable, alias Captain, alias Major.

Arthur. Was my father still in the army, I'd have enlisted a common soldier in his own regiment—then the world might have said, there's Lord Torrendel's son carrying a knapsack—but now let it say, a parent suffers his child to lie in prison for the necessaries of life. Cou'dn't you carry me to gaol by the cattle?

Dick. Constable, you have my authority, take him.

Enter

Enter SIR HANS.

Sir H. No man in England fhall take him.
My prince of bold actions, what are they going
to do with you?

Dick. Conduct him to prifon!

Sir H. I'll bail him.

Arthur. Pray be quiet, Sir.

Sir H. I wo'n't de quiet, Sir.

Dick. But, here's an affault and battery—muft
be bound over to keep the peace for a year and
a quarter—no, a year and a day.

Sir H. I'll anfwer for him! aye, two thoufand
pounds! there's my name; fill up the inftrument. (*figns*)

Dick. Oh! very well: he'll fave his neck, and
you'll lofe your money—let him out now, and
catch him again if you can.

Arthur. Does your little rafcally foul conceive
I'd let a friend fuffer for an act of benevolence,
and to myfelf? No! human laws may punifh
other crimes; but, let the hotteft bolt of heaven ftrike ingratitude.

Timolin. (*without*) Sweet Mr. Conftable, 'pon
my falvation I didn't—

Re-enter CONSTABLE, *with* TIMOLIN (*prifoner*).

Conft. Meafter, here be's an accomplifh.

Timolin. I'm not accomplifh'd, I'm quite a bog
trotter. (*crying*)

Conft. The picture that was robb'd out of——

Dickins. What, you found it upon him?

Conft. Upon his very head.

Dick. You notorious criminal!

Timolin.

Timolin. My mafter to be jumping about with Ladies, and leave me——oh! my dear Sir *(runs to Arthur. Tradefmen whifper. Timolin, pointing to Sir Hans)* did he! then plaife your honour, will you be bound bail for me too?

Sir H. For you! pardon me.

Timolin. No, Sir! afk them to pardon me.

Enter GEORGE.

George. Mr. Dickins, I'm making up a fmall fum,—there was change coming to me yefterday when I bought the half-pound of Six-fhilling Souchong, I'll thank you for it, it was nine-pence.

Dick. Confound your nine-pence, Sir, come into Court for your nine-pence.

Sir H. And burn your Souchong.

Arthur. Come, Come, my fuper-excellent friends, you fhould know each other.—I have not the honor of knowing your name, Sir, but give me leave to introduce you to Sir Hans Bur-gefs, an exceeding worthy Gentleman, who has a fon, a mean fpirited young foaken fot that gets tipfey with water, and dines on bread and cheefe at the Goat in Boots.—Sir Hans, this is Mr.·——however, he has a foul to relieve poor Debtors out of prifon, yet has a father, the very devil of an " old avaricious Curmudgeon."

George. Now, Sir, Give me leave to intreduce my father,—(*pointing to Sir Hans*)

Sir H. My Lord, My Son, (*prefenting George*)

Arthur. Eh! (*furprifed and confufed*)

George. Oh, my friend, where's the fine picture I faw on your head, (*to Timolin.*)

Dick. There he faw it on his head,—Swear it. (*to George*)

Sir H.

Sir H. Get along you rafcal, an Informer too. (*pufhes him off.*)

Dick. Take away your prifoner.

Arthur. I'll bail my fervant.

Dick. You! a rare fhadow! ah! friend, I know you. Thanks to the noble Lord Torrendel's gallantries, we've twenty fuch Lords cutting cabbages, and drudging for oyfters, down at Sandgate Ifland---but becaufe your mother had a pretty face, a great fortune, and no virtue——

Arthur. Throw a refleftion on my honour'd parent! defame the facred memory of the dead —the only univerfal epitaph fhould be——oblivion to the frailties of humanity!—I'll murder him, by heavens!

Timolin. No occafion to fwear, you've faid it, and you'll do it.

Sir H. Hold! the devil's in you; break the peace, and I lofe my two thoufand pounds.

Arthur. True, my dear friend.---oh! I burn with fury---but your Worfhip's wig can't fwear a battery. (*twirls it*) There's Burn's Juftice, Blackftone, and Coke upon Littleton. (*knocks books about*) Come along, Timolin,

Timolin. Mafter, ftay for me---take me---

Sir H. Oh! what a bright model for my fon George!

[*Exeunt all, Conftable with Timolin.*

END OF ACT THE THIRD.

ACT IV.

SCENE I.

An antique Room in LORD TORRENDEL'S

Enter CONSTABLE, *and* L'ŒILLET, *pushing in* TI-
MOLIN.

L'ŒILLET.

THERE, you ſtay faſt, coquin! ſuch audace---
of robbery, take furniture and pictures out of
my Lor's houſe!

Timolin. I'm more guilty than my Maſter, as
the receiver is worſe than the thief.

Conſt. Who is your maſter, the receiver?
ſpeak!

Timolin. Friend, you may take me for a robber,
if you will; but you ſhan't prove me an informer, becauſe I've a regard for my character.

L'Œillet. Stay there till we find Mr. Dickin,
de juſtice, to ſend you to jail; be merry with
that table and chair; ſorry to diſgrace---make a

brown bear of my chamber---there fit and fing
—" de charge is prepared, de lawyers are met."

[*Exit finging.*

Timolin. I wifh they had crammed me into a
jail at once, and not thruft me into this difmal
top of a caftle. Oh did my poor mother ever
think that, before I died, I fhould get myfelf
hanged for a thief? Lord Arthur! Lord Arthur! unlucky was the day that Mr. Felix Timolin hired to be your fervant man. (*locks at
the table*) Here's letters and papers, fcribble fcrab-
ble, eh! why, this is my Lord's own hand I remember it by one of his Franks—" To Monfieur
L'Œillet." What does he write to his fervants;
but what's all this to me; no way to get out of
window, may be in this clofet.   [*Retires.*

Enter at a private door, LADY TORRENDEL, *and*
MARTHA.

Martha. (*furprifed*) Why, I vow my Lady, this
is the valet's room, and none of us ever knew
this door to it.

Lady Tor. I think, Martha, I remember the
caftle better than you, who have lived in it fo
long. Out of that door there's a ftair-cafe to
my Lord's dreffing-room, where I'll wait till he
comes in. I'd wifh to know a little more before
I fee him. Rather mean this lurking about and
tampering with fervants—but no hope of re-
claiming him, except he's certain I know what
then will be out of his power to deny. (*afide*)
My Lord rode out you fay; feemed difcompofed?
well, not a word that I'm here,—(*Exit Martha*)
this houfe feems all wild, no regularity, peace,
or the comforts of a home, but the gratification
of

of paffions which reafon and nature now fhould fubdue, reconciles him to inquietude, meannefs, and difhonour. So, this. room now belongs to his vile agent! it was formerly put to a better purpofe—this is the very room that I converted into a fchool for the poor infant ruftics. Here the young mind was trained to virtue and induftry —here now, are, perhaps, plans laid to corrupt and deftroy the fweet rofe of innocence! Eh, who's here!

Re-enter TIMOLIN.

Timolin. No, looks into a deep court. Oh, I'm very high up, they've double locked the door. (*trying it*) Oh dear! oh dear! (*fits*)

Lady Tor. Dos'nt feem one of the family! (*afide*)

Timolin. This letter, from my Lord to Monfieur, I've a ftrong curiofity to fee.

Lady Tor. How! as I'm here on a voyage of difcovery, the fight of that might prepare me better for this dreaded interview with my Lord. (*afide*)

Timolin. It's ungenerous to look into another man's letter, only I'd like to fee the taftieft mode of writing. I'm told its not the fafhion now to crofs the t's, and put little tittles on the i's; no harm to fee that fure—(*reads*) " The fight of this boy has troubled me exceedingly !"—Boy ! oh, that's my mafter; (*reading*) " Probably, I fhan't be home before evening, but if you can contrive to get Augufta into your power, the better. She may be brought down to Sandgate ifland"—Oh, here's villany ! here's villany !

Lady

Lady Tor. (*aside*) Some poor intended victim!
My coming at such a time is highly fortunate.

Timolin (*reads*). " Pray have an eye upon
that Arthur's ill-looking Irishman"—Oh, that
crowns his rogueries—" No harm to keep Augusta under lock and key." I'll keep this proof
of their wickedness, and if they talk of hanging
me for a bit of an old picture, I'll bring it out
to their shabby red faces—ill looking Irishman.
(*sees Lady Tor.*) What! then they have locked
you up? you most unhappy beautiful soul.

Lady Tor. He takes me for the present object
of pursuit! by giving into this mistake, I may
discover some more of my husband's atchieve-
ments. (*aside*) Are you his Lordship's emissary?

Timolin. I, Miss! I despise such doings:

Lady Tor. I believe it; your face speaks ho-
nesty.

Timolin. Then it speaks truth, and the devil
himself shan't make it tell a lie.

Lady Tor. But, who are you?

Timolin. My master is his Lordship's son that's
at this instant shifting about, and can't get a beef-
steak without venturing his neck for it.

Lady Tor. True—Martha told me of this unhappy destitute youth—Oh, husband! false to
me, and unnaturally cruel to the offspring of
your follies,

Timolin. Miss, I'll assure you, Lord Arthur is
as brave a little boy—

Lady Tor. And bears his forlorn state with
meekness and resignation?

Timolin. Oh yes, Miss, he's as meek and gentle—ah, hem!

Lady Tor. (*aside*). Poor youth, he has a father, and yet an orphan! Then he shall find a
friend

friend in me—though not mine, he belongs to the man I ftill love! but to continue this deception—cou'd you contrive any means for me to fly this manfion of fhame and ruin? (*a noife without*)

Timolin. Offer to touch her, and, by the mighty powers of heaven, I'll flay you. (*fnatches up a chair*).

Lady Tor. Ah! (*runs in. The door burft open.*)

Enter ARTHUR.

Arthur. Suffer me to perifh, and imprifon my faithful fquire for his attachment! Put your arms a-kimbo, firrah, ftump down thofe great ftairs with your hat on, and let me fee who dares fquint at you——Oh! that lovely divine Augufta!

Timolin. What! then you've feen her, Sir— (*winks, and points off where Lady Torrendel went.*)

Arthur. What do you ftand winking and making faces there, firrah? come out.

Timolin. But there's fomebody elfe loek'd up.

Arthur. Kick up your legs boldly, no matter whofe fhins are in the way.

Timolin. But, Sir—

Arthur. By'r leave there for Mr. Timolin.
[*Exeunt.*

S C E N E II.

A Street.

Enter SIR HANS, *and* GEORGE.

Sir. H. Aye! and well George? (*joyful*)

George

George. We had a dance, Sir.

Sir H. As if he had faid we had a funeral.
'Sblood! man, fay—we had a dance. (*capers*)
Arthur was mafter of the ceremonies—you
fhuffled it away? eh, boy?

George. Yes, Sir, I was'nt afraid to fhuffle, for
I had my thick walking fhoes on.

Sir H. Shoes! affes' hoofs! I believe they're
half an inch thick.

George. Sir, they're near an inch. (*afide*) I muft
fee if the poor woman has releafed her hufband.

Sir H. George, then 'twas you rafp'd up the
fiddle for them?

George. Yes, Sir, fo we had no fiddler to pay.

Sir H. Pfha! I'd hire Handel's anniverfary
band to fee you dance the Cameronian Rant
with Augufta. This fcheme of leaving her at
large wo'nt do—fhe'll be fnapt up. Gad, yonder fhe is—I muft clench this bufinefs. Why
do you put on that difmal look, firrah?

George. I was thinking, father, of the cruelty
in keeping people in prifon for fmall debts above
a twelvemonth however; liberty's fo fweet,
they'd purchafe it if in their power, if not, hard
to punifh a man for only being unfortunate.

Sir H. Here comes Mifs Augufta, Devil's in
your thick foal'd fhoes!

Enter AUGUSTA, *and* FANNY.

Augufta. That man certainly whifpered fomething difagreeable that caufed the abrupt departure of Lord Arthur.

Fanny. Dear no, he's a very civil foul, why
'twas papa's conftable. Oh if here is'nt George.

Sir H. Your waiftcoat's buttoned all crooked

—no powder in your hair—by the lord! you look like the duftman. (*apart*) Well Mifs, how do you like your new fituation?—ftop, I want to fpeak to you.

Fanny. Stop, he wants to fpeak to us—how do you do, George?

Sir H. Ha! very free with George! (*afide*) Mifs Woodbine, I've your good at heart. Your uncle's whim, in taking his fortune from you, makes you an object of compaffion.

Augufta. Many would rather be an object of envy—but, to my thinking, an humble ftate is preferable to affluence, built upon the rui of unmerited adverfity.

Sir H. (*afide*) Made for each other! George, to her in her own way—out with your handkerchief, and cry for the poor debtors. (*apart*) My fon, Mifs is fo happy to fee—to be with you—

Fanny. Happy to fee her? but I'm fure its no fuch thing.

Sir H. He expreffed great joy at your coming fo opportunely:

George. Opportunely indeed! (*looking at his ftocking*) Mifs, could you lend me a needle and thread?

Sir H. Go along, fortune! I'll bind you apprentice to a taylor.

Augufta. You're happy, Sir, in having a fon of fo much frugality for his years.

Sir H. Frugal ma'am! he's the moft extravagant—

Fanny. I fee now he only wants them to like each other; I muft prevent this.

Sir H. Why, look now, with his coat over
his

his knuckles; he has on lace ruffles at three guineas a pair. Pull down your ruffles. (*pulls
George's wriftbands down*) by the lord! he has got
into a hopfack. What have you done with all
the fine linen and lace I fent you?

George. The lace was too fine for ufe—but
the Holland made foft child-bed linen for a
poor curate's wife.

Sir H. Yes, madam, the bifhop's lady was the
good woman in the ftraw. He is very frolickfome—it's a fhame for you to be fuch a buck.

Fanny. Mifs, George is no buck! he's a mere
milk fop, an't you George?

Sir H. Get away you little devil, who wants
your prate. (*apart*) Mifs, we'll conceal your lofs of
fortune from my fon—he's fo proud—fee how he
throws his head about. (*apart*) George, with Augufta's cafh, you can do fuch pretty charities! Son,
this lady is worth one hundred thoufand pounds.

Fanny. George, fhe's only my governefs, and
as poor—borrowed five fhillings from me juft
now to releafe her box from the waggon—fay
you did. (*apart to Augufta*)

Sir H. Get along you little bufy thing. (*apart
to Fanny*) You know, ma'am, you're an immenfe
fortune.

Augufta. Sir, I am neither ambitious of compaffion or ridicule.

Sir H. George, never mind—fhe's very rich.

Augufta. Oh no, Sir!

Sir H. Madam, you're a Jew.

Fanny. My governefs is not a Jew, fhe has
more religon than the bifhop.

Sir H. The devil's in me, if I don't make
your father pull your ears! Mifs, my fon has
a moft

a moſt liberal mind, a foul of magnificent extra-vagance.

George. Madam, my father is only jeſting.

Fanny. True, George, now that's very good, of you, Sir Hans is always making his fun of every body.

Sir H. Overthrowing my whole ſcheme. (*aſide*) Hop home you little magpie! (*to Fanny*)

George. Madam, be aſſured, I eſteem œconomy the firſt virtue.

Sir H. Then the devil's in you both! but it's you, you prating monkey, has done it all; you, you raſcal, with your œconomy and aſſes' hoofs, truſſ down to Sampſhire Hall; and you, Miſs, ſtalk with your poverty to Mr. Dickins, the banker's.

George. Madam, your humble ſervant! (*bows and exit*)

Sir H. Civil ſcoundrel! ſome mad gander will tuck her and her fortune under his wing, and fly off to Gretna Green.

Fanny. George ſent down to the rocks, oh! oh! then I know where ſomebody will go. (*aſide*) Sir Hans, your moſt obedient, good morning to you, Sir! (*curtſys and exit*)

Sir H. Oh very polite Ma'am, but I wiſh you had dropt your curtſy half an hour ago.

Auguſta. (*looking out*) The forlorn thoughtleſs Arthur! Sir, tell me—is Miſs Woodbine's ſon my uncle's heir? then why not inſtantly extricate him, from the embarraſſing perplexities that muſt end in his deſtruction.

Sir H. What ſon? (*looking out*) The gay Ar-thur! true, Lord Torrendel's; (*aſide*) oh oh! I ſuſpect there's love here—this was her dancing partner. My dear, as to affection and all that, this Arthur.——

Augusta. Sir, I am only interested for him, on account of my cousin Woodbine.

Sir H. Right! for his heart is engaged to a girl—he told me all over a glass of hock. (*Augusta agitated*) (*aside*) Yes! she likes him—then, in one word, Miss Augusta, my dear, I'll not part with you, till I see you and my son fairly coupled.

Arthur. (*without*) Sir Hans! (*enters*)

Sir H. Yes, Sir! past three. (*exit with Augusta*)

Arthur. Past three! Don't much like his avoiding me, and taking the lady. His bail-bond may keep me from limbo—but mustn't rob me of paradise either.

Enter TIMOLIN.

Run, sirrah, after Miss Augusta, and ——

Timolin. Back again to your father's?

Arthur. You *will* persist, we left Augusta there; (*tears a leaf from his pocket-book, and writes with pencil*) if I can but obtain the love of this charming girl, she's so beautiful, elegant—but then, very modest; I must engage her affections—Timolin, run with this letter.

Timolin. With what?

Arthur. Stop to ask questions with your hows and whats—run, take this letter to the young lady.

Timolin. I'll give no letters to ladies. Do you want, Sir, to carry on your father's profligate rigmarols? but you don't make a French Moun-
seer

feer of me—for the fpirit of Mr. Timolin is a peg above that, I affure you.

Arthur. Walk back, if you pleafe, into Caftle Quod.

Timolin. Then 'pon my word, I won't.

Arthur. How! do you object to go into prifon when I defire you? begone! I difcharge you.

Timolin. Oh! Sir, I difcharge myfelf, and there's a receipt for my wages. (*fnaps his fingers*) I'd hazard my life, to procure you what you might again repay—but, helping you to take the innocence you can never return, is beneath the foul of Mr. Felix Timolin.   [*Exit*

Arthur. I've loft him.   I had no conception of this mighty Irifh honour of his brave foul.   He has had moral, from his ruftic parent in his mud cabin; but, I never knew a father's kind precept or good example.

Enter COACHMAN, *furveys* ARTHUR *at a diftance.*

What does this fellow eye me for.

Coachman. My lady fent me to know his per-fon—yes! that's he, very well.   [*Exit.*

Arthur. You're no Coachman, my friend, you're a bailiff—they take all difguifes.   [*Exit.*

SCENE III.

A Walk near Lord Torrendel's

Enter L'ŒILLET.

L'Œillet. To divert mi Lor from de thought of

of dis tapageur fon of his, I muft get off Mifs Augufta for him ; but, to fee more of this letter of inftruction, (*feeling his pockets*) eh! oh! I have left it on the table in my room—Thomas have borrow Sir Hans's livery to carry her fham meffage; but if dere be danger, we yet want fome ftrong, able, defperate——

Enter TIMOLIN, *melancholy.*

Timolin. I could be contented with one dinner in three days, becaufe it's a thing I've practis'd with fome fuccefs—but, my poor dear mafter——

L'Œillet. Oh! you be got out, where I did lock you————

Timolin. Here, lock me up again; for now I've loft my mafter, I don't care where I am.

L'Œillet. I fuppofe you be not overcharg'd vid money, and I take it you be fripon—in your character, roguery be the leading feature.

Timolin. I judge that your nofe is your leading feature—fo I take it. (*advancing*) I, a rogue! produce a proof that I'm one.

L'Œillet. Here be a ftirling proof. (*fhews money.*)

Timolin. So, becaufe you've money, you've a right to call a poor man out of his name.

L'Œillet. (*gives it*) Dere now, call me out of my name.

Timolin. (*looking at it*) Then, you're an honeft man and a genteel noble lad. If I can find my lord, this will carry us back to town. (*going*)

L'Œillet. Arreté! dat is for fervice you vill do me. (*looking out*) Milor! go! dat footman vill tell you vat it be. Befides, more reward, if you fhould be taken up again for little peccadilloz, milor's intereft vill releafe you. Allez!

Tim-

Timolin. Paid for doing good before hand!
I've gold and a clear confcience, two compa-
nions that are feldom together now a day's.
[*Exit.*

Enter LORD TORRENDEL.

Lord Tor. That fellow of Arthur's ftill lurking
about here!

L'Œillet. Arthur's fervant! pefte! quelle bal-
lourdife! I have made fine confidante in my
Lor's fcheme. (*afide*)

Lord Tor. I hope you hav'nt let this affair go
further than thofe already concerned?

L'Œillet. Oh! no, my Lord! if he knew I had
employed this Irifhman, I am undone. (*afide*)

Lord Tor. You've warned the porter how he
admits them again?

L'Œillet: Ah, my Lor, he vill find hard to
admit himfelf.

Lord Tor. L'Œillet, I've improved upon your
plan. Thomas's being in Sir Hans's livery may
not be fufficient to perfuade Augufta, that fhe
is really fet for by him—now if you could borrow Sir Hans's poft chaife, that would effectually
remove fufpicion—make any excufe, he'll be glad
to oblige me.

L'Œillet, Here I go for Sir Hans's coach to
carry off Mifs Augufta, and have fet Thomas and
de Irifhman to take her off vid horfes. (*afide*)

Lord Tor. Why, you don't feem over hearty
in the caufe now?

L'Œillet. Oh! I'm devote to your Lorfhip's
fervice.

Lord

Lord Tor. Once wheedled into the carriage, a pretext is foon found to get her to Sandgate Ifland.

L'Œillet. Ah! mais ceſt que ceſt excellent ca!

Lord Tor. About it now—I ſhall be there before you.   [*Exit.*

L'Œillet. Pardi! dis is lucky—for now I vill do it myſelf. I viſh tho' I cou'd meet vid dis maroufle, to hinder him meddle in de affair— dat malheureux Iriſh tief vill do me ſome miſ- chief.   [*Exit.*

———————————

SCENE IV.

A Road.

Enter TIMOLIN, *and* THOMAS, in SIR HANS's *Livery.*

Timolin. Well, Mr. Thomas, I know all your plan, now you've told me. So here you've borrowed Sir Hans's livery from one of his fer- vants, and you're to go and tell Mifs Augufta, he has fent you for her—but, as you may be a cowardly kind of a chap, the Mounfeer has bid me affift you with my tight bit of an arm. Huſh! here ſhe comes.

Thomas. I thought ſhe was a little girl juſt left fchool.

Timolin. I don't know, whether ſhe goes to fchool or no—but, this is the very Mifs Au- gufta, that was lock'd up in the caftle with me.

me. (*afide*) Oh! I'll make a neat example of ye
all.   [*they retire.*

Enter LADY TORRENDEL, *and* COACHMAN.

Lady Tor. My mind is in a ftate of the moft
tormenting folicitude! I wifh I knew where to
find this young lady, and apprize her of my
Lord's defigns. Whether to return and wait for
him? I dread the interview, unkind upbraiding
often fhakes the very bafis of affection. Yet I
know he'll endeavour, by fome artful evafion,
to flip from my charge, except I can bring it to
a full conviction—but [firft to afford this poor
young man affiftance.
Timolin. Young man! that muft be me—fhe
faw I was in diftrefs. (*afide*)
Lady Tor. Deliver this to him, without letting
him know who it comes from. (*gives a pocket-
book to Coachman*)   [*Exit Coachman.*
Timolin. Stop! I'm here.
Lady Tor. Oh, his fervant.
Timolin. Now, this goodnefs to me, has determined me, in what I was resolved upon; to
fave her from all danger. (*afide*)
Lady Tor. Perhaps I may now learn, who this
young lady is.
Timolin. (*to Thomas*) Go you, and ftay with
your horfes—I'll deliver the meffage to her my-
felf.
Thomas. But you're not in Sir Hans's livery
—It wo'n't take. '*apart*)
Timolin. How d'ye do, Mifs Augufta?
Lady Tor. (*afide*) My trufty champion's mif-
taking me for her, I find, continues.
Thomas. Mifs, your guardian, Sir Hans Burgefs,

geſs, hopes for your company down at Samphire-hall—he has ſent horſes.

Timolin. I'll whiſper a few words, that ſhall
bring her directly. Harkye, Miſs! don't go,
this is a rogue, that wants to coax you again into the mouſe-trap. (*apart to Lady Torrendel*)

Lady Tor. You miſtake—I'm not the perſon.
(*to Thomas*)

Timolin. That's a good thought to deny yourſelf—I'll ſecond it, (*apart*)—are you ſure you
never ſaw Miſs Auguſta before now?

Thomas. Not I.

Timolin. Then this is not ſhe—ſo go about
your buſineſs.

Thomas. What!

Timolin. He wants to inveigle you, to Lord
Torrendel. (*apart*)

Lady Tor. Indeed! this is charming, as I ſup-
poſed! the moſt lucky opportunity to do good,
prevent evil, ſave the innocent from ruin, and
overwhelm the guilty in the bluſhing ſhame of
his own baſe intentions. (*aſide*) I was apprehen-
ſive of ſome error—you've brought horſes you
ſay—very well, I'll—wait on my guardian. (*to
Thomas.*)　　　　　[*Timolin ſtares, and whiſtles.*

Thomas. Then you are Miſs Auguſta. Why,
what did you mean juſt now by ſaying it was
not. (*to Timolin*)

Lady Tor. Yes, yes, you're right enough.

Timolin. If they take you for a Lady, that
will fly off to an old libertine, they're right
enough indeed; but I was wrong, when I thought
you a bit of an angel.

Lady Tor. Come. (*going*)

Timolin. A word, ma'am! your intentions juſt
now about me, were good—but, ſince you give
your-

yourſelf up to this old reprobate, I ſcorn your
affiſtance, and if a little turn of virtue, ſhould
ever make you repent of your nonſenſe, don't
expect any defence from the ſoul of Mr. Timolin.

Lady Tor. Heavens! I leave a ſhocking im-
preſſion on the mind of this worthy creature.
(aſide) Well, well, we ſhall find a time to clear
my character. [*Exit with Thomas.*

Timolin. An old rotten potatoe for your character! bye and bye, when you're ſeen flouriſhing in curricles, with a different gallant every
day, ſtuck up at your elbow, you'll ſtill be chat-
tering about your character, to all the turnpike-
men.

Enter ARTHUR, *(haſtily)*.

Arthur. Yes! it is a bailiff—he's at my heels.
Timolin, do you ſee any door open? ſtand in
that ſpot, you ſcoundrel.

Timolin. Oh Sir! if any more of thoſe compliments paſs between you and me, it's a toſs up
who's to pay them.

Arthur. If he don't touch me, it's no caption.

Timolin. He's returning with the money, the
gay Miſs gave him for me.

Re-enter COACHMAN.

Coachman. I've had a good chace after you,
Sir.

Arthur. Attempt to give me the tip, and——

Coachman. *(taking papers from his pocket)* Here
it is—this bill for three hundred——

VOL. I. M *Ti-*

Timolin. If it was ten thoufand, I wou'dn't accept it.

Arthur. You villain, do I want you to accept
bills for me?

Coachman. It's a good note, and your own
too.

Arthur. Well, I know I have notes and bonds
enough out—but if I pay one of them, I'll be
damn'd.

Timolin. Sir, don't frighten yourfelf, about
what doesn't concern you.

Arthur. Hold your tongue, firrah; of my own
accord, I came from our dance, when old Wig-
hum, the juftice, fent for me; but, compell'd
I will not be; fo let the plaintiff carry the bills
to my father:

Coachman. Now, Sir, you're too nice. I promifed to do the bufinefs, and I will. (*offers papers.*)

Arthur. Aye! he only wants to touch me.
(*flips round Timolin.*)

Timolin. Arrah! what fignifies your dancing
round me, like a couple of May-poles?

Arthur. Timolin, knock him down—I wonder whether it's a capture if I touch him.

Timolin. What are you at with your caps, and
hats? The English of the thing is—Mifs Augufta, I defpife.

Arthur. Speak fo of my divine charmer!

    [*ftrikes him, and runs off, Coachman follows.*

Timolin. Oh! if he difcharges me, and comes
once a day to give me a knock in my cheek,
I'm to have a bleffed life of it—tho' my honor
wou'd not fuffer me to take relief from this
                            Mifs

Miſs Auguſta, yet I'll try and get the reward from Mounſeer, for, if I was to preach in a pulpit as high as Patrick's ſteeple, the ladies, and gentlemen, would be running after one another, and, till they give roaſt beef for nothing, to mere honeſty, a guinea is convenient in an empty pocket.

[*Exit.*

END OF THE FOURTH ACT.

M 2

ACT V.

SCENE I.

Samphire-hall: SIR HANS's, *and other Houses :—*
A view of the Sea, bathing Machines, &c.

Enter SIR HANS, *and* ROBIN HOOFS.

SIR HANS.

A Month fince I've been down here at my favourite rocks. How do the lodging-houfes go
on? I hope they keep low with their prices, till
the place is known. Aye! I may yet fee Samphire-hall eclipfe Brighton, Weymouth, and Scar-
borough.

Robin H. Yes! your honour ; for the young
Squire has fet up a ftaple commodity of trade,
and already the volks bes fo merry about'n.
You know Humphry Grim, the ftone-mafon, is
famous in the letter cutting way—Meafter
George has gi'n the freedom of the quarry,
and he has eftablifhed a manufacture for tomb-
ftones.

Sir H.

Sir H. Tomb-ftones to make people merry!

Robin H. He has finifhed half a dozen choice epitaphs with:

> " Afflictions zore
> " Long time I bore
> " Phyficians were in wain."

(SIR HANS *walks up enraged.*)

Enter GEORGE.

George. That was certainly Lord Torrendel turn'd into the green lane—muffled up, and feem'd hiding his face. Robin gave me a hint of his defigns upon Fanny.

Sir H. A fweet morning concert for the rooms, of chipping and fawing! Tell Mafter Grim, he muft depart in peace with his merry monuments. Did you hire a new poftillion?

Robin H. Yez, Sir.

George. Oh, Robin! my fcheme of fettling the poor artificers here, requires a kind of agent or fuperior, to regulate it in my abfence; a fenfible perfon of good nature and probity—that I can truft—I've fixt upon a man—he's now over at Sandgate ifland, you muft acquaint him—no only tell him I'd fpeak with him.

Sir H. (feeing George) Don't come near me— get a tin pot and a bit of ftick, and pick up cockles on the beach—you haven't a foul above a cockle-gatherer, you curfed otter. Robin! have they put up the fhelves in the raffling fhop?

George. Sir, the men are working at their looms.

Sir H. Looms!

George.

George. Inſtead of encouraging frauds, cheat-
ing ſtrangers with paltry toys, I have erected
looms, that will give bread to two induſtrious
fam lies. *(loom heard without)*

Sir H. Why, they're Weavers!

George. Yes, Sir, weavers of ſtockings, gloves,
and mittins.

Sir H. A ſtocking loom in the place of my elegant raffling ſhop!

George. There's a ribband loom too. This
was the firſt wove in it; for the motto's ſake,
put it into your hat.

Sir H. (reads) " Succeſs to Commerce, and a
ſpeedy peace." Well, let Induſtry throw the
ſhuttle to this motto with all my heart. What
ſmoke's that yonder? clinking of hammers! by
the lord it's a forge.

George. Yes, Sir, the forge I built for poor old
Grimes.

Sir H. What, a ſmith?

George. Yes, Sir, a worthy blackſmith.

Sir H. Within the very walls of my cold bath,
old Grimes blowing his bellows!

George. What uſe for a cold bath juſt on the
verge of the ocean? and the farmers want the
neceſſary tools for agriculture.

Sir H. I baniſh you for ever, from my faſhion-
able bathing-place. You barbarous young ſavage! after my high puff advertiſements of cold
larders, neat wines, circulating libraries, baths,
concerts, balls, billiards, machines, and bathing-
caps, to expect to drag people of faſhion down
here, amongſt ſtocking-looms, tombſtones, and
bellows-clinkers!

George. Father, my little colony was famiſh-
ing

ing on Lord Torrendel's ifland. Since I have brought them here, in pity don't diflurb them.

Sir H. A fine ragged colony you've planted.

George. Confider, Father, induftry is a flower that fhould be encouraged by the genial warmth of patronage.

Sir H. By the the lord! the fellow's only fit for a plowman, or a weaver.

George. Well, Sir, the one gives bread, the other cloathing; as a plowman and a weaver are the moft ufeful characters, I know of none more noble.

Sir H. Ah! don't talk to me, my very fervants will defpife you, I dare fay not one of 'em would ftir a ftump to fave your foul and body, you young Beaver.

Enter ROBIN HOOFS.

Robin H. Your purfe, Sir—I found it on the road. (*to George*)

George. Thank you, Robin;

Sir H. George's purfe! how much was in it?

Robin. More than I can tell—once I knew it to be mafter George's, I never put finger on the cafh it held.

Sir H. Suppofe it had been my purfe?

Robin H. Ecod! your honor, you might never have feen it again: Gold's a tempting thing, and I don't fet up for more honefty than my neighbours; but young Squire's money already belongs to the poor, and he bez a bad man indeed that wou'd take, what the generous heart is fo ready to give.

George. You've been playing tricks, knocking

IC

it about—its all broke—ftupid fellow, I dare fay
you'd take better care of your own!

Robin H. La, Sir, I have no purfe, only a little bit of a leather bag, to divide a few fhillings
from the halfpence. (*fhewing the bag, George
takes it.*)

George. Whole, and found—tearing one's property—there's my broken one, I fhall keep yours.
(*flings it to Robin Hoofs*)

Robin H. But, Sir, the gold's in it.

George. Never mind, keep it Robin, you're an
honeft fellow; honefty is a true diamond, and
fhould be fet in gold. (*puts him off*)

Sir H. My generous boy, George, build up
and pull down, juft as you pleafe; I fee now the
rich man's fafeft guard, is the bleffings of charity; but gold is the grand ftaple of your trade
of benevolence—I've brought Mifs Woodbine,
and her fortune; go and entertain her.

George. Ifn't that Lord Torrendel's Frenchman. (*looking out*)

Re-enter Robin Hoofs.

Robin H. Your honor, Mounfeer's come from
his Lord, to borrow your poft-chay—going on
a vifit, and his own be broke.

Sir H. Here's an opportunity to oblige my
Lord. He fhall have it, and hanfel my new pof-
tilion too.

George. (*afide*) Some knavery in this poft-
chaife borrowing! Robin, a word.

Sir H. Here ftill! go to the Lady! hold, here
fhe is.

Enter

Enter AUGUSTA.

Augusta. 'Twas certainly Arthur crofs'd the road. (*aside*) Sir, I've walk'd out, to fee your charming place here. (*to Sir Hans*)

Sir H. Hem!—I bid him fpeak to the Lady, and by the lord he's whifpering Robin; George, addrefs her with rapture.

George. Yes, Sir! Madam, the great pleafure of—Robin. [*Exit, talking with Robin Hoofs.*

Sir H. The great pleafure of—Robin! oh! the devil's in you, for a fine amorous fcoundrel! Stop, you Sir. [*Exit.*

Augusta. This young gentleman is an unadorned cafket, enclofing the moft delicate fprings of fenfibility; but that heart is not for me; or rather mine is not for him. I muft not cherifh an hopelefs paffion for Arthur; if, as Sir Hans tells me, another poffeffes his affections.

Enter FANNY.

Fanny!

Fanny. My dear governefs, I've got down to you; I'm only come, becaufe you are here— where's George.

Augusta. You only come becaufe I'm here— where's George! Ah, Fanny!

Fanny. I've made papa bring me too—by a monftrous ftory though. I've told him, Sir Hans wants him on moft prodigious bufinefs.

Enter ARTHUR, (*running*).

Arthur. Diftanced the nabber! my lovely partner! who could expect to find you here,

like

like a fea-nymph fent from old Neptune's palace, to make mortals plunge into the ocean,
enamoured from this divine fpecimen of aquatic
beauty.

Augufta. Moft heroically gallant indeed, Sir.

Fanny. Now for fomething gallant to me—
How d'ye do, Sir? (*curtefies*)

Arthur. Ah! little titmoufe, fuppofe, my love,
you ftep and gather a few honeyfuckles from the
hedge yonder.

Fanny. George might have had the manners
to meet, and make nymphs of other people.
Titmoufe, indeed!　　　　　　　　　　[*Exit.*

Arthur. Madam, you fee before you, a fellow
the moft wretched——(*afide*) fhall I venture to
declare my love? no—farewell.

Augufta. Whither, Sir, are you going?

Arthur. The truth is, Madam, tho' Great-
Britain's large, I'm driven to the water's edge,
where I'll ftep into, and pufh off the firft fifhing
boat I can find; for abandon'd by my father, and purfued by——England, Madam, is
no home for me. If I can get acrofs the channel, amongft camps, and batteries, my empty
fconce may keep a bullet from a head that has
brains in it.

Augufta. Your fortunes, Sir, are not, perhaps,
fo defparate—your mother was—

Arthur. How! Madam, have you heard?—fhe
is I hope an angel—and you my heaven (*kneels.*)

Enter COACHMAN.

Coachman. Overtaken you at laft!

Arthur. I'll be damn'd if you have though.
(*runs off, Coachman purfues.*)

Auguf-

Augusta. Unhappy youth! they'll pursue him to despair; but I'm usurping a concern that belongs to the mistress of his heart; yet, tho' I must not love, am I to reject all feelings of humanity.

Re-enter FANNY.

Fanny. (*joyfully*) Oh! governess, I have asked the postillion to give us a roll on the beach—you don't know half this sweet place.

Augusta. In the chaise I may have a better chance of seeing which way he takes. (*aside.*)

Fanny. (*aside*) Mustn't tell 'twas my Lord's valet proposed our ride, she's so squeamish.

Augusta. Does Sir Hans know of this jaunt?

Fanny. Very true—he may not let us go; I have it, sit in the chaise till I come; I'll fetch your hat and cloak. [*Exit.*

Augusta. Is this prudent, but no time for reflection, Arthur may be lost for ever. [*Exit.*

SCENE II.

A parlour in SIR HANS'S.

Enter DICKINS.

Dick. Devilish good place the Knight has got here; a fine prospect of the sea; a pretty mortgage, and I may pick up such a bit as this, with Torrendel's interest.

Enter

Enter FANNY; *looking about.*

Fanny. My Governefs is fo giddy—where can fhe have left her hat.

Dick. Oh, Fanny, where's your friend Augufta? you feem all upon the fidgets.

Fanny. (confufed) Oh no, Sir.—The two old boys will be running after us—what can I think of to keep them here? oh, true. *(afide)* Papa, I wonder why Sir Hans has fent for you; do you know?

Dick. No, child, but I fhall if I can get to fee him.

Fanny. Here he is, ha, ha, ha! *(afide)* only look papa, what a fine profpect at that window; you can fee, I believe, to the Ifle of Wight.

Dick. Oh no; but very fine. *(looks out of window.)*

Enter SIR HANS.

Sir H. Fanny, where's your papa?

Fanny. He's there, Sir, but his head is fo full of this ferious affair, he's come down to tell you about. *(in an under tone)*

Sir H. Oh, very well.

Fanny. He, he, he! now each will be fo full of expectation of the other telling, when there is nothing to tell, it may bring them into a fquabble, and that will keep them as clofe as a game backgammon—but where's Augufta's hat? [*Exit.*

Sir H. Ah, Dickins! how do you do?

Dick. (turning) Oh, Sir Hans, well, I've trundled down to you.

Sir H. Then the affair is very urgent? fit down.

Dick.

Dick. Of confequence, I hope; for I had a good deal to do.

Sir H. And fo?

Dick. Well.

Sir H. Well? fo fudden, I was alarmed! but does it concern me much?

Dick. That you beft know.

Sir H. How fhould I know!

Dick. (*peevifhly*) Well then, when you tell me, perhaps I may know.

Sir H. When you tell me, perhaps I may not know. But come.

Dick. Aye?

Sir H. He's afraid of being overheard I fuppofe; come, I'll faften the door.

Dick. Oh, if it is of fo much confequence, and fecrecy, I'll faften this door too. (*both rife and go to oppofite doors*) There now, we are quite fafe. (*fits down*) aye?

Sir H. Aye? (*they put their heads together as liftening*)

Dick. What do you fit gaping for, why don't you out with it?

Sir H. Why do you fit ftaring and ftretching your neck? why don't you tell it at once?

Dick. You fent for me down about your bufinefs—and, zounds! what is it? that I may go about mine.

Sir H. I fend for you! you came here to tell me of fomething of great importance—tell it, and fhorten your vifit, when you pleafe, Sir. (*both rife*)

Dick. Sir, your ill manners, in your own houfe, are equal to your impudence in bringing me into it for nothing.

Sir H. Impudence, you vulgar man! it's well
you

you are in my houſe, or by the hand of this body, I'd pitch you out of window.

Dick. Pitch me, you hard-headed old fool! if
Torrendel was to behave ſo, I'd——

Sir H. I ſhall choak.—*(rings)* You're under
my roof—ſo ſay what you will—Robin Hoofs!

Dick. Damn your hoofs, and your horns, Sir!
I can quit your houſe myſelf. You're as impudent as Torrendel. *(puts on his hat, and gloves)*

Enter FANNY, *crying, with Auguſta's hat.*

Fanny. Oh George! George! my Governeſs
has run away with George! falſe fellow! to dreſs
himſelf up as the new poſtilion, and drive off
with my Governeſs, when I only returned to fetch
her hat and cloak.

Sir H. My ſon drive off with Auguſta! Huzza! he's a daſher.

Fanny. And then Lord Torrendel's valet, to
jump up behind the chaiſe—'twas all a pack'd
thing to deceive me. *(cries)*

Sir H. What! the Frenchman gone off with
my ward.

Fanny. Yes, they'll ſurely be married.

Dick. What, the Frenchman?

Fanny. No! George!

Dick. But where are they gone?

Fanny. Rattled down the beach, towards Sandgate Iſland.

Sir H. Robin Hoofs, John, the devil, I've loſt
my ward.   [*Exeunt Dickins, and Sir Hans.*

Fanny. Yes, I heard Sir Hans brought her
down here to marry George; a demure looking
thing, ſhe knew better than to take the mad
                                                  young

young Arthur; and I myfelf to introduce her to
my George; this is female friendfhip indeed,
here's my friend's hat, and my friend's ribbands,
oh that I had herfelf here.

[Exit tearing the bat.

SCENE III; <i>and laft.</i>

Sandgate Ifland; one fhattered houfe, and a few
wretched cottages.

Enter ARTHUR.

Arthur. The ferryman not to run his boat
boldly in the creek—oblige me to dafh through
the water! If I could but get over to the conti-
nent, I'd fight like a true volunteer—the firft
Enfign that dropt, pick up his colours—I wifh
I had a few fhillings, to pay my paffage in fome
fifhing fmack.

Enter COACHMAN.

There again—by heavens! you fha'n't have all
the bailiff-work to yourfelf—we'll have a tufsle
for it—if you are ftronger, I go—if not, I commit your body to mafter fhark—begone, or into
the fea I fling you.

Coachman. Then, there Sir, is three hundred
pound, Bank of England note—now I've at laft
done my job. [*drops it, and exit.*

Arthur. (*picking it up*) It is—and I to miftake my bright angel for the blackeft of all imps,
a catchpole! three hundred! now they fhall fee
who

who is Lord Arthur D'Aumerle—who from ?
my kind father, doubtlefs. Now I've cafh, where
is my poor faithful Timolin.

E..ter ROBINSON, (*out of livery.*)

A dreary Ifland, but one houfe,—you live yonder, mafter.

Robinfon. Live! ah, Sir! (*fighs.*)

Arthur. Complain! Why, in the winter here,
you've ftorms in high perfection—fnow, hail,
rain, lightning and thunder, neat as imported
—no door to your houfe, and fcarce a houfe to
your door! the fplanged canopy your bed-tefters,
and for a clear profpect no glafs to your windows!
nor a tree on your ifland, becaufe you wou'd
not harbour noify rooks to difcompofe your
flumbers!—nor even a bufh! but that's vanity
—that you might have it to fay, you challenge
the globe round to fhew a fpot more defolate.

Robinfon. He doesn't recollect me. (*afide*) I've
only come to-day, Sir, but here I believe I muft
abide till better times. This houfe belongs to a
brother of mine—all poor enough and yet but
for the charity of Mr. George Burgefs, they muft
be worfe. The fquire has unpeopled this ifland,
and fettled them comfortably near his father's.
Since Lord Torrendel, the landlord, leaves them
to his Frenchman and that Mafter Dickins, my
brother wifhes they'd take the houfe off his
hands.

Arthur. They'll be taking it prefently from
about his ears——

Enter ROBIN HOOFS.

Robin II, (*to Robinfon*) I believe it's you I wants
——You're

—You're to come over to-morrow noon to Samphire-Hall, my young Mafter wou'd fpeak to you,
eh!—Sure I know you, why wasn't you porter
to Lord Torrendel? (*looking ftedfaftly at Robinfon*)

Arthur. Indeed!

Robin H. It is—Now I underftands the whole
affair—Squire George is always himfelf.

Arthur. Were not you difcharged from Lord
Torrendel's for admitting me into the Caftle?

Robin H. He was and that he might not lofe
by his good-nature, Mafter George was going to
give him a place of 50 *l.* a year, but Sir Hans has
knock'd up that plan, and wo'n't let the new-
comers fettle there.

Arthur. A man turn'd a-drift into this curfed
world, for a moft kind action towards me, and
I ftand prating here with 300 *l.* in my hand: no
pennyworth of pippins fha'n't have all this work
to himfelf—there, (*gives the note*) that will buy
you cakes and ale till you get a place.

Robinfon. Sir!——

Arthur. Don't talk, I hate talking; I'm abfolute in that particular, Old Crufoe. (*puts them
off*) Ha, ha, ha! I'm tickled with a ftrange ambition—I'll be king of this Ifland from my father's fole inheritance. I'll enchant this houfe
from the court of poverty, to the caftle of comfort.—This ifland is now my territory—here am
I king! oh! for my queen! but plague of my
palace.   [*Exit into houfe.*

Enter L'ŒILLET, *and* BOATMAN.

L'Œillet. Now dat your comrade has brought

lady over in toder boat, let no one elfe crofs but
Milor.   [*Exit Boatman.*
Ah! quel bonheur to find Augufta myfelf! now
Monfieur Thomas and dat villain Irifh terrier
may hunt her for deir own recreation—dis foli-
tary ifle—here milor have no perfon to inter-
rupt.   [*Retires.*

Enter AUGUSTA.

Augufta. The defire of feeing my coufin Arthur once again, before it is too late, can fcarce-
ly reconcile me to this ftep—altogether this
ifland wears a moft forbidding afpeét—I'll return, and fit in the chaife, till Fanny comes.
(*going*).

L'*Œillet.* Ah! ma chere *(preventing her)* You
muft vait for Milor.

Augufta. He here! heavens! I'm betrayed—I
now fee my folly.

L'*Œillet.* I was your laquais, mon ange, and
did fit behind de chaife, and you did not know
it.

Augufta. Pray, Sir, fuffer me to go.

L'*Œillet.* Oui, to Londres! dere Milor vil
buy you fine cloaths and jewels, and you vill
fhine at operas and ball and concert, and he vill
kifs your hand dus. (*offers to kifs her hand*)

Enter ARTHUR.

Arthur. How! (*ftrikes him.*)
L'*Œillet.* Diantre! (*runs off. Arthur purfues. A
plunge, as if in water, is heard without.*)

Re-

Re-enter Arthur.

Angusta. Heavens! fir, what have you done?

Arthur. Only caft my bait into the fea—Lucifer will always bite at a fcoundrel.

Augusta. Sir, he'll be drowned.

Arthur. He's already a pickled dog—don't be alarm'd—you're fafe now from even the fhadow of infult. How came you here in this remote place? fpeak—but no matter—you feem diftrefs'd, Madam.

Augusta. (*afide*) Vice fhould not humble the father in the opinion of the fon.

Arthur. Lean upon me, ma'am—holloo! old Crufoe, where's your dame? come madam: (*leads Augusta in.*)

Enter LORD TORRENDEL.

Lord Tor. Should L'Œillet bring my Augufta fafe, here is no accommodation; I thought I had fome tenants on this Ifland! they've let the place run ftrangely to ruin. Confufion! Sir Hans!

Enter SIR HANS, DICKENS, GEORGE, *and* ROBIN HOOFS.

Dick. But 'fquire, why difguife yourfelf; fure you coud'n't be a confederate with my Lord's pandar, to fteal my daughter's governefs?

Sir H. Aye, George, where was the neceffity of ufing artifice, to run away with Augufta, the very girl I wanted to give you.

George.

George. Then to explain the myftery—fome bafe defigns of others, have funk me into a fchemer of ftratagems. My lord, my name is Burgefs.—I'm no profeffed knight-errand, yet I openly avow that I will endeavour henceforth to protect female innocence from your lordfhip's difhonourable purpofes.   [*Exit.*

Sir H. Bravo! He has been drinking hock with Lord Arthur.—My lord, I'll talk to you.
                                          [*Exit.*
Dick. My lord, to you I'll talk.   [*Exit.*
Lord Tor. Then no fhelter from open fhame, but to turn champion myfelf! befides, the ftorm once blown over, my feeming her protector wins her love by gratitude.

Enter TIMOLIN.

Timolin. Oh, my lord, here flies the fweet creature to you with her character under her arm.

Lord Tor. Then, that villain L'Œillet, has made my fon's fervant a party in this bufinefs.

Enter LADY TORRENDEL, *veiled, and* THOMAS.

Timolin. So Mifs, you wou'dn't be warn'd by me, you wou'd run headlong to the devil. And there he ftands, ready to receive you. (*apart to Lady Torrendel*)

Lord Tor. What's your purpofe, you fcoundrels, in bringing the lady to this lonely place?

Timolin. Our purpofe! well, that's very high!—

Lord Tor. Madam, rely upon my protection.
                                          I am

I am bound by honor to defend you from every infult.

Lady Tor. Certainly, my lord! every gentleman fhould be the protector of—his wife. (*difcovers herfelf.*)

- *Lord Tor.* Lady Torrendel!

Timolin. The Lady herfelf! then 'twas to her hufband fhe was running, oh! here's a wonder, and a blunder!   [*Exit.*

Lady Tor. My Lord, I fee you are confufed, yet could I hope your prefent humiliation proceeded from a forrow that promifed repentance, and confequent reformation, my heart's feelings for the man I did love and honor, fhould melt me to compaffion! (*weeps*) but no! take my refentment! my deferved, and bitter reproach! grief cannot reach a breaft fo callous as your's! it is only the ftings of a wounded pride, and difappointed purpofe, that now agitates you; reflect! return an humble gratitude to heaven for having made my unexpected arrival here the means of fnatching you from the repetition of a crime the moft hoftile to fociety. A felfifh, tranfient gratification, that muft banifh for ever an unhappy female from the paths of honor! fhun'd thro' life by the beft part of her own fex!—and even defpifed by you! the author of her fhame! your wrongs to me are nothing, but your meditated tricks and plans, which you call gallantries, reflect only difgrace on the dignity of manhood!

Lord Tor. Lady Torrendel—I confefs I'm altogether fomewhat fhocked, and wifh—I'm very unhappy to fee—that is—I'm unhappy at your fufpecting——

Lady

Lady Tor. Oh, you mistake, my lord ! I have no suspicions ! mine are all certainties—but even if you consider my throwing the past into the shade of oblivion, any indulgence, I shall insist upon a few conditions, and the first—turn your countenance and protection to your poor deserted youth! you as a parent, are responsible for every violation that your neglect has occasioned him to make on the laws of propriety; if you refuse, I will be his parent, and henceforth regard your poor friendless son, with all the care and tenderness of maternal affection.

Enter ARTHUR.

Arthur. Huzza, the joy that laughs on me, shall smile on all around ; sir, I thank you for your bounty, but——

Enter COACHMAN.

Coachman. My Lady, I gave Lord Arthur the money,

Lady Tor. Well, well!

Arthur. How! was that 300 *l.* sent me by you, Madam.

Lord Tor. Did you give countenance and relief, where wives, in general, look with contempt and even hatred ? Madam, can you pardon ?

Lady Tor. My Lord, your conduct renders you rather an object of pity, than resentment—you have implicitly delivered up your fortune, your character, nay more, my Lord, your honor, to be the sport and property of an infamous

mous parafite—your confidential favourite, your Valet, counteracted the rectitude of your intentions, by embezzling the fums he had for purpofes dictated by duty and nature. Oh! why will thofe who poffefs the godlike power of doing good, delegate a bafe, unworthy agent, for the kind purpofes of humanity.

Enter Sir Hans, Dickins, George, *and* Augusta.

Sir H. Here, boy, take Augufta. (*advancing*).
Arthur. (*advancing*) Thank ye, Sir Hans! (*takes her hand*)
Sir H. Thank ye, indeed, for that! George, will you lofe your wife fo?
George. I've one ready at hand—father, with your leave and her own confent.

Enter Fanny, *and* Timolin, *at the back.*

Dick. To be fure, I confent—and we all confent.
Fanny. Oh! yes! we all confent—my dear governefs, are you going to be married? It feems I'm going to be married. He, he, he! eh! George?
Sir H. To fee my fon taken before my face, with an he, he, he! s'blood, fir! let the girl go, he, he, he, indeed.
Dick. Then I difcover your tricks, Sir, oh, oh, oh! indeed!—Madam, (*to Augufta*) no matter what he fays—you are ftill heirefs to your uncle Woodbine's fortune. Throw it into my bank, chufe me your guardien, I'll recover—I'll fend Sir Nob a fheet of cracklin ramfkin, that

fhall

ſhall reach from Chancery-lane, to Weſtminſter-hall.

Auguſta. Well, even ſo the property of the mother ſhould devolve to the ſon, and to him I reſign it.

Arthur. No! ſooner than take it from you, my generous couſin, Timolin and I will buffet the world again—and, rather than commit further depredations on honeſt tradeſmen, I'll turn to any thing, any one thing in life, except a Poet. Where are you old Bargatrot Caſtle?

Timolin. I'm here, your honor, dead or alive—we'll jump into our boots, before they're bought—away, maſter! I'm your man, thro' thick and thin, fire and ſmoke.

Arthur. I could force myſelf to accept this fortune—that is, with a certain ſweet'ner—Will you, my Auguſta, accompany it?

Auguſta. Then, Sir, for paltry gold, you'd quit your love! oh! fie!

Sir H. Devil's in you, child! I was only joking about the girl over the hock, to make you marry George.

(*Arthur kiſſes her hand.*)

Lord Tor. Why, this is right. Lady Torrendel, your unexampled liberality will reclaim me into a huſband and a father.—My boy, were bleſſings mine, you ſhould have one from me.

Timolin. Then, as you're not worth a bleſſing, ſhow'r a bundle of yellow-boys upon us both.

Dick. A good motion, throw them into my bank.—Eh! is that Monſieur ſhaking his ears like a water dog? (*looking out*)

Arthur. My Lord, father, and you moſt adored Auguſta, if I am deſtined to affluence, here

is

is my model, (*to George*) who can forego the comforts of life to beſtow its neceſſaries on the indigent!

Sir H. Why, my moſt magnificent Arthur, I thought you were to be George's model, and that like you he'd have grace enough, to play the de-vil.

Arthur. So he ſhall—we'll kick Care out of the window, our abode ſhall be the Houſe of Joy, and the firſt card of invitation ſhall be, to the Man of Sorrow.

> My faults how great! but as no foſt'ring care
> Did ever ſmile upon misfortune's heir!
> The outcaſt oh receive! your pardon give,
> And in your favour, let him happy live!

THE END.

THE

CASTLE OF ANDALUSIA.

IN THREE ACTS.

PERFORMED AT THE

THEATRE-ROYAL, COVENT-GARDEN,

IN 1782.

———————

THE MUSICK BY DR. ARNOLD.

P 2

DRAMATIS PERSONÆ.

Don Scipio, ... Mr. WILSON.

Don Cæfar (or Capt. Ramirez), Mr. REINHOLD.

Fernando, ... Mr. MATTOCKS.

Don Juan, ... Mr. FEARON.

Alphonſo, ... Mrs. KENNEDY.

Pedrillo, ... Mr. EDWIN.

Spado, ⎫ ⎧ .... Mr. QUICK.

Sanguino, ⎬ Banditti. ⎨ .... Mr. MAHON.

Calvette, ⎪ ⎪ .... Mr. THOMPSON.

Rapino, ⎭ ⎩ .... Mr. BOYCE.

Philippo, ... Mr. BRETT.

Vaſquez, ... Mr. STEVENS.

Lopez, ... Mr. LEDGER.

Victoria, ... Miſs HARPER.

Lorenza, ... Signora SESTINI.

Iſabella, ... Miſs PLATT.

Catilina, ... Mrs. WILSON.

BANDITTI, SERVANTS, &c.

SCENE, *Spain.*

THE

CASTLE OF ANDALUSIA.

ACT I.

SCENE I.

A Cavern with winding Stairs, and Receſſes cut in the Rock; a large Lamp hanging in the Center, a Table, Wine, Fruits, &c.—At the head Don Cæsar, *on each ſide* Spado, Sanguino, Rapino, *and others of the Banditti.*

CHORUS.

Here we ſons of freedom dwell
In our friendly, rock-hewn cell;
Pleaſure's dictates we obey,
Nature points us out the way
Ever ſocial great and free,
Valour guards our liberty.

AIR.—*Don Cæſar.*

Of ſevere and partial laws,
   Venal judges, Alguazils;
Dreary dungeons's iron jaws,
   Oar and gibbet---Whips or wheels
Let's never think
While thus we drink
Sweet Muſcadine!
O life divine!
    Chorus. Here we ſons of freedom dwell, &c.
                    Don C.

Don C. Come, Cavaliers, our carbines are loaded, our hearts are light, charge your glaſ-ſes, Bacchus gives the word, and a volley makes us immortal as the roſy god.—Fire! *(all drink)*

Spa. Ay, Captain, this is noble firing, Oh, I love a volley of grape-ſhot—Are we to have any ſky-light in our cave? *(looking at Sanguino's glaſs)*

Don C. Oh, no! a brimmer round. Come, a good booty to us to-night. *(all drink)*

Spa. Booty! I love to rob a fat Prieſt.—Stand, ſays I, and then I knock him down.

Sang. My noſe bleeds. *(looks at his handkerchief)* I wonder what colour is a coward's blood!

Spa. Don't you ſee it's red?

Sang. Hah! call me coward, *(riſes in fury)* Sirrah! Captain! Cavaliers! but this ſcar on my forehead contradicts the miſcreant.

Spa. Scar on your forehead! Ay, you will look behind you when you run away.

Sang. I'll ſtab the villain—*(draws ſtilletto)* I will, by heaven.

Don C. Poh, Sanguino! you know when a jeſt offers, Spado regards neither time, place nor perſon.

All. *(interpoſing)* Don't hurt little Spado!

Spa. *(hiding behind)* No, don't hurt little Spado.

Sang. Run away! Armies have confeſs'd my valour—the time has been—but no matter! *(ſits)*

Don C. Come, away with reflection on the paſt, or care for the future; the preſent is the golden moment of poſſeſſion; let us enjoy it.

All. Ay, ay, let us enjoy it.

Don C. You know, Cavaliers, when I enter'd into this noble fraternity, I boaſted only of a lit-tle courage ſharpen'd by neceſſity, the reſult of my

my youthful follies, a father's feverity, and the
malice of a good natur'd dame.

Spa. Captain, here's a fpeedy walk-off to old
women.

All. Ha, ha, ha! *(drink)*

Don C. When you did me the honor to elect
me your captain, for two conditions I ftipulated
—Tho' at war with the world abroad, unity and
focial mirth fhould prefide over our little common-wealth at home.

Spa. Yes, but Sanguino's for no head—he'll
have ours a common-wealth of fifts and elbows.

Don C. The other, unlefs to preferve your
own lives, never to commit a murder.

Spa. I murder'd fince that—a bifhop's coach-
horfe.

All. Ha, ha, ha!

Don C. Hand me that red wine.

AIR.—*Don Cæfar.*

Flow, thou regal purple ftream,
Tinted by the folar beam,
In my goblet fparkling rife,
Cheer my heart and glad my eyes.
My brain afcend on fancy's wing,
'Noint me, wine, a jovial king.
While I live, I'll lave my clay,
When I'm dead and gone away,
Let my thirfty fubjects fay,
A month he reign'd, but that was May.

[*Thunder.*

Don C. Hark, how diftinct we hear the thunder through this vaft body of earth and rock—
Rapino, is Calvette above upon his poft?

Rap. Yes.

Don C. Spado, 'tis your turn to relieve the
centinel.

Spa.

Spa. Relieve ! why what's the matter with him ?

Don C. Come, come, no jesting with duty—
'tis your watch.

Spa. Let the wolves watch for me—my duty
is to get supper ready—*(thunder)* Go up! Od's
fire, do you think I am a Salamander? D'ye
hear !

Sang. No sport I fear.

Don C. Then call Calvette, lock down the
trap-door, and get us some more wine from the
cistern.

Spa. Wine! Ay, Captain, and this being a
night of peace we'll have a dish of olives.

Sang. No peace ! we'll up and scour the forest
presently. But well thought on, a rich old fellow, one Don Scipio has lately come to reside in
the castle on the skirts of the forest—what say
you to plunder there ?

Don C. Not to night—I know my time—I
have my reasons—I shall give command on that
business. But where's the stranger we brought
in at our last excursion ?

Rap. He reposes in yonder recess.

Spa. Ay, there he lies with a face as innocent
as an angel, thought he fought like seven devils.
(aside) If my fellow-rooks wou'd but fly off—I'd
have the pidgeon here within all to myself.

Calv. (*appears at the top of the winding stairs
with a lanthern*) Captain !

Sang. Good news, Cavaliers ; here comes Calvette.

Calv. A booty !

Sang. What? where ?

Calv. Soft—but one man !

Sang. Is he alone ?

Calv. Quite.

                                            Spa.

Spa. One man and alone—that's odd!

Calv. He feems in years, but his habit, (as well as I could diftinguifh,) fpeaks him noble. (*defcends*)

Don C. Then he'll fight. My arms!

Spa. Oh, he'll fight.—Get my arms—no, my legs will do for me. (*afide*)

Sang. Come, my carbine—quick!

Don C. To the attack of one man—paltry! Only you Calvette, and Spado go, the reft prepare for our general excurfion.

Spa. Captain, don't fend me; indeed I'm too rafh!

Don C. Come, come, leave buffoonery and to your duty.

> [CALVETTE *afcends, the reft go in at feveral receffes,* SPADO, *afcends flowly.*]

Enter ALPHONSO:

Alph. I find myfelf fomewhat refrefh'd by fleep—at fuch a time to fall into the hands of thefe ruffians, how unlucky! I'm pent up here; my rival Fernando, once my friend, reaches Don Scipio's Caftle, weds my charming Victoria, and I lofe her for ever; but if I could fecure an interview, love fhould plead my caufe.

AIR.—*Alphonfo.*

The hardy failor braves the ocean,
    Fearlefs of the roaring wind;
Yet his heart, with foft emotion,
    Throbs to leave his love behind.

To dread of foreign foes a ftranger,
    Tho' the youth can dauntlefs roam,
Alarming fears paint every danger
    In a rival, left at home.

SPADO *returns down the stairs.*

Spa. (*aside*) Now for some talk with our prisoner here—Stay, are they all out of ear-shot?
How the poor bird sings in its cage! I know
more of his affairs than he thinks of by overhear-
ing his conversation at the inn at Lorca.

Alph. How shall I escape from these rascals!—
Oh, here is one of the gentlemen. Pray, Sir,
may I take the liberty——

Spa. No liberty for you here—Yet upon certain conditions, indeed—give me your hand.

Alph. (*aside*) Impudent scoundrel!

Spa. Senor, I wish to serve you, and serve
you I will; but I must know the channel before
I make for the coast, therefore to examine you
with the pious severity of an holy Inquisitor, in
heaven's name, who the devil are you?

Alph. A pious adjuration truly! (*aside*) Sir,
my name is Alphonso, and I am son of a banker at Madrid.

Spa. Banker! I thought he sung like a young
gold-finch.

Alph. Perhaps by trusting this fellow I may
make my escape——

Spa. I'll convince him I know his secrets, and
then I hold his purse-strings.

Alph. You won't betray me?

Spa. Honor among thieves.

Alph. Then you must know when your gang
attack'd me yesterday evening——

Spa. You were posting full gallop to Don Scipio's castle on the confines of the forest here.

Alph. Hey! then perhaps you know my passion for——

Spa-

Spa. Donna Victoria his daughter.

Alph. Then you know that she's contracted—

Spa. To your friend Don Fernando de Zelva, who is now on his journey to the castle, and to the destruction of your hopes, weds the lady on his arrival.

Alph. True, while I am pent up in this cursed cavern, but how you got my story, I——

Spa. No matter! I could let you out of this cursed cavern.

Alph. And will you?

Spa. Ah, our trap-door above requires a golden key.

Alph. Your comrades have not left me a piastre.

Spa. Will you give me an order on your father's bank for fifty pieces, and I'll let you out?

Alph. You shall have it.

Spa. A bargain. I'll secure your escape.

Enter Don Cæsar, (*behind*).

Don C. How's this!

Spa. Zounds, the Captain Ramirez! (*aside*) Aye, you dog, I'll secure you from an escape! Do you think I'd set you at liberty without the Captain's orders? Betray my trust for a bribe! What the devil do you take me for? (*in a seeming rage*) Oh, Captain, I didn't see you.

Don C. What's the matter?

Spa. Nothing, only our prisoner here was mistaken in his man—that's all. Let you escape, indeed!

Alph. Here's a rascal!

Spa. Rascal! D'ye hear him? he has been

Q 2   abusing

abuſing me this half hour, becauſe I would not convey him out without your knowledge. Oh, what offers he did make me! but my integrity is proof againſt Gallions, Eſcurials, Peru's, and Mexico's.

Don C. Begone inſtantly to your comrades.

[*Spado aſcends.*

Senor, no occaſion to tamper with my companions; you ſhall owe your liberty to none but me. Some particulars of your ſtory, which I had from Spado, have engaged me in your intereſt—to be free, up in the open air would you venture—ha, ha, ha!—not afraid of a ſprinkle of rain or a flaſh of lightning—no, no. Well, without conſulting my brethren here, as ſoon as they ſally forth, I'll convey you to the cottage of the vines, belonging to the peaſant Philippo, not far from Don Scipio's caſtle; there you may reſt in ſafety to-night, and——

Alph. Ah, Captain! no reſt for me.

Don C. Look ye Senor, I am a ruffian, perhaps worſe, but venture to truſt me—A picklock may be uſed to get at a treaſure—don't wiſh to know more of me than I now chuſe to tell you, but if your miſtreſs loves you as well as you ſeem to love her, to-morrow night ſhe's yours.

Alph. My good friend!

Don C. Now for Philippo—I don't ſuppoſe you wiſh to ſee any of our work above, ha, ha, ha!—Well, well, I was once a lover, but now——

AIR.

AIR.—*Don Cæfar.*

On by the fpur of valour goaded,
Piftols prim'd and carbines loaded,
Courage ftrikes on hearts of fteel ;
    While each fpark
    Through the dark
Gloom of night,
Lends a clear and cheering light,
    Who, a fear or doubt can feel ?

Like ferpents now, through thickets creeping,
Then on our prey, like lions, leaping !
    Calvette to the onfet lead us,
    Let the wand'ring trav'ler dread us!
Struck with terror and amaze,
While our fwords with lightning blaze. (*Thunder*)
Thunder to our carbines roaring,
Burfting clouds in torrents pouring,
    Each a free and roving blade,
    Ours a free and roving trade,
    To the onfet let's away,
    Valour calls, and we obey.   [*Exeunt.*

SCENE II.

A Foreft, (a ftormy night).

Enter FERNANDO.

Fer. Pedrillo ! (*calling*) What a dreadful night, and horrid place to be benighted in ! Pedrillo !—I fear I've loft my fervant, but, by the pace I rode fince I left Ecceija, Don Scipo's caftle can't be very far diftant—this was to have been my wedding night, if I arrived there—and as for my charming bride—Yet I cannot regret
                my

my feparation from beauties, that I can only imagine.

AIR.—*Fernando.*

Serenely fmooth the moments run,
With him, who from his natal hour,
Has ne'er beheld the fplendid Sun,
Nor fovereign Nature's genial power.

But by the bolt of Jove ftruck blind,
Thus fhut from every ray of light,
What poignant grief o'ercafts his mind,
Who once hath known the joys of Sight.

But what keeps Pedrillo, Pedrillo! Pedrillo! (*calling*)

Ped. (*within*) Sir!

Fer. Where are you?

Ped. Quite aftray, Sir.

Fer. This way.

Enter PEDRILLO, (*groping*).

Ped. Any body's way, for I have loft my own —Do you fee me, Sir?

Fer. No, indeed! (*lightning*)

Ped. You faw me then, Sir. (*thunder*) Ah, this muft frighten the mules, they'll break their bridles; I tied the poor beafts to a tree.

Fer. Well, we may find 'em in the morning, if they efcape the banditti which I am told infefts this foreft.

Ped. Banditti! (*a fhot without*) Ah! we are dead men.

Fer. Somebody in trouble!

Ped. No, fomebody's troubles are over.

Fer. Draw, and follow me.

Ped.

Ped. Lord, Sir! ha'nt we troubles enough of our own?

Fer. Follow! who can deny afliftance to his fellow-creature in diftrefs? *(draws)* [*Exit.*

Ped. What fine creatures thefe gentlemen are! But for me, I am a poor, mean fervant—fo I'll ev'n take my chance with the mules.

AIR.—*Pedrillo.*

A mafter I have, and I am his man,
    Galloping, dreary, dun,
And he'll get a wife as faft as he can,
    With a haily, gaily, gambo raily,
      Giggling, niggling,
Galloping galloway, draggle tail, dreary dun.

I faddled his fteed fo fine and fo gay,
    Galloping, dreary dun,
I mounted my mule, and we rode away.
    With our haily, &c.

We canter'd along until it grew dark,
    Galloping, dreary, dun,
The nightingale fung inftead of the lark,
    With her, &c.

We met with a friar, and afk'd him our way,
    Galloping, dreary, dun,
By the Lord, fays the friar, you're both gone aftray,
    With your, &c.

Our journey, I fear, will do us no good,
    Galloping, dreary, dun,
We wander alone, like the babes in the wood,
    With our, &c.

My mafter is fighting, and I'll take a peep,
    Galloping, dreary, dun,
But now I think better, I'd better go fleep,
    With my, &c. [*Exit.*

SCENE

SCENE III:

A thicker part of the forest. Large tree and stone crofs near the front.

Enter SPADO, *runs round terrified, and climbs into the tree.*

Enter DON SCIPIO, *attacked by* SANGUINO, RAPINO, *and* CALVETTE.

Sang. Now, Rapino, lop off his fword-arm.

Don S. Forbear! there's my purfe. (*throws it down*)

Sang. Fire!

Spa. (*peeping from the tree*) No, don't fire.

Sang. I am wounded, hew him to pieces! (*as Don Scipio is nearly overpowered*)

Enter FERNANDO.

Fer. Ha! what murderous ruffians! (*engages the Banditti who precipitately difperfe feveral ways*)

Spa. Holloa! the foreft is furrounded with Inquifitors, Alguazils, Corrigidores, Hangmen, and holy fathers.

Don S. Oh, I hav'nt fought fo much thefe twenty years.

Spa. Eh, we have loft the field, curfed dark; tho' I think I could perceive but one man come to the relief of our old Don here.

Don S. But where are you, Senor? approach my brave deliverer.

Spa. So here's a victory and nobody to claim it! I think I'll go down and pick up the laurel. (*defcends*) I'll take the merit of this exploit, I may get fomething by it.

Don

Don S. I long to thank, embrace, worſhip this generous ſtranger as my guardian angel.

Spa. (*aſide*) I may paſs for this angel in the dark—Villains, ſcoundrels! robbers, to attack an honeſt gentleman! but I made the dogs ſcamper! (*vapouring*)

Don S. Oh, dear! this is my preſerver!

Spa. Who's there? Oh, you are the worthy gentleman I reſcued from theſe raſcal banditti.

Don S. Noble, valiant ſtranger—I—

Spa. No thanks, Senor, I have ſav'd your life and a good action rewards itſelf.

Don S. A gallant fellow faith—Eh, as well as I could diſtinguiſh in the dark, you look'd much taller juſt now? (*looking cloſe at him*)

Spa. When I was fighting? true, anger raiſes me—I always appear ſix foot in a paſſion; beſides my hat and plume added to my height.

Don S. (*by accident treading on the purſe*) Hey, the rogues have run off without my purſe too.

Spa. O, ho! (*aſide*)—What, I have ſav'd your purſe as well as your precious life! Well, of a *poor* fellow, I am the luckieſt dog in all Spain.

Don S. Poor! Good friend, accept it as a ſmall token of my gratitude.

Spa. Nay, dear Sir!

Don S. You ſhall take it.

Spa. Lord, I am ſo aukward at taking a purſe. (*takes it*)

Don S. Hey, if I could find my cane too I dropt it ſomewhere hereabouts when I drew to defend myſelf. (*looking about*)

Spa. Zounds! I fancy here comes the real con-

VOL. I.   R   queror

queror—no matter—I've got the fpoils of the field. (*afide chinks the purfe and retires*)

Don S. Ah, my amber-headed cane! (*ftill looking about*)

Re-enter FERNANDO.

Fer. The villians!

Don S. Ay, you made 'em fly like pigeons, my little game-cock!

Fer. Oh, I fancy this is the gentleman that was attack'd. Not hurt, I hope, Sir,

Don S. No, I'm a tough old blade—Oh, gadfo, well thought on—feel if there's a ring on the purfe, it's a relick of my deceas'd lady, it's with fome regret I afk you to return it.

Fer. Return what, Sir?

Don S. A ring you'll find on the purfe.

Fer. Ring and purfe! really, Sir, I don't understand you.

Don S. Well, well, no matter—A mercenary fellow? (*afide.*)

Fer. The old gentleman has been robb'd, and is willing that I fhould reimburfe his loffes. (*afide*)

Don S. It grows lighter: I think I can diftinguifh the path I loft—follow me, my hero, and —(*going fuddenly turns and looks ftedfaftly at* Fernando.) Zounds, Senor, I hope you are not in a paffion, for I think you look fix foot high again.

Fer. A ftrange, mad old fellow this! (*afide.*)

Don S. Thefe rafcals may rally, fo come along to my caftle, and my daughter Victoria fhall welcome the preferver of her father.

Fer.

Fer. Your daughter, Victoria! Then, perhaps, Sir, you are Don Scipio, my intended father-in-law?

Don S. Eh! Why! is it possible that you can be my expected son, Fernando?

Fer. The same, Sir, and was on my journey to your Castle when benighted in the forest here.

Don S. Oh, my dear boy! (*embraces him.*) Damn'd mean of him to take my purse tho'—(*aside.*) Ah, Fernando, you were resolv'd to touch some of your wife's fortune before-hand.

Fer. Sir—I—

Don S. Hush! You have the money and keep it: aye, and the ring too; I'm glad it's not gone out of the family—Hey, it grows lighter—Come!

Fer. My rascal Pedrillo is fall'n asleep some-where. (*a whistle without*)

Don S. No, we're not safe here—Come then, my dear—brave valiant—Curs'd paltry to take my purse tho'. (*aside.*) [*Exeunt.*

Spa. (*who had been listening, advances.*) So then our old gentleman is father to Victoria, my young banker Alphonso's mistress, and the other is Fernando his dreaded rival—this is the first time they ever saw each other too.——He has a servant too, and his name Pedrillo—a thought strikes me, if I could by cross paths but get to the castle before 'em, I'd raise a most delicious commotion—In troubled waters I throw my fishing-hook—(*Whistle without.*) Excuse me, gen-I'm engag'd.

[*Exit opposite side.*

SCENE

SCENE IV.

An apartment in Don Scipio's *caſtle.*

Enter Victoria *and* Catalina.

Cat. Nay, dear madam, do not ſubmit to go into the nunnery.

Vic. But, Catalina, my father deſires I ſhould take the veil, and a parent's voice is the call of heaven!

ꞌ *Cat.* Heav'n! Well, tho' the fellows ſwear I'm an angel, this world is good enough for me —Dear Ma'm, I wiſh I could but once ſee you in love.

Vic. Heigh ho! Catilina, I wonder what ſort of gentleman this Don Fernando is, who is con- tracted to me, and hourly expected at the caſtle!

Cat. A beautiful man, I warrant—But, Ma'm, your'e not to have him. Huſh! Dame Iſabel, not content with making your father by ſlights and ill-uſage, force your brother, poor Don Cæſar, to run about the world in the Lord knows what wild courſes, but ſhe now has perſuaded the old gentleman to paſs her daughter on Don Fernando for you—There, yonder ſhe is flaunting, ſo be- jewell'd and be-plum'd—Well, if I was you, they might take my birth-right—but my huſband— take my man—the deuce ſhould take them firſt! Ah, no! if I ever do go to heav'n I'll have a ſmart lad in my company. Send you to a nun- nery!

Vic. Was my fond mother alive!—Catilina, my father will certainly marry this Dame Iſabel; I am

I am now an alien to his affections, bereft of every joy and every hope, I fhall quit the world without a figh.

AIR.—*Victoria.*

Ah, folitude, take my diftrefs,
    My griefs I'll unbofom to thee,
Each figh thou can'ft gently reprefs,
    Thy filence is mufic to me.

Yet peace from my fonnet may fpring,
    For peace let me fly the gay throng,
To foften my forrows I fing
    Yet forrow's the theme of my fong.
                    Exit Victoria.

Cat. I'd quit this caftle as foon as ever Donna Victoria enters a nunnery—Shall I go with her? No, I was never made for a nun—Aye, I'll back to the vineyard, and if my fweetheart Philippo, is as fond as ever, who knows—I was his queen of all the girls, tho' the charming youth was the guitar, flute, fiddle and hautboy of our village.

AIR.—*Catilina.*

Like my dear fwain, no youth you'd fee
So blythe, fo gay, fo full of glee,
In all our village who but he
        To foot it up fo featly---
    His lute to hear,
    From far and near,
    Each female came,
    Both girl and dame,
    And all his boon
    For every tune,
        To kifs them round fo fweetly

While

While round him in the jocund ring,
We nimbly danc'd, he'd play or sing,
Of may, the youth was chosen king
    He caught our ears so neatly.
Such music rare,
In his guitar,
But touch his flute
The crowd was mute,
His only boon
For every tune,
    To kiss us round so sweetly.   *[Exit.*

Enter VASQUEZ, *introducing* SPADO.

Vaf. I'll inform dame Isabel, Sir—please to wait a moment.   *[Exit Vafquez.*

Spa. Sir!—This dame Isabel is, it seems, a widow-gentlewoman, whom Don Scipio has retain'd ever since the death of his lady, as supreme directress over his family, has such an ascendancy here, that she has even prevail'd on him, to drive his own son out of his house, and, ha, ha, ha! is now drawing the old Don into a matrimonial noose, ha, ha, ha! I am told, rules the roast here in the castle—Yes, yes, she's my mark—Hem! Now for my story, but my scheme is up if I tell a single truth—Ah, no fear of that.—Oh, this way she moves—

Enter Dame ISABEL *and* VASQUEZ.

If. Don Scipio not return'd! A foolish old man, rambling about at this time of night! Stay, Vasquez, where's this strange, ugly, little fellow you said wanted to speak with me?

Vaf. (*confused.*) Madam, I did not say ugly—

Spa. No matter, young man—Hem!
    [Exit Vafquez.
    If. Well,

If. Well, Sir, pray who are you?

Spa. (*bowing obsequiously.*) Madam, I have the honour to be confidential servant and secretary to Don Juan, father to Don Fernando de Zelva.

If. Don Fernando! Heav'ns! is he arrived? Here, Vasquez, Lopez, Diego! (*calling.*)

Spa. Hold, madam; he is not arriv'd! Most sagacious lady, please to lend your attention for a few moments to an affair of the highest importance to Don Scipio's family. My young master is coming—

If. Well, Sir!

Spa. Incog.

If. Incog!

Spa. Madam, you shall hear—(*aside*) Now for a lie worth twenty pistoles—The morning before his departure, Don Fernando calls me into his closet, and shutting the door, Spado, says he, you know this obstinate father of mine has engag'd me to marry a lady I have never seen, and to-morrow, by his order I set out for Don Scipio her father's castle, for that purpose; but, says he, striking his breast with one hand, twisting his mustachios with the other, and turning up his eyes—if, when I see her, she don't hit my fancy—I'll not marry her, by the ——!! I shan't mention his oath before you, madam.

If. No, pray don't, Sir.

Spa. Therefore, says he, I design to dress Pedrillo, my arch dog of a valet, in a suit of my clothes, and he shall personate me at Don Scipio's castle, while I, in a livery, pass for him—If I like the lady, I resume my own character, and take her hand, if not, the deceit continues, and Pedrillo weds Donna Victoria, just to warn pa-
rental

rental tyranny how it dares to clap up marriage without confulting our inclinations.

If. Here's a difcovery ! fo then, it's my poor child that muft have fall'n into this fnare—(*afide.*) Well, good Sir !

Spa. And, continued he Spado, I appoint you my trufty fpy in this Don Scipio's family ; to cover our defigns, let it be a fecret that you belong to me, and I fhan't feem even to know .you—You'll eafily get a footing in the family, fays he, by impofing fome lie or other upon a foolifh woman I'm told is in the caftle, Dame Ifabel, I think they call her.

If. He fhall find I'm not fo eafily impos'd upon.

Spa. I faid fo, madam ; fays I, a lady of Dame Ifabel's wifdom muft foon find me out were I to tell her a lie.

If. Ay, that I fhould, Sir.

Enter VASQUEZ.

Vaf. Oh, Madam ! my mafter is return'd and Don Fernando de Zelva with him.

[*Exit Vafquez.*

If. Don Fernando! Oh, then, this is the valet, but I'll give him a welcome with a vengeance !

Spa. Hold, Madam ! Suppofe for a little fport, you feem to humour the deceit, only to fee how the fellow acts his part, he'll play the gentleman very well I warrant ; he is an excellent mimic, for, you muft know, Ma'am, this Pedrillo's mother was a Gypfy, his father a Merry Andrew to a Mountebank, and he himfelf five years Trumpeter to a company of Strolling Players.

If. So,

If. So, I was likely to have a hopeful fon-in-law—Good Sir, we are eternally indebted to you for this timely notice of the impofition.

Spa. I have done the common duties of an honeft man—I have been long in the family and can't fee my mafter make fuch a fool of himfelf without endeavouring to prevent any mifchance in confequence.

If. Dear Sir, I befeech you be at home under this roof, pray be free, and want for nothing the houfe affords.

Sp. (*bows.*) Good Madam! I'll want for nothing I can lay my fingers on. (*afide.*)
(*Exit Spado.*)

If. Heaven's! what an honeft foul it is! what a lucky difcovery! Oh, here comes my darling girl!

Enter LORENZA, (*magnificently drefs'd.*)

Lor. Oh, cara Madre! See, behold!—Can I fail of captivating Don Fernando? Don't I look charming?

If. Why, Lorenza, I muft fay the toilet has done it's duty, I'm glad to fee you in fuch fpirits, my dear child!

Lor. Spirits! ever gay, ever fprightly, chearful as a lark—but, my dear mother—

If. Mother! Hufh, my love! you forget you are now to pafs for Donna Victoria, Don Scipio's daughter; and for that purpofe, I had you brought from Italy—It feems your young Madrid Lover, Alphonfo too, thinks you Victoria, but you muft forget him, child.

Lor. Yes—but how fhall I forget my Florence Lover, my dear Ramirez? I love him, Alphonfo

VOL. I. s loves

loves me, and here for the fake of Fortune muft I give my hand to this Don Fernando, when there can't poffibly be any love on either fide.

If. I requeft, my dear, you'll not think of this Ramirez—ev'n from your own account of him, he muft be a perfon of moft diffolute principles— fortunately he knows you only by your name of Lorenza, I hope he won't find you out here.

Lor. Then, farewell, loving Alphonfo—Adieu, belov'd Ramirez! In obedience to your commands, Madam, I fhall accept of this Don Fernando; and as a hufband, I will love him if I can—

AIR *Lorenza.*

Love! gay illufion!
Pleafing delufion,
With fweet intrufion,
    Poffeffes the mind.

Love with love meeting
Paffion is fleeting;
Vows in repeating
    We truft to the wind.

Faith to faith plighted,
Love may be blighted;
Hearts often flighted
    Will ceafe to be kind.

Enter VASQUEZ.

Vaf. Madam—my mafter and Don Fernando.
If. Has Don Fernando a fervant with him?
Vaf. No Madam.
If. Oh, when he comes, take notice of *him.*

Enter

Enter DON SCIPIO *and* FERNANDO.

Don S. Oh, my darling dame, and my delicate daughter, blefs your ftars that you fee poor Scipio alive again—Behold my fon-in-law and the preferver of my life—Don Fernando, there's your fpoufe, and this is Donna Ifabella, a lady of vaft merit, of which my heart is fenfible.

Fer. Madam !   *(falutes Ifabella.)*

If. What an impudent fellow !   *(afide.)*

Don S. Dear Fernando, you are as welcome to this caftle as flattery to a lady, but there fhe is—bill and coo—embrace, carrefs her.

(Ferdinand falutes Lorenza.)

Lor. If I had never feen Ramirez, I fhould think the man tollerable enough !   *(afide)*

Don S. Ha! ha! this fhall be the happy night —Eh, Dame Ifabel, by our agreement, before the lark fings I take poffeffion of this noble tenement.

Fer. Don Scipio, I hop'd to have the honour of feeing your fon.

Don S. My fon! Who, Cæfar? Oh, Lord! He's—He was a—turn'd out a profligate—Sent him to Italy—got into bad company—don't know what's become of him—My dear friend, if you would not offend me, never mention Cæfar in my hearing. Egad—Eh, my dainty dame, is not Don Fernando a fine fellow!

If. Yes, he's well enough for a trumpeter.

Don S. Trumpeter! *(with furprife)* what do you mean by that? Oh, becaufe I found his praife; but, Madam, he's a cavalier of noble birth, title, fortune, and valour——

If. Don Scipio, a word if you pleafe.

(takes him afide)

Lor.

Lor. (*to Fernando*) Si, Signor, our caftle here is rather a gloomy manfion when compared to the beautiful Caffino's on the banks of the Arno.

Fer. Arno! true, Don Scipio faid in his letter, that his daughter had been educated at Florence. (*afide*)

Lor. You have had an unpleafant journey, Signor.

Fer. I have encountered fome difficulties by the way, it is true, Madam ; but am amply repaid by the honour and happinefs I now enjoy. (*bows*)

Lor. Sir!—I fwear he's a polite cavalier. (*afide* Won't you pleafe to fit, Sir ? I fancy you muft be fomewhat weary. (*they fit*)

Don S. Eh, fure—what this fellow only Don Fernando's footman ! how ! it can't be !

If. A fact; and prefently you'll fee Don Fernando himfelf in livery.

Don S. Look at the impudent fon of a gypfey —Sat himfelf down—By St. Iago I'll—

If. Hold ! let him play off a few of his airs.

Don Sc. A footman ! Ay, this accounts for his behaviour in the foreft—Don Fernando would never have accepted my purfe—(*taps Fernando on the fhoulder.*) Hey, what, you've got there !

Fer. Will you pleafe to fit, Sir ? (*rifes*)

Don S. Yes, he looks like a trumpeter. (*afide*) You may fit down, friend. (*with contempt*)

Fer. A ftrange old gentleman !

Enter VASQUEZ.

Vaf. Sir, your fervant Pedrillo, is arriv'd.

[*Exit Vafquez.*

If. Servant Pedrillo ! Ay, this is Fernando himfelf. (*a, art joyfully to Scipio*)

Fer.

Fer. Oh, then the fellow has found his way at laft. Don Scipio—Ladies—excufe me a moment.

[*Exit Fernando.*

Lor. What a charming fellow!

Don S. What an impudent rafcal!

Ped. (*without*) Is my mafter this way?

Don S. Mafter! Ay, this is Fernando.

Enter PEDRILLO *with a Portmanteau.*

Ped. Oh, dear! Ive got among the gentle-folks, I afk pardon.

If. How well he does look and act the fervant!

Don. S. Admirable! Yet I perceive the gran-dee under the livery.

If. Pleafe to fit, Sir. (*with great refpect*)

Lor. A livery fervant fit down by me!

Don S. Pray fit down, Sir. (*ceremonioufly.*)

Ped. Sit down. (*fits*) Oh, thefe muft be the upper fervants of the family—her ladyfhip here is the houfekeeper, I fuppofe—the young tawdry tit, lady's maid—(hey, her miftrefs throws off good clothes) and old Whifkers Don Scipio's butler. (*afide*)

Enter FERNANDO.

Fer. Pedrillo! how! feated? what means this difrefpect?

Ped. Sir. (*rifes*) Old Whifkers the butler there, afked me to fit down by Senorita, Furbelow the waiting-maid, here.

Fer. Sirrah!

Ped. Yes, Sir.

Don S. Sir, and firrah! how rarely they act their parts. I'll give them an item tho' that I underftand the plot of their comedy. (*afide*)

AIR

AIR.—QUINTETTO.

D. Scipio.	Senor! (*to Pedrillo*)
	Your wits muſt be keener,
	Our prudence to elude,
	Your fine plot,
	Tho' ſo pat,
	Will do you little good.
Pedrillo.	My fine plot!
	I'm a ſot,
	If I know what
	Theſe gentlefolks are at.
Fernando.	Paſt the perils of the night,
	Tempeſts, darkneſs, rude alarms;
	Phœbus riſes clear and bright,
	In the luſtre of your charms.
Lorenza.	O, charming, I declare,
	So polite a cavalier!
	He underſtands the duty,
	And homage due to beauty.
D. Scipio	Bravo! O braviſſimo!
Lorenza.	Caro! O cariſſimo!
	How ſweet his honey words,
	How noble is his mien!
D. Scipio.	Fine feathers make fine birds,
	The footman's to be ſeen.
	But both deſerve a baſting!
Pedrillo.	Since morning I've been faſting.
D. Scipio.	Yet I could laugh for anger.
Pedrillo.	Oh, I could cry for hunger.
D. Scipio.	I could laugh.
Pedrillo	I could cry.
D. Scipio.	I could quaff,
Pedrillo.	So could I.
D. Scipio.	Ha, ha, ha! I'm in a fit.
Pedrillo.	Oh, I could pick a little bit.
D. Scipio.	Ha, ha, ha!
Pedrillo.	Oh, oh, oh!
Lorenza.	A very pleaſant party!
Fernando.	A whimſical reception!
D Scipio.	A whimſical deception!
	But maſter and man accept a welcome hearty.
Fernando. ⎫	Accept our thanks ſincere, for ſuch a welcome
Pedrillo ⎭	hearty.

END OF ACT I.

ACT II.

SCENE I.

An Apartment in the Caftle.
Enter DON CÆSAR *(with precaution.)*

DON CÆSAR.

THUS far I've got into the Caftle unperceived
—I'm certain Sanguino means the old gentleman a mifchief, which nature bids me endeavour to prevent. I faw the rafcal flip in at the
poftern below; but where can he have got to!
(*A fliding pannel opens in the wainfcot, Enter thro'*
it SANGUINO.) Yes, yonder he iffues like a rat
or a fpider.—How now, Sanguino!

Sang. Captain Ramirez!

Don C. On enterprize without my knowledge! What's your bufinefs here?

Sang. Revenge! Look—(*fhews a ftilletto.*) if
I meet Don Scipio—

Don

Don C. I command you to quit your purpofe.

Sang. What, no fatisfaction for my wound
laft night, and lofe my booty too!

Don C. Your wound was chance—Put up—
We fhall have noble booty here, and that's our
bufinefs—But you feem to know your ground
here, Sanguino?

Sang. I was formerly Mafter of the Horfe to
Count D'Olivi the laft refident, fo am well acquainted with the galleries, lobbies, windings,
turnings, and every fecret lurking place in the
caftle.

Don C. Ha, ha, ha! Well, I have hope o'er
our booty here, we can afford to laugh at paft
dangers.

AIR.—*Don Cæfar.*

As homeward from the neighb'ring fair,
His grain well fold, difpell'd his care,
With jocound hafte the thrifty fwain
Trips o'er the mead and fkims the plain,
He ftops! He views--.Oh, dire amaze!
His ftock, his cottage all a blaze!

But haft'ning on he looks around,
The heath's on fire---to clear his ground.
His jovial friends to meet him come,
To chaunt the cheerful welcome home;
With heart-felt joy the found he hears,
And laughs away his former fears.

I mift Spado at the mufter this morning—did
he quit the cave with you?

Spa. (without) As fure as I'm alive it's fact,
Sir,—

Don C. Isn't that his voice?

Sang.

Sang. Impoſſible !

Don C. Huſh! (*they retire.*)

Enter Don Scipio *and* Spado.

Don S. Yes, I've heard of ſuch places; but you ſay you've been in the cave where theſe ruffian banditti live ?

Spa. Moſt certainly, ſir; for after having robb'd me of five hundred doubloons, the wicked rogues barbarouſly ſtripp'd, tied me neck and heels, threw me acroſs a mule like a ſack of corn, and led me blindfold to their infernal cavern.

Don S. Poor fellow !

Spa. There, Sir, in this ſkulking hole the villains live in all manner of debauchery, and dart out upon the innocent traveller like beaſts of prey.

Don S. Oh, the tygers! juſt ſo they faſtened upon me laſt night, but your fellow ſervant Pedrillo, our ſham Fernando, made 'em run like hares; I gave him my purſe for his trouble tho'.

Spa. And he took it ! what a mean fellow ! —you ought not to have ventured out unarm'd—I always take a blunderbuſs when I go upon the road—the raſcal banditti are moſt pitiful cowards.

Don S. What a glorious thing to deliver theſe reprobates into the hands of juſtice.

Spa. Ah, Sir, 'twould be a bleſſed affair— Oh, I'd hang 'em up like mad dogs !

Don S. Well, you ſay you know the cave?

Spa. Yes, yes, I ſlipp'd the handkerchief from my eyes and took a peep, made particular ob-

ſervafervations of the fpot; fo get a ftrong guard, and I'll lead you to the very trap door of their den.

Don S. then we'll furprize them, and you'll have the prayers of the whole country, my honeft friend.

Spa. Heav'n knows, Sir, I have no motives for this difcovery but the publick good, fo I expect the country will order me a hundred piftoles as a reward for my honefty.

Don C. Here's a pretty dog! (*apart.*)

Sang. Ay, ay, he han't long to live.

(*apart.*)

Don S. An hundred piftoles!

Spa. Sir, have an eye upon their Captain as they call him, he's the moft abandon'd, impudent, profligate—(*fuddenly turning fees* Don Cæfar, *who fhews a piftol.*) Captain did I fay. (*terrified.*) Oh, no; the Captain's a very worthy good natur'd fellow—I meant a fcoundrel, who thinks he ought to be Captain, one Sanguino, the moft daring, wicked and bloody villain that— (*turning the other way perceives* Sanguino *with a piftol.*) but indeed, I found Sanguino an honeft good natured fellow too—(*with increafed terror*)

Don S. Hey, a bloody, wicked, honeft, good-natur'd fellow! what is all this?

Spa. Yes; then, Sir, I *thought*, I faw thefe two gentlemen, and at that inftant, I *thought* they looked fo terrible, that with the fright, I *awoke*.

Don S. Awoke! what then, is all this but a dream you have been telling me?

Spa. Ay, fir, and the moft frightful dream I ever had in my life. I'm at this inftant fright'ned out of my wits.

Don

Don S. You do look frighten'd indeed——poor man! I thought this cave was——

Spa. Don't mention the cave or I faint—heigho!

Enter VASQUEZ.

Vas. Dame Ifabel would fpeak with you, fir.

Don S. I'll wait on her.

Spa. Yes I'll wait on her. (*going haſtily.*)

Don S. You! fhe don't want you.

Spa. Dear Sir, fhe can't do without me at this time.   [*Exit Don Scipio.*
I come. (*going.*)

Don C. No you ſtay.—(*pulls him back.*)

Spa. Ah, my dear Captain. (*affeƈting furprize and joy.*) What, and my little Sanguino too! Who could of thought of your finding me out here!

Don C. Yes; you are found out.

Spa. Such difcoveries as I have made in the caſtle!—

Don C. You're to make difcoveries in the foreſt too.

Sang. Our cave!

Spa. Oh, you overheard that! Didn't I hum the old fellow finely? Ha, ha, ha!

Sang. And for your reward, traitor, take this to your heart.   [*Offers to ſtab him.*

Don. C. Hold, Sanguino

Spa. Nay, my dear Sanguino, ſtay! What the devil—So here, I can't run a jeſt upon a filly old man, but I muſt be run thro' with a ſtiletto!

Don

T 2

Don. C. Come, Spado, confefs what really brought you here.

Spa. Bufinefs, my dear Sir, bufinefs, all in our own way too, for I defign'd to let every man of you into the caftle this very night, when all the family are in bed, and plunder's the word— Oh, fuch a delicious booty ! pyramids of plate, bags of gold, and little chefts of diamonds !

Sang. Indeed!

Spa. Sanguino, look at that clofet.

Sang. Well !

Spa. A glorious prize !

Sang. Indeed !

Spa. Six chefts of maffy plate ! Look, only look into the clofet ; wait here a moment, and I'll fetch a mafter-key that fhall open every one of them.

Don C. Hey ! Let's fee thofe chefts.

Sang. Maffy plate ! Quick, quick, the mafter key.

Spa. I'll fetch it.

Sang. Do, but make hafte, Spado.

Spa. I will, my dear boy.

[*Exit Sanguino into the clofet.*

My good—honeft—Oh, you two thieves! (*afide.*)

[*Exit Spado.*

Don C. Yes, I'll avail myfelf of the power my influence over our Banditti has put into my hands ; this night fhall give me poffeffion of the caftle ; I'll fee if terror can't reftore that right of which injuftice has deprived me—perform my promife to Alphonfo, quit my honeft compani- ons—carry my fpoil to Florence, and with my fond little Lorenza enjoy the delights of love and competence.

Re-enter

Re-enter SANGUINO.

Sang. A valuable booty, I dare fay, Captain.

Don C. (*Looking in.*) Ay, to judge by the form of the chefts they do feem full of clumfy old plate.

Sang. If we can but convey it off.

Don S. Yes. but I infift, Sanguino, no more of the poniard.

Sang. It's fheath'd—Enough—But, Captain, if this little rafcal, Spado, fhould turn informer and difcover us,——

Don S. (*without*) I'll be with you prefently, Dame.

Don C. Away, a way, to your lurking place.

Sang. Yes, yes, thofe pregnant chefts muft be delivered.

[*they haftily retire into pannel.*

Enter DON SCIPIO.

Don S. Now, Spado, I—hey, where is my little dreamer ? but why is this door open; this clofet contains many valuables—Why will they leave it open ? Let's fee—(*goes into the clofet.*)

Enter SPADO (*with a portmanteau.*)

Spa. (*as entering.*) I have no key—However I have ftol'n Don Fernando's portmanteau as a peace offering for thefe two rafcals! (*lays it on table.*) Are you there! What a pity the coming of my fellow-rogues! I fhould have had the whole caftle to myfelf

felf—Oh, what a charming feat of work for
a man of my induftry—*(fpeaking at clofet door.)*
You find the chefts there—You may convey
them out at night, and as for cutting Don Scipio's throat—that I leave to——

Enter Don Scipio,

Don S. Cut my throat!—What are you at
your dreams again?

Spa. (*afide*) Oh, zounds!—Yes Sir, as I was
telling you.

Don S. Of a little fellow you have the worft
dreams I ever heard.

Spa. Shocking Sir—then I thought—

Don S. Hold, hold, let me hear no more of
your curft dreams.

Spa. I've got off, thanks to his credulity.

[*afide.*

Don S. What portmanteau's that?

Spa. I'm on again! (*afide.*)

Don S. Fernando's I think.

Spa. (*affecting furprife*) What, my mafter's—
fo it is.—But I wonder who could have brought
it here.—Ay, ay, my fellow fervant Pedrillo is
now too grand to mind his bufinefs;—And my
mafter I find, tho' he has taken the habit fcorns
the office of a fervant—So I muft look after the
things myfelf.

Don S. Ay, ay, take care of them.

Spa. Yes, Sir, I'll take care of them!

Don S. Ha, ha, ha! what a ftrange whimfical fellow this mafter of yours! with his plots
and difguifes.—Think to impofe upon me too.—
But I think I'm far from a fool.

Spa.

Spa. (*looking archly at him.*) That's more than I am.

Don S. So he pretends not to know you, tho' he has fent you here as a fpy to fee what you can pick up?

Spa. Yes, Sir, I came here to fee what I can pick up. (*takes up the portmanteau.*)

Don S. What an honeft fervant! he has an eye to every thing. [*Exit Don Scipio.*

Spa. But before I turn honeft, I muft get fomewhat to keep me fo.

AIR—*Spado.*

In the foreft here hard by,
A bold robber late was I,
Sword and blunderbufs in hand,
When I bid a ṭrav'ller ftand :
   Zounds deliver up your cafh,
   Or ftrait I'll pop and flafh,
All among the leaves fo green-o,
    Damme, fir,
    If you ftir,
    Sluice your veins,
    Blow your brains,
    Hey down.
    Ho down,
    Derry, derry down,
All amongft the leaves fo green-o.

II

Soon I'll qnit the roving trade,
When a gentleman I'm made ;
Then fo fpruce and debonnaire,
'Gad, I'll court a lady fair ;
   How I'll prattle, tattle, chat,
   How I'll kifs her, and all that,
All amongft the leaves fo green-o!
    How d'ye do ?
    How are you ?

Why

Why fo coy ?
Let us toy,
Hey down,
Ho down,
Derry, derry down,
All amongft the leaves fo green-o.

III

But ere old, and grey my pate,
I'll fcrape up a fnug eftate ;
With my nimblenefs of thumbs,
I'll foon butter all my crumbs.
    When I'm juftice of the peace,
    Then I'll mafter many a leafe,
All amongft the leaves fo green-o.
    Wig profound,
    Belly round,
    Sit at eafe,
    Snack the fees,
    Hey down,
    Ho down,
Derry, derry down,
All amongft the leaves fo green-o.   [*Exit.*

SCENE II.

A Saloon.

Enter FERNANDO.

Fer. A wild fcheme of my father's to think of
an alliance with this mad family ;—yes, Don
Scipio's brain is certainly touch'd beyond cure,
his daughter, my cara fpofa of Italy don't fuit
my idea of what a wife fhould be—no, the lovely novice, this poor relation of Dame Ifabel has
caught my heart. I'm told to-morrow fhe's to
                                                    be

be immur'd in a convent; what if I aſk Dame
Iſabel, if—but ſhe, and indeed Don Scipio carry
themſelves very ſtrangely towards me—I can't
imagine what's become of my raſcal Pedrillo.

Enter PEDRILLO, *in an elegant morning gown, cap
and ſlippers.*

Ped. Strange, the reſpect I meet with in this family: I hope we don't take horſe after my maſter's wedding: I ſhou'd like to marry here myſelf—before I unrobe I'll attack one of the maids!
—Faith a very modiſh dreſs to go courting in—
hide my livery and I am quite gallant.

Fer. Oh, here's a gentleman I haven't ſeen yet.

Ped. Tol de rol

Fer. Pray, Sir, may I—Pedrillo! *(ſurpriſed)*
where have you—hey! what, ha, ha, ha! what's
the matter with you!

Ped. Matter!—Why Sir, I don't know how
it was, but ſome how or other laſt night, I happen'd to ſit down to a ſupper of only twelve covers, crack'd two bottles of choice wine, ſlept in
an embroider'd bed, where I ſunk in down, and
lay 'till this morning like a diamond in cotton.
—So, indeed, Sir, I don't know what's the matter with me.

Fer. I can't imagine how, or what it all
means.

Ped. Why, Sir, Don Scipio, being a gentleman of diſcernment, perceives my worth, and
values it.

Fer. Then Sir, if you are a gentleman of ſuch
prodigious merit, be ſo obliging, with ſubmiſſion
to your cap and gown, to—pull off my boots.
(Pedrillo ſtoops)

Enter VASQUEZ.

Vaf. Sir, the ladies wait breakfast for you;
(*to Pedrillo, who rises hastily.*)

Fer. My respects, I attend 'em.

Vaf. You! I mean his honour here.

Ped. Oh, you mean my honour here.

Fer. Well, but perhaps my good friend, I
may chufe a dish of chocolate as well as his honour here.

Vaf. Chocolate, ha, ha, ha! (*with a sneer*)

Ped. Chocolate, ha, ha, ha!

Fer. I'll teach you to laugh, Sirrah! (*strikes
Pedrillo*)

Ped. Teach me to laugh! you may be a good
mafter, but you've a very bad method—hey for
chocolate and the ladies.

[*Exeunt Pedrillo and Vasquez.*

Fer. Don Scipio shall render me an account
for this treatment, bear his contempt, and become the butt for the jefts of his infolent fervants! As I don't like his daughter, I have now
a fair excufe, and indeed a juft caufe to break
my contract, and quit his caftle; but then, I
leave behind the miftrefs of my foul.—Suppofe I
make her a tender of my heart—but that might
offend, as she muft know my hand is engaged to
another.—When I look'd, she turn'd her lovely
eyes averted—doom'd to a nunnery!

AIR.—*Fernando.*

My fair one like the blushing rose,
Can fweets to every fenfe difclofe:
Thofe fweets I'd gather, but her fcorn
Then wounds me like the fharpeft thorn.

With

With fighs each grace and charm I fee
Thus doom'd to wither oh the tree,
'Till age fhall chide the thonghtlefs maid,
When all thofe blooming beauties fade.

Hey, who comes here? oh the fmart little Sou-
brette who feems fo much attach'd to the beautiful novice—No harm to fpeak with her——

Enter CATALINA.

So my pretty primrofe!

Cat. How do you do, Mr.—*(pert and fami-
liar)* I don't know your name.

Fer. Not know my name! You muft know
who I am tho', and my bufinefs here, child?

Cat. Lord, man, what fignifies your going
about to fift me when the whole family knows
you're Don Fernando's footman.

Fer. Am I faith? Ha, ha, ha! I'll humor this
—*(afide)* Well, then, my dear, you know that I
am only Don Fernando's footman?

Cat. Yes, yes, we know that, notwithftanding
your fine clothes.

Fer. But where's my mafter?

Cat. Don Fernando! he's parading the gallery
yonder in his fham livery and morning-gown.

Fer. Oh, this accounts for twelve covers at
fupper, and the embroider'd bed; but who could
have fet fuch a jeft a going? I'll carry it on tho'
—*(afide)* So then after all I am known here?

Cat. Ay, and if all the impoftors in the caftle
were as well known, we fhou'd have no wedding
to-morrow night.

Fer. Something elfe will out—I'll feem to be
in the fecret, and perhaps may come at it—

(afide)

(aſide) Ay, ay, that piece of deceit is much worſe than ours:

Cat. That! what then you know that this Italian lady is not Don Scipio's daughter, but Dame Iſabel's, and her true name Lorenza?

Fer. Here's a diſcovery! *(aſide)* Oh yes, I know that.

Cat. You do! Perhaps you know too, that the young lady you ſaw me ſpeak with juſt now is the real Donna Victoria?

Fer. Is it poſſible! Here's a piece of villainy! *(aſide)* Charming! let me kiſs you, my dear girl. *(kiſſes her)*

Cat. Lord, he's a delightful man! *(aſide)*

Fer. My little angel, a thouſand thanks for this precious diſcovery.

Cat. Diſcovery!—Well if you did not know it before, hang your aſſurance, I ſay—but I muſt about my buſineſs, can't play the lady as you play'd the gentleman, I've ſomething elſe to do; ſo I deſire you won't keep kiſſing me here all day.

AIR.—*Catalina.*

I have a lover of my own,
  So kind and true is he;
As true, I love but him alone,
  And he loves none but me.

I boaſt not of his velvet down,
  On cheeks of roſy hue,
His ſpicy breath, his ringlets brown;
  I prize the heart that's true.

So to all elſe I muſt ſay nay;
  They only fret and teaze:
Dear youth, 'tis you alone that may
  Come court me when you pleaſe.

I play'd

I play'd my love a thoufand tricks,
  In feeming coy and fhy;
'Twas only, 'ere my heart I'd fix,
  I thought his love to try.

So to all elfe, &c.   [*Exit.*

Fer. Why what a villain is this Don Scipio! ungrateful to—but I fcorn to think of the fervices I render'd him laſt night in the foreſt, a falfe friend to my father, an nnnatural parent to his amiable daughter! Here my charmer comes. [*Retires.*

Enter VICTORIA.

Vic. Yes Catalina muſt be miſtaken, it is impoffible he can be the fervant, no, no; that dignity of deportment and native elegance of manner can never be aſſum'd, yonder he walks, and my fluttering heart tells me, this is really the amiable Fernando, that I muſt refign to Dame Ifabel's daughter.—

Fer. Stay, lovely Victoria!

Vic. Did you call me, Sir! Heav'ns what have I faid! (*confufed*) I mean, Senor, wou'd you wiſh to fpeak with Donna Victoria? I'll inform her, Sir. (*going*)

Fer. Oh, I cou'd fpeak to her for ever, for ever gaze upon her charms, thus transfix'd with wonder and delight.

Vic. Pray, Senor, fuffer me to withdraw.

Fer. For worlds I wou'd not offend; but think not lady, 'tis the knowledge of your quality that attracts my admiration.

Vic. Nay, Senor——

                                        Fer.

Fer. I know you to be Don Scipio's daughter, the innocent victim of injustice and oppres-
sion, therefore I acknowledge to you, and you
alone, that whatever you may have heard to the
contrary, I really am Fernando de Zelva.

Vic. Senor, how you became acquainted with
the secret of my birth I know not; but from an
acquaintance so recent, your compliment I receive as a mode of polite gallantry without a
purpose.

Fer. What your modesty regards as cold compliments, are sentiments, warm with the dearest
purpose; I came hither to ratify a contract with
Don Scipio's daughter! you are his daughter,
the beautiful Victoria, destin'd for the happy
Fernando.—Concurrent to a parent's will, my
hand is your's already. And thus on my knees
let me make an humble tender of my heart.

Vic. Pray, rise, Senor!—My father perhaps
even to himself cannot justify his conduct to me;
—But to censure that, or to pervert his intentions, wou'd in me be a breach of filial duty.

AIR.—*Victoria.*

By woes thus surrounded, how vain the gay smile
Of the little blind archer, those woes to beguile!
Tho' skilful, he misses, his aim it is cross,
His quiver exhausted, his arrows are lost.
Your love, tho' sincere, on the object you lose,
(*Aside*) How sweet is the passion! Ah, must I refuse?
If filial affection that passion should sway,
Then love's gentle dictates I cannot obey.

Fer. And do you, can you wish me to espouse
Signora Lorenza, Isabella's daughter?—Say you
do not, do but satisfy me so far.

Vic.

Vic. Senor, do not defpife me if I own, that before I faw in you the hufband of Don Scipio's daughter, I did not once regret that I had loft that title.

Fer. A thoufand thanks for this generous, this amiable condefcenfion,—Oh, my Victoria! If fortune but favours my defign, you fhall yet triumph over the malice of your enemies.

Vic. Yonder is Dame Ifabel, if fhe fees you fpeaking to me, fhe'll be early to fruftrate whatever you may purpofe for my advantage. Senor farewell!

Fer. My life, my love adieu!

[*Exit Victoria*

DUET.—*Victoria and Fernando.*

Idalian queen, to thee we pray,
　Record each tender vow;
As night gives place to chearful day,
Let hopes of future blifs allay,
　The pangs we fuffer now.

Fer. This is fortunate; the whole family except Victoria, are firmly poffeft with the idea that I am but the fervant.—Well, fince they will have me an impoftor, they fhall find me one; In heav'n's name, let them continue in their miftake, and beftow their mock Victoria upon my fham Fernando. I fhall have a pleafant and juft revenge for their perfidy; and perhaps obtain Don Scipio's real, lovely daughter, the fum of my wifhes.—Here comes Don Scipio—now to begin my operations.

Enter

Enter DON SCIPIO.

Don S. Ay here's the impudent Valet.

Fer. (*as wishing Don Scipio to overhear him*) I'm quite weary of playing the gentleman, I long to get into my livery again.

Don S. Get into his livery! (*aside*)

Fer. These cloaths fall to my share however; my master will never wear 'em after me.

Don S. His master! ay, ay! (*aside*)

Fer. I wish he'd own himself, for I'm certain Don Scipio suspects who I am.

Don S. Suspect! I know who you are, (*advancing*) So get into your livery again as fast as you can.

Fer. Ha, my dear friend, Don Scipio, I was——

Don S. Friend! you impudent rascal! I'll break your head if you make so free with me. None of your swaggering, Sirrah.—How the fellow acts, 'twasn't for nothing he was among the strolling players, but harkee, my lad, be quiet, for you're blown here without the help of your trumpet.

Fer. Lord your honor, how came you to know that I am Pedrillo?

Don S. Why I was told of it by your fellow—hold, I must not betray my little dreamer tho' (*aside*) No matter who told me;—I—but here comes your master.

Fer. Pedrillo! The fellow will spoil all; I wish I had given him his lesson before I began with Don Scipio. (*aside*)

Don S. I hope he'll now ha' done with his gambols.

Fer.

Fer. Sir, my mafter is fuch an obftinate gentleman, as fure as you ftand here, he'll ftill deny
himfelf to be Don Fernando.

Don S. Will he? then I'll write his Father an
account of his vagaries.

Enter PEDRILLO.

Ped. Mafter! fhall I fhave you this morning?

Don S. Shave! Oh, my dear Sir, time to give
over your tricks and fancies.

Ped. (furprifed) My tricks and fancies!

Fer. Yes Sir, you are found out.

Ped. I am found out!

Don S. So you may as well confefs.

Ped. What the devil fhall I confefs.

Don S. He ftill perfifts! Harkee, young gentleman, I'll fend your father an account of your
pranks, and he'll trim your jacket for you.

Ped. Nay, Sir, for the matter o' that, my father could trim your jacket for you.

Don S. Trim my jacket, young gentleman!

Ped. Why, he's the beft taylor in Cordova!

Don S. His father a taylor in Cordova!

Fer. Ay, he'll ruin all—*(afide)* Let me fpeak
to him.—Tell Don Scipio you are the mafter.
(apart to Pedrillo)

Ped. I will, Sir.—Don Scipio you are the
mafter.

Don S. What!

Fer. Stupid dog!—*(apart to Pedrillo)* Say you
are Fernando, and I am Pedrillo.

Ped. I will—Sir, you are Fernando, and I am
Pedrillo.

Fer. Dull rogue! *(afide)* I told you, Sir, he'd
perfift in it! *(apart to Don Scipio)*

Don

Don. S. Yes, I fee it; but I tell you what Don Fernando——

LORENZA *fings without.*

My daughter! don't let your miftrefs fee you any more in this curfed livery.——Look the gentleman, hold up your head—egad, Pedrillo's acting was better than your natural manner.

Fer. Ah, Sir, if you were to fee my mafter drefs'd—the livery makes fuch an alteration!

Don S. True! curfe the livery.

Ped. It's bad enough; but my mafter gives new liveries on his marriage.

Fer. An infenfible fcoundrel! (*afide*)

Enter LORENZA.

Lor. Oh, Caro Signor, every body fays that you are (*to Fernando*) not Don Fernando.

Don S. Every body's right, for here he ftands like a young taylor of Cordova. (*to Pedrillo*)

Lor. Oh, what? then this is Pedrillo?
(to Fernando)

Fer. At your fervice, Ma'm. *(bowing)*

Ped. That Pedrillo! then, who am I?

Fer. Here rogue, this purfe is yours—fay you are Don Fernando. *(apart to Pedrillo)*

Ped. Oh, Sir—now I underftand you. True, Don Scipio, I am—all that he fays.

Don S. Hey! Now that's right and fenfible, and like yourfelf, but I'll go buftle about our bufinefs—for, we'll have all our love affairs fettled this evening.
[Exeunt Don Scipio and Fernando.

Lor. So, then, you're to be my hufband, ha,
ha,

ha, ha! Well, who is to have me, or who am I to have at laft? This? *(looking at Pedrillo)* ha, ha, ha! Why this is ftill worfe and worfe—every degree of lover farther remov'd from the perfections of my Ramirez.

Ped. Ma'm—wou'd you be fo obliging as—to be fo kind as—to tell a body what you intend to get talking about now in this here cafe?

Lor. Ah, Lord! Ha, ha, ha! Why, Signor, I was reflecting what a lucky thing it is for fome people that they are born to a great fortune. *(fneeringly)*

Ped. Eh? *(looks grave)* Ha, ha, ha! Ma'am, I'm fo puzzld here—that—my brain turns about like a te-:o-tum, and I don't know which is coming up, A for all or P. for put down.

Lor. Ha, ha, ha! Will you love me, pray?

Ped. Eh!

Lor. Well, if not I can be as cold as you are indifferent.

AIR.—*Lorenza.*

'If I my heart furrender
Be ever fond and tender,
And fweet connubial joys fhall crown
Each foft rofy hour,
In pure delight each heart fhall own
Love's triumphant pow'r.
See brilliant belles admiring,
See fplendid beaux defiring,
All for a fmile expiring,
Wheree'r Lorenza moves.
To balls and routs reforting
Oh blifs fupreme, tranfporting!
Yet ogling, flirting, courting,
'Tis you alone that loves.
If I my heart furrender, &c.

[*Exeunt*
SCENE

SCENE III.

A Vineyard and Cottage.

Enter ALPHONSO, (*with a letter.*)

Alph. How cruel is my situation! Though Captain Ramirez has set me at liberty, to what purpose, while my heart is Victoria's prisoner! This generous Ramirez, means well, I believe; but to enter into any league with a man of his description—Can she love this Fernando? With all my ardour of passion, to me she was cold and insensible?——Her marriage with Fernando is determined on; but, if possible, I'll prevent it—Yes, Philippo, the youth of the cottage here shall bear him this challenge.

Enter PHILIPPO *from the Cottage,* (*with a Fruit-basket.*)

Phil. Are you here, Sir! Lord, Senor, why would not you eat some dinner with us?

Alph. Ah, Philippo! were you in love, you'd have little appetite.

Phil. Why, I like a pretty little girl—ha, ha, ha!—Catalina above at the castle, and next Martlemas I intend to fall in love with her, for then we shall certainly be married—may be—Do step in, Sir, and eat a bit.

Alph. No, no.

Phil. As nice an Ollo Podrida—

Alph. But where now, Philippo? Going to sell your grapes?

Phil. Sell! Oh, no, Sir; I am going to make
a present

a prefent of the earlieft and fineft clufters to Don Scipio up at the caftle.

Alph. Why, you're vaftly generous.

Phil. Oh, yes, Sir; I like to make a prefent to gentlefolks, becaufe they always give me twice the value of 'em; and then my Catalina gives me a kifs—her lips, fweet, foft, and pouting as this plump Mufcadel.

AIR.—PHILIPPO.

In autumn ev'ry fruit I fee,
  Brings Catilina to my mind;
I carve her name on ev'ry tree,
  And fing love-fonnets in the rind.

Her forehead as the nectrine fleek,
  And brown as hazle-nut her hair is;
The downy peach, her blufhing cheek,
  Her pouting lips—two May-Duke cherries.

The birds by faireft fruits allur'd,
And I'm fweet Catilina's bird;
I peck, hop, flutter on my fpray,
And chirp and carrol all the day.

Alph. Well, Philippo, you'll find one Don Fernando at the caftle and—

Phil. Oh, ay, the great grandee that's to marry Donna Victoria.

Alph. Diftraction! (*afide*) Give him this letter from me.

Phil. Yes, Sir, what is't about?

Alph. Ah—its only—an—invitation to Don Fernando and his intended bride to an entertainment I defign to give to a few felect friends at my villa.

Phil. To a feaft, ha, ha!

Alph.

Alph. But ftop! Pray, Philippo, do you know who this Captain Ramirez is?

Phil. Don't even know where he lives—fometimes he rides, fometimes he walks,—fometimes he runs here—travels about—Mayhap a hunting in the foreft—often takes a bed at our cottage, and he pays fo handfome that he's always welcome.

Alph. Ha, ha, ha! Philippo, you're the moft generous—difinterefted lad! (*gives money*)

Phil. So I am, Sir, (*looking at it*) Good bye!

Alph. You'll deliver my letter.

Phil. Ha, ha, ha! yes, Sir—(*looking at the money*) Ha, ha, ha! to think, Senor, what a pair of lovers you and I be!

AIR DUET.—Alphonso *and* Philippo.

Alph.	So faithful to my fair I'll prove,
Phil.	So kind and conftant to my love,
Alph.	I'd never range,
Phil.	I'd never change,
Both.	Nor time, nor chance, my faith fhould move.

Phil.	No ruby clufters grace the vine,
Alph.	Ye fparkling ftars forget to fhine,
Phil.	Sweet flowers to fpring,
Alph.	Gay birds to fing,
Both.	Thofe hearts then part that love fhall join,

[*Exeunt feverally.*

END OF ACT II.

ACT III.

SCENE I.

The Saloon.

Enter Don Scipio *and* Vasquez.

DON SCIPIO.

D'YE hear, Vasquez, run to Father Benedict, tell him to wipe his chin, go up to the chapel, put on his spectacles, open his Breviary,—find out matrimony, and wait 'till we come to him—
[*Exit Vasquez.*
Then hey for a brace of weddings. I wonder is Don Fernando dreft—Oh, here comes the servant in his proper habiliments.

Enter Fernando *in a livery.*

Ay, now, my lad, you look fomething like.

Fer. Yes, your honour, I was quite tired of my grandeur—My paffing fo well in this difguife gives me a very humble opinion of myfelf. (*afide*)

Don S. But, Pedrillo, is your mafter equipp'd! faith, I long to fee him in his proper garb.

Fer. Why, no, Sir, we're a little behind hand
with

with our finery on account of a portmanteau of
clothes that's mislaid somewhere or other.

Don S. Portmanteau! Oh, it's safe enough—
Your fellow servant has it.

Fer. Fellow servant!

Don S. Ay! the little spy has taken it in charge,
Oh, here comes the very beagle.

Enter SPADO.

Don S. Well, my little dreamer, look; Pedrillo has got into his own cloaths again.

Spa. (*surprised and aside.*) Don Fernando in a
livery! or is this really the servant! sure I han't
been telling truth all this while! we must face it
tho'—Ah, my dear old friend!—Glad to see
you yourself again.
                                        [*shakes hands.*

Fer. My dear boy, I thank you.—(*aside.*) So,
here's an old friend I never saw before.

Don S. Tell Pedrillo where you have left your
master's portmanteau. While I go lead him in
triumph to his bride.   [*Exit.*

Fer. Pray, my good, new, old friend, where
has your care deposited this portmanteau?

Spa. Gone! (*looking after Don Scipio.*)

Fer. The portmanteau gone!

Spa. Ay, his senses quite——

Fer. Where's the portmanteau that Don Scipio
says you took charge of?

Spa. Portmanteau! Ah, the dear gentleman!
Portmanteau did he say? yes, yes, all's over
with his poor brain; yesterday his head ran upon
purses and trumpeters and the lord knows what,
and to-day he talks of nothing but dreamers,
spies, and portmanteaus.—Yes, yes, his wits are
going.   *Fer.*

Fer. It muſt be ſo, he talk'd to me laſt night and to-day of I know not what in a ſtrange incoherent ſtile.

Spa. Grief—all grief.

Fer. If ſo, this whim of my being Pedrillo, is perhaps the creation of his own brain,—but then, how cou'd it have run thro' the whole family.—This is the firſt time I ever heard Don Scipio was diſorder'd in his mind.

Spa. Ay, we'd all wiſh to conceal it from your maſter, leaſt it might induce him to break off the match, for I don't ſuppoſe he'd be very ready to marry into a mad family.

Fer. And pray what are you, Sir, in this mad family ?

Spa. Don Scipio's own gentleman, theſe ten years—Yet, you heard him juſt now call me your fellow ſervant.—How you did ſtare when I accoſted you as an old aequaintance !——But we always humour him, I ſhou'd not have contradicted him if he ſaid I was the pope's nuncio.

Fer. (*aſide*) Oh, then I don't wonder at Dame Iſabel taking advantage of his weakneſs.

Spa. Another new whim of his,——he has taken a fancy that every body has got a ring from him, which he imagines belong'd to his deceas'd lady.

Fer. True, he aſked me ſomething about a ring.

Don S. (*without*) I'll wait on you preſently.

Enter DON SCIPIO.

Don S. Ha, Pedrillo, now your diſguiſes are over return me the ring. (*to Fernando*)

Spa. (*apart to Fernando*) You ſee he's at the ring again.

Don S. Come-let me have it, lad, I'll give you something better, but that ring belong'd to my deceas'd lady.

Spa. (*to Fernando*) His deceas'd lady—Ay there's the touch—grief for her death.

Fer. Poor gentleman! (*aside.*)

Don S. Do, let me have it,—Here's five pistoles, and the gold of the ring is not worth a dollar.

Spa. We always humour him, give him this ring and take the money.

[*apart. gives Fernando a ring.*

Fer. (*presents it to Don Scipio.*) There, Sir.

Don S. (*gives money.*) And there, Sir,—Oh you mercenary rascal. (*aside*) I knew it was on the purse I gave you last night in the forest.

Spa. Give me the cash, I must account for his pocket money.

[*apart to and taking the money from Fernando.*

Ped. (*without*) Pedrillo! Pedrillo! Sirrah!

Don S. Run, don't you hear your master, you brace of rascals?—Fly!   [*Exit Spado.*

Don S. (*looking out*) What an alteration!

Enter Pedrillo richly dress'd.

Ped. (*to Fernando*) How now, Sirrah? loitering here, and leave me to dress myself, hey! (*with great authority.*)

Fer. Sir, I was—(*with humility*)

Ped. Was!—and are—and will be, a lounging rascal, but you fancy you are still in your finery, you idle vagabond!

Don S. Bless me, Don Fernando is very passionate just like his father.

                                        Fer.

Fer. The fellow, I fee, will play his part to the top. (*afide*)

Ped. Well, Don Scipio,—A hey! an't I the man for the ladies? I am, for I have ftudied Ovid's art of Love.

Don S. Yes, and Ovid's Metamorphofes too, ha, ha, ha!

Ped. (*afide*) He, he, he! what a fneaking figure my poor mafter cuts.—Egad, I'll pay him back all his domineering over me. (*fits*) Pedrillo?

Fer. Your honour.

Ped. Fill this box with Naquatoch. [*Gives box.*

Fer. Yes, Sir. (*going*)

Ped. Pedrillo!

Fer. Sir?

Ped. Perfume my handkerchief.

Fer. Yes, Sir. (*going*)

Ped. Pedrillo.

Fer. Sir?

Ped. Get me a tooth-pick:

Fer. Yes Sir, (*going*)

Ped. Pedrillo!

Fer. (*afide.*) What an impudent dog!—Sir!

Ped. Nothing—Abfcond.

Fer. (*afide*) If this be my picture, I blufh for the original.

Ped. Mafter! to be like you, do let me give you one kick. (*afide to Fernando.*)

Fer. What!

Ped. Why, I won't hurt you much.

Fer. I'll break your bones, you villain:

Ped. Ahem, tol de rol.

Don S. Pedrillo!

Ped. Sir? (*forgetting himfelf*)

Fer. (*apart*) What are you at you rafcal?

Ped. Ay, what are you at you rafcal? avoid! (*to Fernando*)

Fer.

Fer. I'm gone, Sir.   [*Exit*,

Ped. Curft ill-natur'd of him, not to let me give him one kick. (*afide*)

Don S. Don Fernando, I like you viftly.

Ped. So you ought.—Tol de rol.—Who cou'd now fufpect me to be the fon of a taylor, and that four hours ago, I was a footman. (*afide*) Tol de rol.

Don S. Son-in-law, you're a flaming beau!— Egad you have a princely perfon.

Ped. All the young girls—whenever I got be-hind—infide of the coach—all the ladies of dif-tinction, whether they were making their beds, or dreffing the— dreffing themfelves at the toi-lette, wou'd run to the windows,—peep thro' their fingers, their fans, I mean, fimper behind their handkerchiefs, and lifp out in the fofteft, fweeteft tones, Oh, dear me, upon my honour and reputation, there is not fuch a beautiful gentleman in the world, as this fame Don Pe-drill—Fernando.

Don S. Ha, ha, ha! can't forget Pedrillo.— But come, ha' done with your Pedrillo's now— Be yourfelf, fon-in-law.

Ped. Yes, I will be yourfelf's fon-in-law, you are fure of that honor, Don Scipio, but pray what fortune am I to have with your daughter? You are a grey-headed old fellow Don Scipio, and by the courfe of nature, you know you can-not live long.

Don S. Pardon me, Sir, I don't know any fuch thing.

Ped. So when we put a ftone upon your head—

Don S. Put a ftone upon my head !

Ped.

Ped. Yes, when you are fettled—fcrewed down, I fhall have your daughter to maintain, you know.

Don S. (*afide*) A narrow-minded fpark!

Ped. Not that I wou'd think much of that, I am fo generous.

Don S. Yes, generous as a Dutch ufurer.

[*afide.*

Ped. The truth is, Don Scipio—I was always a fmart young gentleman.

[*Dances and fings.*

Don S. Since Don Fernando turns out to be fuch a coxcomb, faith I'm not forry that my old child has efcap'd him:—A convent itfelf is better than a marriage with a monkey.—The poor thing's fortune tho'! And then my fon—I begin now to think I was too hard upon Cæfar—to compare him with this puppy, but I muft forget my Children, Dame Ifabel will have me upon no other terms. (*afide.*)

Ped. D'ye hear, Don Scipio, let us have a plentiful feaft.

Don S. Was ever fuch a conceited, empty, impudent—

[*Exit.*

Ped. Yes, I'm a capital fellow, ha, ha! So my fool of a mafter fets his wits to work after a poor girl that I am told they are packing into a convent, and he dreffes me up as himfelf to carry the rich heirefs. Donna Victoria! Well I'm not a capital fellow! but I was made for a gentleman—gentleman! I'm the neat pattern for a Lord—I have a little honour about me, a bit of love too; ay, and a fcrap of courage, perhaps—hem! I wifh I'd a rival to try it tho'—od, I think I could fight at any weapon from a needle to a hatchet.

Enter

Enter PHILLIPPO, *with a letter and Baſket.*

Phil. Senor, are you Don Fernando de Zelva ?

Ped Yes, boy.

Phil Here's a letter for you, Sir, from Don Alphonſo.

Ped. I don't know any Don Alphonſo, boy. What's the letter about ?

Phil. I think, Sir, 'tis to invite you to a feaſt.

Ped. A feaſt !—Oh, I recolleƈt now, Don Alphonſo, what? my old acquaintance I give it me, boy.

Phil. But, are you ſure, Sir, you're Don Fernando ?

Ped. Sure, you dog !—don't you think I know myſelf—let's ſee, let's ſee—(*Opens the letter and reads.*)—" Senor, tho' you ſeem ready to fall " to on a love-feaſt, I hope a ſmall repaſt in the " field won't ſpoil your ſtomach"—Oh, this is only a ſnack before ſupper.—" I ſhall be at ſix o'clock this evening"—You dog it's paſt ſix now —" in the meadow near the Cottage of the Vines, where I expeƈt you'll meet me."—Oh dear, I ſhall be too late!—" As you aſpire to " Donna Viƈtoria, your ſword muſt be long " enough to reach my heart, Alphonſo." My ſword long enough ! (*frightened*) Feaſt ! this is a downright challenge.

Phil. I beg your pardon, Senor, but if I hadn't met my ſweetheart, Catalina, you would have had that letter two hours ago.

Ped. Oh, you have given it time enough my brave boy.

Phil.

Phil. Well, Sir, you'll come?

Ped. Eh! Yes, I dare fay he'll come.

Phil. He!

Ped. Yes, I'll give it him, my brave boy.

Phil. Him! Sir, didn't you fay you were——

Ped. Never fear, child, Don Fernando fhall have it.

Phil. Why, Sir, an't you Don Fernando?

Ped. Me, not I, child, no, no. I'm not Fernando, but, my boy, I would go to the feaft, but you have delay'd the letter fo long, that I have quite loft my appetite—Go, my fine boy.

Phil. Sir, I——

Ped. Go along, child, go! *(puts Philippo off)* however Don Fernando fhall attend you—but here comes my fpofa——

Enter LORENZA, *reading a letter.*

" Deareft Lorenza!—By accident I heard of
" your being in the caftle—if you don't wifh to
" be the inftrument of your mother's impofi-
" tion, an impending blow, (which means you
" no harm) " this night fhall difcover an impor-
" tant fecret relative to him who defires to re-
" fign ev'n life itfelf, if not your RAMIREZ."

(Kiffes the letter) I wifh to be nothing, if not your Lorenza; this foolifh Fernando! *(looking at Pedrillo)* but, ha, ha, ha! I'll amufe myfelf with him—looks tolerably now he's drefs'd, not fo agreeable as my difcarded lover Alphonfo tho'. *(afide)*

Ped. I'll accoft her with elegance—How do you do, Senora.

Lor. Very well, Signor, at your fervice.— Dreffes exactly like Prince Radifocani!

Ped.

Ped. Now I'll pay her a fine compliment—Senora, you're a clever little. body—Will you fit
down, Senora ? (*hands a chair*)

Lor. So polite too !

Ped. Oh I admire politenefs. (*fits*)

Lor. This would not be good manners in Florence tho' Signor.

Ped. Oh ! (*rifes*) I beg pardon—Well, fit in
that chair; I'll affure you, Donna Victoria, I
don't grudge a little trouble for the fake of good
manners. (*places another chair*)

Lor. Voi cette molto gentile. (*curtfies*)

Ped. Yes, I fit on my feat genteelly—I find I
underftand a good deal of Italian.—Now to
court her, hem! hem! what fhall I fay? Hang
it, I wifh my mafter had gone through the whole
bufinefs to the very drawing of the curtains.—
I believe I ought to kneel tho'.—(*afide*) (*Kneels*)
Oh, you moft beautiful Goddefs, you angelic
angel ! (*repeats.*

> For you, my fair, I'd be a rofe
> 'To bloom beneath that comely nofe ;
> Or, you the flower and I the bee,
> My fweets I'd fip from none but thee.
> Was I a pen, you paper white,
> Ye gods, what billet doux I'd write !
> My lips the feal, what am'rous fmacks
> I'd print on yours, if fealing-wax.
> No more I'll fay, you ftop my breath,
> My only life, you'll be my death.   [*rifes.*

—Well faid, little Pedrillo! (*wipes his knees*)

Lor. There is fomething in Don Fernando's
paffion extremely tender, though romantic and
extravaganza.

Ped. Oh, for fome fweet founds, Senora, if
you'll

you'll fing me a fong, I'll ftay and hear it, I'm fo civil.

Lor. With pleafure, Signor.

AIR.—*Lorenza.*

Heart beating,
Repeating,
Vows in palpitation,
Sweetly anfwers each fond hope;
Prithee leave me,
You'll deceive me
After other beauties running;
Smiles fo roguifh, eyes fo cunning
Shew where points the inclination.   [*Exeunt.*

SCENE II.

A Gallery in the Caftle.

Enter FERNANDO, ALPHONSO *and* VICTORIA.

Fer. Give me joy, Alphonfo, father Benedict in this dear and wifh'd for union has this moment made me the happieft of mankind.

Alph. Then it is certain all you have told me of my Victoria?

Vic. True indeed, Alphonfo, that name really belongs to me.

Alph. No matter, as neither lineage, name or fortune caught my heart, let her forfeit all, fhe is ftill dear to her Alphonfo.

Fer. Courage, I'll anfwer you fhall be no exception to the general joy of this happy night.

Alph. Happy, indeed, if bleſt with my Lorenza.

AIR.—*Alphonſo.*

Come ye hours, with blifs replete,
Bear me to my charmer's feet !
Cheerlefs winter muſt I prove,
Abſent from the maid I love ;
But the joys our meetings bring
Shew the glad return of ſpring·   [*Exeunt.*

SCENE III.

*A view of the outſide of the Caſtle, with Moat and
Drawbridge.*

Enter DON CÆSAR, *and* SPADO.

Don C. You gave my letter to the lady ?
Spa. Yes, I did, Captain Ramirez.
Don C. Lucky ſhe knows me only by that
name. (*aſide*)

AIR.—*Don Cæſar.*

The Billet Doux, ah, didſt thou bear,
To my Lorenza charming fair ?
I ſee how look'd the modeſt maid,
I hear the gentle things ſhe ſaid.
The mantling blood her cheek forſakes,
But quick returns the roſy hue ;
With trembling haſte the ſeal ſhe breaks,
And reads my tender Billet Doux.

The Billet Doux when I receive,
I preſs it to my throbbing heart;
Sweet words I cry, ſuch joys you give,
Oh, never never thence depart,

And

And now it to my lips is preft,
But when the magic name I view,
Again I clafp it to my breaft,
My fond, my tender Billet Doux!

Spa. A love-affair, hey,—Oh, fly!

Don C. Hufh! Mind you let us all in by the little wicket in the eaft rampart.

Spa. I'll let you in, Captain, and a banditti is like a cat, where the head can get in the body will follow.

Don C. Soft! Letting down the drawbridge for me now, may attract obfervation. (*looking out*) Yonder I can crofs the moat.

Spa. But my dear Captain! If you fall into the water, you may take cold.—I wifh you were at the bottom with a ftone about your neck. (*afide*)

AIR.—*Don Cæfar.*

At the peaceful midnight hour,
Ev'ry fenfe, and ev'ry pow'r,
   Fetter'd lies in downy fleep;
   Then our careful watch we keep;
While the wolf in nightly prowl,
Bays the moon with hideous howl,
Gates are barr'd, a vain refiftance!
Females fhriek; but no affiftance,
   Silence, or you meet your fate;
   Your keys, your jewels, cafh and plate;
   Locks, bolts, bars, foon fly afunder,
   Then to rifle, rob and plunder.

[*Exit Don Cæfar.*

Spa. I fee how this is—our Captain's to carry off the lady and my brethren all the booty, what's left for me then? No, devil a bit they'll give me—Oh, I muft take care to help myfelf in time—Got nothing yet but that portman-

z 2   teau,

teau, a few filver fpoons and tops of pepper-
caftors; let's fee, I've my tools here ftill—(*takes
outs piftols*) I'll try and fecure a little before thefe
fellows come, and make a general fweep—Eh,
(*looks out*) My made-up Fernando!   [*Retires.*

Enter PEDRILLO.

Ped. He, he, he! Yes, my mafter has certainly married the little nunnery-girl—Ha, ha, ha!
Don Alphonfo to demand fatisfaction of me! no,
no, Don Fernando is a mafter for the gentlemen,
I am a man for the ladies.

AIR.—*Pedrillo.*

A foldier I am for a lady,
    What beau was e'er arm'd compleater?
        When face to face,
        Her chamber the place,
I'm able and willing to meet her.
Gad's curfe, my dear laffes, I'm ready
    To give you all fatisfaction;
        I am the man
        For the crack of your fan,
Tho' I die at your feet in the action.
Your bobbins may beat up a row-de-dow,
Your lap-dog may out with his bow-wow-wow,
        The challenge in love,
        I take up the glove,
Tho' I die at your feet in the action.

Spa. (*advances*) That's a fine fong, Senor.
Ped. Hey! did you hear me fing?
Spa. I did, 'twas charming.
Ped. Then take a pinch of my Macquabah.
(*offers, Spado takes.*)
Spa. Now, Senor, you'll pleafe to difcharge
my little bill.
                                          Ped.

Ped. Bill! I don't owe you any——

Spa. Yes, you do, Sir; recollect, didn't you ever hire any thing of me?

Ped. Me! no!

Spa. Oh, yes; I lent you the use of my two fine ears to hear your song, and the use of my most capital nose to snuff up your Macquabah.

Ped. Eh! what do you hire out your senses and organs.

Spa. Yes, and if you don't instantly pay the hire, I'll strike up a symphonia on this little barrel-organ here. (*shews a pistol*)

Ped. Hold, my dear Sir—there—(*gives money*) I refuse to pay my debts!—Sir, I'm the most punctual—(*frighten'd*) but if you please, rather than hire them again, I'd chuse to buy your fine nose and your capital ears out and out.

Spa. Hark'ee (*in a low tone*) You owe your Donship to a finesse of mine, so mention this, and you are undone, Sirrah!

Ped. Sir! (*frighten'd*) Dear Sir! (*Spado presents pistol*)—Oh, lord, Sir!   [*Exit.*

Spa. Ha, ha, ha! They call me little Spado—why I am not big but even Sanguino allow'd I was a clever little fellow. Astonishing how a soul like mine, cou'd be pack'd in so small a compass, but if worth is to be estimated by bulk, then must the Orient pearl give way to the goose's egg, and the moss rose to the red cabbage.

AIR.—*Spado.*

Tho' born to be little's my fate,
  Why so was the great Alexander;
And when I march under a gate,
  I've no need to stoop like a gander;

I'm

I'm no linkum long hoddy-doddy,
  Whofe paper kite fails in the fky;
If two feet I want in my body,
  In foul I am thirty feet high!

II.

Sweet lafs, of fweet love can you fail,
  With fuch a compact little lovy?
Tho' no one can tafte the big whale,
  All relifh the little anchovy.
The eagle, tho' for an high flyer,
  Of fine-feather'd fowl is the crack,
Yet when he cou'd fly up no higher,
  The little wren jump'd on his back.

Enter PHILIPPO *towards the clofe of the air.*

Phil. Lord, Sir! I do vaftly like your finging.
Spa. Oh, then you heard my fine fong.
Phil. Yes, Sir.
Spa. How did you get in?
Phil. In!
Spa. Did you pay at the door?
Phil. What door, Sir?
Spa. What door, Sir! the door of this fpacious theatre.
Phil. Theatre! Lord, Sir, are'nt we out in the open air?
Spa. You little equivocating fneaking fcoundrel! wou'd you cheat, defraud a man of genius out of the reward of his talents?—What, hear my fweet fong, and not pay or your mufick.
Phil. Pay!
Spa. O, ho! I fee fomebody's likely to be robb'd here! Look'e friend, I'm not to be bilk'd, fo if you don't this inftant pay, I muft
                                        difcharge

difcharge my door-keeper, here he is——*(fhews a piftol)*

Phil. (*crying*) And muft I give all the money Don Scipio gave me for my whole bafket of grapes. (*gives money*) A plague o' your mufick! Oh, oh!   [*Exit crying.*

Spa. What, you villain! I fufpect prefently this houfe will be too hot for me, yet the devil tempts me ftrongly to venture in once more, if I cou'd but pick up a few more articles—Ecod, I'll venture, tho' I feel an ugly fort of tickling under my left ear—Oh, poor Spado!   [*Exit.*

SCENE IV; *and laft.*

A Hall in the Caftle.

Enter SPADO.

Spa. So many eyes about—I can do nothing; if I cou'd but raife a commotion to employ their attention—Oh! here's Don Juan, father to Fernando, juft arriv'd—Yes, to mix up a fine confufion now—aye, that's the time to pick up the loofe things—but hold, I am told this Don Juan is very paffionate—heh! to fet him and Don Scipio together by the ears—Ears!—I have it.

Enter DON JUAN *in a travelling drefs, and Servant.*

Don J. My coming will furprize my fon Fernando, and Don Scipio too—tell him, I'm here—I hope I'm time enough for the wedding.
                          [*Exit Serv.*

Spa. A grim looking old gentleman!
                          (*Bows obfequioufly.*)
                          Don J.

Don J. Who's dog are you ?

Spa. How do you do, Senor ?

Don J. Why, are you a phyfician ?

Spa. Me a phyfician ! Alack-a-day, no, your honour, I am poor Spado.

Don J. Where's Don Scipio ? What is this his hofpitality ? he has heard that I am here ?

Spa. He hear ! Ah, poor gentleman—hear ! his misfortune !

Don J. Misfortune! what, he's married again ?

Spa. At the brink.

Don J. Marry and near threefcore, what, has he loft his fenfes ?

Spa. He has loft nearly one, Sir.

Don J. But where is he ? I want to afk him about it.

Spa. Afk, then you muft fpeak very loud, Sir.

Don. J. Why, is he deaf?

Spa. Almoft Sir, the dear gentleman can fcarce hear a word.

Don J. Ah, poor fellow ! Hey ! Isn't yonder my fon ? (*walks up.*)

Spa. Now if I could bring the old ones together, I fhouldn't doubt of a quarrel.

Enter DON SCIPIO.

Don S. Ah, here's my friend Don Juan ! Spado, I hope he han't heard of his fon's pranks !

Spa. Hear ! Ah, poor Don Juan's hearing ! I've been roaring to him thefe five minutes.

Don S. Roaring to him !

Spa. He's almoft deaf.

Don S. Blefs me !

Spa. You muft bellow to him like a fpeaking-trumpet.   [*Exit Spado.*
                                                          Don S.

Don S. (*very loud.*) Don Juan, you are welcome.

Don. J. (*ftarting.*) Hey! Strange that your deaf people always fpeak loud—(*very loud.*) I'm very glad to fee you, Don Scipio.

Don S. When people are deaf themfelves, they think every body elfe is fo—How long have you been this way. (*bawling.*)

Don. J. Juft arriv'd. (*bawling in his ear.*)

Don. S. I mean as to the hearing?

[*Very loud.*

Don J. Aye, I find it's very bad with you. (*bawling.*) I fhall roar myfelf as hoarfe as a raven.

Don S. My lungs can't hold out a converfation: I muft fpeak by figns— (*makes figns*)

Don J. What now, are you dumb too?

Enter VASQUEZ. *Whifpers Don* SCIPIO.

Don S. Oh, you may fpeak out, nobody can hear but me.

Don J. [*to* Vafquez] Pray, is this crazy fool your mafter here going to be married?

Don S. What! (*fuprifed.*)

Vaf. Don Fernando wou'd fpeak with you, Sir. (*to Don* Scipio.) [*Exit* VASQUEZ.

Don S. I wifh he'd come here, and fpeak, to this old blockhead his father—Don Juan, you are welcome to my houfe—but I wifh you had ftaid at home. (*in a low tone.*)

Don J. I am—much oblig'd to you. (*enraged*)

Don S. You'll foon fee your fon: as great an afs as yourfelf. (*in a low toue.*)

Don J. An afs! you fhall find me a tyger, you old whelp!

Don S. Why, zounds, you're not deaf!

Don J. A mad—ridiculous!——

Enter FERNANDO *and* VICTORIA.

Fernando! hey, boy, what drefs is this?

Fer. My father—Sir—I---I---

Don S. (*to* Victoria.) What are you doing with that fellow?

Vic. Your pardon, deareft father, when I own that he is now my hufband.

Don S. By this ruin, this eternal difgrace upon my houfe am I punifh'd for my unjuft feverity to my poor fon---married to that rafcal.

Don J. Call my fon, a rafcal!

Don S. Zounds, man! who's thinking of your fon? But this fellow to marry the girl and difgrace my family.

Don J. Difgrace! He has honoured your family, you crack-brained old fool!

Don S. A footman honour my family, you fuperannuated deaf old ideot!

Enter Dame ISABEL.

Oh, Dame, fine doings! Pedrillo here has married my daughter.

Don J. But why this difguife---what is all this about? tell me, Fernando.

Ifa. What, is this really Don Fernando?

Don S. Do you fay fo, Don Juan?

Don J. To be fure.

Don S. Hey! then, Dame, your daughter is left to the valet---no fault of mine tho'.

Ifa. What a vile contrivance?

Fer. No, Madam, your's was the contrivance, which love and accident have counteracted in juftice to this injured lady.

Ifa. Oh, that villain Spado.

Don J. Spado! why that's he that told me you were deaf.   *Don S.*

Don S. Why, he made me believe you cou'd not hear a word.

Ifa. And led me into this unlucky error.

[*Exit* ISABELLA.

Don J. Oh, what a lying fcoundrel!

Enter SPADO. (*bebind.*)

Spa. I wonder how my work goes on here! (*Roars in Don* JUAN's *ear.*) I give you joy, Sir.

Don J. I'll give you forrow, you rafcal!

(*beats him.*)

Don S. I'll have you hang'd, you villain!

Spa. Hang'd! dear Sir, 'twould be the death of me.

Ped. (*without.*) Come along, my Cara Spofa--- tol-de-rol---(*Enters*) How do you do, boys and girls.---Zounds! my old mafter!

Don J. Pedrillo! hey day! here's finery!

Ped. I muft brazen it out: Ah, Don Juan, my worthy dad!

Don J. Why, what in the name of---but I'll beat you to a mummy, firrah!

Ped. Don't do that-- I'm going to be married to an heirefs, fo muftn't be beat to a mummy--- Lady ftand before me, (*gets bebind* Victoria).

Don J. Let me come at him.

Spa. Stay where you are, he don't want you.

Spa. Dear Sir.

Don S. Patience, Don Juan, your fon has got my daughter, fo our contract's fulfill'd.

Don J. Yes, Sir; but who's to fatisfy me for your intended affront, hey!

Don S. How fhall I get out of this---I'll revenge all upon you, you little rafcal! to prifon you go---Here, a brace of Alguazils, and a pair of hand-cuffs.

Spa.

Spa. For me! the beft friend you have in the world!

Don S. Friend, that fhan't fave your neck.

Spa. Why I've fav'd your throat.

Don S. How, Sirrah?

Spa. Only two of the banditti here in the caftle this morning.

Don S. Oh, dear me!

Spa. But I got 'em out.

Don S. How, how!

Spa. I told 'em they fhould come and murder you this evening.

Don S. Much oblig'd to you.---Oh, lord!

[*A crafh and tumultuous noife without, bandit-ti rufh in arm'd,* Don Cæfar *at their head,* Fernando *draws and ftands before* Victoria.]

Band. This way!

Don S. Oh, ruin! I'm a miferable old man! Where's now my Cæfar, if I hadn't banifh'd him I fhould now have a protector in my child.

Don C. Then you fhall—Hold! (*to Banditti*) My father! (*kneels to Don Scipio.*)

Don S. How! Cæfar!

Don C. Yes, Sir—drove to defperation by— my follies were my own---but my vices——

Don S. Were the confequence of my rigour--- My child! let thefe tears wafh away the remem-brance of the paft.

Don C. My father! I am unworthy of this goodnefs---I confefs ev'n now I entered the caftle with an impious determination to extort by force---

Sang. Captain, we didn't come here to *talk---* Give the word for plunder.

Band. Aye, plunder! (*very tumultuous.*)

Don C. Hold!

Spa. Captain, let's have a choice rumaging.

(*cocks his piftol.*)

Ped.

Ped. Oh, Lord! there's the barrel-organ!

Don C. Stop! hold! I command you.

Don S. Oh, heav'ns then is Ramirez the terrible Captain of the cut-throats, the grand tyger of the cave?—but all my fault! the un-natural parent fhould be punifh'd in a rebellious child! My life is yours.

Don C. And I'll preferve it as my own.   Retire and wait your orders.

[Exeunt all Banditti but Spado.]

Don S. What, then, you are my protector. My dear boy! Forgive me! I, I, I pardon all.

Don C. Then, Sir, I fhall firft beg it for my companions, if reclaim'd by the example of their leader, their future lives fhew them worthy of mercy, if not, with mine let them be forfeit to the hand of juftice.

Don S. Some, I believe, may go up—Eh; little Spado, could you dance upon nothing?

Spa. Yes, Sir; but our captain, your fon muft lead up the ball.   (*Bows.*)

Don S. Ha, ha, ha; Well, though ill-beftow'd, I muft try my intereft at Madrid.   Children, I afk your pardon; forgive me Victoria; and take my blefling in return.

Vic. And do you, Sir, acknowledge me for your child?

Don S. I do, I do, and my future kindnefs fhall make amends for my paft cruelty.

Ped. Ha, here comes my fpofa---Eh! got a Cicefbeo already?

Enter ALPHONSO and LORENZA.

Don C. My beloved Lorenza!   (*They Embrace.*)
Lor. My deareft,
Alph.

Alph. My good Captain! as I knew this Lady
only by the name of Victoria, you little imagined
in your friendly promifes to me, you were giving
away your Lorenza; but, had I then known we
both loved the fame miftrefs, I fhould e're now
have relinquifhed my pretenfions.

Lor. My good-natured Alphonfo!   Accept
my gratitude, my efteem, but my love is, and
ever was, in the poffeffion of—Don Cæfar.

Don C. Dear father, this is the individual Lady
whofe beauty, grace, and angelic voice, capti-
vated my foul at Florence; if fhe can abafe her
fpotlefs mind to think upon a wretch degraded
by his lawlefs irregularities, accompany her pardon with your approbation to our union.

Lor. My Cæfar! let every look be forward to
happinefs.

DUET—*Cæfar and Lorenza.*

My foul, my life, my love how great !
  Sweet flower fo long neglected,
Our joys are rapture when we meet,
  A bleffing unexpected.

The envious clouds now chafe away,
Behold the radient god of day,
Arife with light eternal crown'd,
To guild the glorious landfcape round.

Don S. Ifabel has been too good, and I too
bad a parent! ha, ha, ha! then fate has decreed
you are to be my daughter fome way or other.
Eh, Signora.

Ped. Yes, but has fate decreed that my fpofa
is to be another man's wife ?

Spa. And, Sir, (*to Scipio.*) if fate has decreed
that your fon is not to be hanged, let the indulgence extend to the humbleft of his followers.
(*Bows.*)

Don S.

Don S. Ha, ha, ha! Well, tho' I believe you a great, little rogue, yet it feems you have been the inftrument of bringing about things juft as they fhould be. .

Don J. They are not as they fhould be, and I tell you again, Don Scipio, I will have,——

Don S. Well, and fhall have—a bottle of the beft wine in Andalufia, fparkling Mufcadel, bright as Victoria's eye, and fweet as Lorenza's lip; hey, now for our brace of Weddings— where are the violins, lutes, and cymbals? I fay let us be merry in future, and paft faults, our good-humour'd friends will forget and forgive.

Finale.—GLEE.

Social powers at pleafure's call
Welcome here to Hymen's hall;
Bacchus, Ceres, blefs the feaft,
Momus lend the fprightly jeft,
Songs of joy elate the foul,
Hebe fill the rofy bowl,
Every chafte and dear delight,
Crown with joy this happy night.

THE END.

LE

GRENADIER.

IN THREE PARTS.

INTENDED TO HAVE BEEN PERFORMED AT THE

THEATRE-ROYAL, COVENT-GARDEN,

IN 1789.

———————

THE MUSICK BY MR. SHIELD.

VOL. I.   B B

DRAMATIS PERSONÆ.

Count Clementin, ... Mr. BANNISTER.
Count de Lorge, ...
Governor of the Baſtille, ...
M. Pincemaille, ...
Dubois (a Grenadier, ſon to Ambroiſe), Mr. JOHNSTONE.
Acorn (an Engliſhman), ...
Martin, (a Soldier), ... Mr. DUFFY.
Ambroiſe (a veteran Officer), ... Mr. DARLEY.
Auſtin (a Prieſt), ... Mr. POWELL.
Arnold (an Exempt), ...
Robert (an Invalid), ...
Savetier (a Cobler), ... Mr. EDWIN.
Thomas ⎰ (Chrildren of the Military ⎱
Jaques ⎱ School, and ſons to Am-⎰
broiſe), ...
Alderfeldt (an Officer in the German
ſervice), ...,..
Pere Anthony (a Brother of St. Lazare),

Madame Clementine, ... Miſs PLATT.
Henriette, ... Mrs. MOUNTAIN.
Alice, ...
Madelaine, ...,.......... Mrs. MARTYR.

Friars of all orders, German Guards, French Guards,
Invalids, Nobleſſe, Citizens, Children of the De-
pôt des gardes Françoiſes, Peaſants, Jailors,
Exempts, Women, Children, Priſoners, &c.

SCENE, Paris.

LE

GRENADIER.

PART I.

SCENE I.

A view near Menilmontant in the vicinity of the Fauxbourg St. Antoine; on one fide Madame Clementine's Houfe—A Court and Gate on the other—a Tree with a Seat under it near the front.

ENTER *Thomas and Jaques* hand in hand, in their uniforms—they look, laugh and jump with great joy; then run and hide behind a tree, and archly peep out.

 Enter Ambroife—looks about him for Thomas and Jaques—they fuddenly ftart out from behind the tree, and with joy fpring into his arms.

 Enter Dubois—Tender and affectionate to his father and brothers, who bring Ambroife off with great glee.—Henriette appears at a window of Madame Clementine's houfe, fmiles at Dubois; he falutes refpectfully; fhe enters haftily from the houfe through the gate—Dubois with gallantry and complaifance invites her to fit down

on

on the feat under the tree; he paffionate and tender; fhe liftens with affection.

AIR.—*Dubois*.

Hark to the tinkling of yon brook,
Upon it's flow'ry margin look;
   Thro' this green mead, tho' free to ftray,
   While you are here it feems to fay,
   In plaintive murmurs, Let me ftay,
Ah cruel Seine why afk me yet,
I cannot leave fweet Henriette.

II.

For thee my fair the violets fpring,
To pleafe my love, the fweet birds fing;
   Or was't thy thrilling voice dear maid?
   No, Cupid calls from yonder fhade,
   And he muft ever be obey'd.
Beneath that tree the loves are met,
And there I'll court my Henriette.

III.

To look around thro' all mankind,
Some darling paffion fways the mind.
   The greedy mifer pants for gold,
   A nation's for ambition fold,
   And fame leads on the foldier bold.
Fame, gold, ambition, all are met,
In one fweet fmile from Henriette.

He leads her to the bench; they fit.—Diftant fhouts—Dubois and Henriette liften.

Enter Martin.—Acquaints Dubois that the people are affembling to repair to M. Pincemaile's houfe, with defign to make him give up his monopolized corn. Dubois draws his fword.—Henriette endeavours to diffuade him from going; they part tenderly, [*Exeunt Dubois and Martin.* The former in his ardour having forgot his muf-

quet

quet and grenadier's hat on the bench. Henriette diftreffed.

Enter Madame Clementine from the houfe, introducing the Governor; prefents him to Henriette as a lover. She rejects him with difdain. He entreats Madame Clementine to interpofe her authority in his favor; this fhe declines, unwilling to force her daughter's inclinations. The Governor looking on the bench, fees Dubois' hat with the national green cockade and the mufquet, fnatches up the hat in great fury, upbraids Henriette with giving the preference to fo mean a rival, tears out the cockade, throws it on the ground, and treads on it.——Madame Clementine with indignation againft the Governor, picks up the cockade, prefents it to her daughter, commands her to wear it next her heart, and defires the Governor to fee Henriette no more.—He greatly enraged, ftill having Dubois' hat in his hand, who returns for his mufquet, fees the hat and claims it.——Madame Clementine points to the cockade in Henriette's breaft, afking him if it is his; he acknowledges it—Madame Clementine with great joy looks on Du Bois, authorifes Henriette to receive his addreffes.——The Governor filled with much anger and contempt feems greatly mortified.—Shouting without; the Governor alarm'd; Dubois fmiles at him with exultation, acquaints Madame Clementine that the people are going to break open Pincemaille's granaries, and diftribute to the poor the corn at a reafonable price.

[Exit the Governor haftily and agitated.
Madame Clementine with fpirit, encourages Du bois to go and affift the people, to which Henriette with reluctance agrees.——

DUET.

DUET.

Henriette and Dubois.

Hen.	Generous foldier do not go To fight, when there's no foreign foe.
Dub.	Do not wrong the glorious caufe, Againft the abufe but not the laws. At firft the godlike flame began, To give mankind the claims of Man.
Hen.	My fears fuch boding ills prefage, Bleft Angels ftill my foldier guard; A nation's good his thoughts engage, A nation's praife the bright reward.
Dub.	Sweeteft, beft, of womankind, Sooth my love thy troubl'd mind; When tempeftuous tumults roll, This affurance calm thy foul. Thy Guillaume fcorns a rebel's name, Nor treafon ftain his fword with fhame.
Hen.	Ah me!
Dub.	My Henriette!
Hen.	Go.---
Dub.	The proud humanity fhall know.] With patriotic zeal I burn.
Hen.	Go, and in civic wreaths return.

[*Exit Dubois.*

Shouts encreafe.
Madame Clementine looks after him with joy
and zeal: Henriette expreffing doubts and fears
for his fafety, determines to follow. Madame
Clementine chears her, [*Exeunt.*
SCENE

SCENE II.

A street before Pincemaille's magazine.

People of all defcription, men, women, and children forcibly carrying facks of flour from it. Acorn confpicuoufly active. *Enter Pincemaille* at the fide in rage and forrow, endeavours in vain to prevent them, runs in defpair imploring the feveral characters, as they are carrying off the flour ; they deride him and ftill proceed. *Enter Alderfelt* with a body of the Royal Allemande. *Pincemaille,* gives them all money, befeaching him to oppofe the plunder of his granary : they attack the people, recover great part of the flour and replace it in the houfe. Pincemaille with joy fpirits them up. *Enter Dubois and Martin* heading a party of grenadiers with the national cockades. They engage the Royal Allemande with great vigour, oblige them to retire, the people rally, headed by Acorn, again feize the corn and bear it off with acclamations. *Enter Henriette,* joyful to find Dubois fafe, they embrace. *Re-enter Acorn,* fhakes Dubois heartily by the hand and applauds his valour. *Enter Madame Clementine and Auftin,* fhe addreffes Dubois with great affection and praife for his laft action. *Enter* feveral old people meagre and wretched, they return thanks to Dubois. Madame Clementine comments on their mifery to Pincemaille, upbraids him as the caufe; then looking on the granary with the doors broke open, turns and fmiles on Pincemaille with contempt and exultation at this piece of juftice for his trampling on the national cockade, and his oppreffion of the poor; gives Henriette's hand to Dubois. *Enter Martin* and
some

- fome refpectable citizens. They give Pincemaille a written paper and a bag of money, gold, filver, and copper, the produce of his flour, which they had fold at the halle at a moderate price to the poor : Pincemaille with rage flings it on the ground. Dubois takes it up and gives it to the poor people. Pincemaille endeavours to take it from them, but is prevented by Acorn, who puts them off. Pincemaille with frantic rage pointing to the granary threatens revenge upon 'em all. This at laft irritates the foldiers ; they rufh on, feize him, and Martin makes a ftroke of his fword as to behead him, but his life is fpared by the interceffion of Henriette and Madame Clementine, who are led off by Dubois.   *Exeunt.*

SCENE III.

Le Palais Royal.   Sieur Curtius's cabinet of wax-work conspicuous.

    Enter citizens and people of all ranks expreffing filent forrow. Some go to Sieur Curtius's cabinet he enters from it. They demand the wax bufts of the Duc D'Orleans and M. Necker, he brings them out, the people cover part of them with black crape, carry them high over their heads, they all take off their hats and huzza.   *Enter Martin* and his party of French grenadiers. They join with the people in doing honours to the two bufts.   [*Exeunt fhouting.*

SCENE

SCENE IV.

*A Street.—Savetier difcover'd in his ftall, working,
finging and drinking.*

Sav. I have juft finifh'd my work—(*takes up a
bottle.—Goes to fill out a glafs.*)—Yes I have finifh'd
(*Turns the bottle up*). Some man they fay, roll'd
a ftone up a hill, and no fooner up than it roll'd
down: fo there was all that lads work to do over
again—now when I empty the bottle it ftays
empty—tho' I have no objection to do all that
work over again. I'd take a nap if I thought
nobody would attack my property.—(*Yawns and
falls afleep.*)

Enter MADELAINE *with a Bafket of Flowers.*

Mad. Achetez ma belle Rofe, mon beaux.
Jafmin D'efpagne, ma belle Giroflee blanche me
beaux oieletts deux.

AIR.—*Madelaine.*

Mad. Mes beaux oieletts doux---come my pretty pinks
buy,
How brilliant the feafon, how fweet is the cry,
The Lady, the Bifhop, the Count and Marquis;
The Pinks of gay Paris, their pinks buy of me;
They always pay double, yet fmile on me too,
When they hear the fweet cry of my beaux oieletts
doux.

II.

To the gard'ner I offer my money to pay,
For the pinks I buy of him; my dear he fays nay;
Since I faw your lov'd foot when you ftepp'd o'er
yon ftyle;
I'd give my whole garden to you for a fmile.
At his word I then took him, with dear Sir, adieu,
Yet I paid him his fmile---and then beaux oieletts
doux.

III

A very fine Lord ; but a vile naughty man,
Would purchaſe my pinks---but my perſon trepan ;
He took out his ſnuff-box, and cried with an air,
" Ah ma chere mon ange ; you are deviliſh fair.''
He fain would have kiſs'd me.---I cried taiſez vous,
Yet his Louis I took, and then beaux oillets doux.

Ay, if my drunken huſband was as induſtrious as I am, we ſhould live as happy as any
couple in the Fauxbuorg St. Antoine.—Lord if
he is'nt fallen aſleep—(*looking at him.*) Why
you lazy devil.— Here's a dainty huſband for
ſuch a pretty girl as me !—I've heard of one Miſs
Venus that us'd to ſell myrtles, ſhe married a
Mr. Vulcan, a blackſmith.—I'm ſure I've made
a mere Venus of myſelf to marry a cobler ; why
Savetier ! Savetier ! here's a bit of ſweet briar for
you my dear, the patriotic colour—My Hero,
and a nettle for you my darling-ŗ-(*pats him with
the flowers.*)

Sav. (*Starting out of his ſleep.*) My property.
Heels, ſoals, ſhoes, pumps, ſtraps, lapſtone, ends
and pegging-awls !

Mad. Ha, ha, ha!

Sav. Oh, wife is it you. (*Yawns, gets out of
his ſtall.*)—Oh you awoke me from the ſweeteſt
dream.———

Mad. Ay, but are your children to get bread
by your dreaming ?

Sav. My dear, I thought :—Kiſs me Madelaine.

Mad. You're not ſo fond of kiſſing in the houſe
that you ſhou'd get to it in the open ſtreets.

Sav. Such a dream ! I thought that I was Arch
Biſhop of Paris, that I was preaching a ſermon
at Notre Dame, and that as I was explicatifying
on the text, flouriſhing my arms over my head
like

like a mad kettle drummer, and beating the unfortunate cuſhion with as little mercy as if t'was
my own poor lapſtone.—Out flys from one of my
ſleeves a ſlipper of the Queens, it ſkims round
the church; the piqued toe hits the king in tho
eye, whizzing down, knock'd the ſceptre out of
his left hand into his right; rebounding up at
the breaſt of the Governor of the Baſtile ſlaps
off his upper button, and ſtriking the elbow of
an Engliſh baker, with an oak ſtick in his fiſt,
it fell on the toupee of Dubois the grenadier,
and it inſtantly ſprouted into green leaves round
his forehead; and my dear Madelaine, as you
were offering me one of your ſweet roſes, 1
thought at that moment in ſtepped the devil.—
(*Enter Pere Anthony*) He! he! he! wife, did you
ever ſee any thing ſo apropos.

Ant. Save you.

Sav. Ay ſave us from thee.—If I had mention'd the black gentleman ſooner, I ſhould have
been cut off in the middle of my dream—he! he!
he!—talk of the—he! he! he!—and—he! he!
he! (*looks at father Anthony ſignificantly.*)

Mad. Throw out ſuch inunendes upon his
reverence. Oh! upon my reputation my dear—
you are a reprobate.

Ant. Madelaine you have confeſſed but twelve
times ſince Eaſter.

Mad. Oh holy father, my huſband here is the
worſt man.—

Sav. You jade confeſs your own wickedneſs
and never mind mine.

Ant. Come with me child and let his ſins fall
upon his own head.

Sav. If ſhe goes with you I am afraid her ſins
will fall upon my head.

Mad.

Mad. Why hufband do you know what a Friar is ? Dont you know he can punifh you—, bring you into the church.

Sav. Ay and let him bring my ftall into his church and then I'll be a Prebend.

Mad. Do you hear him Father ? he's the moft curfedeft—do you know—

AIR—*Savetier.*

Gay|friends we'll have a jovial bout,
 Our wine and care difpatching,
And he that's fad, why, turn him out,
 For grief they fay is catching.

Then fhake your heel and fhake your toe,
 Since freedom there's rare news of,
We'll now kick high, and now kick low,
 And kick our wooden fhoes off.

And where they'll drop, may puzzle all,
 The doctors of the Sorbonne,
The globe turns round and let them fall
 Upon a Turkifh turban.

The felfifh patriot may prate
 Of King and people vapour,
Let nothing trouble now your pate
 But how to cut a caper.
  Then fhake your heel, &c.

        Exeunt,

SCENE V.

La Place Louis XV. the Garden and Palace of the Thuleries with the Pont Tournant in view.

Enter Guards and people with the bufts. A ftate
         fedan

sedan chair, brought on preceded by footmen in green laced liveries, the people surround the chair, draw the curtains, finding it open, they break it to pieces, and seize the footmen, one of whom looking at the people's green cockade sneeringly remarks, that with all their patriotism they wear the livery of the Count, they look at his coat and then tear out their cockades, fling them away; some rush into the milliners shops and return instantly with red and blue cockades, which they put in their hats.

[*Exit in tumult.*

Enter SAVETIER MADELAINE *and* PERE ANTHONY.
Savetier seems seized with ardour—discontented with his dress—Madelaine weeps—Pere Anthony comforts, and in condolence takes her off.

Enter a concourse of people with wheelbarrows, pick-axes, shovels, &c. &c. shouts of " Au champs de Mars."

AIR.—*Savetier.*

Come men and boys, widows and maids,
   For fiddles quit musket and trigger,
Since Sire is now King of Spades,
   Each noble should turn turf digger.
The altar we'll raise in the field,
   The heavens our pæns shall greet,
For power got tipsey and reel'd
   And tumbled at liberty's feet.

[*Exeunt.*
SCENE

SCENE VI.

Le Rue Richleau.

Enter People carrying the Buſt in triumph.

Enter SAVETIER, *dreſſed in Regimentals, a label on his back, "Un Capitaine a Louer."*

AIR—*Savetier.*

Tho ſome me a cobler will call,
    I was a neat ſtitcher of pumps,
At laſt I left hammer and awl,
    And now I'm a dealer in thumps.
I've taken ſuch courage of late,
    Nor Gentles nor Nobles I dreads;
I've leather'd the feet of the great,
    And now Sir, I'll leather their heads.
        Hah! Faralibobette,
      Faralibobo,
           Savatt Form Selette,
          Sabre tire Marteau,
             Faralibobette.
      Faralibobo.

II.

With lapſtone I'll bang the Baſtile,
    Then Inſtep the Maſter to vamp,
His ſoul caſe I'll tap on the heel,
    And I'll make him kick out at the lamp.
My buſineſs of late ſo decay'd,
    No caſh could I raiſe for the booze,
But I'll ſoon have a flouriſhing trade,
    Since no more we ſhall wear wooden ſhoes.
           Hah! Fara. &c.

III.

My wax end I'll give to the Pope,
    To the German I'll give a few knocks,
An Iriſhman taught me to tope,
    And an Engliſh Jew learn'd me to box.

                           For

For liberty now I will fight,
  When I can't I'll perhaps run away,
I'm Crifpin Swifs, Hector fo tight,
  Cobler, captain for all that will pay.
                          Hah ! Fara. &c.

Enter ALDERFELT, and the Royal Alemande, fome of them throw out gibes at the bufts, are reproved by Robert, he's pufh'd down, one of the Germans makes a ftroke with his fword at one of the bufts, it's broken, the people incenfed, attack the Soldiers, with ftones, clubs, &c.---Mufquetry is heard without---Alarm bell rings and a general cry " Aux Armes."---German Guards are driving off the people.---Enter Dubois and Martin heading a party of grenadiers, with national cockades, (blue and red,) they engage the Royal Allemande with vigour---oblige them to retire.---*Enter Henriette, Madame Clementine and Auftin.* Proceffion of men and women, as to the marriage of Dubois and Henriette.

AIR *and* CHORUS.

Gentle Venus for a while
Calm the tumult with a fmile,
Let no care difturb the rite,
Blefs with joy the wedding night.
Women. So brave is the youth !
Men. And fo handfome the maid.
Women. 'Tis valour.
Men. 'Tis beauty.
All. Now call for thy aid.
Chorus. Yet if the ftorm needs muft blow,
  ·   And dangers fierce impending ;
Women. He courage has to ftrike the foe,
Men. She beauty worth defending.
Chorus. Yet if the ftorm, &c.   [*Exeunt.*

*The proceffion led by Auftin, as to the marriage of
          Henriette and Dubois.*
      END OF THE FIRST PART.

PART II.

SCENE I.

The Boulevards, with a View of the Depôt des Gardes Francoise's.

THOMAS, Jaques, and the other children of the school armed and in uniforms, drawn up before it. Ambroise ftanding before them fhouldering a large ftick.

AIR—*Ambroife.*

Come, Come to your arms my boys,
     Your firelocks poize,
       Shoulder,
       Bolder,
With your quick manœuvre charm each beholder,
     Ground! Fort Bien! recover!
A petit paté! when exercife is over,
       Alons,
     Charge---prefent---Fire---Bon!

(The Children Exercife.)

Enter

Enter MADAME CLEMENTINE, DUBOIS,
HENRIETTE, &c.

Dubois takes Jaques and Thomas by the hand
and introduces them to Madame Clementine and
Henriette as his brothers.—The Ladies prefent
Ambroife and all the Children with National
Cockades, they put them in their hats and
huzza ! Dubois and the Ladies defire the Children to retire into the fchool out of the way of
danger, they affent, break their ranks, play and
walk about promifcuoufly—Dubois and the Ladies take a tender leave of Thomas and Jaques;
afk Ambroife to go with them, he fays he'll ftay
fome time longer with the boys.

[*Exeunt Dubois, Mad. Clementine, Henriette, &c.*

Ambroife takes papers of cakes out of his
pocket, and diftributes them among the children, they eat, laugh, play and are without any
regularity going into the fchool. A volley of fhot
at a diftance. The Children inftantly return;
form themfelves in order of battle, charge their
pieces with exact military difcipine—Ambroife
ftands looking at them with furprife and admiration.

Enter Acorn, Save'ier, and People, flying with
precipitation. Acorn with fpirit, endeavours
to rally them—Another volley—Cries of diftrefs.

Enter Alderfeldt and the Royal Alemande pur-
fuing them—the people prepare to fly—The
Royal Allemande to follow—The Children interpofe, form themfelves into regular lines before them, difcharge a volley of fmall fhot; thus
repulfed, the Royal Allemande make a ftand.—
Alderfelt commands them to fire on the Children,
they refufe. Acorn rushes forward and knocks

Alderfeldt down, but is himfelf furrounded and taken by fome of the Royal Allemande and borne off.   The Children again charge, the Royal Allemande afhamed to attack them, yet many wounded and fome fallen, they are obliged to retreat.   The People take courage, and purfue them; the Women very active in this—Some of the loweft of the rabble attempt to rifle thofe of the Royal Allemande that had fallen; the Children prefent their pieces at them, and they run off in confufion feveral ways.—The Children and Ambroife exprefs pity for the wounded, and with a fhew of compaffion call out the Servants of the fchool, and Surgeons who have them brought in.

AIR—*Ambroife.*

A Soldier I was and I buftled in wars,
On my old fhining pate I can fhew many fcars,
The Army I left when I found the wars ceafe,
For little is thought of a Soldier in peace.

I fit me down quiet upon a fmall farm,
In the funfhine of comfort how happy I fing,
And all my rent paid and the tax to the king,
I ftill had a bottle to keep my nofe warm.

The fnow of December tho' fhook on my head,
The full rofe of June o'er my jolly cheeks fpread,
In the dance on the green, when my legs chanced to fail,
I had breath enough left for a merry old tale.

But tho' I fowed, my wheat would ne'er come to flour,
Three things ere I reap'd, would my crop all devour,
The Partridge picks the grain up, the blade the Rabbit gobbles,
And all my corn that grew to ears, was threfh'd out by the Nobles.

So

So my flail I fling away and up with my Cockade,
And hoof along the furrows away for the Parade,
Then roufe ye valiant Tiers Etat, fuccefs and triumph
    wait us,
My Ploughfhare leads you on my boys, Huzza! Old
    Cincinatus.

CHORUS of CHILDREN.

Then roufe ye valiant Tiers Etat, fuccefs and triumph
    wait us,
His Ploughfhare leads the way my boys, Huzza! Old
    Cincinatus.

The Children, headed by Ambroife, march
round, and go into the fchool huzzaing.

———————

SCENE II.

*Fauxbourgh St. Laurent—The Convent of St. Lazarre
in view.*

Shouting without on every fide.
Enter from the Convent many of the Priefts in
terror and amazement, with their effects, furniture, plate, Wines, &c.
Enter People at the fides, run into a Blackfmith's
fhop, and bring out various implements as wea-
pons, they go to the gates of St. Lazarre—the
Priefts endeavour by perfuafion to ftop them.
Enter at the fide a body of reputable Citizens
well armed, they try to quell the tumult, but in
vain; the people rufh into the Convent—The
Citizens deliberate—the People return from the
Convent with their plunder of Wines, Provifi-
ons, Sacks of Corn, Plate, &c.

Enter

Enter from the Convent Pere Anthony, walking before a coffin, borne by four priests as to burial. The people give way with reverence; but Savetier more busy than the rest, getting close, perceives a piece of drapery hanging out of the coffin ; calls the people aside, points and laughs; they by force take and set the coffin an end, Savetier opens the lid, and Madelaine walks out of it.

DUET.

Savetier and Madelaine:

Sav.	A Miracle this!
	The dead come to life !
	It isn't——
Mad.	It is
Sav.	By the Lord it's my wife!
Mad.	I died the day, that very day
	That you unkind forsook me ;
	And from the Grave,
	My Soul to save,
	The holy Father took me.
Sav.	You should have died at home sweet spouse,
	Oh, what a funeral feast ;
	Of all the cold meat in the house,
	A dead wife is the best :
	But tell me Father Anthony,
	Did you make my Tantony.
	Piggin,
	Riggin,
	Squeak a few ?
	Tell me this, and tell me true ?
Mad.	Never mind him reverend Sir,
	He's a whelp they call a cur,
	That in Manger takes much box,
	Not Eat himself, nor let the Ox.
Sav.	Little fubsy there you lie,
	The Priest's the Dog, the Ox am I.
Mad.	That your manners! (*strikes him*) how d'ye like it ?

                                                        Sav.

Sav.	By my Captain's fword and pike, it
	Is againft the Salique Law,
	That fceptre wags in female Paw.
Mad.	Captain ftrut without a tizzy.
Sav.	Ma'am be Babylonifh Miffy.
Mad.	March and lead tag-rag to battle.
Sav.	Giggle, ogle, leer and gig it.
Mad.	Powder, frizzle, and be wig it.
Sav.	Lifp and fimper, fneer and tattle.
Both. }	Captain ftrutt, &c.
	Ma'am be, &c.

Ambroife and a great number of the opulent citizens and of the moft refpectable of the Tiers Etat ftill endeavour to quiet the people, and difarm the moft defperate; then form themfelves into order, and propofe to repair to the Hotel de Ville to deliberate.

AIR.—*Ambroife.*

Each Champion for his Nation,
All danger now defies;
Our wrongs in acclamation,
In thunder, fhall arife.

And tho' we draw the fword,
'Tis not to lead a faction;
Our Country! that's the word,
To dignify the Action.

Night coming on, many of the people have lighted torches. [*Exeunt.*

SCENE III.

Infide of the Baftille.—A dark paffage.

The double doors are unlock'd, and grate upon the hinges.——

Enter

Enter the Governor, Lieutenant de Roi, Exempts, Guards, Gaolers with bunches of keys, and Arnold with a bundle.—The Governor tells that by the help of this, (taking a friar's drefs out of the bundle) he hopes to have Henriette in his power, and revenge himfelf on her family. He affifts Arnold to put on the drefs, paufes, fays that he'll make her father Count Clementin (now a prifoner in the Baftille,) the inftrument to draw her into the fnare. [*Exit with Arnold.*

SCENE IV.

Infide of the Baftille, an octagonal Chamber of one of the Towers, marked with every circumftance of horror agreeable to defcription; double barr'd windows very high from the floor, double Iron door in the back flat, the perfpective fo contrived as to fhew the thicknefs of the Wall, by the fpace between the two Doors.—In one corner a large Iron Cage.—A gloomy Lamp hanging in the centre of the room.—A dreadful clanking of chains, grating of bolts, bars and hinges of Iron Gates.

Enter Count Clementin, his head enclofed in an iron mafk, his drefs tatter'd and wretchedly neglected, he feems in the deepeft defpair.

AIR.—*Count Clementin.*

Author of good, a Sun thou'ft giv'n,
To all beneath the cope of Heav'n:
Oh glorious orb! oh joy fupreme!
For ever loft thy chearing beam;
Ah what's to him Celeftial Light,
Imprifon'd here in endlefs night.

CHO-

CHORUS of PRISONERS.
(Suppofed from their refpeƈtive Dungeons).

Ah what's to us celeftial light,
Imprifon'd here in endlefs night.

A ferocious Turnkey (after much noife of locking and unlocking of doors, and grating of hinges, &c.) enters with food, which the Count feems to loath.

[*Exit Turnkey with the food.*

The Count appears in extreme agitation of diftrefs.—Takes a filver plate and fork, looks round with caution and conceals them.

AIR.—*Count Clementin.*

From my lov'd wife, my babe juft born,
A hufband, a fond father torn,
   My anguifh can I bear !
This breaft with Loyalty tho' fraught,
A Traitor to my Prince I'm thought ;
   No comfort but defpair.

Chor. of Prifoners.   No comfort but defpair.

My food is loathfome, bed is hard,
And chilling cold my ftony ward ;
   Ungentle valets tend.
Drop fcalding tears corrode my face,
Still fatal cafque my head embrace,
   My life and forrows end.

Chor. of Prifoners.   Our grief with life muft end.

The flower may wither in its bloom,
The lamp can wafte within the tomb,
   And fountains are exhal'd.
My Senfes to my Griefs awake,
Why ftubborn heart refufe to break,
   When even Hope has fail'd ?

Chor. of Prifoners.   Why ftubborn heart refufe to break,
                 When even Hope has fail'd ?

Du-

During the air re-enter Turnkey, at the back appears to be taking down the words.

Enter the Governor, Guards, &c.—The Governor places himself between the door and Count Clement'n. The centinels at it are doubled. The Governor unlocks the Count's mask, they sit and enter into conversation. A commissaire unseen by the Count takes down his answers, then puts the book in his pocket. The Governor sees a ring on the Count's finger, requests it with a mixture of politeness and servility; the Count appears to set the highest value on it, and cannot be prevailed on to part with it. The Governor changes his manner, orders the Iron Cage forward, and commands two of the Guards to hold him; then forces off the Ring, and claps the Mask on, which he locks. The Count dashes himself on the ground as overwhelm'd with anguish.

Enter Arnold in the friars dress:—The Governor with great joy gives Arnold the Ring tells him to take it to Madame Clementine, who by that pledge will know her husband lives, and will obey instructions. 　　　　　　　　[*Scene closes.*

SCENE V.

A Room in Madame Clementine's House.

Madame Clementine, Dubois, Henriette, Martin, Ambroise, Jaques, Thomas, and company discovered, supper over.—Dubois and Henriette as bride and bridegroom.

GLEE.

GLEE.

I have been drinking, drinking I have been;
I fee by your arch blinking,
 You do the fame,
 Then can you blame,
My eyes fly rogue for winking;
 While wine is good,
 Youthful our blood,
Gay friends be blithe and bonny;
While time is now in merry mood,
Let's banifh care if he intrude.
  · With hey nony nony.

II.

I'm giving to loving, love is my delight;
I fee by your arch blinking,
 Love's fweet to you;
 Elfe why archly woo
My eyes fond rogue in winking;
 From your bright lip,
 Sweets let me fip,
As bees from flowers take honey:
We'll laugh and kifs, and drink and fill,
And let the pleafing burthen ftill,
  Be hey nony nony.

Madame Clementine looks at Henriette with
tendernefs and concern, then at a whole length
portrait of a man, weeps, and feems to invoke it
for a blefling on Henriette and Dubois. They
look on it with reverence and affection, Dubois
compares the face with Henriette's; and Madam
Clementine exprefles, by pointing to her widow's
weeds, that 'tis her deceafed Hufband. Henriette appears to comfort her.

AIR.—*Ambroife.*

Now fhall the honeft man be priz'd,
    His blood with Tinkers blended;
And let the villain be defpis'd,
    From Clovis tho' defeended.
That fools fhou'd rev'rence claim from blood,
    Fly hence the vile delufion,
He's truly noble who is good,
    -And this is Conftitution.

Hard knocks abroad, when I was young,
    I got upon this hard head,
With little crofs on button hung,
    I was at home rewarded.
But to make up for tides of blood,
    A patriot effufion,
I drink my own and country's good,
    And this is Conftitution.

Henriette propofes a family dance—the feveral domeftics men and maids are call'd in—

A BALLET.

The Dance over, *Enter Alice,* (abruptly) an-
nouncing a perfon to Madame Clementine, this
raifes the company's curiofity.   [*Exit Alice.*
    She re-enters introducing *Arnold* in his friar's
drefs; with actions fuiting his affumed character,
he delivers Madame Clementine the Ring : at the
firft fight of it fhe's feized with afhonifhment ;
fucceeded by joy, communicates the reafon of
it to the company—their fuprize and pleafure.
—Henriette takes the ring, looks up at the portrait, preffes the Ring to her lips, and puts it on
her finger.   Arnold looks at the picture, points
alternately at that and the ring with feeming emotions of pleafure.—Madame Clementine prepares
with Henriette to accompany him, as to meet
the Count according to his directions; the reft
                                              of

of the company attempt to go with them—oppos'd by Arnold's advice who takes off Madame Clementine and Henriette by the hand. [*Exeunt.*

SCENE VI.

Night, before Madame Clementine's House.

A Coach at a litttle diftance, the Governor fhews himfelf at the windows of it, the four Guards and Exempts endeavour to hide themfelves ftanding up clofe to the wall; Madame Clementine's door opens. Enter from it Alice with a light, Arnold, Madame Clementine and Henriette. Arnold as by accident knocks the Candle out of Alice's hand, then with many apologies and feeming complaifance, leads the Ladies to the Coach door. Henriette fteps into the Coach, Madame Clementine following her—Arnold fuddenly plucks her back. *Enter Savetier,* obferves flyly what is going forward, makes figns that he'll call the people to their refcue.—Two of the guards feize him, and thruft him into the Coach, fhut the door, and ftep up behind; the Guards furround it, and it drives rapidly off.——Madame Clementine fwoons, Alice fhrieks.—Enter from the houfe Dubois, Auftin, Ambroife and company—Alice in contufion and fright tells the circumftance— Madame Clementine and all, much diftrefs'd, Dubois enraged.— [*Shouting without* *Enter Martin, Grenadiers, Citizens* armed, and a concourfe of pe ple as to the demo ithion of the Baftille, Dubois hears this with joy, encou-

rages them with fpirit, examines their arms, finds
them infufficient for the enterprife; expreffes
want of cannon.—Robert advances, and propofes to go to the Hotel des Invalids.

AIR.—*Dubois.*

Dear Paris, native city beft belov'd,
Forgive thy fons by hard oppreffion mov'd;
Though tumults banifh thy internal peace,
Our Rights eftablifhed, then fierce clamours ceafe.
    March on! we do not draw the fword,
    To fheath it in our Country's breaft;
    But till her freedom is reftor'd,
    Oh never fhall this arm have reft.

While Nature with a bounteous hand,
Has fhower'd her bleffings o'er our land,
How fmall alas! the poor man's fhare;
The Galling Yoke no longer bear.
To keep us flaves the Great combine;
And fhake the lafh if we repine.
    Come on brave youths, let's ftrike the blow,
    Our wrongs in acclamation,
    Shall let our haughty Tyrants know,
    The People are the Nation.

               [*Exeunt led by Dubois.*

END OF THE SECOND PART.

PART III.

SCENE I.

Inside of the Bastille.

ENTER Savetier groping his way.

RECITATIVE.

Sav. What the devil! who's that?
        Bless me!
        It certainly must be——
        Nobody
        Very odd! I
Two pair of feet hear
        A Cat?
        A Rat?
Toad or Lizard---
What's the matter?
        Tho' nought before my eyes is
My teeth chatter
        My hair uprises
And together knock my knees hard.

AIR.

AIR.

I've got into a dungeon, but how to get out
Becaufe I don't know is a matter of doubt,
Should the Governor find me, it runs in my head
If my life he fhould take, then its odds but I'm dead
My two pretty ears he'll cut off fo clean,
But may be he'd leave my head fticking between
For the good of my country myfelf I expofe,
And glory to follow---I'll follow---my nofe.

II

And if I fhould chance to get into the air
Of my fine dainty body he'll kindly take care,
Left by a great fall I my little toe break,
I think that he'll tie me up faft by the neck
Before the vile gibbet deprives me of life
Like Brutus, or Çato I'll fall on my knife
I'll let out my heart's blood here on this cold ftone,
And I'll let out---I'll let---and I'll let it alone.

A fmall door opens, Enter from it the Governor with a da:k lantern leading in Henriette: Savetier retires; the Governor forceably puts Hen-
riettte in at another door, Savetier getting out of
his way falls; the Governor liftens; Savetier
fneaks round the place crouching, ftooping, creeping, and many ludicrous pofitions to conceal himfelf, mews like a cat, fqueaks like a rat; the Governor ftill liftening and looking about; Savetier
to conceal himfelf gets behind him, and ftill as the
Governor walks about with the light Savetier keeps
behind, at length falling on his hands and knees
the Governor fuddenly ftarting back ftumbles over
him, at firft alarmed but rifes, puts the light to
Savetiers face, who kneels befeeching mercy; the
Governor paufes, looks at the door where he had
fecreted Henriette and concluding that fhe muft
have been feen by Savetier, determines to deftroy
　　　　　　　　　　　　　　　　　　　him,

him, goes fome paces back and with actions of
kindnefs and encouragement defires Savetier to approach ; Savetier walking towards him, a trap-
door fuddenly opens under him, and he difappears,
the Governor expreffes joy in felf-fecurity. Going
towards the room where he had placed Henriette,
a noife without, he makes to the door he came in
at, blows out his light, and *exit, haftily.*

SCENE II.

*Dawn.—Before the Hotel des Invalids. Two old
Invalids on guard at the Gates.*

*Enter Dubois, Martin, French Guards, Am-
broife, Citizens, People.*—They demand entrance are
obftinately refufed by the two Centinels who prefent their bayonets : The Soldiers, &c. attempt
to kill them, but are prevented by Dubois.
Enter at the fide *Robert* haftily, he tells his
comrades (the Centinels) how ill he had been ufed
by the Royal Allemande—gives them national
cockades, they put them in their hats, huzza, and
admit Dubois, Soldiers, People, &c. into the Hotel. A party of Soldiers wait without to cover the
entrance : Re-enter thofe who went in, bringing
out cannon, mufkets, and all kind of warlike
ftores : The ardour of the old drummers, trumpeters and fifers whimfically characteriftic.
Shouts of " *A bas la Baftille.*"

AIR—*Martin.*

Too long we've to oppreffion ftoop'd
Or lets be free or ceafe to live ;

Sweet

Sweet lily that fo long hath droop'd
In glorious fun-fhine now revive :
Behold the lurking fpider watch
He fpreads his cruel fangs,
The thoughtlefs fly in web to catch
The infeſt dies in pangs.

Amb.   Let's drag the fpider from his den
The Baſtille is the web of men,
The wretch that built yon manfion drear,
Within it languiſh'd many a year :
When Phalaris the tyrant curſt
Of Brazen-bull much boaſted,
The artful maker was the firſt
Within his fine bull roaſted.

Dub.   Now fell the tree whofe lofty pride
Hath hid its beauties in the ſhade,
Fame to the patriot brow decide
The laurel that can never fade :
The noble theme with joy repeat
Our caufe ſhall with fuccefs be crown'd
To rattling drums our hearts ſhall beat
Our voices to the trumpet round :

Cho.   Down with bolts bars and iron door,
The guiltlefs prifoner ſhall be free
Our cannon with tremendous roar,
Shall join the cry of Liberty.

                                    [*Exeunt.*

SCENE III.

Before the front Gates of the Baſtille : The two Draw-bridges and Moats :   On the one fide a few Houfes of the Fauxbourg St. Antoine, on the other the Governor's houfe.

Enter down the Street Citizens headed by Auſtin armed—they demand entrance ; refufed, they fet fire to the Governor's houfe, this foon extinguiſh'd, the drawbridge is let down ; Lieutenant Du-Roy
                                                    comes

comes over it bearing a white flag; Drum within beats a parley; he invites the people in with courteous action; Auftin and many others crofs the Foffé; the bridge is inftantly raifed and an explofion of cannon is heard within fucceeded by cries and groans; the People without are enraged, to defperation at the Governors treachery. A cannon is fir'd among them from the Baftille, they run in diforder to the other fide; Robert points out danger in fome brambles that appear on the Boulevard, clofe by where they ftand; They quit their ftation, and a cannon fhot is fired from the thicket; The people then retire into the adjacent houfes with precipitation and are feen at the windows, and on the tops, from whence they fire at the Invalids placed on the battlements, ramparts, and at the Embraffures of the Baftille.

Enter down the Street St. Antoine, Dubois, Martin, Ambroife, Thomas, Jacques, Guards, Citizens, Women, Children, &c. with the cannon of the Hotel dés Invalids, a white flag is feen hoifted on a tower of the Baftille, and at the inftant a cannon is fhot from it down the Street St. Antoine. Dubois directs the Soldiers and people to play their cannon againft the gates of the Baftille; they are batter'd down, they then point againft the chains of the draw-bridge which falls and they pafs by it over the firft foffé. A handkerchief is feen to drop from a fmall window of the Baftille, and from a grated aperture a filver plate falls; Dubois knows the handkerchief to be Henriette's, and Martin fhews him the name of Count Clementin infcribed on the plate; they return over the drawbridge with the greateft rapidity; Cannon continues playing, the Women and Children ferve them with ball.

[*Scene clofes.*

SCENE

SCENE IV.

Inside of the Baftille.

Enter the Governor, Pincemaille, Exempts, turn-keys, &c. much terrified : the Governor in great diftraction giving confufed orders to his officers. They run about in terror. The noife without increafes. The Governor goes off with emotions of defpair.   [*Exeunt all.*

Enter from a chamber *Henriette,* frightened. The noife ftill encreafing—She feized with difmay and terror falls on her knees and turns her eyes to heaven in fervent prayer.

Enter from another chamber in a flow and folemn pace, Count Clementin. His iron mafk on. He approaches Henriette. She turns fud-denly, and at the fight of him fhrieks and fwoons, he gently raifes her. She revives, he takes off his mafk, fhe fhews the ring, they recognizing each other for father and daughter, are ftruck with furprife and affection. She kneels to him, he tenderly embraces her. The noife without now approaching, he takes her by the hand, and haftily leads her to an adjoining room.

Enter in wild tumult of fury Dubois, Martin, Ambroife, foldiers, citizens, people, &c. All hurry from place to place, killing the guards, forcing keys from the jailors, opening the cham-bers and dungeons, releafing the prifoners, and bringing out and difplaying the feveral inftru-ments of torture.

Enter Madeleine, Pere Anthony, Priefts, women, children, &c. &c. The old Count de Lorge brought from his cell much emaciated, his beard very long, filled with joy and wonder but can

fcarce

scarce bear the light. Many of the people re-
cognize in the prifoners their former friends
and relatives. Dubois runs precipitately from
cell to cell in fearch of Henriette. Opens a
dungeon fhaped like a cone reverfed, from whence
Acorn afcends, but unable to ftand, falls:
mutual joy; Acorn pointing to the place of his
confinement fhows the fituation his feet were in.
The fight of the unhappy pris'ners and various
implements of torture roufe the indignation of the
multitude high againft the Governor, and many
difperfe feveral ways in fearch of him with fhouts
of vengeance.

Dubois, Ambroife, Martin and their friends
continuing their fearch for Henriette, Dubois
difcovers Arnold in his friars drefs, they drag
him forth from his concealment, he falls on his
knees, implores for mercy. Dubois drawing
demands where Henriette's fecreted. She enters
haftily, runs to Dubois, who quitting Arnold,
clafps her in his arms.

Enter Madame Clementine, and from the room
adjoining Count Clementin with his mafk in his
hand. Madame Clementine feized with aftonifh-
ment and joy at finding her hufband. Each
character full of rapture and congratulation.
Savetier's voice is heard at fome diftance under-
neath. All furprized liften The voice feems
nearer. The different characters liften at feveral
parts of the ground, from whence they think the
voice proceeds. It feems to come from under
where Amb oife ftands. He jumps afide. Madelaine laughs, and the voice is heard near her, fhe
leaps afide frightned. Dubois runs to the place.
Liftens. Searches, and pulls up a ftone difcover-
ing the circular entrance of a fubterraneous paff-

age.

age. Savetier cries loud from below, they with difficulty help him out. He very much foil'd runs about in frantic joy embracing every body, particularly Madelaine. Shouts of triumph without.

Enter citizens, foldiers, &c. dragging on the governor. He proftrates himfelf in an agony of grief and remorfe, weeps and befeeches their compaffion. They tear off his badges of honour, he throws himfelf into the arms of Dubois for protection, who touched with pity weeps, but recovering his fortitude firmly acquaints him that juftice for his treafon to the people demands his life, and all hurry him off for the place de Greve. [*Exeunt.*

SCENE LAST.

Place de Greve—View of the Hotel de Ville.

Pincemaille, The Governor, Arnold, and other unpopular Characters led to execution, the former with a halter of ftraw round his neck, and a bunch of thiftles hanging down his breaft, the trophies confift of large locks, keys, bolts, bars, chains, the iron mafk, and other inftruments of torture, fufpen led on poles.

*The Stage clear.—Grand Proceffion.—*in which Dubois, as having firft mounted the Breach, at the D ftruction of the Baftille, is carried in Triumph.

AIR—*Ambroife,* and CHORUS.

Sufpended high above his reach,
 Was hung this civic crown,
With glory fired he mounts the breach,
 And plucks the trophy down.

Intre-

Intrepid youth, the well earned wreath,
 Thy grateful country gives, *(Drops a wreath of*
  Laurel on Dubois' head.)
Who in her caufe defpifing death,
 In honour ever lives.

No intereft in the land had he,
 Our good was all he fought,
And for our rights, for liberty,
 Alone the Hero fought.

Cho. Sufpended high above his reach,
 Was hung the civic crown,
With glory fired he mounts the breach,
 And plucks the trophy down.

Enter Count Clementin, Madame Clementine, Henriette, Acorn, &c. Dubois defcends, and embraces Henriette, the Count joins their hands.

FINALE.

Savetier.

To fettle all our new difputes,
 Let's to the tavern gang man,
We'll drink and fing, and burn our boots,
 But firft we'll hang the hangman.

RECITATIVE—*Ambroife.*

At Satans fell beheft, uprofe thofe hated walls,
Now at an Angels voice the curfed fabric falls.

Martin.

Juftice in awful ftate has claim'd her own,
Difplaced the Fury, that ufurp'd her throne,
Defpotic power fhall wear a robe no more,
The iron hand her fword muft now reftore.

Count

Count Clementin—RECITATIVE, Accompanied.

Nor at the great event, shall we alone rejoice,
Man, born free! so should remain, 'tis natures general voice.

Dubois.

Let every heart with rapture glow,
 For a joyful moments near;
Tho' from the eye, that fount of woe,
 The pallid cheek, drank up the tear:
  That eye shall beam a living ray.
  That cheek shall bloom the rose of May,

CHORUS.

Every heart with rapture glow,
For a joyful moments near.

Ambroise.

(To those Released from the Bastile.)

From the Dark Dungeon's hideous gloom,
Of the free soul the loathsome tomb,
From solitude and pain and strife,
Immerge to all the joys of life.

DUET—Dubois and Henriette.

(To Count Clementine.)

Come view the beauties of the year,
 The fragrance of the flowers inhale,
 And while the lark floats on the gale,
His liquid notes shall charm thine ear.

Henriette.

To long lost love and friendship sweet,
Let meeting hearts with rapture beat,

       And

And focial interchange of mind,
And fmile benign, and converfe kind.

Dubois.

Launch into the world, new born,
And hail with fong, this bleffed morn !

CHORUS.

Revifit the glad world, new born,
And hail with fong, this bleffed morn.

THE END.

TONY LUMPKIN IN TOWN.

IN TWO ACTS.

PERFORMED AT THE

THEATRE-ROYAL, HAY-MARKET,

IN 1776.

DRAMATIS PERSONÆ.

Jonquil, ... Mr. LAMASH.
Tony Lumpkin, ... Mr. PARSONS.
Doctor Minum, ... Mr. R. PALMER.
Pulville, ... Mr. BLISSET.
Tim Tickle, ... Mr. BANNISTER.
Frank, ... Mr. EGAN.
Diggory, ... Mr. MASSEY.
Shoemaker, ... Mr. KENNY.
Taylor, ... Mr. PIERCE.
Painter, ... Mr. DAVIS.
Footman, ... Mr. PAINTER.

Mrs. Jonquil, ... Mrs. HITCHCOCK.
Lavender, ... Miss HALE.

SCENE, *London*.

TONY LUMPKIN IN TOWN.

ACT I.

SCENE I.

A Hall.——Horn founds.

Enter DIGGORY, *meeting* FRANK. DIGGORY *carrying a diſh of cold beef, and a tankard. A footman following* FRANK *with a tea-board.*

FRANK.

MR. DIGGORY, your maſter's up; I hear his horn.

Dig. Aye, Maſter Frank, I've got his breakfaſt here.

Frank. Beef and porter! his ſtomach is delicate this morning.

Dig. Why, yes, he's always a little puny after a night's hard drinking. Aye, about a pound and half, or ſo, will make him eaſy 'till near two, and then----- (*bell rings.*)

Frank.

Frank. Ha! I think my mafter's a little impatient too for his breakfaft.

Foot. Shall I take up the things, Mr. Frank?

Frank. 'Sdeath! what do you wait here for?
Fly! I imagined you had left 'em above this half
hour.

Foot. Why I thought—

Frank. You thought! Ah! this thinking is
the ruin of us. Now if you wou'd not think,
but do as you are defired, it would make—

Foot. I fuppofe a man may have leave.

Frank. No converfation, I befeech you: (*bell
rings.*) Have you any ears?

Foot. I have, and hands too, and that you
fhall find fome time or other.—Takes more airs
upon himfelf than the mafter! [*Half afide, and
exit with the tea things.*]

Frank. The impertinence and freedom of thefe
fcoundrels is abfolutely intolerable.

Dig. Who fhould he make free with, if he
çan't with his fellow fervants?

Frank. Fellow fervants, Mr. Diggory! Do you
make no difference between a fervant in livery,
and a gentleman's gentleman? In the country,
I fuppofe, it's " hail fellow well met;" but here,
fir, we are delicate, nice, in our diftinctions;
for a valet moves in a fphere, and lives in a
ftile as fuperior to a footman, as a Pall-mall groom
porter to the marker of a tennis-court.

Dig. For certain, fir, we valet-de-fhams are
grand fellows; but you'll fee more of that when
I get on my new regimen—I mean my new liver;
—pfha! my new clothes, I mean. Did you
breakfaft, fir?

Frank. Yes, I've had my chocolate.

Dig. Do take one flice of beef.

Frank.

Frank. What a vulgar breakfaſt ! beef ! ſhocking !

Dig. I don't know as to that, Sir, but I have heard
beef was Queen Elizabeth's breakfaſt ; and, if
that's the caſe, I think it's good enough for I.

Frank. But isn't that for your maſter ?

Dig. O, I'll leave enough for he, I'll warrant. *(bell rings)*

Frank. That muſt be for me, Mr. Diggory.
Serviteur !   [*Exit.*

Dig. How genteel he looks in his maſter's old
clothes !

Enter TIM TICKLE.

Tic. Ha, Diggory ! the London air agrees
with you, I find ; keep working, lad ; ſtrong
beer is our ſtream of life, and in good beef lies
the marrow of an Engliſh conſtitution—that's ·
in the genteel way. *(horn ſounds)*

Dig. I muſt follow the ſound of the horn.

                              [*Exit with beef, ſinging.*

Re-enter FRANK.

Frank. Mr. Tickle, ſeveral perſons are waiting below for Mr. Lumpkin, and they aſk to
ſee you.

Tic. Perſons !

Frank Yes, ſir ; there are tailors, ſhoemak-
ers, milliners, perfumers, dancing-maſters, mu-
ſic-maſters and boxing maſters.

Tic. I'll be with them in a pig's whiſper !

Frank. What a catiff for a gentleman's tutor !
O ! he's ſhocking !

                                      [*Exit.*
                                      Tic.

Tic. Aye! now how could he do without me? If he wants a coat cut in the kick, who can fhew him? I—A tafty nab? Why Tim.—— Handfome pumps? I know the go. If he'd have a tune from his mufic-mafter, a thruft from his pufhing-mafter, a ftep from his dancing-maf- ter, or a fquare from his boxing-mafter, I'm the boy that can fhew him life in the genteel way.

Enter DIGGORY.

Dig. Mafter Tickle, the fquire wants you.
Tic. I ftir.
Dig. I'll tell him fo. [*Exit.*
Tic. They can do nothing without me. To- ny Lumpkin's nobody without Tim Tickle. I'll go—no—I think I'll ftep firft and give my bear his breakfaft; poor foul! many a good one he has got me; aye, and may again for aught I know. The fquire's good at a promife, that's certain; but what's a promife? Pye-cruft. I'd no more depend upon a gemman's promife, than I would upon a broken ftaff, or a candidate for the county after he had gained his election.
[*Exit.*

SCENE II.

A Chamber.

JONQUIL *difcovered in a morning undrefs,* FRANK *attending with chocolate.*

Jon. Frank, has your lady quitted her apart- ment.

Frank.

Frank. Yes, fir, I think I heard Mrs. Lavender fay—Oh, fir, here is my lady. [*Exit.*

Enter Mrs. Jonquil *and* Lavender.

Jon. Good morning to you, madam.

Mrs. Jon. Thank you, Sir. Lavender, give
thofe cards to Pompey, and defire him to deliver them agreeable to their addrefs. I have an
immenfity of vifits, but muft pay them this morning in paper ; or, Shock, you dear polite toad,
will you take the chair, and be my reprefenta-
tive to the ladies ? (*to a lap-dog, which Lavender
carries under her arm.*) [*Exit Lavender.*
Oh, my head ! fuch a night ! Mr. Jonquil, when
did you break up at the mafquerade ?

Jon. I fancy, my dear, 'twas five.

Mrs. Jon. I might as well have accompanied
you there, for I counted the clock 'till four. A
mafquerade to this houfe laft night, was a Quaker's
meeting. Such a noife aud uproar !

Jon. Uproar !—What was the matter ?

Mrs. Jon. Only your coufin Tony holding his
nocturnal revels.

Jon. Tony ! So, fo, 'twas here he came,
when he flipped from me at the Pantheon.

Mrs. Jon. Yes, here he came indeed ; and
fuch a ball as he held with the bear and the fervants, and the mob out of the ftreet, I believe !

Enter Lavender.

Lav. Madam, I'm forry I'm obliged to complain of a fervant, but don't blame me ma'm ;
but indeed there's no fuch thing as living in the
houfe.

Mrs.

Mrs. Jon. What is all this?

Lav. Why ma'am, Mr. Diggory, 'Squire Lumpkin's man, ran into your ladyship's dressing-room, and snatched your cold cream off the toilet.

Jon. Ha! ha! ha! what in the name of delicacy could Diggory want with the cold cream?

Lav. He said it would do to oil his wig, Sir.

Jon. Ha! ha! ha!

Mrs. Jon. Nay, but Mr. Jonquil, this is beyond bearing. I'll assure you I'll—

Jon. Come, my dear, don't be discomposed, 'twill soon be at an end.   [*Exit. Lavender.* Let me see what time his mother proposes to be in town, for I think she says she'll take a house for him. I have her letter here. I wish he was in a house of his own, from my soul, for in a fortnight I should not know mine from a carrier's inn.

Mrs. Jon. What gives me most singular amazement is, that you chuse to be seen in public with him.

Jon. I grant that he is not the most eligible companion for a man of fashion: but at a masquerade I was safe from censure, for every body imagined the uncouthness of his appearance, and rusticity of his manners, merely the effect of his imitative genius. The company thought his behaviour all assumed, .put on *pour l'occasion*; for he threw off his domino, and I'll assure you, simple nature got him infinite reputation. He gaped at the masks, roared most stentoriously discordant with the musick; overset the pyramids, pocketed the sweetmeats, broke the glasses, made love to an Arcadian dairy maid, tripped up the heels of a harlequin, beat a hermit, who
                                                  happened

happened to be a captain of the guards, and gave a bifhop a black eye.

Mrs. Jon. But his mother's epiftle ; I languifh to hear it.

Jon. I afk your pardon, here it is. *(takes out a letter and reads.)*

     " Dear Coufin,
     " In the bearer of this, I introduce to your
" care and friendfhip my dear fon Tony. I'll
" affure you, coufin, Tony with your help will
" make a bright man, as he's already humour-
" fome and comical. I fhall be in town myfelf
" in about a fortnight, or three weeks, and then
" I intend taking a houfe for him, in fome airy,
" fafhionable part, fomewhere near Duke's
" Place, as I'd have him near the King's Palace.
" No more at prefent from your loving coufin,
          " DOROTHEA HARDCASTLE.
     " P. S. Mr. Hardcaftle's and my love to
" coufin Emilia. I requeft you'll take Tony to
" Sadler's Wells, as I'm fure he'll like operas."
          (A horn founds without.

Mrs. Jon. Blefs me, what's that?

Jon. Oh, that's Tony's fummons for his man ; he fays he hates the ringing of bells, therefore has invented that polite fubftitute.

          (Tony calls without.

Tony. Hollo, Diggory, hollo.

Jon. Oh, here he comes.

Tony. *(without.)* Hollo ! flap up the bear.

Mrs. Jon. Heaven defend us, fure he won't drive in a bear here.

Jon. No, no, my dear, don't be alarmed.

Tony. *(without.)* Come along, Bruin.

VOL. I.   H H   *Enter*

Enter TONY LUMPKIN.

Come in; I long to introduce Bruin to my relations. Coufin Milly, will you fee the bear,
ma'am, if you pleafe?

Mrs. Jon. Bear, oh, heavens!   [*Exit haftily.*

Tony. Coufin Milly's very timberfome, fure;
Bruin is a mighty civil beaft; why he's as gentle as the good-natured lion in the Tower, that
let's the dog lie in his den with him.

Jon. I don't entertain a doubt of his politenefs or good-nature; but you'll eternally oblige
me by fending him down.

Tony. Now would it oblige you in downright
earneft.

Jon. Beyond meafure.

Tony. Tim, walk Bruin down again: bid
him firft make his honours at the door tho'.
Come here—only, coufin, look,—only look at
him. Servant, Sir; why he learned among the
grown gentlemen at Hatton-garden. Ah do
now let him in, and he, and I, and you, will
dance the hay. He's muzzled! Tim, an't he
muzzled?

Tim. (without.) Yes, Sir.

Tony. Oh! then there's no danger; you fee he
cou'dn't bite you, if he had a mind; he can
only fcratch you a little.

Jon. Gads curfe, but I'm not difpofed to be
fcratch'd this morning.

Tony. Oh! very well; any other time. Only
fay the word, and Bruin's the boy for it. Slap
him down lad.

Jon. I wifh the devil had you and him together,

gether. Such a fellow!—Mr. Lumkin, have you a fancy for this houfe?

Tony. Anan?

Jon. I fay, do you like this houfe?

Tony. Like it? for certain I do.

Jon. Then to you and the bear, I muft abfolutely refign it.

Tony. I thank you, for your kind offer; but if you were to give me your houfe, and your pyebalds. and your vifee vie, I would not thank you; becaufe them that give all, give nothing at all. But indeed if you'd let me bring in a little queen with me fome time or other, unknown to coufin Milly, you'd make me as happy as a king.

Jon. Oh, fie!

Tony. Oh, fie! Baw! fhake hands! Why don't you get drunk fometimes? It's mighty pleafant! Ay, and very wholefome once a week. Dr. What-d'ye-call-um fays fo, in the book that lies in my mama's window: what fay you to a bout, coufin, ha?

Jon. Excufe me; drinking is, in my opinion, the moft favage and barbarous method, that ever brutality invented, to murder time and intellects.

Tony. by jingo, then mama is the firft timekiller within ten miles of Quagmire Marfh: Oh! fhe loves a fup dearly.

Jon. For fhame! Mr. Lumpkin.

Tony. Oh! take me, it's all in the genteel way, tho'; for my mama always fipp'd her cordial out of a tea-pot; and then, before folks, it was only a drop of cold tea, you know.

Jon. Ha, ha, ha!

Tony. Ay, and Coufin Con, Mifs Nevill, that
was

was courting me, used to drink like a glass-
blower, all in the sentimental way. Over a
love-story book, she and my mama would read
and sip till it came out of their eyes. Sure Cousin
Con was in love with me; Oh! how sweetly
she'd kiss me after a chapter of Mildmay, and a
twist of the tea-pot.

Jon. Yes, yes, what I've always found;
curse me! if there's a woman in the world easier
had, than the die-away romantic novellist.

Tony. How fine I tell lies! he swallows them
like syllabub. (*aside.*)

Jon. But you gave me the slip last night, at
the Pantheon; why did not you wait for supper?

Tony. Why, I love my supper as well as any
body, especially after a day's hunting; because
then we have something to talk of. But the
snug way for my money; and we had our own
gig here at home; I never saw the bear so
airy.

Jon. But what think you of the splendor of
the Pantheon? Is'n't it the temple of elegance?
an Olympus Hall, worthy the Gods to revel
in?

Tony. Gods do you call 'em? I took some of
'em for rascals. A fool of a fellow would have
it, that I was a lady; now I am sure I have not
a bit of the lady about me, except the softness of
my voice, but the monkey was a macaroni;
and those beaux, I fancy, make as much use of
a woman, as they do of a sword; they keep
both merely for shew. Oh, now I talk of that
by jingo, I saw a power of fine shews yesterday,
o'top of Ludgate-hill.

Jon. Shews?

Tony.

Tony. Ay, I believe I've feen all the fine fhews
now; aye, Gog and Magog, St. Paul's and the
Tower, and the hight poft near the Bridge,
that's going to fall upon the neighbours heads;
and I've feen a hanging, and a houfe on fire;
and I paid a halfpenny to walk over the Thames
at Blackfriars; and I eat calves-head turtle, oppofite the Bank; and faw Lord Thingumme's
fine coach, and the Lilliputian Patagonians,
and the Stock-brokers on 'Change; the mad
folks in Bedlam, and the actor-folks at the
Play-houfes; one of the play men at What-d'ye-
call-it play-houfe was very like you,——

Jon. But, Mr. Lumpkin, I imagine 'tis time
for you to begin to drefs; fome of the Scavoir
Vivre and Dilettante dine with me to-day, and
you'll be a precious exhibition. (*afide.*)

Tony. Ay, ay, I'll be as fine as the fheriffs
horfe, by-and-by.

Enter DIGGORY,

(*In a new livery; ftruts aukwardly acrofs the Stage.
Tony leads him by the arm back to the door.*)

Get out!

Dig. Why, fure, 'Squire, you'll be proud
enough yourfelf of your new cloaths when you
get into them.

Tony. Yes, but there's fome difference between
the miller and his dog. Pray know your diftance,
and I defire, Diggory, you'll never dare to be fo
fuperftitious with me, before company

Dig. Well, I won't.

Tony. You won't?—I think you might call
me,

me, my honour, and not wafte much of your manners.

Dig. If that's the cafe, there's all kinds of tradesfolks, and ingenous learners, of all fizes, waiting below for My Honour.

Tony. Your honour, it's my honour they want.

Dig. I'll tell them fo, Sir; my—your honour, mean.   [*Exit.*

Tony. Well, now, coufin, I'll go; and—

Jon. Sir, Mr. Lumpkin, I have a trifling re-queft to make.

Tony. What is it? I'll give you any thing you afk.

Jon. That you will drefs with all poffible cele-rity; for I languifh to fee you one of us.

Tony. Hollo, for lace and powder. Hollo, Diggory; hey, for grandeur—yoics—hark for-ward, taylors, milliners, and glorious haber-dafhers! hollo, hollo!   (*Exit.*

Jon. Makes more noife than a kennel of hounds.   [*Exit.*

SCENE III.

An Antichamber.

Several TRADESPEOPLE, *and* TIM TICKLE, *difcovered.*

Tic. He will, I fent his man to tell him.

Tay. Greatly obliged to you, Sir.

Tic. You are fo, if you kew all; but, for my good word, 'Squire Jonquil wou'd have taken

Mon-

Monſieur Frippery, the new faſhion French taylor.

Enter DIGGORY.

Dig. He's coming; pray ſit down, gentlemen, it's as cheap ſitting as ſtanding.

Tic. Diggory, keep your own ſtation. I do
all in the gentleman-uſher way, d'ye ſee; becauſe why, I know the genteel thing; but take
me neighbours, I don't want you to ſtand, d'ye
mind me'; only, Diggory, your encroaching
upon my compartment, is juſt as tho'f, as how,
as if my bear was to ſnath my hurdy-gurdy out
of my hand, and pok'd me till I moved a horn-
pipe.

Dig. For certain, that would not be manners;
but I was only——

Tic. Say no more! you're an ignorant man,
and you don't know the genteel thing.

Enter TONY.

Tony. Hey, for grandeur, lace and powder!
which of you is my taylor?

Tay I'm the man, Sir.

Tony. Have you my clothes, Mr. Taylor?

Tay. Here they are, Sir, and a more faſhion-
able ſuit never hung upon the ſhoulders of an
Ambaſſador.

Tony. Tim, do they fit me?

Tic. Quite the kick.

Tay. But won't your honour try them on?

Tony. No, it's too much trouble. I make
Tim try on all my new clothes for me.

Shoe. Your ſhoes, Sir.

Tony.

Tony: Black fattin, beautiful! ah, Tim, if I had my filver Artois buckles here!

(*Dr. Minum fings without.*)

Tony. Hey! what merry fellow's this? Get along, boys, leave your goods, and fend your bills to Tim.　　　[*Exeunt tradefmen.*
Here, Diggory, lay my clothes ready.
　　　　　　[*Exit Diggory with the clothes.*

Enter FRANK.

Frank. Doctor Minum, Sir.　　[*Exit Frank.*

Enter DOCTOR MINUM, *finging.*

Doct. (*fings*) Tol de rol, loll. Gentlemen, I afk ten thoufand pardons: I thought Mr. Jonquil had been here; but if I don't miftake, Mr. Lumpkin, I prefume. (*to Tic.*)

Tic. You're wrong tight boy, that there's the 'Squire; I'm Tim Tickle his tutor.

Doct. Sir, I'm very glad to fee you well.

Tony. That's a lie, if you're a right doctor, and know I've got fifteen hundred a year. (*afide.*)

Doct. If your auricular organs be happily humaniz'd to the celeftial fcience of harmony, from your affinity to a gentleman of Mr. Jonquil's tafte, you may command my affiftance.

Tony. Oh, I'm not long enough in London to ftand in need of a doctor.

Tic. No, d'ye fee, lad, we want no doctors nor poticaries yet. I don't know how long we may remain fo.

Doct. Your pardon, gentlemem—but, I fancy——
　　　　　　　　　　　　　Tony.

Tic. Did you know Jack Slang, the horfe doctor?

Doct. Entirely unacquainted with any of the faculty; but under favour, there's a trifling miftake in this overture to our acquaintance. Give me leave to inform you, gentlemen, I am not one of the prefcribing performers, who convey this human inftrument, the body, to its mortal cafe, by pill, bolus, or draught; but I fhift the foul above the ftars, in founds feraphic, by minum, crochet, and quaver. And pleafe to obferve, that tho' I am a doctor, I've no more fkill in the *materia medica* than an advertifing quack; I am a profeffor of mufic, and compofer of original pieces, in that elegant and mellifluous fcience; and, to oblige my friends, a felect fett of the firft rank and dictinction, I inftruct on the violin.

Tony. Then ten to one, but you know how to play the fiddle.

Doct. I'd venture to accompany you in that bett.

Tony. Zounds man, could not you fay at once that you were a fidler, and not come round about us with fuch a circumbendibus?

Doct. Fiddler, in the name of Orpheus! Eh! what! fiddler? allow me, Sir, a da capo to my own introduction?

Tic. A what?

Doct. Three bar refts, if you pleafe. Sir; I am furpriz'd you can be fo much out of tune, gentlemen. I am one of the connoigfcenti—have had the honour to be balloted a member of three felect private concerts, compofed of perfons of the firft rank, aye the Alto Primo of tafte—had the refufal of the band of Carlifle Houfe—led

for five feasons at Vauxhall—had fome
thoughts of purchafing the gardens myfelf—I
have compofed two oratorios, ten ferenatas,
three fets of overtures, concertos for Signor Flo-
rentini's violoncello, fongs for the Capricci of
Palermo, and folos for Madam Sermont's violin,
grand ballets for Signor Georgettini, Signora
Caperini, Signora Baccini, Signora———

Tic. Damn your Signioras and your Signiors,
your Inis and Winis; can you play, Water
Parted, or Lango-lee ?—that's the genteel
thing.

Tony. Oh, mayhap they're too hard for him.
Give me your hand; I love a fiddler, becaufe
one may make him play till he's tir'd, give him
a fhilling, then kick him down ftairs—Do, dine
with me to-morrow.

Doct. I'll promife you any thing, to get from
you to day. (*afide.*) I fhall pofitively do myfelf that
honour, fir,

Tony. That's a good fellow; but bring your
fiddle under your coat, will you? you fhall have
as much liquor as you can carry.

Doct. You're fuperlatively good, fir.

Tony. The devil a better-- You fhall hear Tim
Tickle touch up his hurdy-gurdy.

Doct. Oh, fir !

Tony. You fhall fee the bear dance too.

Doct. That muft be fine indeed !

Tic. Why, it's the genteel thing; 'Squire will
have the dulcimer man.

Doct. Ah, Caro Divino! we fhall have a delightful concert---I fhall certainly attend you, gentlemen; but a moft particular engagement obli-
ges me to deprive myfelf of the felicity of your
company at prefent.

Tony.

Tony. Hold, hold, doctor ; you muſt give us a
raſp before you go ; Tim, fetch me the fiddle out
of the next room ; couſin Jonquil was playing on
it juſt now.

Tic. I ſtir.   [*Exit.*

Doct. Oh, heavens. (*aſide.*)

Tony. You will give us a ſcrape ; ha, boy ?

Doct. Oh, ſir ! (*bows*) how ſhall I get out of
this ſcrape ? (*aſide.*)

Tony. (*capering before a glaſs*) Ay, do you find
fiddling ; I'll find dancing.

Doct. (*ſtealing towards the door*) Andante, An-
dantino, Piano, Pianiſſimo, Allegro, Preſto !
                                   (*Runs off.*

Re-enter TICKLE *with a Violin.*

Tic. Here's the coal box, Doctor ; what ! he
has borrowed himſelf !

Tony. Gone !---voics---hollo, fiddler, hollo !
(*Running out is met by* FRANK) Where's this fiddler ?

Frank. Fiddler, ſir ! oh, Doctor Minum, I
ſuppoſe, you mean ; lord, ſir, he flies as if twenty
Dutch concerts were in the wind.

Tony. The next time I catch the raſcal, I'll
make him play for me, and kick him all the
whiſe.

Frank. But, ſir, my maſter's compliments,
and wiſhes vou'd pleaſe to get dreſſed; it's now
cloſe upon three. (*Looks at his watch and exit.*)

Tic. The fellow has got a tattler, ſtrike him
plump. (*aſide*)

Tony. Zounds ! I wiſh I cou'd get a watch,
that the figures of it were not in letters ; I never
can know what a clock it is, by the X's and the V's
                                   and

and the I's---I wifh I could get a watch with the
figures in figures upon it.

Tic. 'Squire, that's becaufe you know how to
cypher.

Tony. I fuppofe fo---Hollo, Diggory, my new
clothes ; and then for grandeur, lace and powder---
Hollo, hollo.   [*Exeunt.*

END OF THE FIRST ACT.

A C T II.

SCENE I.

A Dreſſing Room.

Mrs. Jonquil *at her Toilet, and* Lavender, *attending.*

MRS. JONQUIL.

Ha! ha! ha! Indeed, Lavender, I think ſo too but where is the ſavage now?

Lav. Ma'am, I fancy by this time he's almoſt transformed into a very fine gentleman. He's gone to dreſs.

Mrs. Jon. Dreſs! Ah! his native ruſticity is invincible to the powerful combination of art and elegance. His tutor a bear dancer, you tell me; ha! ha! with ſuch a pupil a bear-leader we muſt grant him.

Lav. Ma'am, he has brought this Mr: Tickle purpoſely to London with him, to ſhew him taſte and high life in the genteel way as he ſays.

Mrs.

Mrs. Jou. Yes, tafte and gentility at a Sunday tea-garden, and high life at the top of St. Pauls.

Enter TICKLE *and* PAINTER.

Tic. Come, mafter Painter, come along; this way, 1 believe, we can take a fhort cut to the 'Squire's room.

Mrs. Jon Who are thefe ? what's the matter ?

Tic. Only going to quarter the ground.

Lav. Fye, Mr. Tickle ! what bufinefs have you here ? and why would you bring fellows.into my lady's apartment ?

Tic. Fellows ! why, ma'am, this is Jack Raddle, the fign-painter. Why it was this here Jack that painted the Three Jolly Pigeons at Quagmire marfh, down in our parts.

Paint. Yes, and the Saracen's Head Tim.

Lav. Come, come, get you along out of this, with your jolly pigeons.

Tic Get out ! Strike me plump ! is that your manners, ma'am ?

Lav. Go, man ? pray take your Saracen's head out of this room.

Tic. Hark'ee, if you deny that you paint a head every morning, your tongue gives the lie to your cheeks.

Paint. Tim, that was a dafh with the pound brufh !

Tic. Ay, ay; I'm the boy for it. Come along; Ha ! ha ! ha !

Paint. Ha ! ha ! ha ! [*Exeunt Tickle and Painter.*

Lav. An impudent fellow ! I paint indeed . A pretty difcerning tutor for a young gentleman !

Mrs. Jon. Lavender, hand me the eau-de-luce. I die ! oh heav'ns, throw up that fafh ! I fhall expire !

Lav. And no wonder, ma'am: I'm fure the
cham-

chamber fmells of oil worfe than a floor-cloth ware-
houfe.

Enter DIGGORY, *fearches round the room.*

Mrs. Jon. Heavens! what's this now? what do
you want,?

Lav. Why is the deuce in the fellow? For fhame
Diggory! why do you come into my Lady's apartment this way?

Dig. This way! why would you have me come
in at the window?

Mrs. Jon. For mercy's fake, do, good man,
withdraw.

Lav. What do you want?

Dig. I want my mafter's boots.

Lav. What the mifchief could bring his boots
into my lady's dreffing-room?

Dig. His legs, I believe; for I think 'twas here
he took them off.

Mrs. J. Do, pray retire, I befeech you, fir.

Dig. I beg pardon, ma'am, I fee the boots are
not here; fo I'll go look in the ftable.

(*A tapping at the door.*)

Mrs. Jon. What monfter have we now?

Jon. (*without.*) Avec permiffion!

Lav. My mafter! madam.

Mrs. Jon. Entrez, monfieur.

Enter JONQUIL.

Jon. This way, for wonder fake, quick, quick.
Ha! ha! ha! fuch a fight, tranfcending all So-
ho!

Mrs. Jon. I think it muft be fomething fuper-
natural that can excite my wonder now. But
allons for this miracle.

[*Exeunt* Mr. *and* Mrs. JONQUIL.

Lav. (*looks in the glafs*) A Saracen's head?
Yes, it muft be my lady he meant.   [*Exit.*

SCENE

SCENE II.

A Gallery hung with Pictures.

Enter Mr. *and* Mrs. JONQUIL.

Jon. Now, settle your features.

Mrs. Jon. O, I set risibility at defiance.

Mr. Jon. Mr. Lumpkin, are you apparell'd, quite completely a-la-mode ?

Enter TONY, *dressed.*

Tony. O yes, I think I'm the very colliflower of the mode. Tell me in downright earnest, how do you like me, (*turns round*) Eh! Cousin Milly ? I believe, now I'm something like a tanzy ; how do you like my hair, tho'?

Mrs. Jon. Charming!

Jon. The style most happily fancied.

Tony. So it is, cousin Milly ; you've a fine head of hair, if it's all your own---it's very like some of the heads I saw in the barbers windows.

Mrs. Jon. Now, that's so civil.

Tony. That's what every body says of me, that I'm so civil; but do you know that my mama used to dress up my hair herself every Sunday, whether I would or no ? she'd rub it up with soap, and put a paper in the top, just like the sign of the unicorn.

Enter LAVENDER *whispers* Mrs. JONQUIL.

Mrs. Jon. Presently ; Mr. Lumpkin, allow me the liberty to withdraw myself for a moment or two.

Tony.

Tony. Ma'am, I'll excufe your going away with a great deal of pleafure. How polite fine clothes make a body! (*afide*)

[*Exeunt Mrs. Jonquil and Lavender.*

Enter TICKLE.

Tic. 'Squire, the Painter's ready. (*to Tony*)

Tony. Mum. (*apart to Tickle*)

Jon. Pardon my curiofity, Mr. —— excufe me, Sir—you fpoke of a painter; are you acquainted—I mean have you a penchant?

Tic. A what?

Jon. That is, do you admire the art?

Tony. Oh, yes, Sir; my tutor's very knowing in the picture way. Tim, fhall I tell coufin you carried a fhew-box' (*apart to Tickle*)

Tic. You need not mind it now. (*apart to Tony*)

Jon. There are fome tolerable paintings here, Sir. (*loooking round*)

Tic. Yes; they are quite genteel.

Tony. I warrant, now, they ftood you in a matter of fifteen or twenty pounds.

Jon. Above ten thoufand.

Tony. Pounds?

Jon. Pofitively.

Tony. What a ftud and a kennel of hounds that would buy a man!

Tic. What a collection of wild beaftiffes!

Jon. Befides the money I have expended in my Flemifh and Italian acquifitions, during my tour, I have, at this moment, a pecuniary underftanding with moft of the eminent picture-dealers and auctioneers in town; and, confequently, the refufal of antiques, coins, china, lap-dogs and original pictures.

Tic. How do you order it?

Jon. Briefly thus: if an extraordinary engagement prevents me from a private peep, previous to the fale, fuppofe me in the auction-room: a full fale, good pictures, my favourite piece up, friend Mallet, in the heat of his oration, cafts me an eye fignificant; I, unperceived by the company, return an affirmative fignal; and one, two—down, the picture's mine for one third of the value.

Tic. What then becomes of his poundage?

Jon. That, Sir, I make good by an ample douceur.

Tony. Well, let them fay what they will of flock paper, pretty pictures for my money; coufin, you muft choofe me fome nice ones, when my mama takes a new houfe for me.

Tic. Ay, I dare fay, 'Squire Jonquil knows all the painters in town, in the genteel way.

Jon. In town?—no—no—Mr.—Sir—if a modern ever intrudes upon a pannel of mine, tafte muft give the preference to Flemifh and Italian; if the contrary fhould tranfpire, Sir, I'd be excluded the *ton,* as void of all virtu.

Tony. Virtue! It does not fhew much virtue to encourage foreigners, and let your own countrymen want bread; damn me, if I do that; and damn them that do.

Tic. Well faid, tight boy; there's a fine fellow, and I'm his tutor.

Jon. I own, Sir, I'm of your opinion; but powerful fafhion!——

Tony.

Tony. Tim, there's a clever fellow, running after a pretty girl among the bushes!

Jon. Apollo, pursuing Daphne, by Corregio; observe the modest grace in the flight of Daphne; and that figure of Apollo, what fine proportion in the outline! what an attitude!

Tic. Now, that there I call a tall woman.

Jon. A Vandyke!

Tony. Mrs. Vandyke?

Jon. No, no; it is the portrait of Beatrix Constantia Contacroyana, painted by that master. The Judgment of Paris, the sleeping Venus, and that delightful picture of the Cardinal Virtues, Faith, Hope and Charity, are by Carraci; a most enchanting piece! observe how finely the Hope is relieved.

Tony. Relieved by Charity; poor soul!

Tic. That's a pretty woman that's looking up at the sky.

Jon. A Cleopatra, by Guido.

Tony. See the little eel in her hand! that's a dark looking man in the black bonnet.

Jon. A Rembrandt, by himself.

Tony. Yes; he's all alone, there's a woman riding on a white cow.

Jon. Europa, an undoubted Raphael.

Tony. No!

Jon. As true as the cartoons.

Tic. Riding on a bull! strike her plump; 'Squire the woman and the goose!

Jon. Jupiter and Leda; upon my honour I never saw a more capital picture!—but, dear Sir, the goose happens to be a swan.

Tony. Mayhap 'twas only a goose before you got it.—Tim, who is that like in the black wig.

Jon.

Jon. That is the portrait of Charles the Second.

Tony. He's mighty like Matt Muggins the exciseman.

Jon. It's a Sir Godfrey Kneller; but I fancy king Charles never sat for it.

Tic. And so they've drawn him standing. Who is the lad with the long hair?

Jon. Lad, Sir? that's a Magdalen, by Guido.

Tony. She's a plump Mag. Who is that thin ill-looking fellow?

Jon. It's a picture of Cassius, that stabb'd Cæsar—It's a Rubens, very bold.

Tic. Yes, he was a bold fellow.

Jon. Good keeping!

Tic. Fast enough; I remember they kept him in Newgate.

Jon. Charmingly brought out!

Tic. He was brought out in a white cap, tied with black ribbon.

Jon. What a glow of colouring!

Tic. I never saw a 'man look better upon the occasion.

Jon. Greatly designed! forcibly executed!

Tic. Only the peace-officers at his execution, no calling in the military; we have had enough of that already.

Jon. What harmony of light and shade! What noble masses!

Tic. Masses! He a Papish! I'll bett half an ounce, that Tom Cassius, that stabb'd 'Squire Cæsar, died a Presbyterian.

Tony. How knowing my tutor is!

(*During the above speeches of Tickle, Jonquil stands enraptur'd with the picture, not attending him.*)

Cousin,

Coufin, Coufin Jonquil, hollo !

(*Slaps him on the fhoulder.*)

Jon. Sir !

Tony. I intend to have my picture taken off fome evening or other.

Enter FRANK.

Frank. Sir, Lord Spindle has fent to let you know, he waits for you at the Thatched-houfe.

Jon. The chariot at the door ?

Frank. Yes, Sir. [*Exit.*

Jon. Adieu, [*Exit.*

Tic. Abfolutely, 'Squire, this coufin of your's is a tip-top macaroni.

Tony. Yes, he's a famous mac.

Tony. But tho' he feems to love his pictures, as I do my horfes, he does not take half fo great care of 'em. Think of old bonnets and black and brown heads! Coft him ten thoufand pounds too. Why my little Robin, my Whipper-in, looks more decent than the beft of them.

Tic. Aye! but when my friend Jack Raddle the painter comes brufh upon 'em, they'll be quite another thing.

Tony. But what keeps him?

Tic. Here he is.

Enter PAINTER, *with a pot of paint and large brufh.*

Are you there, Jack? Come, fall to.

Tony. Hold, you remember the bargain: Tickle, be witnefs. You're to paint five large powder'd pretty wigs upon every head in this
om,

room, at the rate of half-a-crown a nob all round.

Tic. That's the bargain.

Paint. And I fcorn to go back, tho' it's a tight price, your honour.

Tony. How charmingly they'll look!

Tic. Yes, they'll be quite genteel. Hark'ee, Jack, d'ye fee, I recommend you to this here 'fquire; fo do the job neatly. None of your little ftarv'd caxons, with one buckle, and that no larger than a pipe-ftopper; but let me fee the browneft face againft this wall, wigg'd like an alderman.

Paint. Say no more.

Tony. But quick, quick, buftle; you muft have 'em done before coufin comes back.

Enter DIGGORY.

Dig. Sir, the gentleman's come.

Tony. What gentleman?

Tic. How fhould he know? I'll go fee myfelf.
                      [*Exit.*

Tony. Come, come, fall to.

Paint. Don't fear, fir; they fhall foon be quite another thing.

Tony. Come along, we'll be with you foon again. Come; Lord! how delighted coufin Jonquil will be!   [*Exeunt Tony and Diggory.*
(*The Painter, whiftling, takes one of the pictures down, and as he fits to it, the fcene clofes.*

                                SCENE

SCENE III.

The Antichamber.

Enter PULVILLE, *meeting* TONY, TICKLE, *and* DIGGORY.

Dig. Here's my mafter.

Pulv. Sir. your humble fervant.

Dig. Sir, this the——

Tic. Diggory, I tell you once for all, if you come the gentleman ufher, while I am by, you'll abfolutely knock your head again my fiftes.

Dig. Why fure i——

Tony. Go, go, you fool, and fee that the painter flaps away brifkly.   [*Exit Diggory.*
Well, Sir, are you a barber?

Pulv. A barber! no, Sir; my name is Pulville.

Tony. But what are you?

Pulv. I am a perfumer, Sir.

Tony. Now, bang me, if I know what trade that is. (*afide*) Tickle, do you talk to him.

Tic. A perfumer? I'm at home, tho' he's too fine for that: I fuppofe he moulted in Monmouth. (*afide; ftruts up to Pulville*) Mafter, how do ye take 'em.

Pulv. Sir?

Tic. Do you fhoot 'em.

Tony. Aye, do you fhoot 'em?—What, Tickle? (*apart to Tickle*)

Pulv. I fhoot, Sir!

Tic. Aye, how do you order it?

Pulv. If you mean my bufinefs, Sir; by cal-
                                        cination,

cination, infuſion, mixtures, compoſitions, phil-
ters, and diſtillation.

Tic. What, then maphap you don't uſe the
ferret ?

Pulv. No, Sir, the only eſſential animal is the
civet cat.

Tic. The cat will catch them, I allow; but
then they mangle them ſo curſedly.

Pulv. Mangle who, good Sir ?

Tic. Ever while you live, take rabbits with a
ferret, that's the genteel thing. Mayhap, lad,
you're in the hedge-hog way. Have a care, tho',
for ſince ſome buſy fellow put it into the news-
paper, that they were as good as a partridge—
—my bear to a lap-dog, if hedge-hogs don't
ſoon be included in the game-act. You're the
firſt rabbit catcher I ever knew that——

Pulv. I a rabbit catcher! I don't underſtand
you, gentlemen. I'd have you to know, I keep
one of the firſt perfumer's ſhops in St. James's
pariſh; I can't imagine what you mean, by talking to me about rabbit-catchers and hedge-hogs.

Tony. I belive my tutor knows every thing.

Pulv. Sir, I thought every body knew Mr.
Pulville. However, Sir, I have the honour to
be very well known to the nobility, as my book-
debts of ten years ſtanding can ſufficiently teſ-
tify. Rabbit catcher! Sir! I'm original inven-
tor of the genuine Circaſſian beautifying coſme-
tic lotion, cream of roſes, and powder of pearl.
Step into my ſhop a crocus, and you walk out
a narciſſus; my ſweet lip-ſalve can change a
blubber to a pouting—a walnut to a cherry-lip.
Then, Sir, my perfumed powders conquer nature; I can give a lady a pink head, a green
head, or a blue head. Do you know, Sir, that
I make

I make the chymical Paphian wash, for eradicating hair; so innocent it may be used by infants just born, and yet so powerful, that three ablutions give an Esau the hand of a Jacob? And now, Sir, with me, and me alone, the elderly maiden ladies deal, for their sweet-scented shaving powder.

Tony. I said he was a barber.

Pul. Rabbit-catcher!—Why, Sir, my bear's grease—

Tic. Do you dance a bear, tight boy?

Pul. Sir, do I look like such a scoundrel?

Tic. Scoundrel! Strike you plump, am I a scoundrel?

Pul. You, Sir! I——

Tic. Aye, poke you well—I dance the sprightlieft bear in all England, that's in the genteel way.

Pul. Hem!—Sir!—when you want any thing in my way, you'll see my name, P. Pulville, over the door. Rabbit catcher! [*Exit Pulville.*

Tic. A bear dancer, a scoundrel! you rascal, I'll—he's gone—he was right; my name is Tim Tickle; and now you've told me your place of abode, call upon me when you will. (*calling off*)

Tony. Tim knows all the points of honour.

Enter Diggory.

Dig. Oh, Sir, the pictures are done; and 'Squire Jonquil is walking out of his carriage.

Tic. I told you, 'Squire, Jack Raddle cou'd touch them up in the genteel way, because he's the boy for it; come, we'll take a squint at his handy work.

VOL. I.   L L   *Tony.*

Tony. Come, I'm as glad as a guinea; how my coufin Jonquil will be delighted!

[*Exeunt.*

SCENE IV.

Difcovers the Picture Gallery, moft of the portraits with large white wigs ; the Painter fits daubing a wig upon a picture, which he has on a chair. DIGGORY *officioufly attending.*

Dig. Do, let me give him another curl.

Paint. I can't ftand it, man ;—be ftill, I fay ; let him be.

Enter JONQUIL.

Jon. What do I fee! confufion! what is all this? (*Stands amazed*)

Dig. I knew he'd be delighted.

Jon. Stop your facrilegious hands, you pro-phane villain.

Paint. Blefs your heart, mafter, I don't grudge you a curl or two more. (*whiftles and paints*)

Jon. My Rembrandt! from the Florentine gallery! You affaffin, why did you murder me? (*Seizes the painter*)

Paint. Sir!

Jon. Anfwer me, you mifcreant; who brought you here? what mortal enemy to the arts, what Gothick fiend, whifper'd you to perpetrate fuch infernal action?

Paint. If this moment was my laft, Sir, it was white lead of eightpence a pound.

Jon. White lead, you caitiff!

Paint.

Paint. How cou'd a poor fellow, like me, afford flake-white for the price?

Jon. What price? you barbarian; explain, firrah: confefs, or I'll have you flay'd like Marfyas.

Paint. Sir, 'Squire Lumpkin, the little, round, fine gentleman, employ'd me to paint white wigs, upon all the pictures, at half-a-crown a head.

Dig. Indeed Sir, I'm fure my mafter would not grudge twice the money, to make them look decent, as they belong to your honour.

Jon. I'm undone!

Enter TONY *and* TICKLE.

Tony: Eh, Tim! (*looks exultingly at the pictures*) I believe they are the thing.

Tic. Bang me, but they are quite genteel!

Jon. Mr. Lumpkin, I thank you, Sir.

Tony. You're mightily welcome.

Jon. I am infinitely oblig'd to you, Sir.

Tony. I guefs'd you wou'd.

Jon. I am eternally your debtor.

Tony. I'll never charge you a penny for it. I believe now they look like gentlemen. How pleas'd I am that I thought of it!

Dig. I thought of it firft.

Tony. You lie.

Tic. You do, Diggory! 'twas I advis'd the 'Squire to it, becaufe I knew the genteel thing.

Jon. Oh, pray, no contention for the brilliancy of the thought; for I'd give three or five thoufand pounds to undo what you have done.

Tony. What!

Jon. You have ruin'd me.

Tony. Anan!

L L

Jon.

Jon. You've undone me, Sir!

Tony. Who, I! as how?

Jon. You've fpoil'd my pictures.

Tony. Tim!

Tic. I faid, at firft, it was a damn'd ftupid thing of you.

Dig. And you know, 'Squire, I told you, that none but an afs could think of fuch nonfenfe.

Tony. Can you unwig 'em again?

Paint. What will I get by that?

Jon. I'll give you fifty guineas.

Paint. Lay it here.

Jon. There's the money; (*takes out his pocket-book and gives a note*) charm my longing eyes, once more, with the fight of my Rembrandt's dear, dear, black bonnet.

Paint. Then, Sir, they're only done in water colour; fo a wet towel and a little foap fettles their wigs in five minutes.

Jon. Give me your hand; I was dreadfully alarmed; but now I can laugh at it. Ha! ha! ha! what a whimfical thought! but, you ftupid rogue, why would you put wigs upon the ladies?

Paint. Sure it's the fafhion now for all ladies to wear wigs. How charming they look! Poor fellows, ye muft foon lofe your grandeur!

Enter FRANK.

Frank. Sir, the company are come.

Jon. Very well.

[*Frank looks at the pictures, laughs and exit.*

Dig. Pleafe your honour, may I laugh at them a little?

Tony. Tutor, kick Diggory out of the room, if you pleafe.

Tic.

Tic. To oblige you, 'Squire.

Dig. I'll save you the trouble. [*Exit.*

Jon. All is now very well; but I have one request to make you.

Tony. What is it, pray?

Jon. Only to dismiss one of your retinue.

Tic. That's Diggory. (*aside*)

Tony. Who?

Jon. The bear?

Tony. What! the bear?

Jon. That's the gentleman.

Tony. Why, Tim, d'ye hear my cousin? Will you?

Tic. Look'ee, 'Squire; this here harmless soul, this bear of mine, has maintained me some years, when I could not do for myself; and though, thanks to my good breeding, I'm grown polite enough to be a gentleman's tutor, yet I'll never be so much in the fashion as to forsake an old benefactor. [*Exit Tic.*

Tony. I wish I could get any regular family to board the bear: enquire among your acquaintance Sir.

Jon. Sir, I'll do myself that honour.

Tony. Bruin's a lad of few words, but he's as civil a fellow as ever stood upon two legs. But, cousin Jonquil, I won't offer you the fifty guineas you gave the painter.

Tony. Say no more; you meant well, and that palliates the consequence. But, for Rubens' sake forego your pretensions in future to a taste in pictures.

Tony. Well, I know the points of a horse, and that's made by a better workman.

Jon. Therefore, to the knowledge of horses and dogs, like a true 'Squire, from this moment confine

confine your claim; for if a man will, in oppo-
fition to nature, meddle with matters of which
he is fo extremely ignorant, he muft inevitably
render himfelf the object of ridicule and laughter.

Tony. Laughter! and what's pleafanter than a
laugh? By jingo, a laugh is all I wanted.

If I've rais'd fome fweet fmiles on thofe lovely
    fair faces,
I am glad I put wigs on their fifters, the
    Graces:
I would not offend you for more than I'll
    mention;
To pleafe all my friends, was my only in-
    tention.

THE END.

THE

POOR SOLDIER,

IN TWO ACTS.

PERFORMED AT THE

THEATRE-ROYAL, COVENT-GARDEN,

IN 1782.

The MUSICK By Mr. SHIELD.

DRAMATIS PERSONÆ.

Captain Fitzroy, ...	Mr. BANNISTER.
Father Luke, ...	Mr. WILSON.
Patrick, ...	Mrs. KENNEDY.
Dermott, ...	Mr. JOHNSTON.
Darby, ...	Mr. EDWIN.
Bagatelle, ...	Mr. WEWITZER.
Boy, ...	Master SIMMONDS.
Norah, ...	Mrs. BANNISTER.
Kathlane, ...	Mrs. MARTYR.

SCENE, *Carton, near the Seat of the Duke of Leinster in Ireland.*

THE

POOR SOLDIER.

A C T I.

S C E N E I.

*The Country—Sun rife—a large Manfion at fome dif-
tance—near the front, on one fide, a fmall
Houfe ; on the other a Cottage.*

DARBY, (*without.*)

NOW what harm, Dermot ?
   Der. (*without.*) Why 'tis harm ; fo ftay where
you are.

Enter DERMOT *and* DARBY.

   Dar. Upon my faith I won't fay a word.
   Der. Go away I tell you.
   Dar. Lord, I never faw fuch a man as you:
fure I'll only ftand by.
   Der. But I tell you it's not proper for any
one to be by when one's along with one's fweetheart.

Dar. Well, I always like to be by when I'm along with my fweetheart—She's afleep—I'll call her up, halloo! Kathlane!

Der. Will you be quiet, Darby. Can't you go make a noife there, under Father Luke's window?

Dar. Ecod if I do, he'll put me in the Bifhop's Court.

Der. If I wasn't fo fond of Kathlane, I fhou'd think Norah, his Neice there, a very handfome girl.

Dar. Why fo fhe is, but fince her own fweet-heart, Patrick, run away from her and lifted for a Soldier, fhe dont care a pin for the prettieft of us; by the lord fhe even flouts me.

Der. Well, well, you'll fee how it will be; fomebody I know——

Dar. Ay, you mean the foreign ferving man, to the ftrange Officer that's above at the Duke's. Eh, why faith Dermot, it would indeed be a fhame, to let a black muzzled Mounfeer carry off a pretty girl, from a parcel of tight Irifh boys like us.

Der. So, 'twou'd Darby; but my fweet Kathlane is faft afleep, and never dreams that her poor Dermot is here under her window.

Dar. Ay, never dreams poor Darby's under her window—but I'll have her up—Kathlane—Kath——

Der. Hufh!

AIR—*Dermot.*

Sleep on, fleep on, my Kathlane dear,
  May peace poffefs thy breaft,
Yet doft thou dream thy true love's here,
  Depriv'd of peace and reft.

The

The birds fing fweet, the morning breaks,
　　Thefe joys are none to me,
Tho' fleep is fled, poor Dermot wakes,
　　To none but love and thee.

[Exit

Dar. What a dull dog that is! Ah, poor Dermot! ha, ha, why fuch a fong cou'dn't wake an Owl out of his fleep, let alone a pretty girl that's dreaming of me. Kathlane!—upon my confcience I'll,—yes, I'll roufe her.

AIR—Darby.

Dear Kathlane you no doubt,
　　Find fleep how very fweet 'tis,
Dogs bark, and cocks have crow'd out,
　　You never dream how late 'tis,
　　　　This morning gay,
　　　　I poft away,
To have with you a bit of play,
　　　　On two legs rid,
　　　　Along to bid,
Good morrow to your night cap.

II.

Laft night a little bowfy,
　　With Whifkey, Ale, and Cyder,
I afk'd young Betty Blowfy,
　　To let me fit befide her,
　　　　Her anger rofe,
　　　　And four as floes,
The little gypfey cock'd her nofe,
　　　　Yet here I've rid,
　　　　Along to bid,
Good morrow to your night cap.

III.

Beneath the Honey-fuckle,
　　The Daify, and the Vi'let,
Compofe fo fweet a truckle,
　　They'll tempt you fure to fpoil it,
M M 2

Sweet

Young Sall and Bell,
I've pleafed fo well,
But hold, I musn't kifs and tell,
So here I've rid,
Along to bid,
Good morrow to your night cap.

(Kathlane opens the Cottage window.

Dar. Ay there fhe is, oh I'm the boy for it.

Kath. Is that Dermot?

Dar. (*hiding under the penthoufe*) O dear, fhe takes me for Dermot, he, he, he!

Kath. Who's there?

Dar. Sure it's only I.

Kath. What Dermot?

Dar. Yes—I am—Darby. (*afide*)

Kath. I'm coming down. (*Retires.*)

Dar. I thought I'd bring her down: I'm a fure markfman.

Enter KATHLANE *from the Cottage.*

Kath. Where are you, my dear Dermot?

Dar. (*Comes forward.*) " Good morrow to your nightcap." (*fings.*)

Kath. (*Starling.*) Darby! Now hang you for an impudent fellow.

Dar. Then hang me about your neck, my fweet Kathlane.

Kath. It's a fine thing that people can't take their reft of a morning, but you muft come roaring under their windows.

Dar. Now what need you be fo crofs with a body—when you know I love you.

Kath. Love!—ha,—I like you for that.

Dar. I'm oblig'd to you.

Kath. You love, ha, ha, ha!

Dar.

Dar. I do, upon my confcience.

Kath. Well, let me alone, Darby : once for all I will not have you.

Dar. No !

Kath. No, as I hope for man, I won't.

Dar. Ha, ha, ha ! hope for man, and yet won't have me.

Kath. Yes, but I'll tell you what fort of a man ; then look into the river, and fee if you're he.

Dar. And if not—I'll pop in head foremoft.

Kath. Do Darby ; and then you may whiftle for me.

AIR.—*Kathlane.*

Since love is the plan
I'll love if I can,
But firft let me tell you what fort of a man.
In addrefs how complete
And in drefs fpruce and neat,
No matter how tall, fo he's over five feet :
Nor dull, nor too witty
His eyes I'll think pretty
If fparkling with pleafure whenever we meet.

II.

Tho' gentle he be,
His man he fhould fee
Yet never be conquer'd by any but me.
In a fong bear a bob
In a glafs a hob nob
Yet drink of his reafon his noddle ne'er rob,
This is my fancy
If fuch a man can fee,
I'm his, if he's mine, until then I am free.

Dar. So then you won't have me.

Kath. No, that I won't.

Dar. Now you might if you pleas'd.

Kath.

Kath. I might if you pleas'd.

Dar. Well sure I do please.

Kath. Ay, but you don't please me.

Dar. Why I'm a better match for you than Dermot.

Kath. No.

Dar. No ? Havn't I every thing comfortable about me? cows, sheep, geese and turkies for you to look after in the week days, and a pretty pad for you to ride to chapel on a Sunday : a little cabin for you to live in, and a neat bit of a potatoe garden for ycu to walk in ; and for a husband I'm as pretty a lad as you'd meet with of a long summer's day.

Kath. Get along: don't talk to me of your geese and your turkies, man, with your conceit and your nonsense.

Dar. My nonsense! Oh very well : you say that to me, do you ?

Kath. To be sure I do.

Dar. Then marry hang me if I don't.—

Kath. What—what'ill you do?

Dar. Do, why I'll—tell the Priest of you.

Kath. Ah do——do your worst, you ninney hammer !

Dar. I'm a ninney hammer, oh very well— I tell you what Kathlane——I'll say no more.

DUET.

Kath.	Out of my sight or I'll box your ears.
Dar.	I'll fit you soon for your jibes and jeers.
Kath.	I'll set my cap at a smart young man,
Dar.	Another I'll wed this day if I can.
Kath.	In courtship funny.
Dar.	Once sweet as honey,
Kath.	You drone.
Dar.	No Kate, I'm your humble Bee.

Kath.

Kath.   Go dance your dogs with your fiddle de dee
            For a fprightly lad is the tune for me.

II.

Kath.   Like fweet milk turn'd now to me feems love.
Dar.   The fragrant Rofe does a Nettle prove.
Kath.   Sour Curds I tafte, tho' fweet Cream I chofe.
Dar.   And with a flower I fting my nofe.
Kath.   In courtfhip funny, &c.
                              [*Exeunt feverally.*

Enter FITZROY.

Fitz. Ay, here's Father Luke's houfe : I doubt if his charming niece is up yet. (*Looks at his watch*) I fhall be back before the family are ftirring, and even if not, drawn hither by the devout hopes of paying my adoration to this Sylvan Deity, the beauty and frefhnefs of the morning exhilirates and delights.

AIR.—*Fitzroy.*

The Twins of Latona, fo kind to my boon,
   Arife to partake of the chafe,
And Sol lends a ray to chafte Dian's fair Moon,
   And a fmile to the fmiles of her face.
For the fport I delight in, the bright Queen of Love
   With myrtles my brow fhall adorn,
While Pan breaks his Chaunter, and fkulks in the Grove,
   Excell'd by the found of the horn.

The dogs are uncoupled, and fweet is their cry,
Yet fweeter the notes of fweet Echo's reply.
Hark forward, my Honies! The game is in view
But love is the game that I wifh to purfue.

                                  The

II.

The Stag from his Chamber of Woodbine peeps out,
   His fentence he hears in the gale,
Yet flies, till entangled in fear and in doubt,
   His courage and conftancy fail.
Surrounded by foes, he prepares for the 'fray,
   Defpair taking place of his fear,
With Antlers erected awhile ftands at bay,
   Then furrenders his life with a tear.
           The dogs, &c.

Oh here comes the Prieft her uncle, and now for his final anfwer, which muft determine my happinefs. (*Enter Father Luke*) Good morning to you, Sir.

F. Luke. And a good morrow, and a hundred and a thoufand good morrows to you worthy Sir.

Fitz. As many thanks to you my reverend Sir.

F. Luke. True, Sir, I am reverend, becaufe I'm the Prieft of the Parifh. Blefs you, Sir, but you're an early rifer.

Fitz. Why you muft imagine that the pillow has no great charms for one whofe heart can take little reft 'till lull'd to peace by your friendly benediction.—Oh! Father Luke your charming Niece.—

F. Luke. My Niece— you told me of that, but you never told me your fortune, fo it's gone quite out of my memory.

Fitz. Why Father, if you muft peep into my rent-roll, I fancy you'll find it fomething above 2000l. a year

F. Luke. Two thoufand!—You fhall have my niece: but there's two things which perhaps you have not confider'd on.

Fitz. What are thofe?

F. Luke. Her religion and her country.

Fitz.

Fitz. My dear Sir, be affured I am incapable of an illiberal prejudice againſt any one, for not having firſt breath'd the fame air with me, or for worſhiping the fame Deity in another manner. We are common children of one parent, and the honeſt man who thinks with moral rectitude, and acts according to his thoughts, is my countryman let him be born where he will.

F. Luke. Juſt my thoughts, Sir, I don't mind a man's country ſo he has—You've 2000l. a year ? *(Fitz. bows)* Your hand, you ſhall marry my niece.

Fitz. My dear good man you're the beſt of Prieſts ; but there's one thing that I'd wiſh to be certain of—Are you ſure your niece's heart is totally difengag'd ?

F. Luke. Why Sir ſhe did give her heart away but I made her take it back again, ſhe had a ſort of a Lover that I think ſhe was a little fond of.

Fitz. How ?

F. Luke. Don't be alarm'd, Sir, for lord knows what's become of poor Patrick ſince he was ſent off for America : upon my refuſing Norah to him, he took on ſo, that one day, full of ale and vexation, the fool went and liſted for a ſoldier.

Fitz. Ah, I cou'd wiſh that———

F. Luke. You can wiſh for no more than you ſhall have : ſhe's your's : I ſay the word ; and I'm her uncle, her Guardian, and her Clergy. Here, Norah, child, *(calls at the window)* I fancy ſhe's not awake yet. *(Going in.)*

Fitz. Hold Sir, I wouldn't have her diſturb'd for the world.

F. Luke. Well faith, you're good natur'd enough conſidering you've been fighting in America.

Fitz. My dear Father Luke, you know I'm down here at the Duke's upon a visit, and you have sense enough to know likewise, that notwithstanding your niece's beauty and merit, and the reverence due to your character, such is the ridiculous pride, and assum'd privilege of birth and fortune, that I should be most egregiously rallied, and perhaps obstacles thrown in the way of my happiness, shou'd this affair be talked of there.

F. Luke. Not a word, my lips are seal'd.

Fitz. That's right, my dear friend, the ceremony once over, with pride I shall publish my felicity to the world. I have already sent up to Dublin, for some trifling ornaments for my sweet Norah; I expect them every hour, this night you shall join our hands, and then I'll introduce my lovely bride as such, to my friends at Carton House.

Enter DARBY.

Dar. Father Luke, I want to speak a word with you if you please, Sir. (*Fitzroy walks up the Stage.*)

F. Luke. What do you mean you free fellow? Don't you see I'm in company, and in company with a gentleman too? Eh, you wicked boy?

Dar. I'm not wicked.

F. Luke. Eh, how child, what, an't I your Priest, and don't I know what wickedness is.

Dar. Well Sir, to be sure I have been a young rake, as a body may say, but now I'm going to take a wife to myself.

F Luke. (*to Darby*) Get away.——I beg your worship's pardon. *to Fitzroy*)

Fitz. Oh no apology, Sir. The Shepherd must look to his flock.

F. Luke.

F. Luke. Ah ! I'm shepherd to a blessed flock of goats: Now would you think it, Sir ? that Darby, that fellow that looks so sheepish, is the most notorious reprobate in the whole parish.

Dar. (*to Fitzroy*) Sir, I'll tell you why Father Luke's always at me. He, he, he! when one plays or so, among the girls, you know one must give them a kifs or two, to keep them in good humour ; and then the long winter nights before a fine fire, I'm so frolickfome among 'em, that when we play at forfeits, it may come to twenty or thirty kifses a piece: thefe they must all confefs to him, and ecod, of a cold morning they keep Father Luke, 'till his fingers are numb'd, and his nofe is blue, he, he, he! you know, Sir, you know that's the reafon you don't like poor Darby.

F. Luke. Get along you profligate.

Dar. Well, Sir, I'll go.

F. Luke. Come back here: Where are you going now ? I warrant you're pofting away to the alehoufe; but I'll follow you; I'll meet you there, and if I catch you guzzling, if you dare call for a quart of ale before me.——

Dar. You'll drink half of it.

F. Luke. Go along, go. (*pufhes him off*) Oh! dear me! I'm only a poor parifh priest here ; and I profefs I have more to do than a bifhop.

Fitz. I wifh father you were a bifhop.

F. Luke. I wifh to Heaven I was

Fitz. Well, well—who knows—all in good time—We fhall have his Grace's intereft—Such a thing may be done.

F. Luke. Oh, that nothing may hinder it !

AIR

AIR.—*Father Luke.*

An humble curate here am I,
  The boys and girls director;
Yet fomething whifpers by and by,
  I may be made a Rector:
    Then I'll preach
    And teach,
  My fheep and rams.
So well I'll mind my duty;
  And Oh, my pretty ewes and lambs!
Your paftor fhall be true t'ye.

For tho' a fimple fifherman,
  A dean'ry if I fifh up,
So good I'll do the beft I can,
  And pray---to be a Bifhop.
    To my preaching,
    Teaching,
    Then farewell.
No more with duty hamper'd,
  But plump and fleek,
  My Rev'rend cheek;
Oh, how my lordfhip's pamper'd.

But, Sir, you're fure of my niece Norah; and now I muft attend fome duties of my function among my parifhioners.   [*Exit.*

Fitz. Love for a young man! this is not fo well: The firft impreffion of love upon the heart of an innocent young woman, is not eafily, if ever eras'd; yet, the coldnefs of her carriage to me, rather checks my hopes than abates the ardor of my affections. (*F. Luke's door opens*) 'Tis fhe; I fear to fpeak to her, left I fhou'd be obferv'd by fome of the villagers. (*retires*)

Enter

Enter NORAH, *from the Houfe.*

AIR.—*Norah.*

The meadows look chearful, the birds fweetly fing,
So gaily they carrol the praifes of fpring ;
Tho' nature rejoices, poor Norah fhall mourn,
Until her dear Patrick again fhall return.

. II.

Ye laffes of Dublin, ah, hide your gay charms!
Nor lure her dear Patrick from Norah's fond arms ;
Tho' fattins and ribbons and laces are fine,
They hide not a heart with fuch feelings as mine.

What a beautiful morning! The primrofes and violets feem to have fprung up fince the fun went down: If the grafs is not too wet, perhaps Kathlane will take a walk with me—but, fhe's gone to walk with her fweetheart Dermot: Well, if Patrick had'nt forfook me, I fhou'dn't now want a companion.—Oh dear! here's the gentleman that my uncle is always teazing me about.

Fitz. A fine morning, Madam ; but your prefence gives an additional luftre to the beauties of this charming fcene.

Nor. Sir. (*curtfies*)

Fitz. Beautiful Norah, has your uncle appriz'd you of the felicity I hope to derive from your compliance with his will, and my ardent wifhes?

Nor. I don't know, Sir ; he talk'd to me a great deal, but——

Fitz. (*taking her hand*) Nay, do not avert thofe lovely eyes—look kindly on me.

AIR.

AIR.—*Fitzroy.*

For you deareſt maiden the pride of the village,
  The town and it's pleaſures I freely reſign.
Delight ſprings from labor, and ſcience from tillage,
  Where love, peace and innocence ſweetly combine.
    Soft tender affeƈtion, what bliſs in poſſeſſing,
      How bleſt when 'tis love that inſures us the
        bleſſing.
      Careſs'd, Oh what rapture in mutual careſſing,
  What joy can I wiſh for, was Norah but mine.

II.

The feaſts of gay faſhion with ſplendour invite us,
  Where luxury, pride and her follies attend ;
The banquet of reaſon alone ſhould delight us,
  How ſweet the enjoyment when ſhar'd with a friend.
    Be thou that dear friend then, my comfort, my
      pleaſure,
    A look is my ſunſhine, a ſmile is my treaſure,
      Thy lips if conſenting, give joy beyond meaſure,
  A rapture ſo perfeƈt, what joy can tranſcend !

Nor. Do, Sir, permit me to withdraw ; our village is very cenſorious ; and a gentleman be_ing ſeen with me, will neither add to your ho_nor or my reputation.   [*Exit into houſe.*

Enter BAGATELLE. (*haſtily*)

Bag. Ah, Monſieur !
Fitz. Well, what's the matter ?
Bag. Ah, Monſieur ! I'm come—I'm come— to tell you—that—I'm out of breath.
Fitz. What's the matter ?
Bag. It is all blown——
Fitz. I ſuppoſe my love affair here is diſcover'd. (*half aſide*)
Bag. Oui Monſieur, I have diſcover.——

Fitz.

Fitz. How, you?

Bag. All blown.

Fitz. The devil!

Bag. We muſt go to town.

Fitz. Diſcover'd—all blown—and we muſt go to town—

Bag. Oui Monſieur. I have diſcover dat all your Mareſchal poudre is blown out of de vindre, and I muſt go to town for more.

Fitz. And is this the diſcovery that has made you run about the roads after me?

Bag. Non Monſieur ; but I am come on de affaire of grande importance.

Fitz. Quick, what is it?

Bag. To know Monſieur, if you will dreſs to-day en queue or de twiſted club.

Fit. Is this your affair of grand importance?

Bag. Oui, I muſt make de preparation ; oh, I did like to forget to tell you, dat his Grace, and all de fine Ladies wait for your honor's company in de breakfaſt parlour.

Fitz. Damn your impertinence, ſirrah ; why didn't you tell me this at firſt? I ſhall have fifty ſcouts after me; follow and be in the way, as I ſhall want to dreſs.

[*Exit.*

Bag. Ah !—ah, ah, begar dis is de Prieſt's houſe, and I did meet him in de village. Fort bien, ah, 'tis bon opportunité to make de love to his neice; I vil finiſh de affaire with coup d'eclat—Somebody come—Now for Mademoiſelle Norah. [*Exit into Father Luke's houſe.*

Enter

Enter Patrick.

Pat. Well, here I am, after all the dangers of war return'd to my native village, two years older than I went; not much wiser, up to the heart in love, and not a fixpence in my pocket. (*Darby fings without*) Isn't that Darby? 'tis indeed, and as foolifh as ever.

Enter Darby, *finging, ftops fhort, looks with furprize at* Patrick.

Dar. Is it——Pat? (*runs to him*) My dear boy you're welcome, you're welcome my dear boy.

Pat. Thank you Darby: how are all friends fince I left them.

Dar. Finely; except a cow of mine that died laft Michaelmas.

Pat. But how is my dear Norah?

Dar. As pretty as ever. I muftn't tell him of the Mounfeer that's about her houfe. (*afide*) 'Twas a fhame for you to turn foldier, and run away from her.

Pat. Cou'd I help it, when her ill-natur'd uncle refus'd me his confent, and fhe wou'dn't marry me without it.

Dar. Why Father Luke's very crofs indeed to us young lovers.—Eh, Pat, but let's look at you. Egad you make a tight little foldier enough; you'll have Norah: oh, if I thought I cou'd get Kathlane by turning foldier, I'd lift to-morrow.

Pat. Well, I'll introduce you to the Serjeant.

Dar. Ay, do, if you pleafe. I think I'd look

very

pretty in a red coat, ha, ha, ha! (*seems delighted with Patrick's drefs*) Let's fee how the hat and feather becomes me? (*takes off Patrick's hat, and difcovers a large fcar on his forehead*) What's that?

Pat. Only a wound I got in battle.

Dar. Hem, take your hat; I don't think regimentals wou'd become me at all.

Pat. How! ha, ha, ha! what terrified at a fcar, eh, Darby?

Dar. Me terrified! not I, I don't mind twenty fcars, only it looks fo conceited for a man to have a black patch upon his face; but how did you get that beauty fpot?

Pat. In my attempt to fave the life of an officer, I fell, and the bayonet of an American grenadier left me for dead, bleeding on the field.

Dar. Left for dead!

Pat. There was glory for you.

Dar. Hem! and fo they found you bleeding in your glory?

Pat. Come now, I'll introduce you to the Serjeant.

Dar. (*looks out*) Hem! yes, I'm coming, Sir. (*feems as if anfwering fomebody without*)

Pat. Oh, yonder is the Serjeant. (*looking out*) Where are you going?

Dar. To meet him. (*going the contrary way*) I'll be with you prefently, Sir. (*looks at Patrick*) Hem —glory—row de dow.   [*Exit.*

Pat. Ha, ha, ha! the fight of a wound is enough for poor Darby—but now to fee my fweet Norah, and then for a pitcher of friendfhip with my old companions.

AIR.—*Patrick.*

The wealthy fool with gold in ſtore,
  Will ſtill deſire to grow richer;
Give me but health, I aſk no more,
  My little girl, my friend, and pitcher.

    My friend ſo rare,
    My girl ſo fair,
With ſuch what mortal can be richer;
Poſſeſs'd of theſe, a fig for care,
My little girl, my friend and pitcher.

II.

From morning ſun, I'd never grieve,
  To toil, a Hedger, or a Ditcher;
If that when I come home at eve,
  I might enjoy my friend and pitcher.

My friend, &c.

III.

Tho' fortune ever ſhuns my door,
  (I know not what can thus bewitch her;)
With all my heart; can I be poor,
  With my ſweet girl, my friend and pitcher.

My friend, &c.

              [Exit into houſe:

SCENE II.

Inſide of FATHER LUKE's *Houſe.*

BAGATELLE *diſcover'd, ſpeaking at a chamber door.*

Bag. I wou'd only ſpeak von vord vit you. Ouvrez la porte, ma chere; do open de door, Mademoiſelle Norah.

              Nor.

Nor. (*within*) I requeſt, Sir, you'll go away.

Bag. Firſt give me de von little kiſs.

Nor. (*within*) Upon my word this is exceeding rude behaviour, and if my uncle finds you there, ſee what he'll ſay to you.

Bag. (*aſide*) Oh de Father Luke; begar he may be enragé—vel, I am going; Mademoiſelle Norah, I am going.

Pat. (*without*) Where is my charming Norah?

Bag. Ah, mal peſte! begar, I am all take. I vill hide. (*goes into a cloſet*)

Enter PATRICK.

Pat. Eh! all the doors open, and nobody at home. (*knocks at the chamber door*) Who's here?

Nor. (*within*) You're a very rude man, and I deſire you'll leave the houſe.

Pat. Leave the houſe! a kind reception after two year's abſence.

Nor. Sure I know that voice.

Enter NORAH.

My Patrick!

Pat. My dear, dear Norah!

Nor. If I was dear to you, ah Patrick, how cou'd you leave me?

Pat. And were you ſorry for my going?

Nor. Judge of my ſorrow at your abſence, by theſe tears of joy for your return.

Pat. My ſweet girl! this precious moment makes amends for all the dangers and fatigues I've ſuffer'd ſince our parting.

Bag. Ah, pauvre Bagatelle! (*aſide*)

Pat.

Pat. I heard a noife!

Nor. Oh heav'ns, if it fhou'd be my uncle, —what fhall I do? he's more averfe to our union than ever.—Hold, I'll run to the door.

Pat. And if you hear Father Luke coming up ftairs, I'll ftep in here. (*opens door, and difcovers Bagatelle*) Is this your forrow for my abfence, and tears for my return?

Bag. Begar Monfieur, I am forry for your return.

Nor. How unlucky!

Bag. Monfieur, votre ferviteur.

Pat. Shut up here with a rafcally Hair-dreffer!

Bag. Hair-dreffer! Monfieur, you fhall give me de fatisfaction; I vill challenge you, and I vill meet you vid——

Pat. With your Curling Irons.

Bag. Curling Irons! Ah, facre Dieu!

Pat. Hold your tongue, except you like to walk out of a window.

Bag. Monfieur, to oblige you, I vill valk out of de vindre, but I vou'd rather valk down ftairs: I'm not particular in dat point.

Pat. March Sirrah! or I'll cudgel you while I can hold a fplinter of Shelelah.

Bag. Cudgel! Monfieur, vill you take a pinch of fnuff?—non! oh den I put up my box, and bid you bon jour, ferviteur Mademoifelle Norah.
[*Exit.*

Pat. Ah, Norah! cou'd I have believed this of you?

Nor. Cou'd I have believ'd Patrick wou'd have harbour'd a thought to my difadvantage? —And can you think me falfe?

Pat.

Pat. If I do Norah, my heart is the only suf-
ferer.

DUET.

Pat. A Rofe tree full in bearing,
    Had fweet flowers fair to fee ;
One Rofe beyond comparing,
    For beauty attracted me.
Tho' eager once to win it,
    Lovely, blooming, frefh, and gay ;
I find a Canker in it,
    And now throw it far away.

Nor. How fine this morning early,
    All fun-fhiny, clear and bright ;
So late I lov'd you dearly,
    Tho' loft now each fond delight.
The clouds feem big with fhowers,
    Sunny beams no more are feen ;
Farewell ye happy hours,
    Your falfehood has chang'd the fcene.
                      [Exeunt feverally.

END OF THE FIRST ACT.

ACT II.

SCENE I.

The Country.

Enter PATRICK.

PATRICK.

AY, I'm but a common rank and file; it is not of this Frenchman I fhou'd be jealous: my Norah I find has given her heart to an officer—no matter.

AIR.—*Patrick.*

Why breathe fo rude, thou northern wind
    Be gentle unto me;
I lov'd a maiden moft unkind,
    No fairer fhall you fee:
Her vows were foft as weftern gale,
    Whilft flocks are penn'd in fold;
I thought fhe liften'd to my tale,
    She left me, ah! for Gold.

Full featly fexton with thy fpade,
    Oh make my bed a boon;
Yet tho' to reft is Patrick laid,
    Thy bells ring out this tune.

Beneath

Beneath this bank of tufted grafs,
   Ye faithful fwains be told,
Is laid the youth that lov'd the lafs,
   Who left him, ah! for Gold.

                              [Exit.

Enter DARBY.

Dar. Ho Pat! Paddy! Ay there he goes finging about the roads like a difcarded fowl; fo am I, but why fhou'd Kathleen like Dermot better nor I? Well, well, I'm fure I'm as—fhew me a compleater fellow—I can wreftle—I'm a good hurler—I can cudgel—I can play upon the pipes, and I can dance—(*dances*) and I can—fhew me a compleater fellow, that's all —(*Kathlane fings without*) Oh, here fhe comes.

Enter KATHLANE.

Kath. What are you there, foolifh Darby?

Dar. Now am I puzzled whether to take a friendly glafs of punch with Patrick yonder, or ftay here and kifs you.

Kath. So betwixt my lips and a glafs of punch, you're the afs between two bundles of——

Dar. Now I'm an afs—you're a bundle of fweet—fince nobody's by I'll make hay while the fun fhines—kifs me Kathlane and then I'll be in clover.

Kath. No, I'll not take fuch a rake as you when I go a hay-making, I affure you.

Dar. See there now!

Kath. Ay, and fee there again now, you know Darby I'am an heirefs, and fo take your anfwer; you're no match for me.

                              Dar.

Dar. An heirefs! Why tho' your father, old Jorum that kept the Harp and Crown, left you well enough in the world, as a body may fay, yet—

Kath. Well enough, you difparaging fellow! Did'nt my poor father leave me a fortune of eleven pounds—a barrel of ale upon draught— the dappled mare, befides the furniture of the whole houfe, which 'prais'd to the matter of thirty eight fhillings! Well enough indeed!

Dar. (*foothing.*) Nay, but Kathlane—

Kath. (*Paffionate.*) Well enough! And did'nt he leave me the bald filley, you puppy?

Dar. Oh, now fhe's got upon the bald filley— the devil ca'n't take her down—

Kath. A pretty thing to fay to a girl of my fortune.

AIR.—*Kathlane.*

Dermot's welcome as the May,
Chearful, handfome, and good natur'd;
Foolifh Darby, get away,
Aukward, clumfy, and ill-featur'd:
Dermot prattles pretty chat;
Darby gapes like any oven:
Dermot's neat from fhoe to hat;
Darby's but a dirty floven.
        Lout looby,
        Silly booby,
Come no more to me courting:
Was my deareft Dermot here,
        All is joy and gay fporting.

II.

Dermot's teeth are white as egg,
Breath as fweet as fugar-candy:
Then he's fuch a handfome leg;
Darby's knocky-kneed and bandy:

Dermot

Dermot walks a comely pace;
Darby like an Aſs goes ſtumping:
Dermot dances with ſuch grace:
Darby's dance is only jumping.
Lout looby,
Silly booby, &c.

[*Exit.*

Dar. So I muſt fall in love, I wiſh I'd firſt fell in the river; Oh dear! (*ſighs*)

Bag. (*without*) Oh, Monſieur Darby!

Dar. Lord this is Mr. Bag and tail the Monſieur.

Enter BAGATELLE.

Bag. Ah, ha! Monſieur Darby, begar I did look all about and I could no find you.

Dar. That's becauſe I'm ſo wrap'd in love.

Bag. Monſieur Pat ſhall fight a me.

Dar. Oh, you're going to fight Pat.

Bag. Oui, and dis is the deadly challenge, de lettee de mort.

Dar. Oh, what you'll leather him more.

Bag. Dis ſoldier Patrick did affront me before Mademoiſelle Norah, and I vil have de ſatisfaction—Begar I vill kill ſoldier Pat, and you ſall be my friend.

Dar. Can't you as well kill Dermot, and then you'll be my friend—but why kill Pat?

Bag. Ce Monſieur Pat, quel Barbare!

Dar. Oh, becauſe you're a barber.

Bag. Voud you affront me?

Dar. Not I.

Bag. You vil be my friend, if you vil give dis challenge to Monſieur Patrick.

Dar. Give it me—by the Lord Harry, man, he ſhall have it.

VOL. I. P P *Bag.*

Bag. I vill not truft dat Lord Harry's man—
Give it yourfelf,

Dar. Well, I will.

Bag. Dere it is—Le Duc's coachman did write
it for me as he is Englis.

Dar. Let's fee. (*Opens it and reads.*) " Sir,
" this comes hopping," " Hopping ! I'll run
all the way if that will do—" that you're in good
" health, as I am at this prefent writing—I tell
" you what friend, tho' you think yourfelf a
" great officer, you don't make me walk out
" of a window, and this comes to let you know
" I'll have Norah in fpite of you, I'll be damn'd
" if I don't, and moreover than that, meet me
" in the Elm Grove, at Seven in the Evening,
" when you muft give me fatisfaction, but not
" with curling irons, till then I'm yours, as in
" duty bound."

Bag. Oui, dat is de etiquette of the challenge,
I put no name for fear of de law.

Dar. It is not directed, but Pat fhall have it.

Bag. Fort bien.

Dar. I know Pat is Norah's fweetheart—but
how did he affront you?

Bag. Affront, begar he did take off his hat
and make me a low bow.

Dar. That was an affront indeed.

Bag. And den fays he, Monfieur, I fhould be
much oblige to you if you vil do me the honour
to valk out of the window.

Dar. Well you could not do lefs, he was fo
civil.

Bag. Ah ha, Monfieur, fays I, begar I vil
make you walk down ftairs, vid dat I did lift
my leg and give him one blow dat did kick him
from de top to de bottom.

Dar.

Dar. You kickt him down ſtairs! and for that he muſt give you ſatisfaction.

Bag. Dat is it,—Monſieur Darby, I voud not truſt de upper domeſtiques at the Dukes, nor employ de lower ſervants upon dis affair of honour—You muſt come to de fight vid me—I have de piſtols.

Dar. Piſtols!

Bag. Oui, you ſall be my ſeconde.

Dar. Piſtols! Second—Eh, coud'nt I be third or fourth?

Bag. Ah, Monſieur, you are wrong, toute autre choſe.

Dar. Oh, I muſt get two other ſhoes.

(looking at his feet.

Bag. Non—Vel, Monſieur Darby, now I have ſent my challenge, I am ready in de duel to decide de point of honour, and ſo I vil go—bruſh my Maſter's coat.   [*Exit.*

Dar. Piſtols! I don't much like giving this challenge to Pat—he's a devil of a fellow ſince he turned Soldier; the boy at the alehouſe ſhall give it him, for as Pat bid Monſieur walk out of a window, he may deſire me to walk up the chimney.   [*Exit.*

SCENE II.

Enter NORAH.

Nor. No where can I find him, and I fear my uncle will miſs me from home.—My letter muſt have convinc'd him how he wrong'd me by his ſuſpiçions.

AIR

AIR.—*Norah.*

Dearest youth why thus delay,
    And leave me here a mourning;
Ceaseless tears while thou'rt away,
    Must flow for thy returning.
Winding brooks if by your side,
    My careless love is straying;
Gently murmur, softly chide,
    And say for him I'm staying.

II.

Meads and Groves I've wander'd o'er,
    In vain dear youth to find thee;
Come, ah come and part no more,
    Nor leave thy love behind thee.
On yon green hill I'll sit till night,
    My careful watch still keeping;
But if he then not bless my sight,
    I'll lay me down a weeping.

He comes—My Patrick!

Enter PATRICK.

Pat. My dear Norah, excuse my delay; but so many old acquaintances in the village.

Nor. You had my letter?

Pat. Yes, and I'm asham'd of my folly, to be jealous of such a Baboon too.

Nor. Aye, he'd be soon discharg'd if his master Capt. Fitzroy knew of his presumption.

Pat. Ah, Norah, I feel more terror at that one Captain's name, than I did at the sight of a whole army of enemies, drawn up in battle array against me.

Nor. My dearest Patrick only be constant, love me as I think you do, and mine is fixt on
                                                        such

such a basis of permanent affection, as never to be shaken.

Pat. And can you prefer a poor foot soldier to a Captain, my sweet Norah?

Nor. Ah, my Patrick, you may be only a private in the army, but you're a Field Officer here, (*lays her hand to her heart*)

Pat. Charming, generous girl!

AIR.—*Patrick.*

Tho' Leixslip is proud of it's close shady bowers,
  It's clear falling waters and murmuring cascades,
Its groves of fine myrtle, its beds of sweet flowers,
  Its lads so well dress'd and its neat pretty maids.
As each his own village must still make the most of,
  In praise of dear Carton I hope I'm not wrong;
Dear Carton containing what kingdoms may boast of,
  'Tis Norah, dear Norah the theme of my song.

II.

Be gentlemen fine with their spurs and nice boots on,
  Their horses to start on the Currah Kildare,
  Or dance at a ball with their sunday new suits on,
Lac'd waistcoat, white gloves and their neat powder'd
    hair.
Poor Pat while so blest in his mean humble station,
  For gold or for acres he never shall long;
One sweet smile can give him the wealth of a nation,
  From Norah, dear Norah, the theme of my song.

Enter FITZROY *behind in a plain scarlet frock and round hat.*

Fit. (*aside*) My little country wife in company with a common soldier!

Nor. Don't fail to come to our house as you promis'd, for at that time my uncle will be down at Dermot's.—I've a notion 'twill be a
                                    match

match between him and Kathleen, my uncle's her guardian—Adieu my Patrick. You'll come early. (*parting tenderly*)   [*Exit Norah.*

Pat. Happy Dermot! his Kathleen had not charms to attract the attention of this gentleman, but becaufe Norah is moft beautiful, Patrick is moft unhappy.

Fitz. (*afide*) This is a timely and fortunate difcovery—If I had married her, I fhould have been in a hopeful way—I'll endeavour to conceal my emotions and fpeak to this fellow. (*advancing*) A pretty girl you've got there, brother foldier.

Pat. She's handfome, Sir.

Fitz. You feem to be well with her—eh?

Pat. (*fighs*) But without her.—

Fitz. Oh, then you think you fhall be without her?

Pat. Yes, Sir.

Fitz. What parts you?

Pat. My poverty.

Fitz. Why, fhe don't feem to be rich.

Pat. No, Sir, but my rival is.

Fitz. Oh, you've a rival?

Pat. I have, Sir.

Fitz. Now for a character of myfelf. (*afide*) Some rich rafcal, I fuppofe.

Pat. Sir, I envy his riches only, becaufe they give him a fuperior claim to my Norah; and for your other epithet, I'm fure he don't deferve it.

Fitz. How fo?

Pat. Becaufe he's an officer, and therefore a man of honor.

Fitz. It's a pity, my friend, that you're not an officer, you feem to know fo well what an officer fhould be—pray, have you been in any action?

Pat.

Pat. I have feen fome fervice in America, Sir.

Fitz. Carolina ?

Pat. Yes, Sir ; I was at the croffing of Beattie's Ford.

Fitz. (*with emotion*) Indeed !

Pat. I'd an humble fhare too, in our victory of the 15th March at Guilford, under our brave officers, Webfter, Leflie, and Tarleton.

Fitz Were you in the action at Beattie's Ford ?

Pat. Here's my witnefs, Sir. (*takes off his hat*) I receiv'd this wound in the refcue of an officer who, having fall'n, muft have perifh'd by a determin'd bayonet.

Fitz. By heav'n ! the very foldier that fav'd my life. (*afide*) then I fuppofe he rewarded you handfomely ?

Pat. I look't for no reward, Sir.—I fought—'twas my duty as a foldier; to protect a fall'n man was but an office of humanity.—Good morning to your honor.—

Fitz. Where are you going now my friend ?

Pat. To abandon my country for ever.

Fitz. (*afide*) Poor fellow !—But, my lad, I think you'd beft keep the field, for if the girl likes you, fhe'll certainly prefer you to your wealthy rival.

Pat. And for that reafon I'll refign her to him. As I love her, I'll leave her to the good fortune fhe merits ; 'twould be only love to myfelf fhould I involve her in my indigence.

Fitz. You'll take your leave of her tho' ?

Pat. No, Sir—I told her I'd meet her at her uncle's, but I think it better even to break a promife, than expofe her to the pangs of a feparation, which, without felf-flattery, I know muft grieve her tender heart.

Fitz.

Fitz. Well, but my lad, take my advice and fee the girl once again before you go.

Pat. Sir, I'm oblig'd to you—you muſt be a good natur'd gentleman, and I'll take your advice.—Then I will venture to ſee my Norah once more, for if even Father Luke turns me out of his houſe, I ſhan't be much diſappointed.

AIR.—*Patrick.*

Farewell my dear Norah, adieu to ſweet peace,
Ah, ſay cruel fate, when my ſorrow ſhall ceaſe ;
I fear'd neither muſket nor cannon nor ſword,
Farewell is my terror, for death's in that word !
Yet farewell to Norah, adieu to ſweet peace,
Ah, ſay, cruel fate when my ſorrow ſhall ceaſe.

[*Exit Patrick.*

Fitz. What a noble ſpirit—there let the embroider'd epaulet take a cheap leſſon of bravery, honor and generoſity from ſixpence a day and worſted lace.

Enter Boy *with a letter.*

Boy. Pray, Sir, are you the man in the red coat ?

Fitz Ha, ha, ha ! Why, yes, my little hero, I think I am the man in the red coat.

Boy. Then Darby deſir'd me to give you that.

[*Exit unperceived.*

Fitz. (*opening the letter*) Darby ! a new correſpondent—(*reads*) " This comes hopping,——duty bound."—A curious challenge, and pray my little friend, where is this Mr. Darby. (*looks round*) Eh ! why the herald is off—my Norah ſeems to have plenty of lovers here—but how has my attachment tranſpir'd ? Seven o'clock in the

the Elmgrove—Well, we fhall fee what fort of Hero Mr. Darby is.—This charming girl! A pretty fnare mafter Cupid has led me into. How unlucky, to erect fo fair a manfion on another man's foundation !

AIR.—*Fitzroy.*

Thou little eheat, return my heart,
  For if you've loft your own,
'Tis but at beft a roguifh art,
To coax poor me with mine to part
  And yours for ever gone,

Hence ye graces, fmiles, and loves.
  Tender figh and falling tear,
Venus harnefs all thy doves,
  Cupid quit thy manfion here,

Heal my wound and footh my pain,
  Rofy Bacchus chear my foul ;
If the urchin comes again,
  Drown him in thy flowing bowl.

[*Exit.*

SCENE III.

Outfide of DERMOT'S *Cottage.*

Enter FATHER LUKE *and* DERMOT.

F. Luke. Well now Dermot, I've come to your houfe with you—what is this bufinefs ?

Der. Oh, Sir, I ll tell you.

F. Luke. Unburthen your confcience to me, child—fpeak freely—you know I'm your fpiritual confeffor, fo I muft examine into the ftate of your foul—tell me—have you tapp'd the barrel of ale yet ?

Der. That I have, Sir, and you shall taste it.

[*Exit.*

F. Luke. Aye, he wants to come round me for my ward Kathlane.

Re-enter DERMOT *with Ale.*

My dear child, what's that?

Der. Only your favorite brown jug, Sir.——

F. Luke. (*taking it*) Now, child, why will you do these things? (*drinks*)

Der. I'll prime him well before I mention Kathlane.——Its a hard heart that a sup can't soften. (*aside*)

F. Luke. Boy, what signifies your jug, you know I don't think of it without a tender song——you're a country lad and a shepherd, and a lover.

Der. All that I surely am, Sir.

AIR.——DERMOT.

My sheep feast on flowers, and fine is their wool,
My dog he is faithful my bottle is full:
And green is the pasture, and blue is the sky,
And Aura soft whispers in amorous sigh.
A note from my pipe is the joy of the plain,
That couples in dancing the nymph and the swain.
Tho' smiles of bright summer encircle my year,
Alas! all is nothing---Kathlena's not here!

Gay Shelah presents me a bowl of sweet cream,
Fond Oonah requests I'd interpret her dream;
For saving two lambs that fell into the brook,
Each wove me a chaplet to hang on my crook.
All mine are the meadows that round I behold,
And mine are the flocks that at sun-set I fold,
My neighbours are cheerful, their friendship sincere,
Alas! all is nothing---Kathlena's not here;

[*Exit into the House.*

Enter

Enter DARBY.

Dar. How do you do, Father Luke ?

F. Luke. Go away Darby, you're a rogue.

Dar. Father Luke, confent that I fhall marry Kathlane.

F. Luke. You marry Kathlane, you reprobate !

Dar. Give her to me, and I'll give your rev'rence a fheep.

F. Luke. Oh, well, I always thought you were a boy that woud come to good—a fheep !—You fhall have Kathlane—You've been very wicked.

Dar. Not I, Sir.

F. Luke. What ! an't I your prieft, and know what wickednefs is—but repent it and marry.

Dar. Yes, Sir, I'll marry and repent it.

AIR.—*F. Luke.*

You know I'm your Prieft and your confcience is mine,
But if you grow wicked it's not a good fign,
So leave off your raking and marry a Wife
And then my dear Darby you're fettled for life.
  Sing Ballynomona Oro,
  A good merry wedding for me.

II

The banns being publifh'd to Chapel we go,
The Bride and the Bride-groom in coats white as fnow,
So modeft her air and fo fheepifh your look,
You out with your ring and I pull out my book.
  Sing, Ballynomona Oro,
  A good merry wedding for me.

I thumb

III.

I thumb out the place and I then read away,
She blufhes at love, and fhe whifpers obey,
You take her dear hand to have and to hold,
I fhut up my Book and I pocket your gold.
                    Sing Ballynomona Oro,
                    The fnug little Guinea for me.

IV.

The neighbours wifh joy to the Bridegroom and Bride,
The piper before us, you march fide by fide,
A plentiful dinner gives mirth to each face,
The piper plays up, myfelf I fay grace.
                    Sing Ballynomona Oro,
                    A good wedding dinner for me.

You fhall have Kathlane and here fhe comes.
Dar. (*Bowing.*) Thank you, Sir. [*Both retire.*

Enter KATHLANE, *with a bird in a Cage.*

AIR.—*Kathlane.*

Sweet bird I caught thee in thy neft
And fondling plac'd thee in my breaft,
        When thou wert helplefs, weak and young,
Unfledg'd thou couds't not wing the air,
I cherifh'd thee with tender care,
        Be grateful pay me with a fong.

Ah what to thee are groves and fields,
The tempting gifts gay Flora yields,
        Why pant and flutter to be free ?
Ten thoufand dangers are abroad,
Then in thy fmall, but fafe abode,
        Content and cheerful fing for me.

                                    Thou

Thou thinks't not of the various ills
The wintry blaft that often kills,
 I'd fain thy little life prolong,
The ruffian Hawk prefcribes it's date,
The levell'd gun is charg'd with fate,
 Here brave them in thy warbling fong.

Oh, Father, is Dermot within, Sir ?

F. Luke. Kathlane, don't think of Dermot.—
To her man, put your beft leg foremoft.

Dar. I don't know which is my beft leg.

F. Luke. Go—(*makes figns to Darby.*)

Dar. Oh, I muft go and give her a kifs.
(*kiffes her.*) He, he, he !—what fweet lips !
he, he, he !—Speak for me, Sir.

F. Luke. Hem !—Child Kathlane—Is the fheep
fat ?

Dar. As bacon!

F. Luke. Child, this boy will make you a good
hufband, won't you Darby ?

Dar. Yes, Sir.

Kath. Indeed Father Luke, I'll have nobody
but Dermot.

F. Luke. I tell you child, Dermot's an ugly
man and a bad chriftian.

Enter DERMOT.

Dar. Yes Dermot's a bad man and an ugly
chriftian.

F. Luke. Come here Dermot, take your mug,
you empty fellow, *(throws it away)* I am going
to marry Kathlane here, and you muft give her
away.

Der. Give her away ! I muft have her firft, and
it was to afk your confent that I—

F. Luke. Fh, what ! you marry her ! no fuch
thing—put it out of your head.

Der.

Der. If that's the cafe, Father Luke, the two fheep that I intended as a prefent for you, I'll drive to the fair to-morrow and get drunk with the money. [*Going.*

F. Luke. (*paufes.*) Hey, two fheep! (*afide.*) Come back here; it's a fin to get drunk.—Darby if you've nothing to do, get about your bufinefs.

Dar. Sir!

F. Luke. Dermot, Child! Is'nt it this evening I am to marry you to Kathlane?

Dar. Him! why lord Sir, it's me that you're to marry to her.

F. Luke. You, you ordinary fellow!

Dar. Yes Sir, you know I'm to give you—

F. Luke. (*Apart to Dermot.*) Two fheep? (*loud to Darby.*) You don't marry Kathlane.

Dar. No!

F. Luke. No, 'tis two to one againft you. So get away Darby.

Kath. and Der. Aye, get away Darby.

F. Luke. (*To Kath. and Der.*) Children, I expect Capt. Fitzroy at my houfe for my niece Norah and I'll couple you all as foon as I clap my thumb upon matrimony.

QUARTETTE.—*F. Luke, Dermot, Darby and Kathlane.*

Kath. to Der.	You the point may carry If a while you tarry.
To Dar.	But for you I tell you true, No, you I'll never marry.
Cho.	You the point, &c.
Der.	Care our fouls difowning, Punch our forrows drowning, Laugh and love, And ever prove Joys, joys our wifhes crowning.
Cho.	Care our, &c.

Dar.

Der. To the church I'll hand her,
  (*Offers to take her hand, she refuses.*)
  Then thro' the world I'll wander,
  I'll fob and figh
  Until I die,
  A poor forfaken Gander.
Cho.   To the church, &c.

F. Luke. Each pious Prieft fince Mofes,
  One mighty truth difclofes,
  You're never vext,
  If this the text
  Go fuddle all your nofes.
Cho.   Each pious, &c.
                          [*Exeunt.*

SCENE IV.

A Grove.

Enter FITZROY.

Fitz. Who can this challenger be ? Some hay-maker perhaps meet me with a reaping hook, ha, ha, ha!

Bag. (*without.*) Venez ici.

Fitz. (*Looking out.*) Eh, my man Bagatelle.—Ah, the officious puppy I fuppofe has heard of the affair, and is come to prevent mifchief.

Bag. (*Without.*) Come along Monfieur Darby.

Fitz. Darby ! the name the boy mentioned—Let's fee.   [*Retires.*

                          Enter

Enter DARBY, *with a Piſtol, and* BAGATELLE,
with a Sword.

Dar. Mr. Bag and Tail.

Bag. Well?

Dar. When I fall, as to be fure I ſhall—that is, if Pat's ſecond is as wicked as I am, bring my corpſe to Dermot and Kathlane's wedding.

Bag. I vil Monſieur Darby.

Dar. But do you think I may be kill'd?

Bag. Very like.

Dar. Hem!—He's not here—we'll go home.

Bag. Ah, ha! firſt I vill fight him vid de piſtol and den I vil fight him vid de ſword.

Dar. I'd rather you'd fight him with the ſword firſt.

Bag. Pourquoi—why ſo?

Dar. Becauſe I long to ſee a little ſword play, and if you ſhould be killed with the piſtols, then I'm diſappointed.

Fitz. (*aſide.*) Can Bagatelle be the challenger?

Dar. When Pat ſhoots I get behind you.----
(*ſtands at his back*) You're curſed thin, one might as well ſtand behind a pitch foik; I w'ſh you were fatter.

Bag. Ah, Diable! wou'd you have me Dutchman?

Dar. Indeed I wou'd upon this occaſion---I'd rather fight behind a Dutch Weaver than a French Churchwarden.

Bag. Soldier Pat did bid me valk out of de vinder.---Ah, ha, begar I vil make him valk out of de vorld.

Fitz. (*Advances.*) Servant Gentlemen.

Bag. Mon Maitre!

Fitz.

Fitz. So you fend challenges, you rafcal.
(*fhews letter to Darby*)

Dar. Me, Sir! Not I, Sir—Oh! yes, Sir, I—
No, Sir, I got it from Monfieur Bag and Tail.
(*frightened*)

Bag. (*afide*) Ah diantre!

Fitz. (*to Bagatelle*) Had you the impudence
to write fuch a letter as this?

Bag. Non, Monfieur—the Duke's coachman.

Fitz. Coachman, firrah!

Bag. Oui, Monfieur—I vil tell your Honor all
touchant cet affaire. Sir, I was—

Dar. Hold your jabbering—I'll tell the whole
ftory in three words. Sir, you muft know,
Pat, the foldier—No—Monfieur Bag and Tail—
was—Father Luke's houfe—come up ftairs—
no—Norah bid him—fays Pat, fays he—(*to
Bagatelle*) What did he fay? Oh, fhe fhut the
door—out of the window: and before Pat could
—no—after—how was it? (*to Bagatelle*)

Bag. Oui, dat vas de whole affair.

Dar. Yes, Sir, that was the whole affair.

Fitz. Upon my word, very clearly explain'd.

Dar. Yes, I didn't go to fchool for nothing.

Fitz. I find my little Norah is the object of
univerfal gallantry. (*afide*)

Bag. Ah, Monfieur.

Fitz. Begone, firrah; and if ever I find you
concern'd in letters of this kind again, you get a
lettre de catchet.

Bag. Ah malheureux! [*Exit.*

Dar. (*calling after him*) Yes, Monfieur, you'd
better ftick to the curling irons.

Fitz. Yes, my friend, and you had better
ftick to your flail and fpade than meddle with
fword and piftol. None but gentlemen fhou'd

have privilege to murder one another in an honorable way; but, when duelling thus defcends, let them be afham'd of a practice, the fatal confequences of which precludes him from hope of mercy who dies in the commiffion of a premeditated crime, and delivers the survivor to the fharpeft pains of remórfe. (*going*)

Dar. One word, Sir, if you pleafe.

Fitz. (*returning*) Well, my honeft friend!

Dar. Now, Sir, Kathlane's quite loft, there's one thing troubles me; and I'll leave it to you which of the two, Dermot or I, is the prettieft boy for it?

Fitz. Ha, ha, ha! Stupid fcoundrel! [*Exit.*

Dar. Stupid fcoundrel! You a captain! Halloo, corporal! (*calls after Fitzroy*)

Re-enter FITZROY.

Fitz. (*threat'ning*) How!

Dar. (*turning and calling to the other fide*) I fay you, corporal. [*Exit Fitzroy.*

Dar. Such a fwaggerer! Aye, I muft go to town, and learn to talk to thefe people.

AIR.—*Darby.*

Since Kathlane has prov'd fo untrue,
Poor Darby, ah! what can you do?
No longer I'll ftay here a clown,
But fell off, and gallop to town:
I'll drefs, and I'll ftrut with an air,
The barber fhall frizzle my hair.

II.

In Dublin I'll cut a great dafh;
But how for to compafs the cafh?

A:

At gaming, perhaps. I may win,
With cards I can take the flats in:
Or trundle falfe dice, and they're nick'd;
If found out, I fhall only be kick'd.

III.

But, firft, for to get a great name
A duel eftablifh my fame;
To my man then a challenge I'll write,
But, firft, I'll take care he won't fight:
We'll fwear not to part 'till we fall,
Then fhoot with our powder, and---the devil a ball.

[*Exit.*

SCENE V; *and laft.*

Infide of FATHER LUKE's *Houfe.*

F. Luke. (*within*) Aye, I'll teach you to run after foldiers.

Nor. (*within*) Dear, Sir!

Enter FATHER LUKE *and* NORAH.

F. Luke. Come along. If you won't have Captain Fitzroy you go to Boulogne. Pat, the foldier, indeed! I'll fend you to a convent—I will by my function.

Nor. Sir, I am contented.

F. Luke. Contented! Very fine. So you put me into a paffion, and now you're contented. Go—get in there, Mrs. Knapfack, (*puts her in, and locks the door*) (*tapr at the door with the key*) confent to marry Captain Fitzroy, or there y ..
ftay 'till I fhip you for France.

Enter

Enter FITZROY.

Fitz. Eh, Father Luke! Who's going to France?

F. Luke. Only a young lady here within, Sir, that's a little refractory. She won't marry you, Sir.

Fitz. Refuse my hand! Well, that I did not expect. But do you resign her to me, Sir?

F. Luke. There, with that key, I deliver up my authority. (*gives key*) And now, if I can find Mr. Patrick, her soldier, he goes to the county gaol for a vagabond. A jade! to lose the opportunity of making herself a lady, and me a bishop.   [*Exit.*

Fitz. Oh! here is her soldier. Now, " I must seem cruel only to be kind."

Enter PATRICK.

Pat. Well, Sir, by your advice I have ventur'd here, like a spy, into the enemy's camp.

Fitz (*sternly*) Pray, my friend, were you ever brought to the halberts?

Pat. Sir!

Fitz. How came you absent from your regiment? have you a furlough?

Pat. (*confus'd*) Not about me, Sir.

Fitz. I have the honor to bear the King's commission, and am oblig'd to take you up for a deserter.

Pat. Sir, it was a reliance on your honor and good nature that trapann'd me here; therefore, I hope you won't exert an authority which I had no suspicion, at that time, you had a right to.

Fitz.

Fitz. No talk, Sir; it was for the good of the
fervice I trapann'd you hither, as you call it.
I've a proper perfon prepar'd here, into whofe
cuftody I fhall deliver you. (*unlocks the door*)

Pat, What a cruel piece of treachery! (*afide*)

Fitz. (*prefenting Norah*) Since you rejeĉt me,
madam, here's one that will know how to deal
with you.

Nor. My Patrick!

Pat. Oh, Norah! if this is real, let's kneel
and thank our benefaĉtor.

Fitz. No, Patrick, you were my deliverer;
I am that very officer whofe life you fav'd at
Beatti's Ford, and the identical Captain Fitzroy who wou'd have depriv'd you of a treafure I
now deliver to you with joy, as the reward of
your generofity, valour, and conftancy.

F. Luke. (*without*) No, I can't find the run-
away-rafcal.

Pat. Your uncle!

Nor. Oh, heavens!

Fitz. Don't be alarm'd.

Enter FATHER LUKE, DERMOT, DARBY, *and*
KATHLANE.

F. Luke. What's here! Patrick! Dermot and
Darby, lay hold of him.

Der. Not I.

Dar. I'm no conftable.

F. Luke. I fay take him. The ferjeant fhall
lay hold of him.

Dar. Why, Sir, the white ferjeant has laid
hold of him.

Fitz. Dear Sir, don't be fo violent againft a
young man that you'll prefently marry to your
niece.

F. Luke.

F. Luke. Me!

Fitz. Don't you wiſh to be a biſhop?

F. Luke. A fine road to bring a foot ſoldier into my family; then a halbert muſt be my croſier, and my mitre a grenadiers cap, a common ſoldier indeed!

Fitz. He's no longer ſo, I have a commiſſion to diſpoſe of, and I cannot ſet a higher value on it, than by beſtowing it on one ſo worthy.

F. Luke. An officer! Oh, that's another thing.

Dar. Pat an officer! I'll liſt to-morrow in ſpite of the black patch.

Pat. Sir, tho' it's a vain attempt, my ſweet Norah and I ſhall endeavour to deſerve your patronage and goodneſs.

Kath. (to Norah.) My dear Norah, I wiſh you joy.

Dar. (apart to Kathlane) How dare you make ſo free with an officer's lady?

F. Luke. But Captain, why do you give up my Niece?

Fitz. Sir, the Captain thought himſelf unworthy of her, when he found ſuperior merit in the poor Soldier.

FINALE.

Fitz.	More true felicity I ſhall find
	When thoſe are join'd, *(to Pat. and Nor.)*
	By fortune kind;
	How pleaſing to me,
	So happy to ſee,
	Such merit and virtue united.
Nor.	No future ſorrows can grieve us,
	If you will pleaſe to forgive us;
	To each kind friend
	We lowly bend, *(curtſies)*
	Your pardon---with joy we're delighted.

Pat.

Pat. With my commiffion, yet deareft life,
        My charming wife,
          When drum and fife
        Shall beat up to arms,
        The plunder your charms,
      In love your poor foldier you'll find me.

Kath. Love my petition has granted,
        I get the dear lad that I wanted,
          Lefs pleas'd with a duke,
          When good Father Luke
      To my own little Dermot has join'd me.

Dar. You impudent huffey, a pretty rate
          Of love you prate,
          But hark ye, Kate,
        Your dear little lad
        Will find that his pad
      Has got a nice---kick in her gallop.

F. Luke. Now, Darby, upon my falvation,
        You merit excommunication,
          In love but agree,
          And fhortly you'll fee
      In marriage I'll foon tie you all up.

Der. The devil a bit o'me cares a bean,
          For neat and clean
          We'll both be feen,
        Myfelf and my lafs
        Next Sunday at mafs,
      And there we'll be coupled for ever.

Pat. The laurel I've won in the field, Sirs,
        Yet now in a garden I yield, Sirs,
          Nor think it a fhame
          Your mercy to claim,
      Your mercy's my fword and my fhield, Sirs.

THE END.

MODERN ANTIQUES;

OR,

THE MERRY MOURNERS.

IN TWO ACTS.

PERFORMED AT THE

THEATRE-ROYAL, COVENT-GARDEN,

IN 1789.

DRAMATIS PERSONÆ.

Cockletop, ... Mr. QUICK.
Frank, ... Mr. MUNDEN.
Hearty, ... Mr. WILSON.
Joey, ... Mr. BLANCHARD.
Napkin, ... Mr. CUBITT.
Thomas, ... Mr. THOMPSON.
John, ... Mr. BLURTON.

Mrs. Cockletop, ... Mrs. MATTOCKS.
Mrs. Camomile, ... Miſs. CHAPMAN.
Belinda, ... Mrs. HARLOWE.
Flounce, ... Mrs. ROCK.
Nan, ... Mrs. WELLS.
Betty, ...

SCENE, *London*.

MODERN ANTIQUES;

OR,

THE MERRY MOURNERS.

A C T I.

S C E N E I.

Mrs. Camomile's *House.*

Enter Mrs. Camomile *and* Betty.

Mrs. Camomile.

Betty, any body here, fince?

Bet. No, Madam, but here's a ftrange Servant.

Mrs. Cam. True, Mrs. Cockletop defired me as I paffed along Charing-Crofs, to enquire for one for her at the Regifter-office.—Ha, ha, ha! She's too fine a lady to look after thefe things herfelf.

Bet. Walk up, young man. [*Exit Betty.*

s s 2   *Enter*

Enter Joey.

Joey. Sarvant. (*nods*)

Mrs. Cam. Quite a ruſtic! How long have you been in Town?

Joey Our Town?

Mrs. Cam. London.

Joey. I thought as how you meant our Town. I com'd from Yerkſop, in the county of Nor-folk, to get a place.

Mrs. Cam. Your name?

Joey. What of it?

Mrs. Cam. What is it?

Joey. Oh, my name is Joey; but volks call'd me Mr. Joey all the way up, thof I com'd upon the Coach roof; for as it's near Chriſtmas time, all the inſide paſſengers were Turkeys. I quitted our village in a huff with one Nan Holliday, my ſweetheart; cauſe why, ſhe got jealous and ſaucy given.

Mrs. Cam. The wages that this Lady gives to her footboy, are eight Guineas a year.

Joey. Guineas! that wo'n't do I muſt have eight Pounds.

Mrs. Cam. Well, if you inſiſt upon pounds, ha, ha, ha!

Joey. Oh, I'm hired. (*lays his hat and ſtick on the table*)

Mrs. Cam. You can give and take a meſſage?

Joey. Yes, ſure.

(*A loud Knocking without.*)

Mrs. Cam. Then let's ſee? Run.

Joey. Where?

Mrs. Cam. To the door, you blockhead.

Joey. (*goes to the room door and ſtands*) Well, I be's at the door—What now?

Mrs. Cam. Open the Street door.

Joey. Oh! (*going*) Here comes a Lady.

Mrs. Cam. Come up when you hear the bell.

Joey. Thefe gentlefolks don't moind what trouble they give a poor zarvant man. 　　　 [*Exit.*

Mrs. Cam. Belinda!

Enter BELINDA.

Bel. My dear friend! I've quitted Southampton Boarding-fchool, without leave tho'.

Mrs. Cam. My fweet girl, I'm very glad to fee you; but is this a prudent ftep?

Bel. To be fure, when I was kept there fo long againft my will, by my aunt.

Mrs. Cam. Ah Belinda, confefs the truth: wasn't it to fee your uncle's nephew Frank, that you have fcamper'd up to town?

Bel. Ha, ha, ha! 'Pon my honor, you're a witch: but fuppofe fo, why not? you and I were fchool-fellows t'other day, yet, here you're married: but, apropos, how is your hufband?

Mrs. Cam. The Doctor is well.

Bel. You're already happy with the man you love, while I'm kept at a boarding-fchool; when I am able, even to teach my dancing-mafter.

Mrs. Cam. Why, my dear Belinda, fince your laft letter, I've been planning fchemes, how to make you happy with the man you love.

Bel. My good creature, do tell me?

Mrs. Cam. You know if your uncle Mr. Cockletop's tooth but aches, he fancies he'll die directly, if he hasn't my hufband Dr. Camomile's advice; he's the grand oracle of his health, the Barometer and Thermometer of his animal fyftem. Now, as the Doctor is at Winchefter on

a vifit

a vifit to fome of his College chums, and w'on't
leave his good orthodox bottle of Old Port to
vifit him here in London; he fhall vifit the Doctor at Winchefter, if we can but get your Uncle
to leave town, on that hangs my grand fcheme
for the eftablifhment of you and Frank.—Your
Aunt's maid Mrs. Flounce, and Mr. Napkin the
butler, are my confederates.

Bel. Oh, charming! but I muft know it tho',

Enter JOEY, (*ftands fome time*).

Joey. Well?

Bel. And well.

Joey. I'm com'd up as you bid me.

Mrs. Cam. But you fhou'dn't have come 'till
you heard the bell.

Joey, And, wounds! it's wringing yonder
enough to pull the Church-fteeple down.

Mrs. Cam. and Bel. Ha, ha, ha!

Mrs. Cam. Joey, carry thofe to your new
mafter's. (*to Belinda*) Plants and fimples, cull'd
for him by the Doctor, your uncle will now be
a Botanift, as well as an Antiquarian. (*Joey takes
up the fack*)

Bel. Ha, ha, ha! But my tonifh aunt's new
fangled rage for private Theatricals are to the
full, as unaccountably ridiculous as my crazy
uncle's paffion for mufty antiquities.

Mrs. Cam. Well Belinda, I'm going there directly on your affairs.

Bel. My kind friend!

Mrs. Cam. Call a coach. (*Joey takes his ftick,
and puts on Belinda's hat*) Ha, ha, ha! why,
you've put on the Lady's hat.

Joey.

Joey. (*Takes it off, then compares them.*) One wou'd think the Lady had put on mine.

[*Exeunt Mrs. Camomile and Belinda.*
Your London Ladies are so manified with their swich rantans, and their coats, and their waist-coats, and watch-chain bobbities, and their tip-top hats, and their cauliflow'r cravats, that, ecod, no mark of their being women, but the Petticoat.   [*Exit.*

SCENE II.

Mrs. Cockletop's *Dressing Room.*

Mrs. Cockletop *discovered at her Toilet,* Flounce *attending.*

Mrs. Coc. What a strange incident, my marrying this old Mr. Cockletop! Pon my honor, were I single, I'd have the most beautiful Theatre in my house, and his nephew Frank should be the manager—of late he looks at me in a very particular manner; I can scarce think it possible for those features to strike him with admiration. (*looking in the glass*)

Flounce. Ma'm those features must strike every body with admiration. (*looking at herself in the glass over Mrs. Cockletop's shoulder*)

Mrs. Coc. You flatter them.

Flounce. Not in the least, Ma'am; but what signifies your beauty, or my skill in setting it off, my master, since he's turn'd his brain—

Mrs.

Mrs. Coc. Ay, fince my hufband has com‑
menced antiquarian, with his curiofities.

Flounce. Foreign cockle-fhells, mouldy far‑
things, and all his old fafhion'd trumperies. I
dare fay he'd fell you for the wing of a but‑
terfly.

Mrs. Coc. Flounce, I'll take you to fee Lear
to-morrow night at Lord Rantum's private
Theatre.

Flounce. Thankye Ma'am. But Mifs Topits
maid told me, all of them except your Ladyfhip,
made a ftrange piece of bungling work of their
play there laft Wednefday.

`Mrs. Coc.` Work! Oh heavens! If Shakefpeare
could have taken a peep at them, ha, ha, ha!—
Romeo and Juliet the play—a hot difpute arofe
on the text—Mrs. Melpomene infifting an error
o'the prefs in, " Juliet is the fun," for, fays fhe,
(*mimicking*) " Isn't Juliet a woman's name!" Cer‑
tainly replies Sir Colly Comment. (*mimicking*)
" And is'nt Romeo talking to this very young
lady in the balcony?"—Moft certain, mem, "Oh,
oh, then, certainly (fays fhe) the poet meant
" Inftead of Juliet is the fon, that Romeo fhould
fay, it is the Eaft, and Juliet is the daughter"—
Ha, ha, ha! then the Romeo and Paris were
real rivals for the love of——I was the Juliet—
you know Flounce, how I look'd when I left
my toilet here.

Flounce. Charming! I don't wonder if they fit
about you.

Mrs. Coc. Flounce, you're near it—for in the
tomb fcene, Romeo, inftead of a foil, (ufual in
thofe cafes) whips out a fword on the noble
County Paris, who fuppofing malice prepence,
prudently before a lunge cou'd be made at him,

lays

lays himfelf down, kicks up his heels, and—
Oh! dies very decently.—Romeo full of remorfe,
looking over the breathlefs body, and going on
with his fpeech in the author's words, fays—
" Who have we here? The noble County Paris!
" one writ with me in four misfortune's book,
" give me thy hand." (*mimicking*) The good
natur'd Count, eager to make up all animofity
on the very word, from the dead, up went the
hand, meeting Romeo's with a cordial fhake.
In the confufion of laugh, occafioned by this
kind conduct, the hero, on breaking open the
tomb, totally forgot what he had to fay next, in
vain the prompter whifpers the word; poor Juliet
might have lain in Capulet's monument 'till
Doomfday—At length impatient, (for't got monftrous cold) I foftly bid him: " Speak, why
don't you fpeak? Ha, ha, ha! He taking it for
what he fhou'd fay, with all the furor of diftracted love, burfts out. " Speak, fpeak, Oh!
why don't you fpeak," ha, ha, ha! (*looks in the
glafs*) Flounce, can I in complexion compare
with my niece Belinda.

Flounce: Can a dafh of cold water compare to
almond pafte, and milk of rofes.

Enter JOEY *with the fack, throws it on the Toilet.*

Joey. My firft piece of farvice in my new place.
                                         [*Exit.*
Mrs. Coc. Ah! (*fcreams*)

Enter COCKLETOP *with a fmall fcroll of Parchment.*

(*angrily*) Aftonifhing, Mr. Cockletop, you won't
even let me have my dreffing-room to myfelf.

Coc. Oh, Mrs. Cockletop what a prize! I have bought one of the long-loft books of Livy, a manufcript fo capitally illegible, that no man on the globe can diftinguifh or read a letter of it.—Let's fee what change he has given me. (*reckoning money*)

Flounce. Full of fnails. (*flinging the plants off the table, knocks the money out of Cockletop's band.*)   [*Exit.*

Coc. The botanical plants from Doctor Camomile! carefully pick them up, every leaf has the virtue.——

Enter FRANK *in a riding drefs.*

Frank. Will they heal my wounded pocket? (*picks up the money*)

Coc. Eh! what, you lizard! (*taking the money from him*) The valuable fimples—

Mrs. Coc. Do, my dear, let poor Frank have a little money.

Coc. From which I'd have diftill'd aqua mirabilis. (*gathers the leaves*)

Frank. Your generofity would be—

Coc. So rare!—

Mrs. Coc. Confider, your nephew making an appearance equal to other young gentlemen is a credit to you, as you're known to be—

Coc. A curiofity!

Mrs. Coc. Give him a few guineas.

Coc. Penny-royal—I'll give him——a colt's foot. (*picking up the leaves*)

Mrs. Coc. Befides often antiques may fall in his way. (*winks at Frank*)

Frank. Ay, if I want to buy curious medals, camios or intaglios for you—

Coc.

Coc. What, would you buy antiques for me, my good antelope?

Frank. I was offer'd a fine old moth eaten Hemings and Condel folio of Shakefpeare t'other day for fourteen and nine pence.

Coc. What? no, matter, could you have it for nine pence? Buy it, here's a fhilling, and keep the change.

Frank. Ay, Sir, a few guineas could never come in better time, as I'm juft whip and fpur you fee, hey! fpank to Southampton.

Mrs. Coc. (alarm'd) Pray, Frank, what bufinefs have you there?

Frank. What, but to fee my lovely coufin.

Coc. Eh! (*puts up the money*)

Mrs. Coc. Oh! is that your bufinefs?

Coc. May be, you like—

Mrs. Coc. Ay, do you admire my niece?

Frank. Admire? I love her to diftraction.

Coc. The fweet girl I doat on myfelf. (*afide*) Get out of my houfe you locuft.

Mrs. Coc. Love her, after all my fond hints to him! (*afide*) Oh, Sir, I remember rehearfing Imogen with you t'other night, when I was to have fainted in your arms.——

Coc. Ay, you villain, you ftept afide, and let my poor wife tumble down, and knock her fine head againft the brafs fender——Take a double hop out of your two boots, you jackdaw, how dare you ftand before your aunt, with a horfewhip in your hand? Do you want to bring her grey hairs with forrow to the grave?

Mrs. Coc. Grey hairs.

Enter FLOUNCE.

Flounce. Ma'am! Mrs. Cammomile.

Mrs.

Mrs. Coc. Sir, command your nephew to think, no more of my niece.—Love another—You an amateur !—Stand from the entrance.

[*Exit in a paſſion, and Flounce.*

Frank. Why, my dear uncle, you are really a good natur'd old lad ; but for this nonſenſical paſſion for antiquities, in which you've no more judgment than my boot.—

Coc. What's that?

Frank. Did'nt you t'other day, give ten pounds for a model of Trajan's pillar, which turn'd out to be a braſs candleſtick ?

Coc. No.

Frank. Had'nt you a ſervant-maid dragg'd before a juſtice for ſecreting three hundred and fifty ſilver ſpoons, which you ſwore were ſhut up in a cherry ſtone.

Coc. No.

Frank. You woud'nt let my aunt go to a poor living actor's benefit, yet gave half a guinea for Roſcius's eye laſh, which proved to be taken from the corps of a cobler in Cripplegate.—

Coc. 'Tis no ſuch thing.

Frank. Didn't you give twenty pounds for the firſt plate ever Hogarth engraved, tho' it was only a pint porter pot from the Barley Mow?

Coc. No.

Frank. Did'nt you throw a lobſter in the fire, ſwearing it was a Salamander ?

Coc. No.

Frank. When my aunt broke her tortoiſeſhell comb, you carefully pick'd up every tooth, ſhewing them about for the quills of a porcupine.

Coc. I did not ſirrah.

Frank. Hearing me whiſtle " the larks ſhrill notes" from the next room, you attempted to perſuade the company, 'twas a humming bird.

Coc.

Coc. Ay, but that was all when I was fick.—
In bodily health my mind is bright and polifh'd ;
but you moft audacious dromedary ! traduce my
fkill in antiques !—Hark'y, when you can prove
to me that it's poffible I can be impofed upon
in antiquities, that is, if I am in health, I
confent to give you Belinda; here's my hand
on it.—Begone, your face is as odious to me as a
new copper penny.   [*Exit.*

Enter HEARTY, *calling after* COCKLETOP.

Hearty. Sir, Here's the receipt—
Frank. Ay, Hearty, you're my uncle's Steward, receiver of his cafh, and yet— —do, give
me a few guineas, cheat him a littte my honeft
fellow.
Hearty. Mufn't.
Frank. Plague of the money, I want it.—Yefterday met a parcel of lads in the Park—a party
propofed for a bafon of turtle at the Spring Garden—I was oblig'd to—" good bye"—afked to
dinner at Mr. Nabob's, Harley Street, fo, as I
dreaded cards in the evening, fneak'd off without
my hat, 'caufe I hadn't half a crown to releafe
it from the butler.—Then my friend, Jack Fro-
lick, the player, franck'd me into Covent Garden ;
fat down in the upper boxes between'Mifs Frump,
and Mrs. Rollabout, when the curft orange woman thrufts her bafket, with " fweet gentleman,
treat the ladies."—I was obliged to clap my
hand upon my pocket, with my purfe gone !
'Pon honor, no entring a public place for
thefe light finger'd gentry."—Coming home
yefterday, caught in a foaking fhower.—" Your
honor,

honor, coach unhir'd.'' In I jumps, not re-
collecting his difmal honor had'nt a fhilling
to pay for it, fo, as the fellow clapt to one door;
out I pops at t'other; but then I got mob'd by
the waterman, and broke my fhins over a poft
running away from the link-boy.

Hearty. Why, Frank, I'll lend you my own
money with all my heart.——

Frank. No, before I ftrip you of what you
may yet want to cherifh your old age, I'll perifh.
—Yet, this is my Belinda's birth day—By heaven
I will wifh, ay, and give her joy, tho' I foot it
every mile to Southampton, and dine on water
creffes by a ditch fide.   [*Exit.*

Hearty. Spirited lad! But I hope by means
of my letter, I fhall be able to affift him—tho'
I thought his uncle too abfurd to tell him, yet
its ftrange what a paffion I've got myfelf, for
fifhing up thofe odd fort of rarities. I'll fell my
old mafter the fmall collection I've made; but
as his knowing them to be mine may leffen their
value in his opinion; this letter roufes his defire to buy them, and then if I can but make
him believe I'm fome traveller that has brought
them from Italy, or——

Enter JOEY *in a Livery.*

You're the new footman?

Joey. Yes, I be's. I've put'n on my livery.

Hearty. Here's a letter was left for your mafter.
You'll give it to him directly.

                    [*gives letter and Exit.*

Joey. So, I muft give this letter too!—They'r
refolv'd in London, to keep no cats that wont
catch mice.

                                        Enter

Enter NAN *with a broom, singing.*

Nan. (*begins to sweep*) " A sarvice in London is no such disgrace."

Joey. Isn't that——

Nan. Why, Joey ! (*surpriz'd*)

Joey. Nan, lord, lord, how glad I be's to see thee. (*they embrace*)

Nan. But what brings you here ; and in this fine lac'd coat.

Joey. Why, I be fix'd here for a sarvant man.

Nan. Zurn ! Lord, how comacle ! and I hired here to-day as maid.

Joey. Hills and mountains will meet—Oh dear! Oh dear !

Nan. I'm now sent in here by Mrs. Flounce to do up Lady's dressing-room, that it seems some clumsy booby has thrown leaves aboutn.

Joey. I'm not a booby, Nan, I find you're as saucy tongu'd as ever.

Nan. Oh law, was it you, Joey? I ask pardon.

Joey. 'Twas all along of your crossness I com'd up to London.

Nan. And 'twas your false heartedness that drove me to seek my bread here.

Joey. Well, since good luck has brought us into one house, we'll never quarrel, nor be unkind no more.

Nan. Nor I never more will be jealous—Oh, Oh ! you've had this letter from Poll Primrose— Ah ! you deceitful—(*snatches Hearty's letter from Joey's waistcoat pocket, breaks it open, and reads*) " Sir, encourag'd"——

Joey. The devil, do you see what you've done

done, this letter was for Meafter—If I havn't a moind——

Nan. Why, Joey, dont be angry—The firft letter I get for my Lady, you fhall open for me, that you fhall—" And better my fortune as other girls do."   [*Exit finging.*

Joey. Egad! you've fpoil'd my fortune! What will become of me! Before I've time to fit down in my new place, I fhall get kick'd out on't.

Enter FRANK.

Frank. Eh! where's Hearty?
(*Joey drops the letter, Frank picks it up and looks at the fuperfcription.*)
For my uncle?
   Joey. (*confufed*) Yes, Sir; I got it to give him.
Frank. But how came it open'd?
   Joey. It's open'd.
Frank. I fee it is.—Do you know, that opening another man's letter is tranfportation.
   Joey. Is it? then I'll take the blame upon myfelf rather than Nan be punifhed. (*afide*) 'Twas I broke it open, Sir—but I meant only to—to—break it open.—all accident——(*trembling*)
Frank. This promifes fomething. (*perufing*) Well, keep your own fecret, and I'll bring you out of this fcrape.
Joey. Do, Sir, do.
Frank. Any paper here. (*fits down, writes, as copying the opened letter; reads*) " Sir, Encouraged by your character, I fhall, in perfon, to-morrow, offer to you for fale fome antique rarities."—My old conceited uncle has engaged to give me Belinda, when I can prove that it's poffible to impofe on him in antiquities—This may do it, and
bring

bring me a convenient fum befides—for with all the ridiculous enthufiafm of a Virtuofo, my Uncle has fmall reading, no tafte, but a plentiful ftock of credulity. (*writes*)

Coc. (*without*) Joey !

Joey. Waunds ! that's Mafter.

Frank. (*Haftily feals and fuperfcribes the letter he had written.*) There, ftand to it ftoutly, that's the very one you receiv'd. (*Gives it.*)

Joey. A thoufand thanks, kind fir.

Frank. Oh, but I fhall want a difguife (*afide.*) You put on your livery fince you came, where are your own cloaths ?

Joey. In the Butler's pantry.

Frank. Quick, go give that letter, (*Puts him off*) Ha, ha, ha! Yes uncle, if you've cafh to buy antiquities, I'm a ftupid fellow indeed if I can't find fome to fell you, and if I fucceed, hey, for Southampton with the triumphant news to Belinda.

[*Exit.*

SCENE III.

Cockletop's Study.

Enter COCKLETOP, *perufing the letter, and* JOEY.

Joey. Yes, fir, I was defired to give it you--- if he fhould find out that Nan broke open t'other ---Indeed, fir, that's the very letter it was never opened.

Coc. The things this learned man mentions here, are really very curious.

Joey. Sir, here be Mr. Napkin the Butler coming.

Enter NAPKIN.

Nap. Sir, a man wants you there below.

Coc. Then fir, do you fend him up here above. (*Perufes.*)

Nap. Eh! what are you idling here? Come, come, I'll fhew you the bufinefs of a Footman--- you muft toaft the muffins for mine and Mrs. Flounce's breakfaft.

Joey. I woll, fir, and broil a beef-fteak for my own.   [*Exit Napkin and Joey.*

Coc. Only that my brain is for ever running on my wife's charming Niece Belinda, (Oh, I love her! I like every thing old except Girls and Guineas)---I fhou'd certainly be a fecond Sir Han's Sloane.--I'd be a Solander and a Monmouth Geoffery! Now, who's this?

Enter FRANK *in Joey's firft Cloaths, with a fmall Hamper.*

Frank. (*afide*) If my Uncle knows me now, he muft have good fpeftacles. Meafter told me, as he told you in letter, he'd call on you to morrow with fome rarities fir. (*In broad country dialeft*)

Coc. Oh, then, you belong to the gentleman who fent me this letter? Where does your mafter live?

Frank. At Brentford; but I be's from Taunton Dean, and as I was coming to town, to day, he thought I might as well drop them here if you'll buy them. Thefe be they. (*fhewing hamper*)

Coc. Oh, what, he's fent you with the things that are mentioned here. (*To the letter.*)

Frank. I warrant them all woundy rich, he gave me fuch a ftrift charge about 'em.

Coc.

Coc. Rich! ah, thefe fordid fouls can't conceive that the moft extream delight to the eye of an Antiquarian, is beautiful brown ruft, and heavenly verdigreafe! Let's fee, (*reads.*) "The firft is a Neptune's Trident from the Barbarini Gallery."

Frank. That's it. (*fhews a toafting-fork.*)

Coc. (*Reads.*) "One of Niobes tears preferv'd in fpirits."

Frank. That. (*Produces a fmall phial.*)

Coc. Curious. (*afide.*) "A piece of Houfehold Furniture from the ruins of Herculanium, comprifing the genuine fection of the Efcurial." Precious indeed. (*afide.*) Section of the Efcurial! Ay, then it muft be in the fhape of—(*Frank fhews a gridiron.*) Wonderful! (*Reads.*) "The cap of William Tell, the celebrated Swifs Patriot, worn when he fhot the apple off his fon's head."

Frank. I've forgot to bring any thing even like that.—What fhall I do? (*afide.*) I warrant it be's here, fir.

Coc. I hope it is; for I will not buy one without all.

Frank. Then all you fhall have (*afide.*) *Pretends to look in the Hamper. Picks up Cockletop's hat and with a penknife cuts off the brim.*) That's it, mayhap. (*Gives the crown*)

Coc. Great! This is indeed the Cap of Liberty. (*Puts it on his head and reads.*) "Half a yard of " cloth from Otaheite, being a part of the mantle " of Queen Oberea, prefented by her to Captain " Cook."

Frank. Zounds, I was in fuch a hurry to get to work, that Iv'e forgot half my tools. (*afide*)

Coc. Where's the cloth from Otaheite?

Frank. I dare fay it's here (*Feels the coat be has on.*) No, mufn't hurt poor Joey. Eh! (*Cuts a large piece off the Skirt of Cockletop's coat while*

he

he is admiring the things.) Belike that's it.
[*Gives it.*

Coc. Indeed! What wonderful foft texture!
We've no fuch cloth in England.—This muft
have been the Fleece of a very fine fheep.

Frank. Ay, taken from the back of an old
ftupid ram.

Coc. Speak of what you underftand, you clown,
much talk may betray little knowledge.—Cut
your coat according to your cloth.

Frank. Yes, fir, I cut your coat according to
your cloth.—I muft fix him in his opinion now,
with a little fineffe (*afide.*) Mafter to expect fifty
pounds for this balderdafh.

Coc. Here's the Money.

Frank. No, no; if he even thought you fuch a
fool to give it, he muft be a rogue to take it, but
he fha'n't make me a party, I'll let him know I'm
an honeft man.—Dom me if I don't throw them
in the kennel and quit his farvice. (*Going to take
them.*)

Coc. (*Haftily*) Leave them there, and take
the money to your mafter, or I'll make him fend
you to the devil, you thickfkull'd Buffalo.
(*Taking out a pocket book*)

Frank. Not a penny of it will I touch.

Enter Napkin.

Nap. Sir, here's the Gentleman that fent you a
letter about calling on you to morrow.

Coc. This muft be your mafter. (*to Frank*)

Frank. Now I'm in a fine way.

Coc. I'll tell him of your rafcality. Shew the
gentleman up.   [*Exit Napkin.*

Frank. Don't tell him—don't get a poor man
turn'd

turn'd out of bread—Quick, give me the money, and I'll take it to him myfelf.

Coc. No, no, I'll give it to him.

Frank. Plague of my fineffe, that I coud'n't take the money when I might.

Enter HEARTLY, (*difguifed*) *with a fhagreen cafe.*

Hearty. Eh! my old mafter feems difguifed as well as I—The fooner I get the money the better for poor Frank's fake. (*afide*)

Coc. Sir! (*Bows*)

Hearty. Sir! (*Bowing*)

Coc. You've been in Italy, fir?

Hearty. I have (*In an affumed voice*)

Frank. I wifh you'd ftaid there. (*afide*)

Hearty. Not to intrude upon your time, we'll proceed to bufinefs.

Coc. Oh, he's in a hurry for his money. (*afide*) No delay on my fide, fir, for I offered the cafh half a dozen times.

Hearty. Sir, it was time enough for you to offer me payment when you received the articles.

Coc. I don't fay I offer'd it to you yourfelf,

Hearty. To who then, fir?

Coc. To Taunton Dean.

Hearty. I underftand you faid;—but I afk pardon—you'll pleafe to look at, and if you approve of them.—

Coc. Oh, yes, I approve, tho' certain people that eat your bread, feem to think that you're a rogue, and I'm a fool.

Frank. Then fir, you will ruin me! (*apart*)

Coc. Yes, I will fir. (*apart*)

Hearty I'm a rogue! fure he don't know me? (*afide.*)

Hevrty.

Hearty. I flatter myſelf ſir, when you ſee the articles—

Coc. I have ſeen them.

Hearty. Pardon me, ſir, but I think not, where how ?

Coc. Why, with my eyes ; how the devil elſe ſhou'd I ſee them.

Frank. I've a mind to knock both their wife heads together and ſnatch the money. (*aſide*)

Coc. Will you diſpoſe of theſe or not ? (*pointing to Franks articles*)

Hearty. Sir !

Coc. And, Sir ! the devil didn't you come here to ſell me rarities? (*in a great paſſion*)

Hearty. Yes, ſir, and will if you will buy them.

Coc. I tell you I do, and have bought them.

Hearty. Have !

Coc. Oh, he repents offering them ſo cheap ; but I'll clench the bargain.—Here's the fifty pounds, tell your maſter you took it before he came in. (*apart to Frank, giving him a note*)

Frank. Yes. (*goes towards door*)

Coc. Hey! ſtop, wo'n't you give it to your maſter ?

Frank. I'm going to give it him directly, Sir. (*going*)

Coc. But, zounds ! What's all this? You'll give it him directly ! Yet, you ſtalk by him as if he was only an old wig-block.

Frank. Stalk by—Who's a wig-block, Sir ?

Coc. Your maſter here.

Frank. That my maſter—no.

Coc. Eh ! Isn't this your ſervant ?

Hearty. No, Sir.

Coc. Didn't you write me this letter ?

(*ſhewing it*)

Hearly

Hearty. No, Sir.

Coc. What, not about the Antiquities?

Hearty. About the Antiquities? Oh, Yes, Sir.

Coc. Yes, Sir; no, Sir; carry your prevaricating pate down ſtairs, Sir.

Frank. This muſt be an Impoſtor. (*apart to Cockletop*) You're too late for after-graſs, for my maſter has already hum'd this old fool.

Coc. Old fool! Get you out of my houſe you ſcoundrel, or——(*takes down a blunderbuſs*)

[*Exit Frank.*

Offer to open your juggling-box here, and I'll blow you to Brentford, you dog, I will. (*preſents*)   [*Exit Hearty.*

Enter MRS. CAMOMILE, *and* MRS. COCKLETOP, *they both ſcream.*

Mrs. Cam. Heavens, Mr. Cockletop, will you kill us?

Mrs. Coc. Lord, what's on your head?

Coc. The Cap of Liberty—Oh, the ſuper-beautiful purchaſe I have juſt made! Such a charming addition to my little curious collection! Mrs. Camomile you've taſte, I'll give you a treat —I'll ſhew her all. (*aſide*)

Mrs. Coc. (*ſeeing the things that Frank had left*) Heavens! who has done this?

Enter FLOUNCE.

Here, take theſe, and fling them——

Coc. Lay your fingers on them, and I'll—Strabo, Campden, and Biſhop Pocock—Madam, you ſhould, (*to Mrs. Camomile*) that is, do you know you're a Dilitante—I ſay you're a celebrated Dille—and—Now what a fine diſcourſe Sir Joſeph Banks wou'd make upon theſe—Madam, I ſay—

Mrs. Coc.

Mrs. Coc. Blefs me! who has trimm'd you this way?

Coc. Sir Afhton Lever!—I wifh your hufband Doctor Camomile was in town—I've fuch a feaft for the venerable Bede.

Mrs. Cam. I wifh we cou'd get you out of town. (*afide*)—Ay, but Mr. Cockletop, a man with money and judgment like you, fhou'd travel himfelf to collect rarities.

Coc. I've no occafion to give myfelf the fatigue and perils of travel, to hazard my neck, dragg'd over Alpine precipices, or get my throat cut in dirty Italian inns, or fuffocated by peftilential fteams from the infernal mouth of Vefuvius; I need not like Pliny the elder, be drown'd in a fhower of cinders. No, no, here I fit at home, quiet, in my eafy chair; while travellers come, and lay at my feet the wonderful fruits of their wife refearches.—Awake, prepare your under-ftanding, here's a tear—the devil, I forgot who cried this tear. (*afide*) Hem! It's a precious drop preferv'd in fpirits.

Flounce. Ha, ha, ha!

Coc. Get along, you moft fcandalous tongued —I defire, Mrs. Cockletop, you'll order your flip-flop out of the mufeum.—Then here is a moft valuable—(*bolds up the Gridiron*)

Enter JOEY, *at the back.*

Joey. I'm fet to broil beef-fteaks, and toaft muffins.—The cook faid Mr. Frank took 'em, and brought 'em out of the kitchen—

Coc. There! all coft me only fifty pounds.— This is a Neptune's Trident, (*bolds up the toafting fork*

fork) and this piece of furniture from Hercula-
nium, the model of the Efcurial, built in honor
of St. Lawrence, who was broil'd on——

Joey. Thankye, Sir, I was looking for the
Toafting-fork and the Gridiron. (*takes them*)
[*Exit.*

Flounce. Ha, ha, ha!

Coc. What's that?

Mrs. Coc. Why, Mr. Cockletop, what have
you been about here?

Mrs. Cam. Only look——

Coc. I believe I'm bit.—Taunton Dean! He
was a rogue. (*looks at his coat and hat*) Is my
face genuine?

Mrs. Coc. Why, 'tis an Antique—But indeed,
my dear, you don't look well.

Coc. Don't I?

Mrs. Cam. This may help my fcheme. (*afide*)
My dear Sir, I wou'dn't fhock you, but you
look——

Coc. Do I?

Mrs. Cam. My hufband the doctor, often told
me, that your bodily illnefs always had an effect
upon your mind.

Coc. No man living underftands my conftitu-
tion but Doctor Camomile—I muft be——(*feeling
his pulfe*)

Mrs. Cam. When a gentleman of your knowledge is fo grofsly duped, it's a certain fign—

Coc. It is, that I'm ill, or I never could have
been taken in.

Mrs. Coc. Lud! I wifh your hufband the doctor was in Town.

Mrs. Cam. I'd advife Mr. Cockletop to go to
him at Winchefter, directly.

Mrs. Coc. Here, Napkin!

Enter NAPKIN.

Order the horses to—your poor master—the doctor—at Winchester.

Nap. (*looks with concern at Cockletop*) Oh, he is —yes Ma'am—here, John, desire Thomas to make Joey put a pair of horses to the chaise.

Mrs. Cam. You'd best let Mr. Napkin attend you.

Mrs. Coc. He's a careful man.

Coc. In this journey, I can view the famous antient abbey of Netley; I have a choice bister drawing of it—I'll climb and bring from the summit of the mould'ring wall——

Mrs. Coc. Yes, you're in a state for climbing! Wou'd you break your neck, my dear love, and your poor wife's heart?

Coc. Kind spouse!—I'll call at Southampton, and see my Belinda, tho' I die at her feet. (*aside*)

Mrs. Coc. When he's out of town, I shall have the uninterrupted company of my dear Frank—(*aside*) Keep up your spirits, my love.

Coc. I live only for you, my dearest.

[*Exeunt Mr. and Mrs. Cockletop.*

Mrs. Cam. Napkin, ha, ha, ha! Here's an opportunity for our plan.—You know as we've all without success, repeatedly endeavour'd to persuade the old couple to settle some provision on their neice and nephew, Frank and Belinda—

Nap. Aye, ma'am we must try stratagem.

Mrs. Cam. The excuse your mistress gives, is the chance of her having children of her own, whom she can't wrong, by lavishing their patrimony on others.

Nap.

Nap. Ha, ha, ha! then to put her out of all hopes of that, as you have fettled, we'll make her believe my mafter's dead, and as I'm now going into the country with him, leave that to me ma'am.

Mrs. Cam. I fancy it will be eafy, as fhe already thinks him ill.

Nap. And feeble.—She heard him threaten to climb up the mould'ring walls of Netley Abbey, in fearch of a fprig of ivy, or an owl's neft; and if I can't invent a ftory to bring the old gentleman tumbling down——

Mrs. Cam. Ha, ha, ha! And make your miftrefs, (the mourning widow) eftablifh the dear, amiable young couple well and happy, it will be an excellent joke to laugh at over their wedding fupper.

Nap. But I muft prepare for the journey.

Mrs. Cam. And I, home, to comfort poor Belinda. Only you act your part moft dolefully natural, and we muft profper.   [*Exeunt.*

END OF THE FIRST ACT.

X X 2

ACT II,

SCENE I.

Mrs. Camomile's *House.*

Enter Frank, *in his disguise.*

FRANK.

Hollo! Mrs. Camomile! here's a nick! ha, ha, ha!

Enter Hearty *in his own cloaths, greatly agitated.*

Hearty. Ay, here's the rascal. (*lays hold on Frank*) Villain ! Tell me this instant.——

Enter Joey, *running.*

Joey. Yes, this is my Coat ; I'll make a Davy of it. (*lays bolds of Frank on the other side*)
Frank. Hey ! Be quiet my good friends!
Herty. (*enraged*) Where's the money you obtain'd under false pretences, rascal?

Joey.

Joey. Peli er my coat, firrah.

Frank. Both deliver me, or with one of you, I'll rattan the other out of the room. (*difengages himfelf*) You fcoundrel, is this your thanks, for faving your neck, when you broke open your mafter's letter. (*apart to Joey*)

Joey. (*Surveying him*) Lud! if it isn't—and here too's the gentleman that gaven me—if he difcovers.—(*afide*) Keep my wearing apparel, and lav no mor aboutn.

Frank. You fay no more aboutn, or you fail for Port Jackfon.—Step down, and bring me word when a faddled horfe comes to the door—Fly!

Joey. Yes, Sir, yes. (*frightened*)   [*Exit.*

Frank. Hallo! Hearty, how do you my buck. (*difcovers himfelf*)

Hearty. Frank! (*furveying him with furprife*)

Frank. Frank and free—Tol, lol, lol!—Eh, only touch'd uncle out of fifty. (*fhews the Bank Note*) Uncle's own Kitchen's now his Hercula-nium, ha, ha, ha! To think how I've left him in his Cap of Liberty, flourifhing his Barbarini toafting-fork. He's to give me Belinda when I can prove he can be impos'd upon in Anti-quities.

Hearty. But how did you——

Frank. Then fuch triumph, to fling the hatch-et even beyond the traveller; but I had a mind to kick him tho'.

Hearty. I'm glad you did not tho'.

Frank. You glad! Why, what is it to you?—I fhall never forget old Muz, the Philofoper; I think I fee him now, with his fcientific wig pull'd over his mulberry nofe.

                                        Hearty.

Hearty. You do? (*in his feign'd voice*)

Frank. Eh! (*furpriz'd*) Really, con'd it have been you my honeſt old friend.

Hearty. Aye, here you fee old Muz, the phi-loſopher, who laid out for a fifty, only to intro-duce it to you, my dear boy. (*ſhakes his hand*)

Frank. (*ruminating*) Well, now, upon my foul, this is—

Hearty. Hang reflection, as long as one of us has ſucceeded; have you heard of your uncle's leaving town.

Frank. Has he?

Hearty. I've fome time upon my hands, I'll go with you to Southampton. My horfe is at the livery-ſtables the other fide of Weſtminſter Bridge.

Frank. You'd beſt ſtep on before me, have him out ready, you'll not have a moment to wait, for I'll mount the inſtant mine comes to the door.

Hearty. You'll tell me how you circumvented me, and fuch roaring laughs as we'll have all the way, ha, ha, ha! " By the Lord, lad, I'm glad you've got the money." [*Exit.*

Frank. Ha, ha, ha! Well, my mock curiofities may have a better effect on my uncle than Heaity's real ones, if they can help to cure him of an abfurd whim that makes him the dupe of impoftors, flinging his money after things of no utility. His very clowniſh terants have now found out his weak fide, and often pay their rent in butterflies, dried leaves, ſtones, and bits of old iron. (*looks at his watch*) Getting late:—I'd like to fee if Mrs. Camomile has any commands for her friend Belinda.

Enter

Enter BELINDA *at the back, and* JOEY *at the side.*

Joey. Sir, the horfe be come.
Frank. Then, hey for love, and my divine Belinda. (*going*)
Bel. Pray, Sir, whither in fuch a monftrous hurry?
Frank. My love!
Joey. Love! Oh, then, I may ride the poney myfelf.   [*Exit.*
Frank. In the name of miracles, how did you get here?
Bel. You know we've the beft friend in the world in dear Mrs. Camomile, the miftrefs of this houfe.

Enter MRS. CAMOMILE.

Mrs. Cam. Come, come, you happy pair of turtles, this room is the ftage for a little comedy I've to act with your aunt; of which, I hope, your union will prove the denouément.

A loud knocking without. Enter FLOUNCE.

Flounce. Ma'am, my miftrefs is juft drove up to the door.
Bel. Oh, heavens! if fhe finds I've run to town (*going*)
Mrs. Cam. Stop—fhe'll meet you on the ftairs.
Bel. This way, Frank: when my aunt comes in here, we'll flip down.
Mrs. Cam. But, Belinda, you'll tell Frank what we're at, and both trip directly home; and you, and all the fervants, on with your fables.

Frank.

Frank. Sables! What, to celebrate my true-love's birth-day!—No, I'll have fuch an elegant entertainment at home.

Bel. Will you hold your tongue, and come along. [*Exeunt.*

Mrs. Cam. If my little plot on their aunt but profpers.—Flounce, run and defire Napkin to con over the leffon I taught him, and look as difmal as an executor left without a legacy.

Flounce. And, Ma'am, I'll bid him keep his handkerchief to his eyes, for fear an unfortunate laugh fhou'd fpoil all: here's my miftrefs, Ma'am; I wifh you fuccefs.

[*Exit Flounce.*

Enter MRS. COCKLETOP, (*elegant and gayly drefsed*)

Mrs. Coc. Oh, Mrs. Camomile!

Mrs. Cam. Well, how do you do?

Mrs. Coc. Our houfe feems fo melancholy fince my poor dear man has left town, that now I can't bear to ftay at home.

Mrs. Cam. And when he was at home, you were always gadding. (*afide*)

Mrs. Coc. I forgot to fhew you my drefs:—I had it made up for Cordelia, in our intended play at Mrs. Pathos's. As you were not there, I put it on to confult your tafte.

Mrs. Cam. Oh, I forgot to thank you for my ticket; but excufe me, an engagement—

Mrs. Coc. Ha, ha, ha! You had no lofs, for our tragedy was converted into a ball.

Mrs. Cam. Ball!

Mrs. Coc. Lear, you know, was our play, which we got up with every poffible care.—Well, Ma'am,

Well, Ma'am, Colonel Toper, who was to have play'd Glo'fter, having conquer'd too many bottles of Burgundy after dinner, (*mimicks*) " No, I'll be for none of your ftage—I'll fit in the fideboxes among the ladies. Begin your tragedy, I'll be very civil—I'll clap, and I'll encore." " But, dear Colonel, (cries Mrs. Pathos) remember you're to play; you muft go on."— " Well, Madam, I'll fit and fee myfelf come on, that muft be monftrous fine, becaufe I'm fo perfect in my part; but, firft, we'll have t'other bottle," and reel'd back into the dining-room. " Oh, diftraction! (cries Mrs. Pathos) my audience all met—I'm eternally difgraced." " By heaven, you fhan't, Mem! (fays Mr. Segoon) I'll make an apology. Ladies and Gentlemen, Colonel Toper having been fuddenly taken ill, my Lord Brainlefs has kindly confented to read the part of Glo'fter, and hopes for your indulgence." " Bravo!" from his Grace, and " bravo!" echoed the furrounding circle. Up went the curtain, on came his Lordfhip, book in hand; he reads, he acts—" braviffimo!" On fmoothly went the play, 'till the fcene where Cornwall orders the unhappy Glo'fter's eyes to be put out, an incident, none of our fafhionable actors ever thought of, 'till the inftant the cruel command was given.— Without eyes (" were all the letters funs") Glo'fter cou'dn't read; the probability of fiction thus deftroy'd the play cou'dn't proceed, a general laugh took place, benches were removed, the fiddles ftruck up Hillifberg's Reel, and audience and actors join'd in a country-dance. Ha, ha, ha! No, I'm determin'd to act no more amongft them. Why can't I have plays in my

own houſe as well as Mrs. Pathos? My huſband's repoſitory wou'd make me a complete
theatre, if I cou'd but get all his ſtupid rarities
out of it. Wasn't that a very abſurd circum-
ſtance? Ha, ha, ha! 'Pon my honor, tho' I
laugh I'm exceedingly melancholy.

Mrs. Cam. You've nothing to make you un-
eaſy :—You're ſure that with my huſband, Doctor
Camomile, Mr. Cockletop is in ſafe hands.

Mrs. Coc. Why, I think he's not worſe, or I
ſhou'd have known it by my dreams ; for, ſleep-
ing or waking, he's my thoughts.

Mrs. Cam. Then there's hope he's better :—
be cheerful.

Mrs. Coc. Well, Mrs. Camomile, it aſtoniſhes
me how you can be cheerful while your huſband's abſent ; but, indeed, it's rather unfortunate when people are formed with hearts of more
ſenſibility than others. I've heard often, but
can't have the ſmalleſt conception, that there
are women that marry old men with no other
view than ſoon to become rich widows, and
then take a young one. Oh! my blood riſes
when I think of ſuch wives! I'd rather die myſelf, nay, I'm ſure I cou'dn't live, if any thing
was to happen to my huſband.

Enter BETTY.

Bet. Why, Ma'am, here's Mr. Napkin juſt
come below.

Mrs. Coc. But is his maſter return'd too?

Mrs. Cam. Well, if even he is not, why ſhou'd
that alarm you?

Mrs. Coc. Then, perhaps, Napkin has brought
—Where is he? Why don't he come up? Napkin;

kin; (*calls*) torture me with fufpence. Oh! Lord, Mrs. Camomile, if any thing's the matter I fhall die. (*with great emotion*)

Mrs. Cam. But don't teaze yourfelf, perhaps without a caufe. Mr. Napkin, pray walk up. (*with compofure*)

Mrs. Coc. How I tremble!

Mrs. Cam. Collect your fortitude; you know we fhould always be prepar'd for the worft.

Enter NAPKIN *in a travelling drefs, fplafh'd, and feemingly fatigued.*

Nap. My dear, good mafter! (*weeps*)

Mrs. Coc. My hufband! Oh, Lord, fpeak! pray fpeak.

Nap. Madam, will you have him brought up to town, or fhall he be buried in the country? (*weeps*)

Mrs. Cam. Dead?

Nap. I wifh Henry the VIIIth had levelled Netley Abbey—my fweet mafter's thirft of knowledge—fuch a height—top of the old fpire —his head giddy—feeble limbs—ftretching too far—a ftone giving way—tho' I caught him—by the heel—head foremoft—corner of a tomb-ftone—dafh—Oh! (*weeps*)

Mrs. Coc. My fears are true. I faint—I die— Pleafe to reach that chair.

MRS. CAMOMILE *places a chair,* MRS. COCKLE-TOP, *with deliberation, brufhes it with her hand-kerchief, feats herfelf, takes out a fmelling-bottle, applies it, and affects to fwoon.*

Mrs. Cam. Nay, now, my dear friend, I thought you were a woman of fenfe. If my jeft

on

on death fhou'd caufe one in earneft! (*afide*)
Pray be comforted.

Mrs. Coc. (*recovering*) Comforted did you fay?
How is that poffible, my dear Mrs. Camomile,
when I've heard you yourfelf remark that black
don't become me, tho' if I was to drefs like
Almeria, in the Mourning Bride?

Mrs. Cam. To confefs the truth, I was afraid
to tell you; but I before knew of this melancholy event: and there that foolifh boy, your
nephew Frank, thro' his zealous refpect for the
memory of his uncle, has (contrary to all cuftom
and decorum) already order'd the whole family
to put on the black clothes that were only
t'other day laid by, when the mourning for your
brother-in-law expired.

Mrs. Coc. Madam, you're very obliging.

Mrs. Cam. I fee this lofs bears hard upon your
mind, therefore it may not be proper fo foon
troubling you with worldly affairs; but now,
my dear, that you'll have no children of your
own, indeed you fhou'd think of fome eftablifhment for your niece Belinda.

Mrs. Coc. I'll firft eftablifh my hufband's nephew, Frank, merely to fhew I prefer my dear
man's relations to my own.

Mrs. Cam. This will anfwer the fame purpofe,
as Frank marries Belinda. (*afide*) Well, fhall
I tell the lad your good intentions towards
him?

Mrs. Coc. You're very kind, I'll tell him
myfelf; but I'll firft confult you, my good
friend, on the thoughts I have had in my mind
how to make him happy; but, in my interview
with the boy, I wou'dn't have any body elfe
by. The hour of forrow's facred; it's a cruel
world,

world, and people luxurious aud fenfual, gay
and fortunate, have little feeling for the dif-
treffes of a difconfolate widow.

Mrs. Cam. My dear creature, endeavour to
keep up your fpirits.

Mrs. Coc. Ah, friend! what fhould a poor
woman do that has loft fo good a hufband, but
try to—to—get a better? *(afide)* [*Exeunt.*

SCENE II.

COCKLETOP'S *Houfe.*

Enter FRANK *elevated with wine, and* BELINDA *in
mourning.*

Frank. Ha, ha, ha! this is the moft whimfical
thought of your friend, Mrs. Camomile!

Bel. Isn't it charming?

Frank. Your aunt, and, indeed, the whole
family, except Flounce and Napkin, who are in
the fecret, actually believe that my uncle's dead.

Enter NAN,

This is your natal day, the birth of beauty: I'll
give an entertainment, upon my foul! Ha, ha!
Mrs. Flounce fays, " Oh, Sir! I can't run any
bills with the tradespeople;" but, bills and
credit!—While we've money my uncle's curiofity guineas fhall fly. Ha, ha, ha! Illuminate
the rooms brilliant, luftres, girandoles, and
chandeliers.

Nan.

Nan. Yes, Sir, La! now where's Joey to do all this? Mr. John, light the clusters, jerry-doles and chanticleers. (*calls off*)

Frank. Prepare the Saloon, Belinda, we will have a ball.

Nan. Air the Balloon, for master's going to play at ball.

Frank. And lay supper; then let Napkin send for a pipe and tabor; a dance we must have.— Tol, lol, lol!

Bel. But indeed now, this extravagance—

Frank. An't my kind aunt to give me my uncle's cash? Then, my Belinda, you and I go to church, and Hymen, in his saffron robe, shall lead us to the rosy bow'r.—Can I resist? you angel! (*kisses her hand*)

Bel. For heaven's sake, Frank, a little decency before the servants. How unfeeling must they think you.

Frank. I'll shew you the feeling of servants for such a master.

Enter JOHN, THOMAS, *and two Maids in mourning.*

Hark'ye, Tom the Coachman, you know your master's no more?

Tom. Ay, Sir, death has whipp'd his horses to their journey's end, to our great sorrow.

Frank. Poor Tom! I'm told you're so griev'd, you've sworn never to touch a drop of punch as long as you live.

Tom. Me! I'll be damn'd if I ever swore any such thing.

Frank. Ha, ha, ha! A jovial bout the servants shall have—we'll celebrate your birth-day.

Bel.

Bel. But where's your friend the steward?

Frank. Right! Holloa, Hearty! Oh, true, I've sent my poor old fellow pacing over Westminster-bridge.—Fly, and every one bring in his hand, something towards the good cheer of the night.   [*Exeunt severally.*

SCENE III.

A Saloon illuminated.

Enter COCKLETOP *in a Storm-cap, Roquelare, &c.*

Coc. All my doors open! this blowy night! reminds me of the Lisbon earthquake; but my storm-cap has protected me.—Odd my not finding Belinda at Southampton.—I wish I had come into town over London bridge, that now, is a sort of young ruin—I love to pass the Tabbard in Southwark, from whence Chaucer's pilgrims went to the shrine of Thomas-a-Becket—Then the monument's growing a pretty rumble-come-tumble, ha, ha, ha! But then over Westminster bridge, to see Hearty mounted like a great equestrian statue! And my man Joey holding his bridle like the Emperor of Morocco's blackamoor—I'm not sorry Napkin left me; nobody knows now I have been at my sweet Belinda's; how glad my wife will be, when she finds I'm come home, and well. (*throws back the storm-cap, and looks about the room*) Eh! my dear has company, this do'nt speak much feeling for my illness.

                                        Enter

Enter TOM *with a cloth, not perceiving* COCKLETOP.

Tom. While Napkin is uncorking the wine, I'll fee if I can't fpread a table as well as a hammer-cloth. (*takes out a large table and begins to lay it—whiftles*) I wonder who drives my old mafter now in t'other world, does he go up or down hill?

Coc. Now, who has put Thomas my coachman into mourning—As I left you a pied zebra, why find you a black bear (*ftrikes him with his cane*)

Tom. Gee up! (*fuddenly turning, furprifed and terrified*)   [*Exit.*

Coc. What's this about?

Enter NAN *with fallad, which fhe places on the table then picks a bit out)*

Nan. I loves beet-root. (*puts it to her mouth*)

Coc. Yes, and fo do I. (*fhe looks at him frighten'd*) Some of my family muft be dead, that they're all fo fuddenly got dipp'd. Tell me young woman, for whom are you in mourning? (*Nan fhakes her head, puts her apron to her eyes and Exit.*)
I hav'nt miftook my houfe, fure I believe I'm at next door.

Enter NAPKIN, FLOUNCE, *and two maid fervants in mourning.*

Nap. Ha, ha, ha! Flounce, if you had feen how capitally doleful I play'd my part.

Flounce.

Flounce. **None** of your dolefuls now. Mafter away, Miftrefs fafe at Mrs. Camomile's; the houfe to ourfelves, and the young pair, fince Mr. Frank will treat us to a little hop.

Nap. Ay, Flounce, for mufic you know I'm no bad fcraper.

Flounce. No, Napkin. Nothing gives fpirit to a dance as a pipe and tabor, fo fend out and fee if one can't be hired.

Enter two Maids, and Footman with a violin.

Nap. My fiddle, John, thanky. (*takes it*) Now liften, Flounce, for our country dance, only mind the violin ; why, I'll lilt up Jackey Bull, fprightly enough to move the dead, ay, even to make our old mafter caper about. (*Napkin plays*)

Coc. " Here, Jacky's return'd from Dover." (*joins in the dance, then feizes Napkin, the reft run off fhrieking*) So, my good friend, I bring you into the country, you leave me fick, fneak away, and here I find you like Nero at Rome, rafping your cremona. Explain, what brings you all in black, if any body's deceafed, why do you celebrate the funeral rites with feafting and fiddling, and if nobody's dead, why change my dove-houfe into a rookery ? (*Napkin puts his handkerchief to his eyes*) Oh then there is fomebody—who is it— Eh I who? tell me—Vexation! an't I to know ? —S'blood ! are people to die in my houfe, and I the mafter, and not be told.

Nap. What, or who fhall I fay ? (*afide*)

Coc. What am I to think of all this?

Nap. Why, Sir, from feeing us all in black—
you're to—think—that——

Coc. What?

Nap. That we're in mourning.——

Coc. But for whom? It can't be my friend
Mrs. Camomile—My nephew Frank?—Oh Lord!
if it fhould be Mifs Belinda—No, no; they
woudn't fiddle and dance for them.—It muft be
for fomebody, for whom ceremony demands the
outward fhews of forrow; but nobody cares
whether they liv'd or died.—Now, there is one
beloved perfon—that I don't care a farthing for.
(*afide*) Yet I left her fo well—I fee they're afraid
to fhock me—Napkin, is it—is it.—(*Napkin
fhakes his head*) It is my—my—wi—wi—wife!
[*Exit Napkin flowly*) 'Tis fo! His filence is a funeral
oration—Oh, my dear wife!—

Enter JOEY, *fhivering as if cold.*

Joey. Oh, oh! It be a bitter fharp night, my
hands are ftone.

Coc. Are you petrified? I wifh you were. I'd
put you on a bracket in my mufeum.

Joey. But, Sir, here we come home, find all
our farvants in mourning, and when I afks for
whom, they fhakes their heads, and walk away.

Coc. Joey, it's for—your—miftrefs.

Joey My lady dead! Lawk how fudden.—I
believe now I ought to cry. (*afide, lifts up the
fkirt of his coat, and watches Cockletop.*)

Coc. The gentle friend, and companion of my
youth. (*weeps*)

Joey. Yes, I fhou'd cry. (*afide*) Oh!

Coc. The beft of wives. (*forrowful*)

Joey.

Joey. The kindeſt miſtreſs. (*imitating*)

Coc. (*recovering.*) Yet my ſervants rejoicing, ſhews how ill ſhe was belov'd.

Joey. Yes, Sir, I ſaid to myſelf when I com'd— Joey, ſaid I, you have got a good maſter, but a bad miſtreſs.

Coc. Stay, now I'm releaſed from her extrava- vagant vagaries—Why, ſhe'd give as much for a little toilet patch box, ay, as would purchaſe the black letter palace of pleaſure, her week's hair dreſſing would buy me Colly Cibber's Fop- pington wig—Then her temper.

Joey. She was a wixen devil.

Coc. Yet ſuch a pretty face.

Joey. She was an angel for beauty, that's the truth on't—Oh ! (*cries*)

Coc. Yet ſhe was getting in years.

Joey. Old enough to be my grandmother.

Coc. With her lace-caps, and her fripperies; her private plays, her Denouément, and Cataſtrophe.

Joey. If I didn't ſuſpeót ſhe play'd in private with that Mr. Denemong behind the tapeſtry.

Coc. I've no right to be ſo ſad.

Joey. Yes, Sir, we mun be glad—Ha, ha, ha ! He, he, he !

Coc. The funeral over, I'll do what I've long wiſh'd—Convert her dreſſing-room into my mu- ſeum.

Joey. Her dreſſing-room would make me a ſnug bed-chamber.

Coc. What ?

Joey. I ſay, Sir, 'twou'd make you a nice bed- room.

Coc. No, a choice repoſitory for my antiquities.

Joey. Yes, Sir ; but indeed they have now got

old

old and rufly, you fhould befpeak an entire new fett.

Coc. The room has an Eaft afpect; the windows face Athens, tho difgraced now by Cockfpur perfumery, and Fleet-ftreet Japanery—I'll remove her things out of it.

Joey. Certainly, Sir; kick them down ftairs—an't you man of the houfe?

Coc. I am. You're but a boy; but I fee you've fpirit, follow me to her dreffing-room.

Joey. Yes, fir, Hem! [*Exeunt.*

Enter Mrs. COCKLETOP *and* NAN, *in mourning.*

Mrs. Coc. Every room, every article of furniture only reminds me of my dear man—My beloved Frank's ill timed mirth does not correfpond with his hafte in getting every body into mourning; but indeed, my poor hufband was never an Uncle to him.

Nan. Oh, Ma'm, you look fo well in your weeds.

Mrs. Coc. Do I?

Nan. Why, your Ladyfhip's arm from the black fleeve looks like the white leg of a fine fowl.

Mrs. Coc. Tho' I revere the memory of my late hufband, yet his ridiculous paffion for fhells, fofsils and antique nonfenfe was got to fuch an intollerable height, I was determined that on the firft opportunity I'd fling his rubbifh out of the houfe, and now I'll do it—it's a good large room, and I think taftily fitted, 'twill make me a moft beautiful little Theatre, the thought charms—but, alas! my charmer is no more!---I'll inftantly go up, and throw all his old Coppers and Crocodiles

diles out of the window---his Mufeum, (as he calls it) is a moft horrid place; but I will have it clear'd out.—Come.

Nan. Yes, an't pleafe you Ma'am.   [*Exeunt.*

Enter Joey, *with Band Boxes, Toilet Furniture, &c.*

Joey. Ho, ho, ho! Now if our Miftrefs coul'd but pop her head out of her coffin and fee what a fine rummage we have made among her fal de rals trinketies, and ginglebobs (*Takes a fmall Phial out of a dreffing box and reads label*) " C--o--s--cos—M--e--t--met—i--c--ic Lotion " for the face". (*Taftes it*) Feace! Eh! this is a good notion for the ftomach—choice Cordial— the very thing that I wanted this cold night to warm my gay little heart, (*puts it into his pocket*) My miftrefs was fond of filken geer, I wonder now how fhe's contented with a fhroud—they fay what people fet their hearts upon in this world runs fo much in their heads, that, even in to'ther, they can't reft if fuch things fhou'd be difturb'd.— Meafter fays he'll give thefe to the flames, I'll afk him to give them to my flame, pretty Nan.--- If fhe gets this here cap upon her pate, and our lady miftrefs was to come ftalking in with a candle in her dead hand

Re-enter Mrs. Cocletop, *with a candle.*

And then fays Nan, with a trembling voice--- " Who's there." (*Not perceiving her*)

Mrs. Coc. Don't be afraid, Joey, it's only me.

Joey. Marcy on us! (*trembling*)

Mrs. Coc. Heavens! who has pull'd my things about in this way. (*feeing them*)

Joey.

Joey. Now the Devil was in our Mafter that he
could not let'n bide *(afide)* I thought we fhould
have her up.

Mrs. Coc. Who did it ?

Joey. Will it quiet your poor foul ? *(folemnly
and frightened)*

Mrs. Coc. Bid Nan make hafte down to me.

Joey. Then fhe's, *(points down)* Ah, thofe ladies
lead fuch rory tory lives. *(afide)*

Mrs. Coc. Nan ! *(calling)*

Joey. Don't hurt Nan, I'll go for the parfon.
                              [*Exit terrified.*

Mrs. Coc. Parfon ! then my intentions to marry
Frank are already known among the fervants.

Enter NAN, *with various Antiquities, which fhe
lays on the table.*

Nan. Here, ma'am I've got a rare bundle of
Antiqui-quackities—Lord Lord Ma'am, what
could bewitch our mafter to heap up fuch a
ftock of lumber ?

Mrs. Coc. Rubbifh indeed ! A neft of moths
and fpiders---Ah ! let them be all thrown out ;
but I'll fee how Flounce dare to let my room be
ranfack'd in this manner.   [*Exit in a paffion.*

Nan. The fkin of fome foreign beaft I fup-
pofe---Something rich here---*(looks in a box)*
Nothing but filthy old rags, he, he, he ! If our
dead meafter's picture don't feem as if it was
looking down directly at me. *(Looking at a
portrait over the chimney)* Tho' grand, this is a
very difmal room.

Enter

Enter COCKLETOP.

Coc. Belinda here in. the houfe !—Iv'e told Hearty to inform her of my intentions to marry her, and I'll compliment my deceafed wife with a Cedar Coffin.—Now muft I promote her dreffing room to the honor of being the Treafury of my Antiques, I wifh Hearty wou'd come to help me to remove my precious—Eh ! they are removed. (*Seeing them*)

Nan. How Mafter's mind when he was alive did run upon thefe fhabby Gimcracks.—Oh ! he cou'd not have priz'd it fo much for nothing.—— No, no, he had fomething good.—Your odd old people are fond of hiding money in holes and corners ; lud ! if here isn't—(*rattling a fmall box*) Ay, don't you look down fo fharp at me, for I will have a peep thou I get a dead man's 'pinch. (*As fhe's opening the box Cockletop pinches her ear ; fhe turns, fees Cockletop, fhrieks and runs off*)

Coc. A moft facriligious petticoat thief !

[*Exit after her.*

SCENE IV; *and laft.*

Another Apartment, a Table covered with a Green Cloth.

Enter JOEY, *with a Candle, (terrified)*

Joey. I've left the parfon in the room—(*ftarts frightened*) who's here ?—But he infifts it be auld mafter that's dead, the good gentleman that juft now with me for madam's death cried fo fine,

all

all alive and merry; but this ftupid minifter won't believe it, fo, if he meets her there, and her fpirit's ftill difturb'd about her rumplified caps, fhe'll claw him for certain. I know nought where mafter's got, and the farvants feem all run to hide—can't find Nan, I wou'd we were both fafe again in the country.—Well, I've fav'd this drop of cordial.—Who's you? Heaven defend us! Oh, fhe is come again! I have no hope now but my bottle and this table. (*Puts out the light, gets behind, and then under the table.*)

Enter Mrs. Cockletop.

Mrs. Coc. Frank! this is the room I defired Mrs. Camomile to bid him meet me in, and here he comes—this way Frank. (*calling off in a low voice*) I'm glad there's no light tho', to difcover my blufhes, at the open declaration I muft make him.

Enter Cockletop.

Coc. As dark as an Egyptian Catacomb—Belinda venturing to town muft be on the report of her aunts death, and if Hearty has told her I'll fpeak to her, here——

Mrs. Coc. Are you there? (*in an under tone*)

Coc. Yes, 'tis fhe, I wifh we had a light, where are you? (*in a low voice*)

Mrs. Coc. Eh! When I bury Mr. Cockletop---

Coc. Bury me! (*afide*) No my dear it's for you I'm to make a mummy of Mrs. Cockletop——

Mrs. Coc.

Mrs. Coc. Make mummy of me !—is it Frank ?

Coc. No, my love, I'm your own Cosey Cockletop.

Mrs. Coc. Angels and ministers ! it's the ghost of my husband come to upbraid me.—Oh, much wrong'd spouse !

Coc. Spouse ! it's the spirit of my wife—Oh, Lord !—oh, great—injured goblin ! (*they fall on their knees opposite sides*)

Joey. (*From under the table*) Here's the parson striving to lay my mistress, but she'll surely tear his head off.—Eh ! why ! it's my poor dear master ! Help ! Murder !

Enter MRS. CAMOMILE, BELINDA, FRANK, *and* HEARTY.

Mrs. Cam. Eh ! what's the matter here ?

Joey. My Lady's ghost tearing auld Master to pieces. (*rising hastily, oversets the table and runs off*)

Mrs Coc. Mr. Cockletop alive !

Coc. My wife not dead !

Frank. Uncle, you promised that when proved to be deceived in antiquities, Belinda should be mine, (*speaks in his feigned voice*) Now, Zur, besides the fifty pounds, give her to poor Taunton Dean.

Coc. Was't you ?—Take her.—I was a wise man, till my brain got love coddled ; so, my dear, let's forgive Frank and Belinda, and forget our own follies.

Hearty. Ay, Sir, and transfer our passion for ancient virtu, to the encouragement of modern genius.—Had not Rome and Athens cherish'd the arts of their times, they'd have left no antiquities now for us to admire.

Bel. Why rake for Gems the afhes of the
  dead,
And fee the living Artift pine for bread.
Frank. Give,
  While you live:
Heirs who find cafh in corners,
Will at your funeral make right Mer-
  ry Mourners.

THE END.

SPRIGS OF LAUREL.

IN TWO ACTS.

PERFORMED AT THE

THEATRE-ROYAL, COVENT-GARDEN,

IN 1793.

THE MUSIC BY MR. SHIELD.

3 A

DEDICATION.

AS a ſmall tribute of congratulation on the patriotic ardour diſplayed by her Majeſty's Illuſtrious Son, His Royal Highneſs Frederick Duke of York, the early and brilliant example he has ſet to the Britiſh Troops of Military ſkill, bravery and Humanity, evincing that he will prove the Defender of his Country;

This Opera is with all poſſible humility laid at her feet, by her Majeſty's faithful ſervant, and

Dutiful Subject,

The AUTHOR.

Brompton,
April the 6th 1793.

DRAMATIS PERSONÆ.

Captain Cruiser, ... Mr. POWELL.
Major Tactic, ... Mr. DAVIS.
Lenox, ... Mr. JOHNSTONE.
Sinclair, ... Mr. INCLEDON.
George Streamer, ... Mrs. MARTYR.
Corporal Squib, ... Mr. DARLEY.
Nipperkin, ... Mr. MUNDEN.

Mary, ... Mrs. CLENDINING.

SCENE, *London and Greenwich.*

ACT I.

SCENE I.

A Chamber at an Inn.

Enter CAPTAIN CRUIZER, *and* NIPPERKIN.

CAPTAIN.

LEAVE my infant in a baſket at a gentleman's door, you villain! when I ordered that your wife ſhou'd bring it up with care and tender-neſs.

Nip. Why, Sir, when my wife ſaid it was my infant, and wou'dn't take charge of it what was a poor honeſt peace-loving huſband to do?

Capt. Well; come, your intelligence?

Nip. The babe was taken in, and chriſten'd Tommy Jones—the gentleman of the houſe in-tended to do well by it; but being given to play, died inſolvent; his family went to ruin, and

poor

poor Tommy to the parifh—the lazy overfeers
farm'd the workhoufe to the village butcher,
who, to feed his calves, ftarved the children;
here, like a young negro, he got hard work,
many blows, and no learning.

Capt. And from this mifery, a charitable
tradefman took him 'prentice.

Nip. Yes, Sir; ferved out his time with honor; but his fpirit too noble for a mechanic, he
lifted, and is this moment a gentleman common
foldier in the foot-guards.

Capt. But how to find him out—?

Nip. In my fearch I got acquainted with two
honeft foldier lads—Ned Lenox and Jack Sinclair, and they're to bring me among the reft—
the ferjeant-major Tactic, that has got the pretty daughter, may know.—I'll run a hum upon
him. (*afide*)

Capt. Nipperkin, you were my fervant twenty years back; but fince that, you've been fuch
a variety of rafcal, there's no trufting you now.

Nip. I want no truft—give me a ready guinea.

Capt. To get drunk and neglect this bufinefs!
—no, difcover my poor loft fon, and you fhall
have a hundred, to fettle you in a farm, firrah.
—John! (*calls*)

Enter a Servant with cane, hat and fwerd.

I muft get off to Greenwich, ready to receive the
Duke. (*going*)

Nip. But, Sir, I intend this evening vifiting
my old father at Chelfea—A little comfort for
the honeft foul.—(*holds out his hand*)

Capt. Chelfea, oh, your father's a penfioner!
well,

well, there. (*gives money*) But ufe every endeavour to find the boy, mind. [*Exit.*

Nip. You fhall fettle on me one hundred a
year or find the boy yourfelf. Lucky, that ftill
keeping an eye to the lad's progrefs through
life, I've this pull upon my old mafter—Till he
bids more I'll not bring father and fon together
—now got loofe from my wife, I'll make a good
ufe of my time—fince I'm come to London, I'll
drink like a foul, and divert myfelf with the
girls ;—if not, I'd be a man in a thoufand !

AIR.—*Nipperkin.*

Shew me a Lawyer refufing a good fee,
Or pious Dean not thinking of a Bifhop's fee,
A Doctor who won't fqueeze fick Ladies by the hand,
'Potticary whom his fcrawl can well underftand,
Dancing-mafter object to dancing off with Mifs,
A Methodift Preacher not in a corner kifs.
Young Enfign not proud of his flafhy large cockade,
Or true Britifh Tar, who of Dutchman is afraid---
Parliament Elector, who never fold his vote,
Parliament Orator, who will not turn his coat,
　　　And that is a man of a thoufand.

II.

Shew me a Right Honorable keeping to his word,
Or a poor poet patroniz'd by a Lord,
An impudent Sharper cloathed all in rags,
Or modeft Genius counting o'er his money-bags,
A Church-warden who fcorns to feaft upon the poor,
Fat Alderman who cannot calipafh endure,
A Groom too honeft to rob horfes of their corn,
Wife Cuckold who blufhes to wear a gilded horn,
Sportfman mind galloping over wheat or ftubble,
Or Secretary of State take nothing for his trouble,
　　　And that is a man in a thoufand.

[*Exit.*

SCENE II.

The Green Park.

Enter SINCLAIR.

Sin. Pleafant enough, on our march from Windfor, Lenox flipping a note into my hand, the inftant I gave him one; but what fays his. (*reads*) " Dear Sinclair, as foon as off guard, " walk into the park, I want to fpeak with you " on particular bufinefs."—Almoft the very words of mine to him; he's my friend; I'll afk his advice before I determine to marry Marry. Determine! oh, my heart!

AIR.—*Sinclair.*

When night, and left upon my guard,
Nor whifp'ring breeze, nor leaf is heard,
And ftars between clofe branches peep,
And birds are hufh'd in downy fleep,
My foul to fofteft thoughts refign'd,
And lovely Mary, fills my mind.
At every noife, for bluff " Who's there!"
I gently figh, " is't thou, my fair?
Thy dying foldier hafte and fee,
Oh come, fweet Mary, come to me."

As on my poft, thro' blaze of day,
The wretched, happy, fad and gay
In quick fucceffion move along,
I fee, nor hear the paffing throng;
My foul fo wrapt in Mary's charms,
I hug my mufket in my arms.
So, all of paffion, joy and grief,
When comrades bring the glad relief,
I cry thy foldier, hafte and fee,
Oh come, fweet Mary, come to me!

Enter

Enter LENOX.

Len. (*reading a note*) " I've a great deal to fay to you"—and I've a great deal to fay to him—. Oh! he's here—Well, Sinclair, what's this affair ?

Sin. Nay, what's your's with me.

Len. Come, you tell firſt.

Sin. No, no; you, let's hear.

Len. Not a word from me till you——

Sin. I'm determin'd that you ſhall—come I'll not ſpeak——

Len. Now I beg you'll——

Both. Then you muſt know, ha, ha, ha!

Len. Why, we're like people in the ſtreet giving each other the way; but here I ſtop, and now you paſs on.

Sin. Then, Ned, " of all the girls in our town," to me there's none like Mary Tactic.

Len. Why, I think ſhe's a moſt charming pretty ſoul.

Sin. Ay, and I love her.

Len. I know *I* love her.

Sin. Oh, you muſt miſtake; it's I that adore her.

Len. Upon my word you're wrong; for I'm the man that wou'd die for her.

Sin. That's as much as to ſay you'd fight for her.

Len. Any man but you.

Sin. Why, Lenox, I ſhou'dn't like to fight you.

Len. But any other, I didn't mind how great. Aye, even the corporal.

Sin. Any fellow that dar'd to think of Mary.

Len. Do you call me fellow, Jack ?

Sin.

Sin. Yes, you're a good fellow.

Len. Was it to tell me that you loved Mary Tactic, that you desired me to meet you?

Sin. Was your only business but to let me know you lov'd her?

Both. It was.

DUET.—*Sinclair and Lenox.*

Len. I like each girl that I come near,
   Tho' none I love but Mary;
   Oh, she's my darling, only dear
   Bewitching little fairy.
   I ask a kiss, and she looks down,
   Her cheeks are spread with blushes,
   By Jove, says I, I'll take the town,
   Me back she gently pushes——
         I like each girl, &c.

Sin. When off 'twas blown, and 'twas my place
   To fly for Mary's bonnet,
   So charming look'd her lovely face,
   There I stood gazing on it.
   Dress'd all in white she tripp'd from home,
   And set my blood a thrilling,
   O, zounds! says I, the French are come,
   Sweet Mary look'd so killing.
         I like each girl, &c.

Len. When to our Colonel at review
   A Dutchess cried, so airy!
   " How does your Royal Highness do?"
   Says I, " I thank you, Mary."

Sin. To quick time, marching t'other day,
   Our fifes play'd Andrew Cary,
   To every girl I gave the way,
   In compliment to Mary.
         I like each girl, &c.

Sin. I've a greater regard for you than for all the men in our regiment put together.

              Len.

Len. I always thought you my friend, and I'm certain I'm your's—Let us leave it to Mary's own choice.

Sin. Why, true; it's a pity to teize a young woman that can never love one.

Len. And it's foolifh and ill-natured to ftand in the way of another man's happinefs, when we can't forward our own by it.

Sin. Here fhe comes; let's afk her in down-right Englifh.

Len. Done.   [*They retire.*

Enter MARY.

AIR.—*Mary.*

Oh, come away,
Come, my foldier bonny;
I am fmart and gay,
But for handfome Johnny.

Enfign pretty doll,
Crimfon fafh fo wrapt in;
Minces, " charming Poll,
" Can you love a Captain?"
                    Oh, come away, &c.

To his fine marque,
At the camp, laft fummer,
He fent for me to tea,
By the little drummer.
                    Oh, come away, &c.

As I crofs parade,
Officers ftand blinking;
Under each cockade,
Sly, an eye cocks winking.
                    Oh, come away, &c.

Johnny fteps in time,
Sweetly plays the hautboy;
Hearts all merry chime,
March, and beat the foe, boy.
                    Oh, come away, &c.

Oh,

Oh, Sinclair, did you fee my father?—Is that Lenox?

Len. (*apart to Sinclair*) Aſk her.

Sin. No, do you? (*apart*)

Len. Mary, you know very well, that I think you a moſt charming girl.

Mary. Well, that's no fault of mine:

Len. No, its no fault—for to be fure you can't help being the fweeteſt foul—you're fure Mary, I love you; but here's Jack Sinclair fays he does.

Mary. Oh yes; he told me fo.

Len. Well; but didn't I tell you I lov'd you?

Mary. Well, and if you do, you can't help that, you know.

Len. We don't want to quarrel, becauſe that woudn't be friendly.

Sin. No; twoudn't be like brother foldiers; fo yourſelf confeſs which of us you love.

Len. Ay, do, Mary, your word ſhall decide it.

Mary. Which of you I love! Upon my honour that's very vain of you both—a pretty decent fort of a confeſſion too for a girl to make; but certainly was I to marry, I muſt chuſe only one.

Len. Ah, but, Mary, wou'd you chuſe one of us?

Mary. Indeed I wou'd.

Len. Sweet girl, but which?

Sin. Ay, which, Mary?

Mary. Well, I will own it, if you'll both pro-miſe not go fight fword and piſtol up in Hyde Park, as the officers do.

Sin. If you chuſe Ned Lenox, may I be whip'd if I wiſh him the leaſt ill-will.

Len. And, my lovely Mary, if you prefer Jack Sinclair to me, if I ever bear him a grudge for it, may I be drum'd out of the regiment.

Mary,

Mary. Heigho ! it's a fevere tafk, but—

AIR.—*Mary.*

When in a garden fweet I walk,
  The charming flowers admiring,
Each nods upon its tender ftalk,
  And feems my touch defiring,
Tho' all of beauties are poffefs'd,
  Too much to be rejefted,
Yet only one, for Mary's breaft,
  By fancy is felefted.

Full confcious of thy faith and truth,   (*to Lenox*)
  No wrong to thee intended,
Ah ! fhould I chufe fome other youth,
             (*giving her hand to Sinclair*)
  Be not fond youth, offended.   (*to Lenox*)
The ftarting tear, the heaving figh,
  True figns, not difregarded ;
But, by a maid more fair than I.
  Oh, be thy love rewarded.

Len. (*cordially fhakes hands with Sinclair*) My dear fellow, I give you joy. (*turns and wipes his eyes*)

Sin. Was it any thing elfe but Mary, I cou'd ——poor Lenox !

Enter NIPPERKIN, *finging.*

Nip. Ah, boys ! Jack Sinclair, Ned Lenox, come from duty at Windfor ?—Rare changes fince you were laft on the parade !
        (*Drum without.*)
Len. The roll-call. (*looking out*)

                    TRIO.

TRIO.—*Lenox, Sinclair, and Mary.*

Len. Tap beats the dub upon my aching heart,
Sin. Sad strikes the sound that bids me hence depart;
Len. Ah! can I from you stay?
Sin. One kiss and then away.
Mary. Go to your duty, go.

[*Exeunt Sinclair and Lenox.*

Mary. Is that to muster the men? For what?

Nip. For what! Why, to draught out a detachment for Holland.

Mary. And do Sinclair and Lenox go?

Nip. To be sure, if so their lot be.

Mary. Oh heavens!   [*Exit hastily.*

Enter Serjeant Major TACTIC.

Tac. (*calling off*) Mary! Ay, off to the parade! I see my daughter will have a soldier—you, Sir, run after that girl.

Nip. I'm a married man; and mus'nt run after the girls.

Tac. What, then you're married?

Nip. Yes, Sir, and so is my wife, a poor woman, Sir—I'm not worth quite a plumb, might have made my fortune by marriage, I have had my opportunities among the dear creatures. I'll see if his majorship won't stand a glass of stout punch (*aside*) Sir, I want to go abroad.

Tac. Why?

Nip. Because, I don't want to stay at home— I've left my wife there.

Tac. Where?

Nip. Why death and ounds! at Dorking in Surry.

Tac. What do you swear so, you rascal!

Nip.

Nip. To.fhew you I'm fit for a foldier.

Tac. But what are you now?

Nip. Nothing; tho' I was every thing—an Auction-porter, Watchman, Town-crier, Monmouth-ftreet Pluck-em-in, Playhoufe Conftable, Dog-ftealer—High and low Life, Sir, from Guard of a Stage-coach, to Waiter in a Cydercellar,—my days have been a round of " paft ten o'clock"—" juft a going"—" nobody bid more" " oh yes," " this is to give notice"—" pray walk in"—handfome fuit of clothes, fit you nicely"— " take care of your pockets"—(*whiftles*) " here, boy!—poor fellow! Ponto, Ponto"—" your pint, Sir—champaign, cackagay!"

[*imitates blowing a horn.*]

Tac. So then, friend, you've come off from your wife to turn foldier?

Nip. Why, Sir, fhe vex'd me into fuch a paffion, that I muft beat fomebody; fo I thought it more honourable to flog the enemies of my country, than the wife of my bofom.

Tac. But how did fhe vex you?

Nip. Sir, I love a drop of ale—'t'other day, we had a mug—fhe puts it to her head; " my dear," fays I, " ftop, the devil is painted at the bottom, and 'twill frighten you if you look on't' —fays fhe " I defy the devil and all his works," and up fhe puts it—" hold, my love," fays I, " you're a bit of a democrat, and it's his Majefty that's painted at the bottom"—" no," fays fhe, " I'm a loyal fubject, and I long to fee the King's jolly face"—So again up went the jug, and the devil a drop fhe left in it for me.

Tac. Ha, ha, ha! what's your name.

Nip. Nipperkin.—Mr. Nipperkin, Sir.

Tac. Then Mr. Nipperkin we'll fee if we can't make a foldier of you.

Nip. Oh, Sir, that's as eafy as making an attorney a rogue, or make this a ftrong arm, when its already at hand—make a foldier! hem! Sir, you do the exercife capital I fuppofe, he, he, he! fhew us a bit—wheel! to the right! ftop, Sir, till I chalk your arm.

Tac. Why do you think I don't know my right from my left?

Nip. Do you? (*gravely*) huzza! the ferjeant major, knows his right hand from his left—(*capers, balloes and waves his hat.*)

Tac. Why, you dog, are you humming me?

Nip. Yes, Sir.

DUET.—*Taƈtic and Nipperkin.*

Tac.	March! before great Juftice Laro.
Nip.	Death and ounds! am I arrefted?
Tac.	Sblood! don't fear, my little hero,
	'Tis only to be attefted.
Nip.	Oh! what then I muft take an oath?
	Here goes; I fwear by Jingo,
	I'll not turn foldier, till we both
	Together tipple ftingo.
Tac.	With all my heart,
	We'll take a quart.
Nip.	Or bowl of punch.
Both.	That's better.
Nip.	But firft a flice
	Of ham fo nice,
	For I approve a whetter.
Both.	For I approve a whetter.
Tac.	You have but to fail o'er to Holland d'ye fee,
	And the French kick back to their nation;
	Then the Emperor, Stadtholder, Pope, you and me,
	Will fit down to a jolly-fication;
Nip.	I'm tir'd of kiffing old Judy, my wife,
	I muft have a pair of new lips,
	So, when I'm in Holland, upon my life,
	I'll be at their fine Dutch tulips.

Both.

Both, Then we have but to fail, o'er to Holland d'ye fee,
And the French kick back to their nation;
Then the Emperor, Stadtholder, Pope, you and me,
Will fit down to a jolly-fication.

[*Exeunt.*

SCENE III.

The Parade in St. James's Park.

Enter MARY.

Mary. No, I can't fee any one to give me a true account how they go on.

Enter LENOX, (*much agitated.*)

Oh, well, Lenox, and how? ay, tell us.

Len. My unlucky fate! curfed chance.

Mary. Oh! then you are one of them that's drafted to go abroad in all thefe dangers.

Len. And, Mary, do you think its that, that could have vex'd me fo? I fee what a mean opinion you have of me—I now don't wonder at your preferring Jack Sinclair to me—you think I'm a cowardly poltroon.

Mary. No, indeed, Lenox: I know you've a very good fpirit—I didn't mean to difparage you; but I tremble to think of the dreadful flaughter thofe poor fellows may be expofed to.

Len. Dreadful! Isn't it glory?

3 C 2   AIR.

AIR.—*Lenox.*

Afpiring thoughts my breaft expand,
    'Ah! why to me is given a foul,
Proudly impatient of command,
    Yet doom'd by fate to bear controul;
Oft at the haughty ferjeant's will,
  A poor recruit at chilling morn,
I've ftood for hours the tedious drill,
    Sad object of his blows and fcorn.

II.

Nor funk my youthful fpirits then.
    'Tho' fierce he poiz'd the dread rattan,
I thus, when taught to conquer men,
    Supprefs'd the feelings of a man;
And now the harveft's warring pride,
    When Englifh triumph, Frenchmen yield,
A ufelefs tool I'm thrown afide,
    Whilft others reap the glorious field.

Enter SINCLAIR.

Sin. Oh, my Polly! we muft part.
Mary. How!
Sin. The lot is caft, and I'm call'd away—I muft leave you.
Mary. And can you? Oh my love!
Len. What then, you go? you have the upper hand of me in every thing. I muft fneak about here in the park, like a watchman—my marches from Story's gate to the ftable yard, and all my war's with the old women to take off their pattens; whilft you, led on by your Prince—I fhall go diftracted!
Sin. You've little caufe to envy me—reflect, I. leave Mary, I leave her with you too—my rival
                                                —with

—with you, that love, that deferve her fo much better than myfelf.

Enter NIPPERKIN *and* TACTIC.

Tac. Not 'lift you rafcal ! after fwallowing a bowl of punch ?

Nip. My dear Sir, don't be in a paffion—I have my reafons for both.

Tac. Your reafons, you rafcal——

Nip. Death and ounds, Sir, don't fwear—but my reafon that I wou'dn't turn foldier, is becaufe I hate fighting ; and I drank up the punch becaufe I love drinking, that fhews that I'm both a fafe and a good companion.

Tac. You're an arch rafcal, and I don't know what to make of you ?

Nip. Then I'll tell you what you'd beft do, Sir.

Tac. What !

Nip. Give me another bowl, Sir, and let me alone.

Tac. Come, Sinclair, quick—you've but little time to prepare your knapfack.

Mary. (*with emotion*) Dear father muft he go ?

Tac. To be fure.

Nip. Oh, certainly : he muft go and protect us all. Egad, I'm like a minifter of ftate ; whilft I fit at peace at home over my bottle, I fend other men out to fight that I may enjoy it in comfort.

Tac. Mary, Sinclair and Lenox are honeft lads—I know they both love you ; but as the mifery or happinefs of marriage will chiefly affect you, I leave the chhice of a hufband entirely to
yourfelf,

yourself, my girl. If Lenox is the man, love favours him; but if Sinclair, what he loses in love, he must make up in honor—give him a kiss, and a few of my best ruffled shirts; drop a tear, and that affair's settled.

Sin. Farewell (*to Lenox*) adieu! (*to Mary.*)

Mary. Oh! my heart will break! dearest father, can't you get him off?

Tac. Child, I wish him too well even to attempt it.

Len. Jack, don't think me a worthless fellow, tho' I am shov'd aside, and you chosen for the post of honor—'tis only blind fortune has done it; for had she fix'd on me,——

Sin. My love, besides your constancy, I rely on the generosity of Lenox; in my absence, don't avoid him; it will be my only comfort to reflect, that I have in England a faithful sweetheart, and a true friend.

Nip. Hem; (*sings*) " My Poll and my Partner Joe." (*looks archly and significantly at Lenox and Mary.*)

Mary. I don't know who you are; but you are a very impudent fellow.

Nip. Dont know who I am and yet know I'm a very impudent fellow.   [*Drum without.* Rub-a-dub, boys, hey, for Holland!

DUET.—*Sinclair and Mary.*

Mary.	Dear youth, keep this for Mary's sake;
Sin.	Sweet maid this poor remembrance take;
	When rivals tender things shall say,
	(*They exchange Tokens*)
	Oh, look on that and turn away!
Mary.	Should rivals win thy 'witching smile,
	Think what thy Mary feels the while.

Sin.

Sin.   When bullets whiftle in the wind,
            My only fear,
            My only dear,
       Is for my treafure left behind.
Mary.   Midft warring fields may angels come,
            And o'er thy head
            Their pinions fpread,
       Then bring my love in fafety home.

Enter Officers, Soldiers, &c. as prepared for the March—A Variety of other Characters taking Leave.

GRAND CHORUS.

Our Gracions George, and Charlotte's Son,
'Tis Royal Frederic leads us on.

AIR.—*Women.*

Britannia fell a fhower of piteous tears
To fee, (alas!) an haplefs Monarch bleed;
   The Royal Widow's mournful plaint fhe hears,
And bids her gen'rous fons revenge the cruel deed.

CHORUS.

To arms, fhe cries, to fave, is now the word,
And 'tis the hand of Mercy draws the fword.

Our Gracious George, and Charlotte's Son,
'Tis Royal Frederic leads us on.

END OF THE FIRST ACT.

A C T II.

SCENE I.

Night.—The Park near Buckingham Houfe.

LENOX *difcovered as Centinel.*

LENOX.

EVERY circumftance turns out fo contrary to what might havè made my friend Sinclair happy, and perhaps banifh for a time the thoughts of Mary from my mind. Since I've no place in Mary's affections, what's in England worth a thought?—I burn, I'm mad with defire to follow the Duke.—— To be left ftuck up here like a lamp-poft, with an ufelefs mufket in my hand—I've a mind to put it to ufe—(*placing it to his head*)—but my life's not my own.—For all Sinclair bid me fee Mary, what now muft he feel, on the reflection that he's left her behind with me?—Tho' I fcorn to take advantage of his abfence—I'll avoid the fight of her.

AIR.

AIR.—*Lenox.*

The Lamp of Hope by rays of Light,
    From thy dear eyes was fed Mary;
Sad hours are come, and shades of night,
    And even hope is fled Mary.
The Sun to all the world but me,
    Will give another dawn Mary;
My only light kind looks from thee,
    For ever they're withdrawn Mary.

I lov'd thee much and for thy fake,
    I ne'er will love again Mary;
If ever yet a heart did break,
    Thou'ft rent this heart in t'wain Mary.
In wild defpair I'll fly to fame,
    And death for thee defy Mary;
When I'm no more, thy true love's name,
    May draw from thee a figh Mary.

Enter NIPPERKIN, (*drunk,*) *with a fmall Keg.*

Nip. Tol, lol, lol!—Now, if I can get out
thro' this fame Buckingham Gate——
Len. Who goes there?
Nip. Brandy—(*holding up the keg*)
Len. You'd better give an anfwer.
Nip. To what?
Len. To me.
Nip. Your queftion?'
Len. I afk'd who went there.
Nip. Then you afk'd a very filly queftion,
when you might fee it was a brave boy—Huzza!
—the town's our own!
Len. Damn your trifling! Give, this inftant,
a proper anfwer, or I'll fire. (*prefenting*)
Nip. (*drops on his knees*) Hold! be quiet. Is
that your politenefs? Juft under the very eye of

the Court? Fire! and wake the maids of honour
—fweet creatures!—that may now be dreaming
of the lords in waiting, and white rod, and gold
ftick, and fuch other grand affairs.

Len. I'm in no jefting humour—Quick, fpeak!

Nip. S'blood! are you deaf? I'm fpeaking as
quick as I can. Stop! your firing will be petty
treafon—Her Majefty may be at this moment
in a fweet dream, that one of her beloved fons,
her gallant Frederic, is returning crown'd with
Laurels.

Len. And I no hand in placing them on his
brow! By heavens I'll not ftay—I'll follow the
detachment, tho' they fhoot me for a deferter.
Hold! this fellow may—why, it's Nipperkin!

Nip. Didn't I tell you it was a brave boy; yet
you wou'dn't believe me—after getting fo nobly
drunk, to frighten me back into fobriety! and
fo I've now all to do over again. Why, you
don't mind what trouble you give a poor man.
(knocks with his knuckles againft the keg) Are you
within? Very well—I'll be with you, or you
fhall be with me.

Len. Where were you going?

Nip. To the college. My father is a Chelfea
penfioner; and about once a quarter, like a dutiful foh, I bring the honeft gentleman, a little
brandy and tobacco, and fuch other dainties, to
comfort his old foul.

Len. You're right to be kind to your father
—Give me your coat.

Nip. " Kind to my father!"—Give me your
coat!"—That's very odd talk at this time of
night.

Len.

Len. You take this—Quick!—(*they change cloaths*)

Nip. I fancy I look better in the King's coat than the King wou'd look in mine.

Len. Give me your hat.

Nip. Sir, take your's off the block. (*pointing to Lenox's head, and bowing*)

Len. (*gives him his musket*) There; now· stand you in my place.

Nip. Did ever I think I shou'd have a place at Court ?—" Who goes there?" (*presents at Lenox*) Speak, or dam'me, I'll fire! I'm in no jesting humour—talk! or I'll blow your brains over the canal, thro' the Horse·Guards, cross the way to Whitehall, into the lottery-wheels.

Len. Silence! (*aside*) The· royal and affecionate parents send a darling son to face the perils of war, to assert his country's honour! What Soldier wou'dn't follow the illustrious example. —Hush! not a word.

> [*Exit with caution.*

Nip. Now that fellow's gone to commit a robbery in my coat, and I shall get hang'd for it: The gate's shut, and I can't get out to give my poor father his drop—Then I must give it to his poor son. (*takes up the keg and drinks*) I'll smoke a pipe too. (*sits on the keg*) Well, he didn't take my match, and my bottle of phosphorus. (*takes a pipe, fills, lights, sits on the keg and smokes*) If my wife was here now, I shou'dn't have all this sport to myself. (*rises, takes up the keg and drinks*) My chair produces good table drink.

3 D 2   AIR.

AIR.—*Nipperkin.*

A glafs is good, and a lafs is good,
    And a pipe to fmoke in cold weather;
The world is good, and the people are good,
    And we're all good fellows together.

A bottle it is a very good thing,
    With a good deal of good wine in it;
A fong is good, when a body can fing,
    And to finifh, we muft begin it,

A table is good, when fpread with good chear,
    And good company fitting round it;
When a good way off, we're not very near,
And for forrow the devil confound it.
                  A glafs is good, &c.

A friend is good, when you're out of good luck
    For that's a good time to try him
For a Juftice good, the haunch of a buck,
    With fuch a good prefent you buy him.

A fine old woman is good when fhe's dead,
    A rogue very good for good hanging,
A fool is good, by the nofe to be led,
    My good fong deferves a good banging.
                  A glafs is good, &c.

But it's getting cool here, il frefco. I'll ftep into my parlour. (*takes up the keg, and goes into the
fentry-box, fits and falls afleep*)

Enter MARY.

Mary. As my dear lover faid, there can't be
the leaft danger in paying fome attention to poor
Lenox whilft he's away. He took on fo at my
refufing him, and the lofs of his comrade, that
I know he hasn't eat a morfel this blefied day.
                                      He

He has a tender and an honeſt heart, and ſure
no harm for me to try if I can comfort him.—
The Park's got ſo ſtill, he may eat and drink
ſome'at, as I'm ſure he wo'nt come to me when
he's reliev'd.—Lenox ! (*goes towards the box, calling ſoftly*) Oh, my heavens ! if he hasn't fallen
aſleep, and here's the corporal coming ! (*looking
down the walk*) If he's caught ſo—Lenox !—
(*calls*)

Nip. (*ſpeaking in his ſleep*) Take care of your
pockets.

Mary. Get up.

Nip. Paſt four o'clock !

Mary. Sure he's been drinking to drive away
his ſorrows. Riſe ! Here's the guard !

Nip. Pray walk in, Sir—I've a pretty coat will
juſt fit you.

Enter CORPORAL, *and Guards.*

Cor. Eh ! Sleep on your poſt ! Holloa !
Centry ! here'll be rare flogging work; take his
arms ! drag him up !

Nip. Fine cloudy morning !

Cor. Ay, dam'me, it will be a fine cloudy
morning with you, peeping through the iron
bars of the Savoy.

Mary. Dear Mr. Corporal—

Cor. Is that Miſs Mary Taﬅic ?

Mary. You know Lenox is a good ſoldier,
and ſhould be excuſed if he's a bit over taken,
conſider, taking leave of his comrades ; you know
he's ſo well belov'd, and ſuch a temptation—then
his ſpirits in ſuch a ſtate, a very little liquor might
have intoxicated——

Nip.

Nip. (*afleep*)—That dogſkin will make a pair of pumps.

Cor. My ſkin!—You'll ſee what the drummer will make of your dogſkin.

Mary. Pray, don't inform the commanding officer.

Cor. Why, Miſs Mary, you know it's not in my power to ſave him, if, as you ſay, he's brought to court-martial for this.

Mary. His Royal Highneſs is good and merciful;—I'm ſure he'd conſider ſo excellent a ſoldier as Lenox—Now do let the poor fellow come to his ſenſes, and ſay nothing of it.

Cor. But then I ſhou'd be puniſhed myſelf, Miſs---Muſt give him up---take him to the Savoy.

Mary. Unhappy creature! and yet I'm aſhamed of Lenox.---However, I'll make my father uſe all his intereſt for his pardon. How have I been deceived in him! and how fortunate that my heart wasn't caught by his kind and obliging manners.---He lov'd me---he is Sinclair's friend, and therefore has a right to my aſſiſtance.

[*Exit.*

Cor. Why, he wou'd ſtand a better chance of mercy from his Royal Highneſs---his ſentence here might be death.---I'll pretend not to know but he's one of the drafts that has ſtaid behind; and to colour it, I'll neither ſee nor talk to him; but at day-break, a guard ſhall take him to Greenwich time enough before the men embark.

CATCH.

CATCH.—CORPORAL, NIPPERKIN, *and Soldiers.*

Corp.   Rare rattling boys, don't let your pris'ner go
           I desire,
      For fudling souls, the Savoy---ho!
Nip.   I'm Captain Muz.---(*All*) Are you so?
Corp.   Hark, ye, 'squire!
        I'm Corporal Squib,
1. I'm Fifer Bob,
2. I'm Drummer Dob,
3. I'm Natty Jack,
4. I'm Paddy Whack,
5. I'm Darby Drill
6. I'm Roving Will,
7. I'm Nimble Nick,
8. I'm a Good stick,
9. I'm Devil Dick.---Zounds! what's your name?
Nip.   Past four o'clock!---(*All*) We'll make you tame!
        S'blood and fire!
Corp. Drink, soldiers, drink, and bear no blame.
                       [*Exeunt.*

SCENE II.

Greenwich.

Enter LENOX *in* NIPPERKIN's *Cloaths, and Capt.*
CRUIZER.

Capt. No such thing friend.

Len. Do, dear, good, worthy sir, let me go on
board your tender.

Capt. But for what?

Len. To partake of the glorious expedition of
my comrades.

                       Capt.

Capt. Your comrades !---Ay, what, are you a foldier ?

Len. (*confufed*)---Yes---fir---no---I am————

Capt. If a foldier, and not one of the drafted men, what brings you to Greenwich ? and if you belong to the detachment, why out of your regimentals, and not with your corps?

Len. Sir, I am as yet, only in wifh a foldier--- I faid " my comrades," becaufe I'm acquainted with a number of the men ; and I've conceived fuch a friendfhip for fome of the honeft fellows, that I can't turn my head to any bufinefs, with the grief of being feparated from them---only let me go, and you'll fee how I'll fight.

Cap. But do you know the caufe ?

Len. Humanity.---To ftop the ravages of war abroad, fecure the bleffings of peace, commerce, plenty and happinefs at home to Old England, where a good King is the common parent---every man is captain of his caftle, and the laws protect his property, wife and children.   Frenchmen give Britons   freedom !---But huzza !---we'll pluck Sprigs of Laurel from their Tree of Liberty.

AIR.—*Lenox.*

The goddefs of mountains, blythe, rofy and free,
As the airs that flew round her, had once a fair tree ;
'Twas Liberty call'd, and a fav'rite of Jove,
And fweet was the fruit to the bright queen of Love ;
In Albion 'twas planted, its branches fpread wide,
Of her fons and her daughters the glory and pride.
         Tranquil pleafures,
         Softeft meafures,
    Then led the dance, and gave Britons to fing ;
         Loving, loyal,
         Good and royal,
People happy, honour'd their king,

Ou

Our fly gallic neighbours peep'd into our grounds,,
And fain would have fcal'd the white wall that furrounds,
They long'd for our tree, when it's beauties were
 known,
But miffing their aim, would have one of their own ;
For this, in poor France, a vile bramble takes root,
Each leaf is a poniard, and bitter the fruit.
  Pity fleeping,
  Angels weeping,
 Saw the favage triumph o'er men ;
  Juftice firing,
  All infpiring !
 Drive the tiger into his den.

Capt. Well, my lad, I muft fay I admire your
fpirit, and am forry we can't take you ; but un-
difciplin'd recruits won't do.—The nature of the
fervice we're order'd on, requires pick'd men.

Len. There's a boat now going off—by heavens
I will get aboard.   [*Exit haftily.*

Capt. By heavens you fhall not tho'—Holloa !
—Stop that fellow—keep him out of the boat.

Enter SERJEANT.

Ser. Sir, his Royal Highnefs's aid-du-camp
wou'd fpeak with you.

Capt. I come.—   [*Exit Serjeant.*
Something in this young fellow that ftrikes me exceedingly — (*looks out*) — No—the boat's gone
without him, and there he walks melancholy
away ; and intimate with the foldiers !—Might
perhaps have given me fome clue to difcover my
fon.—I begin now to defpair ; for if my boy is ftill
in any of thofe regiments, he muft have chang'd
his name,

Re-enter SERJEANT.

Ser. Sir——
Capt. Oh, true.   [*Exeunt.*

Enter MARY.

Mary. The coming spring begins to make the country look delightful. The sweetest season approaching, even the birds join in love—and my love to leave me!

AIR.—*Mary.*

Sing, charming warblers! voice of love!
    The dulcet song
    Now pours along,
For love can harmonize the grove,
    Bid balmy zephyrs gently bear
    The liquid notes thro' yielding air.

Re-enter CAPT. CRUIZER.

Capt. Those men loiter along the road—(*looks out*)
Mary. Oh, your Honor, I hope his Highness isn't yet gone over to the ship!——
Capt. Eh! What, my lass, do you, too, want to go and pull Sprigs of Laurel?
Mary. No, sir: but it's about a young man, a soldier——
Capt. The devil's in the soldiers for bringing the women after them. You're a modest, pretty looking thing---you foolish jade, what business have you with the young men? Take your snivelling good-bye on shore—no petticoats come
                               on

on board my ship. I advise you, child, to modesty and discretion; for your own forwardness
and folly contribute as often to the ruin of innocence, as the base arts of villainous seduction.

[*Exit.*

Mary. I believe that gentleman means well;
but he shou'd have known who he was talking to
—and even then, sweet and welcome is the gentle
monitor! for what we listen to with pleasure, we
follow with delight. I may chance to see my
Sinclair again before he goes—I know he'll conquer; and when he returns—Oh! such a gar-
land as I'll make him!—Aye, and he shall wear
it too.

AIR.—*Mary.*

Fragrant chaplets quaintly twinin·
Thro' the fingers of the fair;
Ev'ry grace and sweet combining
For the soldier's brow prepare.

Gift of Venus, blushing, glowing,
Let the lovely rose be seen;
And the Laurel, Mars bestowing,
Make the wreath an evergreen.

Oh, if here isn't Sinclair and my father.

Enter MAJOR TACTIC *and* SINCLAIR.

Tac. Zounds! how often will they halt?—
Sinclair! Why do you run before the rank?

Sin. Don't you see my attraction?---Oh! my
love! (*embraces Mary*)

Tac. Mary!---Now, girl, what has bewitched
you to follow us?

Sin. My lovely, faithful foul! don't be angry with her.

AIR.---*Sinclair.*

Parted from thee, my ev'ry blifs,
My only joy, the parting kifs;
So fweet! and yet fo fcant a ftore,
I languifh'd to return for more.

And art thou come, and doft thou bring
The fource whence thoufand raptures fpring?
Oh! let me prefs thofe lips again,
Thus parting, ever thus remain.

Mary. Oh! I've fomething to tell you about Lenox---he is——(*mufic, and fhouts without*)

Tac. The men on their march. Get you out of their way, child---you'll fee us at Greenwich. (*fhouts without*)   [*Exit Mary.*

Enter Officers, Soldiers, &c. accompanied and followed by a number of people. All crofs, with fhouting, drums, and martial mufic.

AIR.---*Sinclair.*

Sound trumpets! hard tafks to the foldier belong,
   'Midft dreadful alarms,
The man to deftroy who has done him no wrong.
   Thus founding to arms,
Hoarfe echo now brawls to the loud double drum,
   With, come to fate come;
Let juftice the foldier's bold quarrel ordain,
Tho' dyed all in blood he's yet free from a ftain,
   Then the battle not ceafe,
   'Tis for glory for peace.
         [*Exeunt all but Sinclair and Tactic.*

                            Sin.

Sin. Oh, fir, I've a dreadful boding of Mary's bufinefs.

Tac. Something about Lenox.

Sin. I fee it---he's been bafe and treacherous; and, for all that he feemingly refigned her, no fooner was my back turned, than he has dared to renew his addreffes.

Tac. Plague of your nonfenfical love and jea-loufy---mind your duty---run on and fall into your rank (*pufhes him off*) with their fweethearts and friends, and ftuff! I wifh we had them all fafe on board—fome reafons tho' in Sinclair's fuf-picions! I had a good opinion of Lenox—but this violent friendfhip of your young folks, all a feather—give me an old friend.

AIR—*Major Tactic.*

Midft flaunting fhrubs in vernal green,
 Each finer than his fellow,
A venerable oak I've feen,
 All clad in fober yellow.

Whilft wintry winds could blow around,
 Their leaves all helter-fkelter,
Poor birds within his branches found,
 An hofpitable fhelter.

In life's gay fpring too oft' we find,
 The buds of foft affection,
Scarce knit, when blown by ev'ry wind,
 In this and that direction.

Oh, come, thou friend, that can'ft endure,
 The fhocks of rougheft weather,
Frank, chearful, honeft and mature,
 We'll live and die together.

[*Exit.*

SCENE

SCENE III.

Before Greenwich Hospital—View of the Thames— A Tender at anchor, and boats with Soldiers crossing to it.

Enter GEORGE STREAMER, *attended by Seamen with their oars.*

Officers and Soldiers, &c.

Stream. Chearly my boys, clear the gangway there! here's another boatfull—we'll bring you gentlemen of the red cloth along side of the Frenchmen; I hope 'twill soon be our turn to take a spell at that work. We have a Prince too to lead us on—oh dam'me! how I long to powder their toupees.

AIR—*George Streamer.*

I'm here or there a jolly dog,
At land or sea, I'm all a-gog,
To fight or kiss or touch the grog.
   For I'm a jovial midshipman,
   A smart young midshipman,
   A little midshipman,
To fight or kiss or touch the grog,
   Oh I'm a jovial midshipman.

My honour's free from stain or speck,
The foremast-men are at my beck,
With pride I walk the quarter-deck,
   For I'm a smart young midshipman, &c.

I mix the pudding for our mess,
In uniform then neatly dress;
The captain asks, (no need to press,)
    Come, dine with me, young midshipman, &c.

When

When Royal CLARENCE comes on board,
By England's Navy, all, ador'd,
From him, I fometimes pafs the word,
 Tho' I'm an humble midfhipman,
 A fmart young midfhipman,
 A little midfhipman,
For Royal WILL was once like me,
 A merry little midfhipman.

  [Exeunt with failors &c. into the boat.

Enter MAJOR TACTIC *and* MARY.

Tac. Lenox in this curfed hobble?—An ugly job, faith!

Mary. Father, won't you make the Duke forgive him?

Tac. I make Dukes forgive People! what does the girl take me for?

Enter SINCLAIR, *(greatly agitated.)*

Sin. My beloved Mary, tell me this affair that brought you? ay, well, as I was gone, Lenox——

Mary. Oh! he is——

Sin. A villain!

Mary. How?

Tac. Be quiet—you wronged him in the love bufinefs—egad, poor Lenox has fomething elfe now to think of! Oh, yes, he'll be fhot.

Sin. Who! Sir! Mary, what has he done?

Mary. Is it poffible! I had no idea that his life was in danger.

Sin. What's his crime, and where is he now?
            Tac.

Tac. He has flept on his guard, and he is now in irons at the Savoy.

Enter CAPT. CRUIZER.

Capt. Bring him along, an obftinate young Scoundrel!

Tac. What's the matter, Sir?

Cap. A blockhead that I refufed to take on board, jumps into the river, fwims over to the fhip; and there he was found hiding behind a hen-coop. A brave fellow—but we fhould frighten him a little.

Enter LENOX, *in cuftody of foldiers and failors.*

So, you wou'dn't take my word for it; but now you fhall give an account of yourfelf before his highnefs.

Sin. Why, it's Lenox?

Tac. One of the guards, Sir.

Capt. Indeed! hold him in cuftody!   [*Exit.*

Mary. Ah! Sinclair, doesn't your heart bleed for your unhappy friend?

Tac. Why, how the devil did you fhake off your irons and efcape from the Savoy?

Len. Major, I never was difgrac'd with irons, or in a jail.

Tac. Zounds! Mary, what ftory's this you've been telling us? Oh! I fee it's all a flam, an excufe for her coming after us to Greenwich, and taking another parting kifs with your fweetheart.

Mary. (*cries.*) Indeed, father, I don't know what you mean; Lenox now, has got other
cloaths

cloaths on—but I'm sure I saw him taken into custody, by the Corporal — Think me—so—artful—as—to — invent stories — only — to — compafs—my—own—pleafure !

(fobs.)

Sin. Nay, my love, don't weep—your father cannot suppofe——

Enter CORPORAL.

Corp. Well, Mifs Mary, to oblige you, I've ordered Lenox to be brought before the Duke himfelf—oh! yonder they bring him.

Tac. Why, corporal; you're drunk too;—here they've brought him already.

Corp. I drunk! let me tell you, Major, I can be as fober on my duty, as any man.

Tac. Why, did you pull him from behind the hen-coop?

Corp. Hen-coop! I fay, I found Lenox on his guard moft damnably difguifed.

Tac. Well, you may find him there, difguis'd. (*points to Lenox.*)

Len. You found me drunk! why, corporal, what's the matter with you?

Corp. (*ftaring at Lenox.*) 'Tis Lenox! then who the devil have we got prifoner yonder!

Nipperkin (without.)

"Paft four o'clock!"

Enter NIPPERKIN, (*guarded.*)

Tac. Why, it's the joking rafcal, that cajol'd me out of the bowl of punch.

Len. Nipperkin! Oh! I fee how this has been.

Nip. I'll have juſtice—they took my keg. (*looks at Lenox.*) What, then you have been doing it? I thought ſo—and taken—I deſire he mayn't be hang'd in my coat.

Enter CAPT. CRUIZER.

Nipperkin talks apart to the Soldiers.

Capt. (*to Lenox.*) Young man, I've laid your caſe before his Royal Highneſs—tho' your quit-ing your poſt was a crime, that demands from military diſcipline, a ſevere puniſhment, yet in conſideration of your motive, a brilliant exam-ple of noble ardour for your country's honor, he not only pardons you, but from your high cha-racter as an excellent ſoldier, preſents you with this purſe.

Nip. A purſe for only ſwimming to—by the lord, I once ſwam from Chelſea-reach to Batter-ſea-bridge—give me——

Capt. Nipperkin! why, who made a ſoldier of you? here, my lad! (*offering the purſe to Le-nox.*)

Nip. A hen-coop! to ſmuggle myſelf into a fight I'd hide behind a mouſe-trap.

Len. I humbly thank his Highneſs—pardon is the utmoſt grace I could hope for; my friend (*to Sinclair*) you have never diſobeyed orders—a more finiſhed ſoldier, on the eve of being mar-ried too—and the Duke's bounty will be applied to a better purpoſe in contributing additional comforts to an amiable woman. (*gives the purſe to Sinclair.*

Nip. They won't let me be generous—nobody

will

will give me purſes to give away to poor families.

Len. Sir, if I am only ſuffered but to go with the Duke, ſome future event may offer an occaſion, really to ſignalize myſelf, and by merit win a reward, of which I am now totally unworthy.

Capt. A liberal minded fellow, faith! ſo, my laſs, this is your ſoldier laddie!

Mary. Oh, no, Sir,—I grant he deſerves—ay, the moſt beautiful lady—but here's my humble choice.

Sin. Humble, indeed! yet I have reaſon to be proud with the friendſhip of Lenox, and the love of Mary.

Nip. Captain, lend me a guinea, and I'll tell you a ſecret.

Capt. You drunken ſcoundrel, I'll break your head.

Nip. (*Aſide*) This boy's generoſity has ſo wrought upon my heart, that I can't bear he ſhould longer remain in obſcure wretchedneſs —hearky (*to Lenox.*) down on your knees to the codger. (*points to the Captain.*)

Len. What do you mean?

Nip. Oh! what is this world come to! I bid a ſon aſk his father's bleſſing, and he ſays holloa! death and ouns, what do you mean?

Capt. Son! this——

Len. How!

Nip. I tell you, that's the boy in the baſket, the child of charity, the prentice to—Mr. Dalrumple, the fiddle caſe maker; the private ſoldier, that for glory prefers a French bullet to an Engliſh plumb-pudding.

Len.

Len. Sir, my birth has been a myſtery—and is it thus explained ?

Capt. It muſt be the deſerted ſon——

Nip. Of an abandoned father.

Capt. Nipperkin, you're now privileged—The ſervice you've rendered me by this diſcovery—my boy a brave ſoldier !—muſt make a good officer.

Len. Sir, my higheſt ambition is now to join in glorious enterprize as a private, for if I am to be honoured with promotion I'll firſt, with heart and hand, endeavour to deſerve it.

Enter GEORGE STREAMER, *Officers, Sailors, Soldiers, and a variety of other Characters.*

FINALE.

Sinclair.

Till to your cliffs we turn our face,
Old England be a merry place ;
To pipe and fiddle, jig a-pace,
    Whilſt we take hence our drumming ;

But when we finiſh the campaign,
With wooden leg, or golden chain,
We'll march, or hop to you again,
    You, ſing, our boys are coming.

CHORUS.

Till to your cliffs, &c.

Mary,

Ye warriors, from my ſoldier fly,
The lightnings flaſh his beaming eye ;
Beneath his conqu'ring ſword ye die,
    If to the fight ye dare him.

When

When you my love to battle go   [*To Sinclair.*
Your foot upon the vanquifhed foe,
Your arm raifed high, to give the blow,
    For his love fweetheart, fpare him.
        Till to your cliffs, &c.

Nipperkin.

I'm given much to knock and kill,
This war was made againft my will ;
Some like to fight, but I'll fit ftill,
    And talk in Coffee houfes :

Yet if I took it in my head,
By cutting throats to get my bread,
In moft newfpapers might be read,
    My mighty kicks and douces.
        Till to your cliffs, &c.

Lenox.

But grateful hearts we hence muft bear,
For all thofe noble Britifh Fair,
Who take into their gen'rous care,
    Dear pledges left behind us.

You to protect, the pow'rful charm,
That fires the foul and nerves the arm,
Whilft patriot zeal our bofoms warm,
    Such duties ever bind us,
        Till to your cliffs, &e.

Major Tactic.

We go brave lads at honour's call,
To check the proud, the ruthlefs Gaul,
Let Britain's thunder now appall,
    And bid him think on Creffy.

George Streamer.

I'll weigh for Holland, with a cheer,
And when I've help'd my friend Mynheer,
I'll round for bonny Plymouth fteer,
    And kifs Poll, Sall, and Beffy.
        Till to your cliffs, &c.

1st. Enfign.

Ye Wolfs and Elliots all repair,
Great Britain's ftandard, lo ! I bear ;
My colours flapping in the air,
　　His Majefty was donor.

2d. Enfign.

And, ladies, do not think I jeft,
My courage when put to the teft,
For your dear fakes I'll fight my beft,
　　I will, upon my honor.

CHORUS.

Till to your cliffs we turn our face,
Old England be a merry place ;
To pipe and fiddle, jig a-pace,
　　Whilft we take hence our drumming.

FINIS.

END OF THE FIRST VOLUME.

www.ingramcontent.com/pod-product-compliance
Lightning Source LLC
Chambersburg PA
CBHW021332110726
47900CB00005B/1438